# RED FLAGS

Books by Lisa Black

*Every Kind of Wicked*
*Let Justice Descend*
*Suffer the Children*
*Perish*
*Unpunished*
*That Darkness*
*Close to the Bone*
*The Price of Innocence*
*Blunt Impact*
*Defensive Wounds*
*Trail of Blood*
*Evidence of Murder*
*Takeover*

As Elizabeth Becka:
*Trace Evidence*
*Unknown Means*

# LISA BLACK

# RED FLAGS

KENSINGTON
PUBLISHING CORP.

www.kensingtonbooks.com

KENSINGTON BOOKS are published by

Kensington Publishing Corp.
119 West 40th Street
New York, NY 10018

All Kensington titles, imprints, and distributed lines are available at special quantity discounts for bulk purchases for sales promotion, premiums, fund-raising, educational, or institutional use. Special book excerpts or customized printings can also be created to fit specific needs. For details, write or phone the office of the Kensington Special Sales Manager: Attn. Special Sales Department. Kensington Publishing Corp., 119 West 40th Street, New York, NY 10018. Phone: 1-800-221-2647.

Library of Congress Card Catalogue Number: 2022934638

The K with book logo Reg. US Pat & TM Off.

ISBN-13: 978-1-4967-3690-1
First Kensington Hardcover Edition: August 2022

ISBN: 978-1-4967-3692-5 (ebook)

10 9 8 7 6 5 4 3 2 1

Printed in the United States of America

For Mom and Dad
wish you were here

"Any action of an individual, and obviously, the violent action constituting a crime, cannot occur without leaving a trace."

—Edmond Locard, 1934

# RED FLAGS

# Chapter 1

$F$ew things mobilize people more quickly than a missing child. Usually, that meant scores of volunteers sweeping through the woods, or friends and relatives combing the city streets while the parents made frantic phone calls to every schoolmate the kid had.

Things progressed a little differently when the child in question was only four months old and had not even mastered crawling, much less walking, and hadn't disappeared from a city street but a palatial mansion large enough to house the parliament of a small country.

Ellie Carr parked in the sweeping, curving driveway behind five unmarked but official-looking cars she pegged as fellow FBI. They were too clean for any other agency. A side drive had been turned into a parking lot by the small army of agents now grid-searching the lawn and surrounding woods. Their uniformed bodies walked in straight rows, two outstretched arms apart.

Her white van had been painted with an understated banner reading FBI EVIDENCE RESPONSE TEAM. It wasn't nearly stylish enough for the premises but she didn't care about that. She *did* care about the size of the place—white stone walls and a black slate roof, a center section connecting symmetrical wings, huge windows made up of small panes, second-floor balconies and small dormer windows at the top that must be attic spaces complete with skeletons and ghosts. She estimated thirty rooms, not counting any basement space, and at least fifty windows, and today, thanks to multiple shots fired at a 6th District mall, the "team" consisted of her.

The single available ERT coworker would have been Adam, busying himself with the paperwork that would accompany his promotion to supervisor. Their divorce had been finalized only a few months before, and though they got along quite civilly in the workplace, she had no desire to go elbow-to-elbow dusting windowsills with fingerprint powder or casting shoeprints.

Besides, she had been expecting a regular place, maybe three or four bedrooms and two baths, the kind of house *normal* people lived in. Even in DC.

She snapped a few photos, pivoting to get all of the house exterior, juggling her basic crime scene supplies in a canvas workman's toolbox, her camera, and a clipboard with a scene worksheet attached. The sun beat down through the late summer humidity and she didn't envy the searchers. One good thing about large, wealthy homes—the air conditioners usually worked.

And clearly no one cared about the bill, as the door stood open on this hot day. The foyer she entered could have been featured in *House Beautiful* and smelled of citrus. It had a curved marble staircase she could swear she had seen in a movie. She saw checked tile under a chandelier that appeared too heavy for its chain and a direct view to, after a few more rooms, French doors leading out the back to another green lawn and the Potomac River. Ellie heard emotional voices elsewhere in the house, upstairs—no doubt the parents.

"Dr. Carr."

The man at the foot of the steps introduced himself as special agent in charge Michael Tyler—tall, with somewhat-thinning black hair and a bad scar on his temple, as if someone had once caught him there with a broken bottle. "The parents believe the baby's been kidnapped, but there's no note and nobody on video. CARD is searching—thoroughly—but nothing so far." That did not bode particularly well for the missing child. This very private home wasn't a crowded marketplace where a kid could be snatched in less time it took for their parents to decide on a cheese; and with no obvious outside culprit . . . when bad things happen to small children, it was usually because their parents did bad things to them. Ellie never let herself leap to conclusions, but after nearly eight years in forensics, the thoughts crept in unbidden.

"Though," he added, "ransom would not be a crazy idea—obviously they can afford it. The dad's a big lobbyist and the mom's in Congress."

Ellie felt her eyebrows rise. "Senator? Representative?"

"No, works for a committee."

The FBI's CARD—Child Abduction Rapid Deployment team—could step into any missing-child case, even without a ransom demand or waiting twenty-four hours, and given the proximity to DC, the myriad implications of the political world would always be considered.

Michael Tyler didn't have to emphasize a *thorough* search for her to catch his drift, the same current on which her own thoughts already sailed. Vanished child, no real proof of kidnapping—likely that one of the parents had shook the tiny body too hard, left it unattended in a bath, panicked, and came up with a kidnapping story to protect their reputations in the cutthroat world of Washington, DC. In their turmoil they wouldn't have gone far with the miniature corpse, so the baby might turn up in the back of a closet, the trunk of a car, or somewhere among the trees outside. It was a horrible thought, but not a unique one.

A less malevolent explanation might involve a custody battle, or a disturbed acquaintance who wanted a child and couldn't have their own. Or ransom *would* be demanded—obviously, anyone who lived here could afford it. Much nicer theories, with the baby (boy? girl?) remaining safe and healthy.

She said, "Well, I'm it today. So this might take a while."

"Not a problem. I don't think there will be much to do, forensically speaking—the whole place is in real estate open house order, all apparent openings secure." He meant doors and windows showed no signs of forced entry. "No footprints or tire tracks, and no one larger than a rabbit on the video. Throw some powder in the baby's room, download the video and that should be it."

She just loved it when non-forensic people told her where she'd find forensic evidence, but chose to believe he was trying to be helpful . . . or he had already decided that no outside party had taken the baby at all.

Which did seem the most logical conclusion—but then a woman's voice from above said, "Ellie?"

Ellie tilted her head to see the speaker, though light from the chandelier and the white stone dazzled her eyes.

Rebecca Carlisle had not changed much in the five or six years since they'd last seen each other. Jet-black hair past her shoulder blades and high cheekbones, slender, slightly athletic—very much like Ellie, except for Ellie's auburn hair and blue eyes.

Ellie couldn't think of a single reason why she'd be there. "Becca?"

The woman swept down the steps with unladylike haste, followed by three more men in suits.

"What are—" Ellie's words were cut off as Becca clutched Ellie to her chest with arms packed full of muscle and desperation. "I'm *so* glad to see you! What are you doing here? Oh—your job. You didn't know this was my house?"

"No! Last time I saw you, you had that pretty row house."

"It *has* been a while—we, um, moved."

Up, Ellie thought. Very definitely up.

"You two know each other?" Tyler asked. "How long have you been acquainted?"

"Since birth," Ellie said, thinking that if he hadn't been about to ask her to leave, he would now.

Becca said, "We're cousins. Our mothers are sisters. Ellie used to live with us."

"Cousins," Tyler said, as if hearing other words instead. Family member. Investigational bias. Conflict of interest. Ellie would have to recuse herself from the case.

She looked at her cousin, with whom she'd celebrated teenage birthdays and gone roller-skating at the tiny, run-down rink in Haven, West Virginia. She would be staying in an official capacity or an unofficial one, but she would be staying. To know which it would be, she said to Tyler: "If you want me to recuse myself—"

He exchanged a quick look with one of the other agents, a wiry guy with dark hair, communicating without words.

Then Michael Tyler surprised her by saying: "No. We want you to stay."

# Chapter 2

She used a trip to the van to get supplies as cover to call the ERT supervisor—who was, as so often happened in this lame-duck stage of his career, out celebrating his impending retirement while leaving his handpicked successor in charge: her ex-husband, Adam. "Moved into the office already?" she asked him.

"I heard the phone ringing. Thought I'd take a message."

Too discombobulated to apologize, she summarized the situation.

"And CARD wants you to stay?"

"Yes."

"Huh," Adam said. "That's kinda cool."

"Not really. I would have been okay to stay here as a family member only, but by leaving me in my official capacity, they're setting me up as either spy or scapegoat. Becca and Hunter are automatically suspects, so I can be their inside man. They solve it, then it's 'Yay, FBI!' If they don't, they can let everyone assume it's because I helped Becca cover it up, or simply didn't give it my all. If Tyler and his partner—

guy named Alvarez—want to, they can ruin my reputation just to get their own supervisors off their backs."

"Want me to tell them they can't have you? I could switch you over to the mall shooting. They could use some extra hands out there." He spoke kindly. Adam might have more interest in ambition than effort, but he wasn't a bad guy.

"Not a chance." She rubbed one eye, feeling the pinch of a "rock" on one side of her and a "hard place" on the other. "I'm not leaving Becca."

"The family thing again."

"Yup. If it weren't for them, I'd lack a decent education, soul mates, and a really great cheesecake recipe." The whole Beck clan—the maternal tribe of Ellie and Becca's mothers—had kept her warm and dry and incredibly loved. They were a structure unto themselves, a network of intelligent resources from tying her shoes to where to go for fun, to a couch to flop on to basic auto mechanics.

She heard the soft *clink* of a coffeepot pulled from its burner. "You don't owe them anything, Ellie. It's just cheesecake."

*Just* cheesecake? No wonder they'd divorced.

"Besides, you don't even *like* Becca."

"Of course I do! That—that was just normal girl stuff."

"Glad I was a boy, then. Okay, keep me posted. I could send out someone from swing shift later if you need help, but you should look at this as an opportunity to get CARD in your debt. They're high profile. Can't hurt to have them owe you a favor."

A master class in ambition. She thanked him, picked up an extra roll of fingerprint tape, and went in to find out what had happened to her cousin's child.

The baby's room echoed with a purposeful and malignant emptiness, a beautiful trap. But it was her job to enter such places, and Becca had already pushed past her with customary impatience.

Lush white carpeting spread across the floor like a field of unbroken snow to a credenza full of toys waiting for their owner to get big enough to play with them. Blackout curtains for naptime were hidden behind ruffled baby blue drapes; two dressers painted in whimsical pastels held the tiny wardrobe. The room could have enveloped half the entire footprint of her temporary, post-divorce apartment.

The crib rested in the center of the room like a display case in a museum. Ellie tiptoed over to look inside, as if the four-month-old might have magically reappeared and she didn't want to wake him.

But she knew better than to hope for magic.

She did not touch the railings. The white wood had been rounded and topped with a glossy protective covering, which should hold prints well.

Becca hovered halfway between the door and the crib, glancing at it and then away, as if it were a shameful light that hurt her eyes. Then she turned and crossed to a window.

"This is gorgeous," Ellie told Becca. "Your whole house is . . . amazing. You and Hunter are both lobbyists, I remember that—"

"He's still got the firm, but I'm now policy advisor to the Senate Committee on Commerce, Science, and Transportation. Look at our lawns—there's five hundred feet of grass in every direction, so how would anyone even *get* to one of our doors without a camera picking them up?"

"Do you have any cameras in here?"

"In the bedrooms?" Becca looked disgusted.

"In the house."

"Of course not. Outside only, over the exterior doors. Why do you think no one has called for a ransom? I keep checking for missed calls."

"Has the FBI set up—"

"No. We don't have a landline, and Hunter won't let them tap our cells."

Ellie didn't hide her surprise. "But . . . surely . . ."

"I'm not letting people tap my phone! Once they get in there . . . we'll let them know if someone makes contact."

"But—"

Becca rushed on. "I checked my email, and there's no weird notes shoved under the door. Hunter's office has been alerted and so has mine. With the recess about to end there's hardly anyone there, anyway, but my assistant will keep an eye out. And why not just leave a note here when they took him?"

Luis Alvarez, handsome and friendly and obviously destined to play Good Cop to his partner's Bad during interrogations, appeared in the doorway. "Dr. Carr? Are you going to be processing the exterior doors? We didn't want to touch any until you had—"

"Yes, thank you. I would appreciate you holding off until I can get that done."

"No problem."

He disappeared, his dress shoes clacking down the polished hardwood floors.

"Since when are you a doctor?" Becca asked.

She couldn't blame her cousin for her surprise. Few people held a doctorate in forensic science at all—still a relatively new degree for the planet, despite the field having grown by leaps and bounds since the TV show *CSI* first aired and ushered in a national craze. "It's a PhD. Not strictly necessary to stay in ERT, but it gave me something to focus on during the divorce."

"You're *divorced*?"

"And *that* gave me something to focus on while getting through my thesis." Ellie didn't bother with her personal backstory. Plenty of time for that later. "I know you've probably been through this five times by now, but can you tell me what happened today? Start from the beginning."

Becca obediently began. "I got up with the baby—Mason, did I tell you that? His name is Mason—about six, fed him, he's on formula. Got Taylor up, gave her the usual toast and hot chocolate, with marshmallows, let her linger over the *Post*. She reads it every day. She's precocious. She loves being precocious, and I love that she loves being precocious."

"And how old is Taylor?" Embarrassing to have to ask.

"Eleven. Taylor's eleven, going on forty-five." A bit of a gap between the two kids. Perhaps Mason had been a beautiful surprise. Ellie had last seen Becca at a dinner party at their old house in Georgetown, and she could not remember the occasion or why Becca had invited her to hobnob with the movers and shakers of the country. They had been like sisters, once, the closest thing to a sibling Ellie would have, with Aunt Katey as substitute mother, through most of middle school. Ellie had sent letters and cards, but eventually gave up the one-sided relationship. They hadn't truly communicated in over fifteen years.

Taylor would have been about six at the dinner party. Ellie had only a vague memory of a solemn girl with a long brown braid, quickly packed off to bed by a nanny.

Speaking of which—"You have a nanny." Not a question.

"Yes, but don't even go there. It's not Jenny. She's been with us since Taylor was eight, and right now, she's been in South Korea for over a week, and not due back for five more days. The FBI's checking that she's actually, physically, on the other side of the world, but I'm sure she is. Horrific timing. We should never have let her go with the committee hearing this week, but her grandmother was turning one hundred or some such thing."

Ellie moved over to one of the dressers, topped with an adorable Noah's Ark–themed lamp and three framed photos.

Mason beamed a toothless grin up at her, all dark eyes and long lashes and chubby cheeks. All babies were beautiful to Ellie, but Mason could have won contests—though, as always with the very young, the true appeal of the fresh skin and the wide gaze lay in his utter innocence, his deep faith in his world. His future held infinite possibilities, all of them good and never bad. A sharp hope pierced her heart—let him not find that faith might be false. She had been to too many such crime scenes.

A stack of Pampers (with wetness indicator) topped with Bambo Nature Organic Overnight sat in a neat pile alongside La Mer diaper cream and other accoutrements on the dresser. No matter how much money one had, everybody pooped.

Ellie touched nothing, planning to fingerprint it all, even though none of the items seemed out of place. Two pictures of Mason, one of him with Becca in perfectly coiffed hair and the remaining flush of pregnancy. No pictures with Becca's husband, Hunter, or the sister. Ellie always took keen interest in displayed photos when she made scene visits, who appeared and who didn't, locations and demeanors. They told more than the owners intended, yet never the whole story.

Her cousin continued. "After I dropped her off, Mason and I puttered around until about ten-thirty, when Tara came over."

"Who?"

"Tara Esposito. She's about my best friend. And financial advisor—every DC relationship has to do double duty, after all. We don't have friends we can't use."

Ellie had no idea why that might be significant, but they could get to that. She moved to the large windows with old-fashioned diamond-shaped panes and wondered if the house was truly a hundred or so years old or had been designed to look that way. Outside, the sun turned the beginning-to-change leaves to bursts of red and gold. The nursery sat on a second floor which, in a normal house, would sit high enough to be the third floor. From this window one could fall a sheer twenty or thirty feet to the ground and the architect had left one no drainpipes, balconies, or handy gargoyles to swing from. The windows looked delicate, but the frames were thick, the latches heavy and closed tight with a minuscule white sliver of plastic on the upper corner. The windows had alarms, but no cameras.

Maybe a trained acrobat could have shimmied along the ledges carrying a baby . . . *maybe*. Still, she would process all the windows and the sills inside and outside with black powder. Surely, the acrobat would have worn gloves to grab the rough stone and turn the latch, but one never knew.

Becca went on. "Tara and I were in the sitting room, having some coffee and just yakking. Then Gabriel showed up. That was, maybe, eleven?"

"And who is that?"

"Gabriel Haller, Hunter's BFF—and biggest client, but, honestly, they were friends before he was a client. Maybe I sounded a little cynical about relationships. With this hearing coming up, he and Hunter have been running around like toddlers at Chuck E. Cheese. We all have, really."

"So he came to meet with Hunter?" Ellie photographed each of the four windows, making sure to take a close-up of each latch.

"Hunter wasn't here this morning. He'd been in Missouri, didn't arrive back until—let me go in order."

"Sure, of course. How long had he been there?"

"Two days . . . why?"

"Just placing everyone." Standard part of scene work, trying to picture where people, animals, weapons, vehicles were when the victim died. Except in this case the house went on forever and the victim—she hoped—wasn't dead.

Becca gave a little huff of annoyance, a sound Ellie hadn't heard since the ninth grade, as her body sketched out parts of the story with elbows and fingers. "I put Mason down for a nap, but then remembered I had to pick up Taylor. They had early dismissal today—with the tuition we pay those teachers they have more time off than they have on—but Tara said she'd stay with him. I checked on him, he was sleeping, so I left him here." She halted again, no doubt remembering the last time she'd seen her infant son. Ellie could picture him herself, the tiny, curled fingers, the peach-fuzz hair, the almost imperceptible rise and fall of his fragile chest. She didn't rush her cousin. The time to rush had passed.

"Gabriel drove out at the same time, right behind me. That was probably eleven-fifty?"

"How far away is the school?"

"About eight miles. Potomac Lakes Academy, training future captains of industry for fifty years. The pickup line was a nightmare, as usual . . . I don't know why that place even bothers to provide a bus service that none of the kids will deign to use, including mine. I was stressing because I didn't want to hold Tara up too much. Harper's such a fussy baby—that morning she had been super mellow, sleeping through everything, but once she decides she is over it, she is *over* it."

"Harper?"

"Tara's little girl. And Tara hates breast-feeding anywhere except home—I tell her she's crazy, but it is what it is. So she hustled out of here, Hunter pulled in about five minutes later—that was maybe twelve-thirty? We unpacked him and he disappeared into the basement with the treadmill. He likes to blast seventies rock when he does that. The workout room is right under the kitchen and I thought I might not hear Mason if he cried, the music was that loud. So I went upstairs."

Becca's words ended in an odd little strangled sound. She stood still and listless next to the large white bassinet.

"And?" Ellie prompted.

She seemed to push herself through the next part. "I stood there like an idiot for a second. I actually touched the mattress, even though I could see he wasn't there. Then I started screaming. You know how sometimes your brain works something out long before you do? It was like my head sped through every possible explanation in one instant and I knew, *knew*, that there was no logical explanation. So I screamed. Next thing I knew, Taylor stood here shaking my arm . . . I must have scared the crap out of her, I'm sure she'll be describing that to a therapist someday. I told her to run down the back staircase to get Hunter. He couldn't hear me over the stereo."

"He came up . . . but his bed was just like you see it. Empty." Becca wrapped her arms around herself and Ellie saw emotions she never expected to find in her tough, stubborn cousin's face: grief, and a very real fear. "He was just *gone*. Where is my son, Ellie? Where is my baby?"

# Chapter 3

*2:30 p.m.*

Dr. Rachael Davies felt the usual apprehension before meeting a potential client to discuss what the Locard Institute called "private cases." Clients too often had wildly inaccurate expectations of what the Locard could do for them . . . but they also had deep pockets, so the director insisted she at least take the meeting.

The Locard Institute had been founded to conduct research in forensic topics, from ballistics to DNA analysis, and to train scientists and technicians and law enforcement personnel from around the country in those same areas. Its reputation had grown to the point that those training classes were not cheap, and between those fees, foundation money, and government grants, the Locard had the funds to assemble a smorgasbord of equipment and experts—the envy of labs everywhere.

Yet, given the proximity to Washington, DC, too many government leaders and high-placed CEOs considered them a private detective agency, one that could track down cheating spouses and embezzling employees and all under an inviolable nondisclosure policy. Rachael often took these meetings only to disabuse them of that notion. Gently, of course.

At the first sight of Hunter Carlisle, the former forensic pathologist began rehearsing her speech. *We can conduct any kind of forensic testing, including those often missed in routine law enforcement or insurance investigations—check for obscure poisons or reexamine accident calculations.* Translation: If you *really* believe your great-uncle Frederick was done in by the private nurse to whom he left his entire estate, we can help set your mind at ease. *We have always honored our nondisclosure agreements and have never had information leaked to the likes of* Access Hollywood, *though, of course, we would have to report any crime uncovered to the authorities.* Translation: We're not here to help you hide your offshore accounts or tailor our reports to assist your defense team. *The Locard Institute exists to share our advances in anthropology, electronic and digital analysis, chemistry, botany, and biophysiology with the general public.* Translation: We don't really care if your wife/husband is cheating on you . . . maybe they had a good reason.

Hunter Carlisle's manicured blond hair and Brioni suit made her think she should lead with the last one. From the way he stood in the waiting room instead of sat, then pacing with impatient twitches, she thought he'd understand directness tinged with entitlement.

But as she got close enough to shake his hand, she saw the red-veined eyes and the sagging skin of a deep worry, the hyperalertness that came from consuming lots of coffee, but not food. A cheating spouse could produce that in some people . . . but so could real trouble.

"Mr. Carlisle," she said, "I'm Dr. Davies. My office is this way."

He nodded, but not before his face and body gave away the usual surprise at the position of assistant director being held by a woman, and a Black one at that. Not to mention one that didn't even have gray hair, though at thirty-eight, Rachael wondered how much longer that would last.

Hunter Carlisle got over it quickly, however, and she waved him toward one of the armchairs in front of her desk. He sank into it with an expelled breath as if he hadn't realized how tired he'd become. Shock, she thought. The man was in shock. "Our director tells me this involves your son."

"Yes. Mason." A pause, and then the words spilled out. The boy disappeared from his crib in the middle of an ordinary afternoon, with no trace, no strangers on the property, no ransom demand . . . *yet*. The police and the FBI's CARD team had been called immediately.

"The cops and the feds . . . it already seems like they can't do much, other than check with informants and police reports across the nation. Without a ransom demand, they don't know what to do next. They don't say so, of course, but I can see it."

Rachael's mind raced ahead: Who and how? They now knew when and where, and "how" could wait until, and if, she saw the layout of the house. "Who"—if they didn't want money, then perhaps they wanted the baby. "I'm going to ask indelicate questions, so bear with me."

"Ask anything you want." People rarely meant that. She thought perhaps Hunter Carlisle did.

"Mason is your biological child, not adopted? Not any other birth parents in the situation—no? Any ex-spouses, ex-lovers—not you or your wife? Estranged in-laws, grandparents?" He shook his head at all these suggestions. "Older siblings?"

"We have an eleven-year-old daughter."

"Household staff recently let go?"

He told her a cook had quit a month or two before, but the cleaning ladies, groundskeepers, and nanny were all still employed, no problems or complaints from any. The nanny had been out of the country for the past ten days and the staff only there on certain days. None had been working at the house that morning.

She wanted to ask if they had any acquaintances—it could be someone as remote as their mail carrier—who expressed unusual interest in their baby or in having a baby. But she hesitated . . . no sense prompting suspicion of every female he'd encountered over the past year.

She, likewise, did not yet ask about postpartum depression. If causing him to suspect distant females might be dangerous, making him suspicious of his own wife could be disastrous. She'd save that until she'd met the woman herself, made a mental assessment. Many, many factors came into play around children. People could get crazy.

She ought to know.

If someone *didn't* simply want a baby, and didn't want ransom either . . .

"Do you have any enemies, Mr. Carlisle? You or your wife?"

"I'm a lobbyist. I have a *host* of enemies, that's how you know I'm effective. The old can't-make-an-omelet thing."

For the first time she saw a hint of a smile, a sliver of the cockiness she thought might be his normal mien. "Any current one in particular?"

The smile disappeared into deep thought, and he paused before he spoke. "My agency has thirteen current clients, but most have been with us for years—the Minnesota teachers' union, QuickMart, Dane-Campbell Pharmaceuticals. What's taking up most of my time right now is KidFun."

Rachael considered herself fairly well-informed, but she had no idea what he was talking about.

Her blank expression must have told him this, because he went on: "It's a gaming platform—for online games, not physical setups like PlayStation or Wii. It's surpassed Disney and will take on Nvidia and Stadia if the committee votes the right way after tomorrow. But, of course, Disney and Nvidia and Stadia don't like that and they've set this group of nutcases after us—ChildChallenge is the most vocal, among others who think we don't do enough to protect children's identities. They've picketed KidFun's Georgetown office, protested outside my office, sent my firm and KidFun horrible hate mail. Our IT department is fending off malware attacks by the minute. The child advocates are more than crazy enough to do something like this, and rival gaming companies are more than ruthless enough. You want my enemies? There they are."

"What would be their goal in taking your child?"

"I don't know . . . to get me to skip the hearing tomorrow? The vote on a bill to end Senator Griffyn's ban on direct messaging within the games? We've got our data and our engineers lined up, but my wife tells me that 'concerned experts' have requested to be put on the agenda."

"And your wife is—"

"She's the senior policy advisor to the Senate Committee on Commerce, Science, and Transportation."

"And this is the same committee your—"

"*Yes.* Before you ask, it's not a conflict of interest—everyone encounters their own spouse at some point on the Hill. Is it incestuous? Sure. But that's DC."

Rachael began to feel nostalgic for tales of cheating spouses and thieving stockroom staff. But kidnapping a baby to swing a U.S. Senate vote? A committee vote of no could kill a proposal, while a vote of yes was rarely the final word on anything, with "markup" and alterations and re-wording to come. "Can you postpone this hearing?"

"It would be a freakin' nightmare and I'd lose a couple—a *whole* lot of money, but yes." His shoulders slid farther down the leather wingbacks. "Carlisle Communications makes its living by staying behind the scenes. I can't have any association in the public mind with a crime, even one in which I'm the victim. That's why I need the Locard to investigate this—you helped a friend of mine, Senator Sahir, with a stalker problem he had last year, and he said you were invaluable. And discreet. Discreet is *very* important."

"Of course. But this is an FBI investigation."

"They'll cooperate. If they don't, I'll make a phone call." He flashed a grim smile. "That always works."

*Really? And who are you?* But she was sure they'd get to that, and she didn't care, anyway. For a missing four-month-old, she'd forgive a parent throwing their political weight around.

Hunter Carlisle seemed genuinely distressed about his son. But he also seemed genuinely distressed about his political goal. Which problem held true priority in his mind, Rachael couldn't know.

She didn't give a crap about gaming platforms or Hunter Carlisle's deep pockets—but there was a tiny baby out there somewhere. She would not rest until she'd found out what had happened to him.

Rachael heard a vague buzz, and he pulled his phone out of his pocket to check the screen. Constant interruption by device had become part of life and she didn't resent it. At least he had put it on vibrate.

But then, as she watched, a new force passed through Hunter Carlisle, an electric wave that first shocked and then drained him in a ripple from head to toe. His eyes grew wide and his skin color went from pale tan to ashy gray.

*They found the body,* she thought, the words searing through her with a white hot pain.

"Look at this," he said, and thrust the phone at her. He had received a text: **We have your son. Go to the DM ban hearing tomorrow and speak the truth. Admit you violate 312. Do not delay or cancel hearing or you will not see son again. More instructions soon.**

"Come with me," Rachael said.

# Chapter 4

After Ellie Carr photographed every inch of Mason's nursery, the crib, the closets, each window latch, came the uncomfortable moment when she had to stop being an observer of a crime scene and become a participant—she had to touch things, dirty things with powder and reagents, collect things. With only one chance to get this right, she couldn't afford a misstep. Mason's life might depend on it.

She carried the framed photos and other small items into the attached bathroom to dust them over the sink—it would make for easier cleanup and she didn't have to risk knocking over an open container of incredibly fine black powder onto snow-white, thick pile carpeting. A vacuum would do nothing but spread it around—and water, a complete disaster. White carpeting in a baby's room—a décor choice only made by someone who didn't have to care about cleaning or cleaning bills.

She processed the crib rails and the windows, brushing highly refined carbon dust over the clean surfaces. Each window remained latched from the inside with heavy hardware.

Perhaps someone could have devised a way to slip a wire through and pull the latch back down, while balancing on a three-inch-wide windowsill and carrying a sleeping infant who perhaps was not sleeping by that point, but she couldn't see why they would bother to relock it.

She photographed the carpeting at an angle to look for errant footprints or signs of dragging through the plush fibers—but it hadn't been vacuumed recently and the numerous crisscrossing footprints said nothing to her.

She folded the pale blue crib sheet and blanket inward, to retain any fallen hairs or fibers, and sealed them into a brown paper bag.

She swept the room for hidden cameras with a detector. It would be super handy if Becca kept a nanny cam in some innocent tchotchke or teddy bear, but she found none. Apparently, Jenny Cho had the Carlisles' complete trust.

Then Ellie packed her brushes and cards into her kit, and left the bathroom looking as if it had rained indoors with fine black ash. Becca's housekeeper would have a challenging day on her next visit. Time to move on to the remaining twenty-nine rooms and forty-six windows. Take it slow, don't miss anything.

She found herself enjoying the routine, physical work of applying the powder and lifting the tape, of making herself look at every object in the room—did it seem out of place? Was that window ajar? What had been left in the trash basket? She didn't get to do this every day. Evidence Response duties were collateral, with members of the team on call rather than working ERT all day every day. On days when the Bureau had no need of forensic support, Ellie toiled in the Organized Crime division—interesting enough, but not her favorite. There she listened to surveillance tapes and traced cash payments, waiting for the next ERT mobilization . . . even though 80 percent of the time they'd be responding to a bank robbery. These were also interesting enough, but by now Ellie had worked enough bank robberies to last the rest of her career.

She took careful note of the home's vast layout this trip. The second floor seemed to be guest bedroom after guest bedroom with the master suite at one end and an envy-provoking library at the other. Mason's room rested in the middle, Taylor's next to the library. She checked each room for signs of activity, disturbance, broken windows. She found none. Tyler had been right; the place was as tidy and buttoned up as a model home. The little girl's room had the requisite strewn clothing and YA paperbacks. In Becca and Hunter's bathroom, someone had left the cap off the toothpaste. That was it.

On the first floor she photographed the very solid front door with no scratch marks around its knob or bolt. When it was opened, she could see the searchers outside as they convened, having finished their grids without any shouts of discovery, no excited gestures.

Next a living room—though a space that large couldn't be referred to by any title so mundane. A "Let's invite the entire Senate to tea and the House as well, just to show how egalitarian we are" room might begin to cover it. Then through a dining room, with a table so large that if it couldn't actually seat the entire Senate staff, it could still accommodate a quorum plus their top aides. Burnished wood and velvet upholstery, chandeliers unneeded with sunlight streaming through the tall windows. The faint scent of pine might be a cleaner, might be cleverly concealed scent diffusers, or might be her imagination.

She continued to photograph, dust with powder, lift anything that looked like a print with tape and cards, and move on. She needed to be thorough, but she also needed to get the job done. More FBI might arrive, or friends, and there was an eleven-year-old somewhere in the house. Trying to keep them all from touching areas the kidnapper might have touched would be impossible.

As over-the-top indulgent as the house was, Ellie liked it. Rather than seeming stuffy or imposing, the architect had understood the importance of light and freedom. The copious windows made the place feel airy, the trees and the greenery always in sight as if it were a country cottage. Must be hell to heat in the winter, though.

And the host of windows and doors gave a kidnapper too many options. The place was a sieve. An expensive, gorgeous sieve.

Ellie and her brush left their mark on the south-wing door, then passed through four more rooms. Sprinkling fingerprint powder felt like sacrilege in such beautiful surroundings, but Ellie consoled herself that it would not stain. Usually.

Just as she began to wonder if there were any spaces in the house where Becca and Hunter actually *lived*, perhaps caught a TV show on the couch and heard about their daughter's day at school, she found Becca in a sitting room at the front of the house. A small—relatively speaking, of course—room in cool blues and brilliant whites, friendly and blindingly bright with afternoon sun, with a coffee table of polished mahogany and two overstuffed sofas.

"They didn't find anything outside," Becca said from her seat on one of them. "That FBI guy told me that. I don't think he believes us."

"What? What makes you say that?" Family members always topped the suspect list, but Ellie had hoped the agents would be subtle about it.

"Because of Hunter."

"What about Hunter? Forgive me, but I'm not clear on—"

"He's the owner and founder of Carlisle Communications—lobbyists, not a respectable occupation in this town, despite the fact that any government worker aspires to either be one or marry one. There really is a revolving door between Congress and all its appendages, and the firms. But to laypeople, he's Jack Abramoff, carting around suitcases full of money to bribe people with. I think our very special agents figure this is either a publicity stunt . . . even though Hunter told them that if a *word* of this leaks to the press he'd have both their badges"—

*Yeah*, Ellie thought. *That always works.*

"—or some sort of falling-out among thieves. Then I work for Congress, which everyone *knows* is a den of corruption."

Ellie continued to photograph. "And what does that entail?"

"I am a policy advisor . . . say you and a bunch of CSIs want to, I don't know, outlaw the use of black powder to fingerprint stuff. It causes black lung and you have a pile of studies to show it, you've written a white paper and have drafted a law to ban it. You go to your local senator or congressperson, get them to sponsor it. They will sound out their colleagues to see if they could get support for the bill, though they have a ton of other legislation they're working on, so you're going to have to do a lot of that yourself, talk to industries, chambers of commerce, unions, political parties, people at the Department of Health. You need to get people on your side, get people interested in your issue. If nobody cares about your issue, you might as well stay home and save your money."

Something occurred to Becca and she waved her hand at her cousin. "You've testified in trials—it's a very similar process, only instead of a person on trial, it's an idea, a bill, or a clarification to a law. Committee hearings are like a grand jury—the members have to decide if the case has enough merit to go forward. If a bill can't get past the committee, it probably doesn't have a chance on the floor, anyway."

Being lectured to by the girl that used to steal her nail polish might have felt odd, but Ellie stamped the feeling down. Becca was right to be proud of her stature—how many people could say they directly affect the laws of the nation? Besides, it got her mind off Mason, even if only for a moment. Ellie had seen grief. Ellie had spent seven or eight years facing grief, up close and personal, almost daily. She had seen parents of children insensible, raving, or comatose with loss. But she had also seen loved ones behave exactly as Becca did—focusing on a job, a child, a project, even the funeral with consuming attention. The mind coped as best it could. Victims could ping-pong back and forth between despair and seeming normality, sobbing with deep animal cries one minute and making a joke the next, transitioning through three extreme emotions in the span of one sentence. That was normal.

Or, rather, there *was* no normal when it came to this.

She started on the windows, having not found one yet that seemed to have been opened at any recent time. Not one waft of air-conditioned air had been allowed to escape, until today.

Becca continued. "The committee gets a bunch of bills from all over the country, and I have to research what the bills are about and what they will affect, arrange for the affected parties to come and talk to the committee at hearings, and then rewrite the language of the bill so that it is clear and says what the committee wants it to say."

Ellie knew Becca had gotten a master's in biology from Marshall University, but still couldn't imagine the progression from the emotional tween to one half of a Washington power couple. "That sounds—amazing."

Becca grinned widely now, and gestured to the room with one silk-clad arm. "Yeah. Not bad for a kid from the hills of West Virginia, is it? Wouldn't think our entire grade school only had a hundred kids and a leaky roof, or that my dad was a grease monkey. Not that I'm ashamed of that, mind you—I trade on it. But I'll never go back to that kind of poverty. No way."

"Becca!" Ellie burst out. "You—we—weren't *poor*. You had a solid house and plenty to eat and—obviously—a good education."

The rebuke didn't bother her cousin, who leaned her head back against the crisp white upholstery. "Oh, I know. Maybe just relatively speaking, I mean. Easy for you to say, anyway, *you* got to go live with the rich doctors."

"We only thought they were rich because their house had two bathrooms," Ellie grumbled, brushing powder on another window latch. Uncle Paul and Aunt Joanna had taken her to live in Florida so that she could go to a more stringent high school. They didn't "do" children, but considered fourteen tolerable and said she had a brain that needed to reach its full potential. Maybe it hadn't been necessary, since location hadn't held Becca back, but at least it gave Ellie a chance to slip out from the shadow of her two cousins.

But she spoke truthfully to say: "West Virginia is still my most favorite place in the world. I spent the whole time with you guys pretending I was a wood elf in Lothlórien."

"Yeah, you were always into that fantasy crap. Hardly surprising, given your circumstances."

Ellie moved to the next window and suddenly realized what had been missing: Calls. Texts. Cars in the driveway. An outpouring of support and sympathy and largely unsolicited advice. "You haven't told anyone, have you?"

The grin vanished. "I couldn't. Mom would be so scared that she'd practically stroke out, and my poor dad would have a heart attack. There's no reason to scare them to death."

"And . . . Melissa?" Ellie suggested this cautiously, never knowing if the two sisters were tight or only in a truce. But Melissa was formidable, and good with secrets.

"She's out of the country. I can't make her crazy too, when there's nothing she can do about it. Besides, if the fam even gets a hint of trouble—"

"I know. You'll have at least five more cars in the drive and fifteen text strings going. Mateo will upgrade your alarm system, and Roland will map the estate and calculate angles of approach."

Now Becca did smile at the idea of their personal army. "Aunt Rosalie will drive from Cleveland to bring stuffed cabbage and take me to church."

"While Wayne contacts all his ex-marine buddies and Margery sets up alerts across every national TV channel."

"Exactly," Becca said. "You see why I can't tell anyone, until . . . until I know what to tell them."

Yes, they couldn't call out the forces without a direction in which to deploy them. But Becca did have a husband. "Where *is* Hunter? With the agents?"

"What? No, he left to have a late lunch with the secretary of the interior. Then he was going to go find someone who can help us."

"He's at *work*?" Ellie almost dropped her fingerprint brush. No matter how impressive the secretary of the interior sounded . . .

Becca gave her a look perfected in childhood, incredulous and a bit pitying. "This is DC, Ellie. What we do is *important*. It took him weeks to get this lunch scheduled and he can't afford to cancel. This really is the worst possible timing."

"I see." She did not see. Then the second half of her cousin's words sank in. "But who is Hunter getting to help?"

"The Locard Institute."

"*What?*"

A private institute? Was that even legal, while the official investigation was still going on? "Do the agents in charge know that?"

"Don't care. If they give us any problem, Hunter will

make a phone call. There's always someone who owes us a favor."

Ellie had her doubts about the Bureau bestowing "favors," but didn't argue. She knew of the institute, of course. It had an international reputation and she had asked her supervisors to approve training there once or twice, but it had never been in the budget. The Locard tended to take on cold cases, though, help celebrities with upcoming trials, or identify skeletal remains.

The Bureau went to extremes to coordinate and cooperate with local law enforcement, but the Locard wasn't law enforcement.

Whatever. The SACs, Tyler and Alvarez, would have to deal with that. For Ellie, this was no time to be insular. If the Locard could help, Ellie would share her evidence and her knowledge and even her box of gloves.

Didn't mean she'd be happy about it.

Finally, a window latch not completely secure—the bar had not been pushed all the way into the catch. But no prints appeared.

"That's why I'm so glad you're here," her cousin went on. "I need someone I can *trust*."

"But I'm only—"

"No one in this city is going to look out for us like you will."

Ellie didn't point out that between CARD and the Locard Institute, an ERT tech had little chance of affecting anything, PhD or no PhD. But she didn't bother, because blood was blood. If Becca needed her, she would take some vacation days and dump all her work on her coworkers. No matter what Adam said, she *did* owe them . . . even if that left her bobbing in the waves between Charybdis and Scylla. Tyler and Alvarez were letting her work a scene to which she had a clear personal connection, which could mean only one thing: They meant for her to serve as their canary in a moral coal mine, sniffing the air to detect poison. Becca might confess any guilt to her blood relative. Ellie might function as a spy and solve their case for them, or go bad and serve as a line and hook with which they could draw Becca and/or Hunter out.

Fine for them. Not so great for Ellie, who now had no choice but to make sure this case resolved with every *i* dotted and every *t* crossed. Otherwise, the suspicion that she had helped her cousin get away with murder would linger over her work for the rest of her days. The FBI had put her career against the wall with a gun to its head, and made finding out what happened to Mason its only ransom.

Becca continued as Ellie packed up her equipment. "They even asked me if this could be some sort of custody dispute."

"How could it be that? Forgive me again, but Mason is your biological child? There's no surrogates or exes involved?"

Becca frowned—what had been an ominous sight in their youth—but only said, "One hundred percent. I swelled like Miami Beach during spring break and threw up with the regularity of pop-up ads. My water broke in the middle of a subcommittee hearing, my assistant drove me to George Washington U Hospital, and by the time Hunter got the train back from New York, they had Mason all cleaned up and in one of those Plexiglas bassinets in the window. Eight pounds ten ounces, the biggest one in the unit."

Ellie smiled, though that all sounded rather traumatic. "No medical issues with Mason?"

"None. Aced his last two checkups. Sit down, hon."

"Not after all this powdering. I don't dare sit on anything light-colored."

Becca gave her upholstery a concerned glance, checking its surface for mars, and didn't ask again.

"Who else is regularly on this property besides you? Cook? Maid? Gardener?"

"Cleaners come in twice a week and landscaping staff once, and today isn't the day for any of them. We had a cook, but she quit two months ago—honestly, I can't blame her. Taylor decided to be a vegan one week and went on a paleo diet the next. Then she decided none of us could eat anything that had white rice, white flour, or potatoes— we've been living on takeout since she left. Gained five pounds, after I worked so hard to lose the baby weight! I mean, this isn't LA, we don't have to be a size *zero*, but anything over four is pushing it."

"But the cook didn't leave on bad terms?"

"Not a candidate for babynapper, no. I heard from the gardener that she went right to work for a Supreme Court clerk who's never home, so she's as happy as a pig in . . . in a sty."

"Anyone else who's shown an odd interest in Mason? I'm not trying to make you suspect everyone you know, but—"

"No, I get it. We live in a very exclusive, slightly isolated area. Someone had to know us and know how to get in, and out."

"Exactly. This wasn't random and not impulsive." Women— and it was nearly always women—who kidnapped infants often thought a child would save their marriage or cement a relationship, or needed one to assuage the deep pain of losing their own child, or were simply desperate to be a mother. That should be comforting in its way, but the rosy daydream of having a child could be very different than the exhausting, frustrating, sometimes tedious reality of caring for one. Also, women who thought a baby could save their relationship ran the chance that their significant other might react sensibly and call the police. Neither of those two scenarios bode well for the baby's health if the woman decided to cut her losses.

So Ellie said nothing of them. "Neighbors? People you socialize with? Work friends?"

"With a suspicious interest in the baby? No . . . we haven't really entertained since he was born. And especially not since the cook quit."

"Doctor? Nurse?"

"Nah. They have the sense to make a fuss over anybody who's got a lot of money, but nothing I'd call *abnormal*. Their office is always chaos and there're babies all over the place."

"Hunter's family? I know that sounds harsh, but . . . is he estranged from his parents? Does he have an obsessive sister, brother, a niece—"

"Nope, and nope. His parents are . . . distant, both emotionally and physically. They live in Texas and don't seem terribly interested in either of their grandchildren. He has a brother and a sister, both live in California, are married, have kids of their own, and we haven't seen either of them since his father's seventieth four years ago."

"Okay. Well, that eliminates a lot of possibilities."

"Sorry," Becca said, almost playfully. She glanced around the pretty room. "This is where we hang out."

"You and Hunter?"

"Me and Tara. I call this our situation room. This house has five sitting rooms. I should have kept Mason in here with me, I could have put him on a cushion." She stared at the puffy seat next to her as if picturing her son, cocooned in a blanket, warm in a beam of sun. "Or maybe put Harper in his room with him. Then he wouldn't have been alone. Maybe they'd have taken her instead—isn't that an awful thought?"

"How old is Harper?"

Becca looked up. Only a year older than Ellie, she seemed to have aged much more than the five or six years since they'd seen each other last. "A month younger, five weeks younger. That's what we pretend we're talking about, mommy tips and organic baby foods, when we're actually talking about stocks and tax shelters, because I don't give a crap about organics—don't tell Taylor. But with this committee hearing coming up, we've got lots to talk about."

"The hearing has to do with some business dealing?"

Becca laughed, a quick, harsh sound. "Like saying a Microsoft IPO would be 'some business dealing.' KidFun—Gabriel's company—will be out billions if we don't get this bill through. And that's not an exaggeration, I mean *billions*. It might not affect foreign sales, but most of the income still comes from the good old USA. China has the numbers, but they're so restrictive that those receipts aren't a deciding factor."

Ellie had no idea what Becca was talking about, more interested in who was where when. "And this Gabriel came by yesterday as well?"

"Yes. He brought some stuff he wanted Hunter to see as soon as he got home. They try not to trust email too much. The three of us talked, for about a half hour, about this citizen group and the experts they're going to have testify."

"All three of you?"

"Yeah. Gabriel knows Tara almost as well as I do—she handles part of his personal finances. And they're both over here all the time. Don't even ask—I can see you getting ready—but, no, Gabriel doesn't have any kids . . . Actually, he has two, but they both live with their mothers and he's between wives at the moment. That sounds bad, but he's actually a great guy. Feet of clay when it comes to his own company, but a great guy."

Somehow the enthusiasm in her words didn't bleed into her voice, but then she had other things on her mind than accurate character descriptions. And she went on: "Talks to everyone like they're a person. Answers every random question Taylor comes up with. Parks over by the kitchen instead of in the middle of the circular drive so everyone can see his Bentley. And he's never shown any bizarre obsession with Mason. Or Tara—bizarre obsession with, I mean. But your FBI guys seem convinced that I cooked up this story with somebody. They're just not sure who."

# Chapter 5

Noah Thomas snuck a look at his phone while his teacher explained the difference between metaphors and similes. Phones had to stay in pockets inside the classroom at Virginia Prep Elementary and checked only between classes. But kids lived to break rules and usually got away with it, as long as they kept the screen hidden and at least pretended to pay attention. The ten-year-old didn't really mind English, but he already knew the difference between the two literary devices—a metaphor was saying the Atlanta Braves are a laser beam of energy melting anything in their path, and a simile was saying the Washington Nationals played like a bunch of squirrels on Red Bull. Simple.

But to be fair, the Nats had been doing pretty good all season, so perhaps to say like a squad possibly headed to the play-offs would be more accurate. After all, one had to show some loyalty to the home team. Noah's father was big on loyalty.

And according to his teacher, it didn't matter. The "like" made it a simile, and not a metaphor. Today's lesson completed. So Noah checked his phone.

His dad had texted earlier that day with great news. Weird, but great. Weird that the screen said **Darnell Thomas** instead of **Dad,** and weird that the text started out **Hey dude.** His father never called him or anyone else "dude." But then the IT engineer was always getting a new phone or redesigning his own, and the greeting might be him trying not to sound old. Adults were always trying not to sound old, but that was, as Noah's dad would put it, "a losing battle." And saying it was a losing battle was a metaphor, right?

The earlier text, after the "hey dude" part, let Noah know that Dad had found a great baseball boot camp for him. Only four days so he wouldn't miss that much school—as if Noah cared. When Noah texted back at recess, Dad said it would start that afternoon and their housekeeper would pack up his clothes and iPad Pro for him and get them to the camp counselors. Noah texted back some appreciative emoticons and asked could she please not forget his Braves shirt and his Nintendo Switch. The red one.

At lunchtime his dad had texted again. There would be a lady in a green polo shirt that said HOME RUN CAMP on it to pick him up after school. That name seemed majorly lame, but adults often were. He assured his dad he could handle finding the lady. If his mom wasn't flying back from Germany that day, she'd be insisting on coming to the school and passing Noah off personally. She was hyper about safety—if he went over another kid's house, she'd call to make sure he was there. She'd be the first to take a day off work to volunteer if a field trip needed chaperones or the team needed drivers. His dad had joked once that when Noah started dating, his mom would require two forms of credit and a DNA swab first.

*Dating.* As if.

He'd told his best friend, Ben, about the camp. Ben really wasn't into sports—he didn't even like to play baseball in gym class—and not happy that Noah would get out of coming to school while he didn't. And who ever heard of a camp starting so late in the year? Camps were usually in June.

Not the DC Sports travel team, Noah told him. They practiced year-round in this huge indoor arena out in Bethesda. Noah was determined to get on a travel team, and with his birth year he could try out for the twelve-and-under rather than ten-and-under team. That would be *so* cool.

Now his dad had texted some last instructions: **Office has been notified. Look for the dark green polo shirt. Pickup person will have the number.** Sheesh, he could *handle* it; all he had to do was wait at the pickup office for green-polo-shirt person to give them the right ID number. V Prep was almost as big on safety as his mom—

"Noah. Can you give me a sentence using a metaphor?"

"Baseball camp," he said, "is a bag of M and M's in a candy store in Disney World."

She had to think about that one for a minute, but then said, "Very good."

Yeah, Noah didn't really mind English.

# Chapter 6

*3:40 p.m.*

Ellie had fingerprinted everything that needed to be finger-printed, photographed everything that needed to be photo-graphed, swabbed, measured, sketched, and examined same, and had finally run out of things to do. This was the point in the investigation where she would ask the SAC if there was anything else they needed, while conveying with her expres-sion that the answer had better be a no, because she was due for her lunch/dinner/workout/bedtime. She called her su-pervisor—who, for once, answered his phone—to say she could hang with her cousin all afternoon while on a public payroll, or report back to the lab. She did not say which an-swer she wanted; that wouldn't matter. Her boss said, "That's fine. Stay with your cousin."

She asked, diplomatically, whether he wanted to send out another crime scene tech or two to check her work in light of the circumstances. But he said no; such a crime scene seemed dramatic, but as Tyler had pointed out, with a limited num-ber of things to *do*. There were no bloodstains to document, no stray casings to find or bullet trajectories to follow, no bedsheets to examine for semen, no suspected drugs to test.

SAC Tyler asked if she had found anything of note, where her report would be sent. He volunteered that he and Luis had reviewed the video and saw no signs of any strangers entering the house or any of the three adults spiriting away an infant. The case remained a locked-room mystery.

Becca and Hunter's story made no sense, which meant it was likely to be a lie. And if Becca needed to confess, she might be much more likely to confess to a close family member. Or better yet, a not-so-close family member, one who probably would not help them cover up a crime like—possibly—infanticide.

Thus, the nation's premier law enforcement agency happily left her to putter around her cousin's kitchen rather than string blood spatter or trace bullet trajectories. At least for a day or two.

Because both cousins thought of caffeine as a comfort food—one of the few things they had in common, besides genetics—Ellie had offered to bring Becca a cup of whatever exotic blend could be found in the expensive kitchen.

The kitchen presented as one would expect, an expanse of white marble—walls, floors, counters, island—broken up with gleaming stainless steel and a wall of small-paned windows, openings to the hallway at one end and a small dining room at the other. Not a dish or used spoon in sight, secure windows and two doors. One door opened directly to the driveway outside, shaded by overhanging trees; the other one led to a hallway that led to the five-car garage. As she processed, prints had appeared on both sides of both doors, random and crowded, as one would expect. Those two doors probably got more use than the rest of the home's openings combined.

Ellie found herself stymied by the coffeemaker. Of course this kitchen wouldn't have something as common as a Keurig.

She could have handled a Keurig. This one said Simonelli, with rounded contours like some anthropomorphic Disney prop.

"You have to put the water in there," a voice said from behind her.

She turned to see her first cousin once removed, taller but still a small girl with straight dark hair. She still wore her school uniform, a blue skirt with tiny pinstripes and a white collared shirt.

"Thank you. I'm Ellie, your mother's cousin. It's nice to meet you—again."

Taylor ignored this just long enough to make a point of the absurdity of pretending that life was normal. Then: "Have they found him?"

"No, not yet. I'm sorry about your brother's disappearance. I'm sure you miss him very much."

"Not really. He was a dragon baby. All he did was poop and cry."

Ellie stifled a laugh and didn't ask where the dragons fit in. "That's all most babies do."

"I'm not going to have any." She crossed her arms, daring Ellie to disagree.

"That's entirely up to you. Where are the cups?"

Taylor pointed at a cabinet. "He couldn't walk yet."

"Um—no."

"So somebody must have moved him. If you're making that for Mom, you have to use the hazelnut creamer. It's in the fridge." She didn't offer to help, opting not to curtail Ellie's ineptitude.

Ellie pulled open the massive stainless door. "Who would do that?"

"Anyone. Somebody's always picking him up," Taylor said as if that should be obvious. "But if someone put him somewhere else, like stuffed him in a closet in one of the empty rooms, he'd have started to cry after a while. Like I said, he's always crying."

Ellie pushed a button at random and coffee began to flow. The aroma of some dark roast wafted through the room.

"So he's probably not in the house anymore," Taylor concluded.

*He's not still alive.* Ellie tried not to form that thought in her mind. Becca had already told her: "We did search every room, just on the off chance he had mastered crawling in the past hour. He had begun to roll over—but climb out of the crib? Not a chance." And, of course, the subsequent search had borne this out.

"But it *is* a pretty big house," Taylor added as a qualification. "Are you a lobbyist?"

Ellie started. "Me? No, I'm a crime scene specialist."

"You mean like on TV?"

"That depends on what shows you're watching."

"You cut up dead bodies?" From the sound of her enthusiasm she might have discovered Ellie managed one of her favorite boy bands . . . if she even listened to boy bands.

"No, that's a pathologist. I work with the crime scene to gather evidence like fingerprints, DNA, blood—"

"That is *so cool!*" Taylor cried, smiling for the first time.

*Oh, what the hell,* Ellie thought. *I'm in. Just go with it.*

After delivering the coffee to Becca, still pacing in the sitting room, Taylor insisted on showing Ellie all the places baby Mason wasn't, as well as all points of egress by which he might have been removed by persons or persons unknown. Clearly, if this mystery were to be solved, it would have to be by Taylor, but she didn't mind having the company of someone cool enough to interpret bloodstains.

So Ellie and her small first cousin once removed traipsed

through countless guest rooms and drawing rooms and "conversation nooks" and bathrooms that deserved their own zip code, all resolutely devoid of trails, clues, or personality.

"This is my dad's office." Taylor paused outside one glossy walnut door. "We're not supposed to go in here."

Ellie already had, of course, to examine and process, and saw no need for a return visit. "Well, then, we'd better no—"

Taylor flung herself across the sill without hesitation. "He's in here *all* the time. He's a lobbyist. A lobbyist is a representative of a group of people or a company who want to present a point of view to the government."

"That must be very interesting."

"Oh, it is."

Taylor combed the shelves of a narrow closet for signs of her missing sibling while Ellie observed the habits of Becca's husband. Ellie had been taking a certification exam the day they married, giving her a handy excuse to skip the destination wedding on the Tahitian beach she couldn't have afforded, anyway. Besides, it had been their second wedding, the first a hasty civil ceremony when Becca had become pregnant their second year in college.

Ellie had to hand it to both of them: finishing school and even going on to a master's while caring for a toddler could not have been easy, yet they obviously remained as much a team today as they had been then. Hunter's family had a great deal of money, and that had undoubtedly helped with the financing, but still . . . not easy.

Hunter Carlisle had stacks of paper on nearly every surface, invariably topped with a neon sticky note. One said *COPPA*, the other *ChildChallenge*. A short one had been labeled *Casey*, and seemed to be copies of someone's credit card charges, with *Marriott* and *Métier* highlighted several times each.

The desk would have looked at home in the Oval Office, but it had been so crammed with file folders and papers, two laptops, and three brass paperweights that its owner had perhaps a square foot of space to actually work in. More sticky notes with mysterious titles, sometimes five to a stack, surrounded an ornate silver frame with a photo of a dog.

Not his wife or either child. Not even Hunter with some incredibly famous person. Just an ordinary-looking tan boxer, with perky ears and big brown eyes.

"He's not here," Taylor announced, emerging from the closet.

Ellie asked, "Who's this? Do you have a dog?" The better to foil kidnappers—or not. Perhaps this would be a curious incident of the dog that *didn't* bark.

"No, and Mom says they're too much work so we can't get another one, but we used to," Taylor said. "That's Benjy. Dad's dog. He died."

"Oh, that's too bad. When was that?"

"Come on. We still have the attic. It's haunted."

Ellie replaced the frame exactly as she'd found it. "Haunted?" The kid probably loved her *Goosebumps* TV show and books.

The "attic" was simply an abbreviated third floor, extending over only the main drag of the house and with ceilings only eight feet high instead of twelve. Four rooms were used for storage but even their sheet-draped furniture couldn't rise to the level of creepy, not with the afternoon sun slanting through the panes. Ellie asked what made the floor haunted.

"It makes sounds. I hear things moving up here, when I'm supposed to be sleeping."

"Where do you hear the sounds?"

"All over. Sometimes they're right over my bedroom. Then they move down the hall."

If this frightened her, she did a masterful job of hiding it. Perhaps the "haunted" charge had simply been a carrot to move them out of her father's office. "I can't hear any creaking."

"Well, not now," Taylor said with more than a hint of scorn. "Not in daytime. Nothing's haunted during the *day*. Want to see the secret steps?"

Of course Ellie wanted to see the secret steps, which turned out to be not secret at all, since they opened to the central hallway at each landing. But the narrow column wound from the "haunted" attic past the second floor, past the first floor, and into the basement space stocked with enough workout equipment to supply an LA Fitness and two eighty-five-inch screens to watch while one used it. The ceilings weren't quite as high as on the upper floors, but close. Ellie had largely ignored it on her first pass, since it had no exterior windows.

The room also held an entertainment system and stacks of CDs. Taylor ran to the console and pushed a button. AC/DC poured out of the speakers in a tangible wave that nearly knocked Ellie into the Technogym equipment.

"Can you turn that off?" Ellie shouted, though she could barely hear her own words above the din.

Taylor did not. She merely stood next to the pulsing speaker, stared at Ellie, and smiled.

Blood relative or not, Ellie would not be jerked around by a middle schooler. She stalked over and pushed the button again, creating an abrupt silence. "It's a wonder your father isn't deaf, playing stuff that loud."

"Come on," Taylor said. "This way."

The girl led her quickly through the rest of the basement, apparently not interested in the more utilitarian areas of the home. Ellie recalled the JonBenét Ramsey case with a shudder. She saw evidence of the police/FBI search—items had clearly been moved, storage boxes slid away from the wall. Given the extreme order of the rest of the house, Ellie felt confident that even these dusty spaces would not have looked like this before the search. She'd been working with law enforcement personnel for eight years and chose to trust their competence: Mason Carlisle was no longer on the property.

Moving back up to the ground floors, Taylor insisted they check out Becca's home office as well. The empty room appeared equally as lavish as her husband's, but with a better filing system—literally. Several of the bookcases, Taylor showed her, were hidden filing cabinets. Short shelves and the books on them rolled outward, revealing drawer after drawer of alphabetized—what, exactly?

"My mother," Taylor explained, "is the senior policy advisor to the Senate Committee on Commerce, Science, and Transportation."

"She told me that," Ellie said. "It sounds important."

"It's *extremely* important. That's why they have to work so much, to keep the country going."

Nice that the little girl was clearly proud of her parents . . . or at least their occupations. Or at least her own ability to describe their occupations. Ellie hadn't even been aware that congressional committees *had* their own policy advisors.

Several words jumped out from Becca's paperwork on a regular basis: KidFun, FTC, *Reno* v. *ACLU*, and Xanga Corp. Three neat stacks on her desk were held in place with decorative replicas of chips from the MGM National Harbor casino, a bit of whimsy not in keeping with the rest of the house. Heavy textbooks lined the shelves, with topics from mycology to water pollution to anthropology and criminal justice.

Becca kept more photos around her than her spouse—two of the couple, several of Taylor alone or with her parents, one of Becca, Taylor, and Mason on the same couch in the sunny room where Becca and Tara liked to chat. It was the only nonstudio shot Ellie had seen, other than the one of Benjy.

"And here's another door," Taylor pointed out. While Hunter's office had been on the second floor, Becca's sat on the ground floor, with French doors leading to a patio. As Ellie watched, the little girl pulled up the bolts from the floor and turned a dead bolt, which freed both doors to swing out. Then she examined her hands, now patchily coated with black.

"Sorry," Ellie said. "I had to process all the doors for finger-prints."

"Cool!" Taylor clapped her hands together, as if she could dislodge it like chalk dust from an eraser. Then she gave up and wiped them on her skirt. Ellie had no time to protest, and it would wash out anyway. "But see, there's a camera."

Taylor pointed to a dark bubble mounted over the top of the door. It was subtle, barely bowing out of the frame. No one approaching the house would notice it unless they looked, but surely a kidnapper would look?

"There's also an alarm." Ellie noted the unobtrusive wires connected to the door frame.

"But it's not on during the day. The lady who used to do the cooking used to turn it on all the time because she said it was creepy being out here in the middle of nowhere with no one around, but Dad kept setting it off when he'd come home and yelled at her and she stopped doing it. Do you think it's creepy here?"

Ellie gazed around at the rolling lawn and the shimmering Potomac. The place looked like the outdoor setting of an

F. Scott Fitzgerald novel. She couldn't imagine what it must have cost to buy this type of privacy so close to teeming DC. "I think it's beautiful."

"I like nobody being around," Taylor said, and did a little hop down the flagstones. The open patio ended after thirty feet, a pair of stone lions flanking the three wide steps to the lawn proper. Taylor patted the paw of one of the Sphinx-like lions. "This is George."

"George is pretty cool. Who's his partner?"

"He doesn't have a name. Come see the river."

Taylor crossed the expanse of grass, still perfectly green in these fall days, reached the wooden dock and ran pell-mell toward the end as if about to throw herself off. The sight made Ellie's heart clutch, but her head overruled it: Taylor seemed much too sensible a girl to wet her clothes. Instead, when she reached the end of the dock, she flung herself onto her stomach, head over the edge, feet waving above stocky knees.

Ellie followed. The thick planks of the dock barely stirred, but the wood had seen better days, possibly too far from the house to demand its level of maintenance. No boat clung to the posts, but Ellie saw a small boathouse off to their right. The water rushed by, spanning at least two hundred feet and they seemed to be opposite a park or preserve, an unbroken line of trees.

Taylor could just touch the water from her prone position, washing the powder from her palms. Its deep green color didn't allow a lot of visibility, but in the bright light Ellie could see the bottom with its silt, stones, and small, darting fish.

Taylor's shoulders gave a little quake when Ellie's reflection appeared in the water next to hers, but she only waved her arms to rough up the surface. Then she pointed to a flowery growth on the dock post. "You can eat those."

"No, thanks. I only eat things that have been vetted by experts." She had let Becca and her sister, Missy, talk her into trying too much of the West Virginia plant life. One sweet-looking berry patch had sent her to bed for two days.

"Seriously," Taylor said. "They call it the 'chicken of the woods.' Its real name is *Laetiporus*."

"I believe you."

"You can fish in this river too. There's white perch and stuff. When we first moved here, one time Daddy and me fished here. He caught a fish. He said it was a striped bass, but it wriggled off the line and got away and he called it a 'striped bastard.'" The naughty word made her giggle anew.

"This looks like a great fishing spot. It's so peaceful. I don't see any other houses—do you play with other kids in the neighborhood?"

The girl's face twisted in scorn, reflecting in the wavy water. "I don't *play*."

"That's too bad. Everyone deserves to play."

"I don't need to play. Because *I'm* exceptional."

*And because you have no one to play* with, Ellie thought. The scorn turned to a more considering look, almost . . . mischievous, but that sounded too innocent for the girl's sudden body language. She waved her hands over the dark water. "He's in here, you know."

Ellie tried very, very hard not to react. And failed. She could feel her face freeze in place and her lungs stop. She could not help but picture the helpless infant tossed in to drown, silently and quick. This would save the kidnapper the work of keeping a child fed and dry, and destroy the only evidence that could convict them. "Who is? Your brother?"

"No!" Taylor shot to her feet, bouncing with impatience. "Benjy."

Oh. "The dog?"

"Yes, the dog! He got old and tried to swim and drowned. His hair had gotten all white. But Mom said it's okay because he had arther-itis really bad so it was just like going to sleep and not feeling any pain ever again." She walked along the very edge as if it were a balance beam, arms outstretched, daring Ellie to tell her to stop. This time she did resist.

"My dad's hair is getting white in spots too. I wonder if he won't be able to swim much longer."

"Your dad—"

"Hey," Becca called from the lawn. "Come inside. Hunter's back."

# Chapter 7

Ellie reentered the large kitchen to meet her cousin's husband once again. From Becca's comments she expected a cross between Alexander Hamilton and Godzilla—but at the moment he seemed calm enough, relatively speaking, a slender blond man of average height in a perfectly fitted suit. Even Ellie could tell the material alone cost more than she would budget for a year's wardrobe. Taylor threw her arms around her father's waist and he clamped her to his side, briefly, without looking at her.

Before Ellie could re-introduce herself, Hunter said, "I got a text."

The three females in the room stared at him without comprehension and waited.

He thrust his phone onto the counter and all three leaned over the marble to peer at the screen: **We have your son. Go to the DM ban hearing tomorrow and speak the truth. Admit you violate 312. Do not delay or cancel hearing or you will not see son again. More instructions soon.**

Becca clapped her hands over her mouth, stifling a scream or a sob.

Hunter rushed on. "I was at the Locard when I got it. The doc ran us off to some chick in IT who tried to trace it, but it came back to a burner that wasn't on a network anywhere she could find."

"They didn't keep the phone?" Ellie spoke without thinking.

"More instructions are coming!" Hunter snapped. "Who are you again?"

"That's Ellie, Hunter. But this is about the *hearing*?" Becca cried. Now her daughter clasped her small arms around her mother's waist as if offering comfort, but the woman didn't seem to notice. "They took Mason because of the *hearing*? How is that possible?"

Ellie tried again, with perhaps a more relevant question. "What's three-twelve?"

"CFR three-twelve." Hunter ran one hand through his hair, then absently patted Taylor's shoulder. "It's the federal regulation regarding children's online privacy, says we can only collect personal information if necessary for game participation—which we *do*—and have to make sure all third-party users keep it safe—which we *also* do. But these nutcases think we gather it just to sell it on the dark web."

"Fine," Becca said. "We'll say anything they want. But then when do we get Mason back? And what if the committee votes in our favor, anyway?"

"I don't know." Worry for his son seemed to be eating him alive, leaving his skin chalky and his legs twitchy. Ellie had no trouble believing that he would disregard the FBI and bring in his own experts from the most prestigious private forensic lab in the country.

As if reading her thoughts, he said, "The woman from the Locard will be here any minute, should be pulling in right behind me."

"Are you sure this is a good idea?" Becca asked. "What if the kidnappers didn't want us to call the police?"

"Too late for that! We've already had an army out there beating the bushes—if anyone's watching, they're going to know we called the cops. Besides, we need them now. I doubt the FBI has the resources they have." He turned sharply to Ellie. "I'll expect your complete cooperation."

"Of course," she said . . . not at all sure she meant it.

Becca spoke impatiently. "Ellie always cooperates. And she's my *cousin*."

He said that was good, but didn't seem convinced. Ellie tried not to take this personally, supposing a lobbyist got used to looking for spies everywhere and besides, she didn't care what he thought. She wasn't there to impress either her cousin's husband or his hired gun.

Because Ellie *was* always cooperative.

Until she wasn't.

One happy thought—if Hunter and Becca *were* guilty and had disappeared their own child, they would hardly call in either the FBI or a premier consultant with access to the best in cutting-edge technology. They would have wanted to stick with the underfunded, overworked local cops.

Unless they thought they could pay Locard to look the other way—and they were delusional if they thought that.

A car sounded in the drive, rubber tires grinding against the concrete, and a Black woman stepped out of a sleek Audi as Michael Tyler stood in the driveway. Ellie wished she had had a chance to confer with him before the woman's arrival—how exactly was this going to work?—but hadn't been able to find him. Fine. *Let the Locard and the FBI duke it out. The winner gets my services. And no matter who wins, this will go down in my personal history as one of the weirdest cases I've ever worked.*

But of course the two agencies didn't come to blows. In fact, Michael Tyler politely opened the door for the woman, and they both came inside.

Dressed casually and well in business attire, Rachael Davies had perfected the neutral face—empathetic but professional, probing but not nosy, observing but not judging. *I could take lessons from her,* Ellie thought with envy. She had been working on her own neutral face since the age of four.

"Who are *you*?" Taylor demanded.

Hunter straightened and introduced Dr. Davies to Becca with a few words of hopeful reverence, his confidence in her evident. Becca only nodded coolly from across the island, either because she thought the FBI could do a better job than a private firm of experts or because nothing would have made her feel better other than Rachael turning up with baby Mason in her arms.

Rachael said something sympathetic to Becca and explained herself to Taylor in concise, noncondescending terms. Then Hunter introduced Ellie as "the FBI's forensic tech" and stopped. Everyone realized at the same time that he had forgotten her name.

No need. Rachael stepped closer and extended her hand. "Dr. Carr. How nice to meet you."

Ellie's surprise must have shown—further evidence that her ability to school her face had not improved even with extended practice—because Rachael leaned in and added quietly, "Your work on that ax murder in Chevy Chase was amazing."

"Thank you." *She's just being nice. Don't fall for it.*

"You've already processed?"

"Yes."

*Very* gently: "I'll need to take custody of your evidence."

"Oh," Ellie said, "*hell* no."


*2:15 p.m.*

Sophie Tran thought seventh-grade history would fry every brain cell she had into an omelet of torture and boredom. They were learning about westward expansion, her teacher droning on and on about how amazing it would have been to have miles and miles of empty space from which you could take your pick. Acre after acre of new land—he slipped and said "virgin territory," which made the dweeb boys laugh. The cooler ones, with more life experience, didn't seem to notice, a mild word like "virgin" having long since lost its ability to titillate. People could work hard and form into farms and ranches, her teacher said—good from their point of view, not so much for the Native Americans, but they would get to that next week. Sophie's teacher stared at the back wall as if wishing himself into those covered wagons; wishing himself anywhere, except locked in this room with twenty fidgeting middle schoolers.

You know what that life sounded like to Sophie? Boring. Incredibly, monumentally boring. It sounded like a cursed existence of heat, bugs, malaria and backbreaking labor. Sure, she had read the Laura Ingalls series from *Little House in the Big Woods* all the way through *The First Four Years*, and thought Laura sounded like a sweet kid, but OMG her life was dull.

Not like Sophie's. Her school had a lot more than one room, and SMART Boards, and field trips like last week's to the Supreme Court, where an actual judge had talked to them for a few minutes. Afterward, her mother had snorted, "For that tuition he ought to teach one of your classes," so Sophie hadn't admitted that he'd been kind of lame, and whatever she went to college for, it wouldn't be law.

And instead of having to wear long dresses everywhere— ugh—Sophie got to wear bike shorts and a sports bra when it was hot. Though her mother still wouldn't let her go to the store or anyplace real in them, so maybe not *everything* had changed since Laura Ingalls's day.

But Laura never had a smartphone, or made the soccer

team, or had a boyfriend. Well, not until she got old. Sophie
didn't have to wait that long. She would be meeting her new
boyfriend after practice that afternoon.

She'd only been chatting with Liam for a month, but he
seemed amazingly mature. She hadn't even known *Lion's
Reach*, her fave online game, *had* a chat feature until he'd
messaged her. She'd looked right past the little box in the
lower right corner, and so, obviously, had her mother, who
was a complete Nazi about the internet. Her mother was a
digital media researcher, which Sophie's father liked to joke
was not a real job. All Sophie knew was it had turned her
mother into a fountain of stories about kids being exploited,
abducted, blackmailed, and bullied into suicide, all because
of online contacts. She insisted on examining all Sophie's
apps, games, emails, texts, and posts, with access, passwords,
and veto power at all times. *Don't like it?* her mom would
say to her. *Get a job and pay for your own electronics.*

She even had screen mirroring on Sophie's stuff, so she
could see Every Single Thing Sophie looked at, every message or email or post or app that existed in Sophie's life.
Delete anything, and she lost the phone. Erase the browser
history, and she lost the phone. Arrange with someone to
move to an app her mother didn't know about, and she lost
the phone. Send a photo to anyone she had not physically
met and knew well enough to have over for dinner, and she
lost the phone. And the tablet, and the laptop—even the one
issued by the school.

Maybe, Sophie thought, Laura Ingalls really had been better off.

# Chapter 8

Ellie modulated her reaction to "I don't think so." Not gentle at all, an outburst of pure reaction, feet planted, spine turned to titanium. This went against every principle she could think of—

Michael Tyler cleared his throat. "The FBI has decided to work in cooperation with the Locard in the interest of expediency. Our lab is a bit overworked at the moment, with that attack at the Alexandria mall . . ." He let his voice trail off, quite discreetly for such a large man.

The wording wasn't lost on her. *The FBI* decided, not *I* or *we* decided. This had come from above his pay grade—meaning it was also above hers. She had no choice.

She said to Rachael, "You'd need an AFIS with access to NGI." Meaning an automated fingerprint identification system that could search the FBI's next generation identification databases, not just a list of whomever the Locard might have collected prints from in the ten years since its founding.

"We have that," Rachael said. "We can search Interpol and military too, if that seems necessary."

Can*not*, Ellie thought. The military would never allow that without all sorts of requests, subpoenas, and a really good reason.

As if feeling the skeptical vibes, Rachael amended, "Though not easily."

"I have a stack of swabs for contact DNA." Many labs had limited circumstances under which they'd analyze "touch" DNA, since it was such a crapshoot, without a visible stain.

"We can do that. And upload to CODIS."

Meaning they could also search their results through the combined DNA index system, though they'd have to go through a state lab to do it. Only law enforcement agencies could upload to CODIS. "Hairs might require mitochondrial."

Hair cells were technically "dead" keratin outgrowths, so contained no nuclear DNA for the standard analysis.

Rachael managed to sound more patient than condescending, something Ellie wasn't sure she could have pulled off if their roles had been reversed. "We can do that too."

Too often in life one had no choice. She hadn't when she'd left her grandmother's home for Aunt Rosalie's, then Aunt Katey's, then Uncle Paul's, or her marriage, or apparently now when she'd be leaving her evidence in some other agency's—a *private* agency!—hands.

Stop whining, she told herself. Forensic work was, by definition, reactive. A crime had occurred and her job was to assist the investigators, not take over. The FBI wrote her checks. If it was okay with the SACs, it would be okay with her. That was how it worked.

Besides, it was Becca. Ellie had to stay in the mix, no matter what.

She summoned up the best neutral face she could and

barely avoided throwing a scorching glare in Michael Tyler's direction. "Okay."

Thus, fifteen minutes later, after a quick tour—this one *not* conducted by Taylor, over her strong objections—Ellie and Rachael were seated cozily in Hunter's study, reviewing the security footage.

They watched without speaking, Ellie uncomfortable even in Hunter's ergonomic, aromatic leather chair nearly wide enough to accommodate two people. She had no idea what to say to a woman whose profile she had read about in the previous month's *Science* magazine, and no idea what expertise she could bear on a surveillance video. She'd viewed many such videos in the course of her work—amazing how many people had camera systems in their homes these days—but that hardly qualified her as a digital image analyst. So she sat in silence and more than a little awe of the woman next to her. Rachael Davies had dark skin, large eyes, striking features, and enough publishing credits to paper a wall.

Rachael had started the playback from Wednesday morning, just in case someone they didn't know about had approached the house in the twenty-four hours preceding the disappearance. The cameras were indeed above each exterior door, six in all, wide enough to cover most of the ground between each door. There would be ground-floor windows outside the reach of the various lenses, but the FBI agents and Ellie had found each one locked and without any signs of disturbance.

The cameras operated on motion activation, but were almost always recording, between bushes waving in the wind and the occasional bird. Two were not perfectly positioned; the one above the French doors leading to Becca's office did not show the four or five feet of space adjacent to the house, only the expanse of lawn out to the small dock at the river.

Then the one above the rear center door on the veranda immediately opposite, through over a hundred feet of house, the front door. That camera skewed toward the south, leaving the rear of the garage unseen.

The two women watched in silence as the picture lightened from grays and blacks to the yellows and pinks of early dawn. A Tesla emerged from one of the garage doors and drove out to the road as the door behind it closed automatically. Ellie could glimpse a blond man through the driver's-side window. Hunter on his way to work.

The pinks and yellows turned to the deep greens of the trees' foliage against a cobalt blue sky. Soon the garage expelled a large gray SUV, Becca at the wheel, the hint of a small head in the backseat. Ellie tried to see the car seat in the back, but couldn't differentiate the gray blocks of colored pixels. Taylor seemed to be hunched over a book. Soon Becca returned alone and the car disappeared into the garage.

After that, not much. The trees swayed gently and the shadows moved across the ground.

Rachael used the mouse to increase the speed from 1x to 2x. Almost immediately a blob of pixels flashed up the driveway.

Rachael gave an annoyed puff and ran it back. "That's the problem with videos. Watch them in real time and they take forever. Speed them up and you miss things."

At regular speed the blob settled into a pickup, loaded with equipment. A middle-aged man in a ball cap emerged with a bag. A younger version of him climbed out of the passenger seat, listlessly waving a pair of pruning shears.

Rachael consulted her tablet. "That's the landscaper. His usual day and time."

Apparently Michael had forwarded the timeline of personnel on the Carlisle estate. Seriously?

They watched as the men unloaded from a trailer in the driveway a riding mower with two huge cutting decks. Then watched as one started trimming the occasional branch on the perfectly shaped bushes as the other flew up and down the sprawling lawns on the mower, trimming the area in record time.

"That's pretty sweet," Rachael said. "I could do my yard in about three minutes with one of those."

Ellie recognized the effort to put them on a collegial setting, which normally she'd be all over—normally, she'd be the one making the effort. But she felt a need to show this woman that Ellie wasn't some new recruit straight out of the academy, all hopped up on binge-watching the ID Channel. And she couldn't think of a response, anyway; at the moment she didn't have a yard. A quick nod would have to suffice.

"I read a few articles about one of your cases," Rachael surprised her by saying as the man trimmed a few azaleas and a blurry truck stopped for the box at the end of the drive. "About analyzing the paper in that stalker murder."

"Um, yeah. That was interesting." Flattery would not sway her . . . though it was nice to hear.

"I did not know that about pen ink. And the jury convicted on all counts—excellent job."

She never knew what to say when someone complimented her work. *Thanks? Glad I could help?* Or: *It wasn't my fault?* She had only told the truth, to let the world and the young woman's family know what had happened to her. Now a second person would die from a lethal injection, while the first one had not been resurrected. So "glad" didn't quite cover it.

The landscaper finished his work, loaded up his equipment, and left the grounds, having never entered the house.

They'd make great suspects, could have snuck behind a camera's arc and gotten in a window, had this not been the day *before* Mason disappeared.

Ellie did not want to be churlish, and never unprofessional. More to the point she didn't want Rachael to think of herself as the only well-read person in the room. "Your study of using Bluestar on skin was very interesting."

"Thanks—" Rachael broke off, attention distracted by the garage door opening again. Becca drove out. The timestamp said *12:30*. Again Ellie could not see Mason's car seat in the vehicle, but surely he must be there. No one else had been home. Rachael hovered the cursor over the speed selection, but didn't increase. They watched as the minutes piled up with agonizing slowness, unable to risk missing a clue in the baby's disappearance. Even if it meant ten minutes of watching the azaleas shimmy.

The SUV returned at 3:10, with Becca and Taylor and, Ellie assumed, Mason. Ellie made a mental note to ask Becca where she had gone before retrieving Taylor from school that afternoon.

As if reading her mind, Rachael asked, "You're Ms. Carlisle's cousin?"

"Yes." She didn't tell her they'd lived in the same house for a few years, that Becca's mom, Katey, was still her favorite substitute mother. Instead, she added the useless factoid, "Our mothers were sisters." Friendly enough without giving up personal info that could be wielded later.

Nothing happened on the screen for so long that Rachael broke down and increased the speed once more. But still nothing occurred until 8:45 p.m., when a Bentley pulled up to camera 4, the kitchen door. A handsome, dark-haired man in a suit emerged and approached. The top of his head hovered at the bottom edge of the screen for a few minutes before disappearing from the camera's viewpoint. Obviously, he had knocked, waited, and been admitted to the household. An hour later he went back out and the Bentley drove away. Then they watched some long and unremarkable hours pass. No one came near any of the six doors to the Carlisle home except a couple of moths and a passing raccoon.

Ellie let her gaze wander over Hunter's desk. The piles of papers forming a ring at the perimeter appeared to be prints of articles or laws, nothing personal. On the blotter in front of her, the top page of one stack detailed the time and place and list of names for the hearing in question. At four p.m. tomorrow the Senate committee would hear testimony regarding the Protect Children's Privacy Act.

Wouldn't the hearing or vote or bill simply be redone once coercion had been revealed? Ellie had seen many crazy motives over the years, but kidnapping a child as an act of political extortion? In the U.S., unheard of. In some areas of the globe, quite common.

The other stack had been topped by an insurance form showing a zero copay for Hunter's prescription meds—atorvastatin and tamsulosin.

Ellie averted her eyes, awash in a sense of guilt. She'd been asked to help guide them through a criminal event, not pry into her cousin's husband's medical history. Hunter's cholesterol level did not suggest any relevancy to the disappearance of the baby.

She got up to stretch her legs and, once again, admire the view from the windows of the rolling grass—still green in the heat, they must have a sprinkler system or the landscapers came more than once a week—and the shimmering Potomac beyond it. The old-fashioned windows lent such an air of old-world money to the place, but she didn't envy the work it must take to clean them. Especially since she'd left a light coating of fingerprint powder over much of their surfaces.

Even the window cranks lined up in perfect order, standing erect at one o'clock. All except on the window centered over the credenza behind Hunter's workspace, the long heavy structure in the same burnished cherry as the desk. It lagged at five o'clock.

And, she now noticed, the latch had not been secured, its tail not tugged all the way down. Had she moved it when she'd fingerprinted? No, why would she?

With one finger she selected a spot on a strip of leading between panes and pushed.

The window edged open, about a single inch.

Touching the crank mechanism on the knob's very edge let her know it had broken, and the handle dangled uselessly. The latch hadn't quite caught because the window wasn't quite shut; she used a magnifying glass to see if the slit had been stuffed with a piece of white cotton or paper so that the hook couldn't catch, but she couldn't see anything in the tiny dark opening.

The alarm wires appeared to be connected, though. It didn't go off because the alarm wasn't turned on, as it wouldn't have been earlier that day. But it would have been at night?

Was this window a means to get in? Or a means to get out? Did Hunter sneak out of his house at night? To go where? Engage in a tryst in the woods with a neighbor, because nothing else was in walking distance, and if he took his car, he wouldn't need to go out the window. He could simply walk through the hallway from the kitchen to the garage.

But again, they were on the second floor. She poked her head out of the window, but didn't see a handy drainpipe or wide ledge or any other means of scaling the building other than an extension ladder. One would have to be a skilled aerialist to avoid a fall onto the flagstones below.

She pulled her flashlight out of a pocket, held it at an angle. Then reached it outside to hold it at more angles against the exterior of the glass. But she didn't see any more fingerprints. She had collected one or two from a bottom pane, she could see from the gaps in the powder coating left by the tape lifts. Perhaps she had pushed the window slightly ajar when doing that.

She turned to point out this anomaly to Rachael, but the woman remained glued to the surveillance video.

"Huh," Rachael said again. "What is that?"

# Chapter 9

Luis Alvarez knocked on Tara Esposito's door. The house looked like a palace compared to his modest brownstone, but not nearly as palatial as her client's. Apparently, managing other people's money wasn't nearly the same as actually having enough money to manage in the first place.

Tara opened the door with a sleeping baby tucked into one arm. "I've been afraid to let go of her after what happened to Becca. I know that's silly." She ushered him into a great-room area consisting of a showplace kitchen, a dining nook, and a family room that fit two full-size sofas, a fireplace under a seventy-inch flatscreen, three bookcases, and a computer desk tucked into a bay window extension. It smelled of cinnamon, which made him hungry. At least one baby toy, blanket, diaper (unused), or bottle marked each surface as testament to the priorities of this household. Tara waved him toward a brown suede couch. "But maybe not that silly. I don't know—someone who would target the Carlisles would hardly notice my tax bracket. But if motherhood has taught me one thing, it's that logic stops applying."

Tara Esposito didn't quite fit the DC power broker image.

She had the looks—honey-gold hair that hung past her shoulder blades, exquisite but comfortable clothes, slender to the point of borderline anorexia. Yet her eyes and face seemed too soft, more suited to kindergarten teacher than financial wizard, her voice uncertain. He said, "I can understand that."

"You have children?" she asked him.

"Two. One more in about four more months."

Which might have been why his partner asked him to do this interview, while Michael stayed at the house. He had insisted all babies looked alike to him, which Luis doubted, since Michael had two kids with his ex, but Luis *could* see right away that the sleeping Harper (a) existed, and (b) had not been switched with Mason. Mason's round little cherub face topped with dark peach-fuzz hair could not be confused with the baby now three feet away from him. Harper had a more oval face, pointing chin, and apparently favored her mother with white-blond tresses already growing in. She had a nose like his second boy, Thiago. They didn't know what their third would be, though he'd been trying to talk his wife into letting the doctor tell them. She said she didn't care, but Luis was dying for a little girl.

He'd been staring too long. "I want to help," Tara prompted. "I can't stand the thought of that sweet baby . . . and what Becca must be feeling! Oh—can I get you anything? Water, soda, coffee? It's no trouble."

He could have killed for a latte, but didn't want to eat up any unnecessary time, couldn't rationalize his own comfort when a baby had been taken . . . every minute without success felt like a needle prick. Besides, witnesses or suspects often fussed with refreshments as an avoidance technique. He made his voice extra calm. "No, thank you. Tell me what happened today."

As she spoke, he checked notes, compared times. She told the same story Becca Carlisle had—not word-for-word, and with slight vagaries in the timing, but those made her sound more truthful and not less. She'd been up early with Harper, fed her, put together a portfolio for another client while Harper napped. "I'm still on maternity leave, technically, though I already did half my work from home, so you could say I'm part-time."

"And you work at—"

"Proctor Wealth Management. I'm a partner. I'll tell you the truth, I'm not even sure I want to go back unless I can work from home full-time." She told him that she threw some papers she needed Becca to sign in her diaper bag and packed up Harper and drove over there. Harper fell asleep on the way, always a good thing. She'd had "a rough night." Tara suspected colic, but the baby doc did not agree.

"Was this a business meeting?"

"No—yes—it was only supposed to be a coffee klatch, new-moms-catching-up kind of thing, but we always wind up on business, one way or another. I handle their investments, accounts, taxes. If we're not talking about their money, we're talking about other people's money or other people's bills or other people's scandals. And the babies too, of course."

"What were the papers for?"

Tara Esposito spoke with unconscious animation, the muscles in her face and the shifting of her body describing each word beyond its technical meaning, the blond tresses quivering like a waterfall. "Okay, look, Becca said I should tell you *anything*, including her financials, even things that would normally be confidential."

"Understood." This wasn't gossip, she had the client's permission. Tara Esposito adhered to her profession's rules.

"It really wasn't anything urgent, I only wanted to move some funds out of her callable notes to Hunter's SEP. Nothing terribly time-sensitive, I mostly just felt like getting out of the house. It's all prep work for the IPO—" Her fingers found the large diamond around her neck and rubbed it; ostensibly straightening the pendant, but also engaging in a classic pacifying action for people who are stressed or fearful. Plenty in this situation to be fearful about—so, why would the mention of KidFun's initial public offering set it off?

"The KidFun IPO?" Luis spoke casually, trying to give the impression he knew all about it. "It's been mentioned. Are you involved with that?"

"No—I handle Hunter's personal finances, not business. He's got his own bookkeepers at Carlisle Communications, and I don't have anything to do with KidFun, or the legislation."

Interesting wording. She handled Hunter's personal finances . . . with a slight inflection on Hunter, not Hunter and Becca, and *personal*.

She went on. "They're hoping for a one hundred, maybe one hundred fifty percent increase in the stock price with the IPO . . . ambitious, but it's been done—Airbnb. DoorDash, almost. With Hunter's stake in the company, he's going to have a huge influx of cash, and needs a plan in place to deal with that."

"Nice problem to have."

"*If* the IPO is successful." She stopped, paused, then inspected her child again, as if the baby had stirred. She had not.

"Why wouldn't it be?"

She laid the baby on the sofa in front of her, surrounded the infant with pillows. The little girl sighed and stretched, but remained blissfully silent, eyes closed. Tara kept her hand on the baby's ankle as if a kidnapper might lurk in the next room. "This direct-messaging ban sank recent revenues. As I'm sure you know—"

He didn't, but nice of her not to assume that.

"—an IPO is quite the undertaking. They had to bring in independent auditors to look at their historical financials, as well as their history of general 'governance,' board meetings held, meeting minutes taken, the compensation committee that oversees executive pay, company bonus programs—so on and so forth. This all has to go into the S-1 document. And the SEC takes a close look at all of it."

"Is that a problem?"

"No . . . but with all that scrutiny it won't go unnoticed that KidFun's revenues took this dip. And if that ban isn't overturned, they will continue to dip. No one's going to be clamoring to buy shares, Hunter and Gabriel won't be able to make it a huge news event and whip up a buying frenzy if share prices are going down instead of up."

In his pocket his phone gave a tiny, silent quiver. He ignored it. Never break up the momentum with a witness, even a completely cooperative one. "And that depends on tomorrow's hearing."

"Yes, very much."

"But even if it fails, they could cancel the IPO and try again with a future hearing?"

"Yes, but they've already invested so much in the process. They had to hire the independent auditing firm, bring on extra staff to prepare all the records and paperwork for inspection. It's a huge investment, and they'd lose every penny of it. Hunter would—he started thinking about doing a SPAC, he felt so desperate."

Luis didn't even pretend to know what that meant. He raised his eyebrows, which sufficed.

"A special purpose acquisition company is sort of an end run around all the disclosure—in *some* cases. In a SPAC a management group forms a shell company that is basically nothing, no assets, no history, and sells shares at an IPO. The shares usually come with a warrant for investors to buy a certain number of shares at a certain price, after the IPO. The money generated goes into a trust, and the management company has to buy an existing company with the money in the trust. If that doesn't happen, investors get their money, or some money, back. If they do buy a company, the investors can decide if they want to keep their shares or sell them before that company is combined with the shell. It has some advantages, and can be really great investments."

"Sounds a bit—"

"Shady? They kind of were, for a long time. Finally the SEC began regulating them, so they're actually booming right now. But everything depends on the people running both the shell and the real company—do you trust them to make money, or not? Are they wizards or wannabes? Hunter thought Gabriel's reputation would be enough to get them anything they wanted."

"You don't think so?"

"I do! The problem is Gabriel *didn't.* He believed nothing would counteract KidFun's problems. Hunter couldn't convince him. I think that's why—" She stopped, patted the bundle of cloth that wrapped her baby's body. Either Harper could communicate telepathically with her mother, or Tara used the kid as an excuse to stop talking.

He pressed, "That's why what?"

She continued to hesitate, and the business-related clues— to which he hadn't paid much attention in what seemed to be a domestic incident—clicked for him. He said: "Hunter's going to sell out after the IPO. The value of the shares go up, he sells them all. That's why he needs places to put the funds."

Tara neither confirmed nor denied. "It's a huge amount of money. Enough to ensure anything they could want in the future, and anything the kids"—she hesitated, then purposely used the plural—"the kids might need."

"So this hearing really is vital." No longer a question.

"Completely vital."

For the first time Luis could understand why Hunter and Becca might be preoccupied with their work in the face of their child's loss. Not understand, exactly. But it made them less nuts than he had originally thought.

How did the former figure into the latter, though? Becca might have been so stressed that she accidentally killed Mason. They might be planning to ask for a ransom that they themselves would steal, in order to hide some of their funds from the tax man in case their bank account took a hit. Maybe they *sold* Mason to raise money to pay for the IPO. No theory seemed too outrageous to consider, but none even wobbled toward convincing either. "Okay. Sorry—I got sidetracked. We were going over your day. You arrived at the Carlisle house?"

Tara coughed, and Harper's tiny fist jerked. They both inspected the baby, waited, then continued. "I'd brought over my proposals, and we were going over them. And chitchatting, of course. It's rare that we both have a low-key day. Then Gabriel showed up."

"What time was that?"

She should say eleven, according to Becca.

"Eleven, I think. Maybe five to? I can't be sure, but I'd been checking my watch . . . I'm trying to keep track of how long Harper sleeps and when."

"You've met Gabriel Haller before?"

Tara made a sound between a snort and a chuckle. "Yes, of course. He and Hunter are thick as—they're very close. I've run into him over there lots of times, parties, dinners out with my husband and me."

"So the three of you talked about the hearing?"

"Mostly Gabriel and Becca talked, and I sat around because I didn't feel like going home and getting back to work. And then it was time to pick up Taylor and I offered to stay with—with Mason."

"Where was Mason?"

She blinked. "What?"

A simple question. "Where was Mason all this time?"

"Oh! He fell asleep and Becca put him down for a nap."

"When?"

"I'm not sure—ten after eleven? Quarter after?" Tara sat back, away from him, but with her fingers still on the baby's foot. "Is it important?"

"No. I'm simply trying to picture everyone's movements. So when you got there, Becca had Mason in the sitting room?"

"Yeah."

"And then she carried him upstairs and put him in his crib?"

"Uh-huh."

She spoke as if that should be obvious, and, he thought, that very routine maternal action should be. He'd just wanted to confirm that both Tara and Gabriel Haller had put eyes on Mason that morning. "And you didn't see him after that?"

"No. The whole house was so silent, I was sure I would hear him if he cried. He has—had—*has* a piercing cry." Sitting rather than standing did not help Luis to pick up non-verbal clues, because feet were never as schooled in deception as heads and hands. But Tara did shift herself back—only another inch away from him, but even that small bit of distancing could signify her discomfort with a topic.

But a missing child would always be a discomforting topic, especially to a woman obviously enthralled with her own infant. She went on to say that Harper had been snoring away. Her face broke into a wide, utterly genuine smile, so sweet that Luis found himself smiling along. "She actually snores, it's the cutest thing. Anyway, we just stayed in the sitting room. Becca and Gabriel walked out together, and I heard the cars start up and drive away. I sat on the couch and checked my email."

"You didn't go up to Mason's room?"

"No." The smile faded to a great sadness, as if she could

have stopped the kidnapping if only she hadn't been so interested in her social media. "Becca came back in, I don't know, twenty or thirty minutes. Harper had begun to stir, and I knew she'd want to eat as soon as she woke, so I had already packed up my stuff, Becca gave me a hug, and I left." Weariness showed in the beautiful face, and she rubbed one eyebrow with the back of a hand. "That was it."

Luis waited to see if she would add anything more, but, provided this had all been the truth, she had nothing more to give. "What can you tell me about the nanny?"

The expressive face reacted to the change in topics, but without apprehension. "Jenny? She's great. Puts up with Taylor, who . . . can be a challenge. And she isn't here, you know."

All the players had made it abundantly clear that Jenny Cho had not been in the country when the kidnapping occurred. Just as Becca had made it clear that Tara had not left the house with Mason tucked under one arm.

His phone shivered again. This time she heard it, gaze flickering to his pocket, but he said, "Any other difficulties with Jenny's work here? Any tensions that she might have felt for the Carlisles, or vice versa?"

"Nothing that I know of."

"All right. Can you think of anyone who would want Mason badly enough to kidnap him?"

"Like some baby-obsessed woman? I can totally understand if someone couldn't have . . . I don't know what I'd do without Harper, but no. All of our friends either have kids of their own, or don't on purpose. I mean, it could be someone we *don't* know, but how could they get in and out of the house without Becca realizing it?"

"That's what I keep coming back to. Okay, last question, then I'll let you go. Can you think of anyone, *anyone*, who would want to do this to the Carlisles?"

"No one. I just can't imagine. If it were Harper . . . I'd have to be sedated." Her eyes filled with tears at the thought of the baby, utterly helpless to affect his fate. Luis felt his own throat tighten up as well—his job required objectivity, but he couldn't help but picture his two, soon to be three. If anything happened to them . . .

"They'd better keep an extra-close eye on Taylor," Tara whispered. "Just to be sure."

# Chapter 10

Noah Thomas saw the woman as she walked up to the pickup office window and typed the security number into the board there. She wore a green polo shirt with a name tag and held a clipboard, from which she checked the number to be sure. The dorky admin working the window that day checked her monitor, fumbled through a pile of papers to make sure there had been a note from Noah's dad delivered, and finally said Noah could leave.

"Noah?" the woman asked as soon as he emerged, her gaze locking on like a laser beam (simile, not metaphor)—not that it was difficult to pick him out. Black kids were a distinct minority at the school. "Noah Thomas?"

"That's me." He tried to look her in the face, but didn't want to—he really hated talking to adults he didn't know. Her name tag read MILLIE underneath HOME RUN CAMP in plain letters. It was one of those plastic sleeves with a paper insert so you can print your own. His mother had made up a bunch for a charity barbecue she had to organize and all the ladies complained because they had to stick pins in their clothes.

"Great." She led him to the kind of van not usually seen waiting for students in the controlled "School's out!" chaos outside Virginia Prep—dull beige paint and a dent in the rear fender. Noah hoped the accommodations would not match it . . . Once he'd gone to a summer camp that showed sparkling pools and fluffy beds in the brochure, but actually the pillows had smelled and there were dead ants stuck around the baseboards. Noah would camp out in a tent with no bug spray for the chance to hone his fastball, but that didn't mean he preferred it.

He stuck right to her side. She might be picking up a group of kids, and if they filled up that van, would he have to wait for another? But no worries, the seats were empty . . . and the tires worn, spots of rust along the doors. Parents had to stay in their cars but substitute picker-uppers had to sign in at the office, and in this town there were always substitutes—nannies, housekeepers, drivers, all the cars tightly regulated. Noah didn't know what the school worried about more—kids being snatched by non-custodial parents or kids getting creamed by some diplomat's Range Rover.

A horn beeped, probably at them—the pickup line got cutthroat. His dad said he'd rather get in the middle of warring biker gangs than pickup line parents.

Millie pulled open the side door. "Your mother already dropped off your stuff at the camp and we took care of all the paperwork online. Hop in."

He grasped the frame, slinging his overstuffed backpack over one shoulder.

"I'll take that," she said, and pulled it from him in one smooth motion.

"You sure? It's heavy."

"What a polite young man you are. But it's fine." She hitched it over her own shoulder as he settled in the seat nearest the door. As she did, the name tag flopped up enough to reveal an embroidered logo underneath it: CARSON'S CAR WASH.

"Anybody else coming?" Noah asked her. He hoped Barry Wilson wouldn't. Barry was a year older than him, and big, and went to baseball camp every summer for weeks and weeks. Barry had tried out for the traveling team twice already.

"Just you from this location." She slid the door shut and walked around the vehicle, got in the driver's seat. Somehow she crammed his backpack in front of her seat, next to the door, practically under her legs, though they had an entire van to store it in. A horn blared again. "We'd better get going," Millie said. "They're pretty impatient here, aren't they?"

*4:32 p.m.*

In the video the colorful landscape had faded to the grays and blacks of the previous night. Pixels shifted and floated and settled into a figure in white, walking away from the house. The time read 11:55.

"What door is that?"

"Becca's office," Ellie said.

Rachael said, "Why didn't the alarm sound? Surely, Becca would have set it before going to sleep."

"Especially with Hunter out of town. Wait, did that sound chauvinistic? It sounded chauvinistic." Ellie spoke without thinking, forgetting to be prickly, but then prickly had never been something she could keep up for very long.

Rachael made a sound between a snort and a chuckle. "Or it was Hunter's nightly habit, and she forgot to do it."

"Or," Ellie said, "Taylor turned it off."

Because as they watched the video progress, the figure gained definition briefly before moving out of range and turning grainy. Straight hair past the shoulder blades, but not as dark as Becca's. The anime graphics on the pajama pants were surely too juvenile for her cousin to wear, and the lilac bush that brushed Ellie's shoulder that afternoon came level with the figure's head. It had to be Taylor.

The little girl walked in a straight line to the dock, moving to the end of it. At this distance Taylor became a light-colored stick with the occasional shard of a limb as appendages, only vaguely recognizable as human. The figure stood still, then made a sharp movement. Then still again.

"Did she just throw something in the water?" Ellie asked aloud. It looked as if Taylor threw a white bundle into the river. A bundle, the size of a small dog. Or a baby. Ellie only then recognized that she had been carrying something, since they'd only seen her from the back as she left the house, something large enough to require both hands.

Taylor stood at the edge for what seemed like a long time, but less than a minute according to the timestamp. Then she turned around and made another straight line back to the door she'd exited. On the flagstones of the patio, she looked up at the camera—perhaps she'd just remembered its existence. Or she wanted to be seen.

Rachael ran the recording back. The white stick at the edge of the dock, a quick flicker of a tiny white blob disappearing into the inky water or simply the night.

"Definitely her," Rachael said. "This raises some questions."

"To put it mildly," Ellie said. "What did she toss, if she threw anything, and it's not some trick of the light . . . maybe her sleeve as she threw a stone? But why in the middle of the night?"

Rachael said, "Videos of dark areas are notoriously unreliable. Photos are all about light, and when the light isn't there, the pixels have to try to fill in the gaps. Then there's dust, clouds across the moon—that's why people think they see ghosts."

Ellie didn't know if she was showing off or trying to prove her objectivity in regard to Ellie's family. "I know that. Or, Taylor murdered her brother and Becca concocted the whole kidnapping story the next day to protect her daughter. It's okay. I might be Becca's cousin, but I'm also a forensic specialist." Juvenile murderers weren't common, but hardly unheard of.

Rachael considered this, looking at Ellie as if she could see through to the back of her skull. "All right, then. That is a possibility. But it would require Oscar-winning performances from both of them. Becca had to fool two close friends, cops, FBI agents, and maybe her own husband. Taylor had to get through a school day without alerting teachers or friends."

"True." Though Ellie suspected Taylor might not have a lot of friends, and anyone who could so calmly kill her baby brother might not have trouble sitting in class as if all were normal.

"What's Taylor like?"

*I think she's an emotionally neglected, very lonely little girl who's in total denial about being a lonely little girl.* But it seemed disloyal to say so, and, besides, what the crap did she know about parenting? So she punted: "I don't know. Today is the first time I've even spoken to her."

"Is she into the paranormal at all?"

"I wouldn't know." She *had* mentioned dragons.

"Preteen girls often are."

"I know. They're old enough to want some personal power, but not old enough to date or get a job, and that frustration—boys fantasize about being James Bond and killing anyone they don't like, and girls fantasize about being a witch. You can have anything you want. That's why the TV show *Charmed* is still in daily syndication."

Rachael laughed. "I thought it was because the girls looked like models in every scene."

"That too. It makes sense. Girls are trained to be unaggressive, maybe nurturing. Being able to blink up a new dress or new house for your bestie doesn't hurt anyone—unless you need it to. And imaginations are so strong at that age."

"Exactly."

But, Ellie thought, two girls Taylor's age had stabbed and left for dead a friend of theirs in order to please an urban legend known as "Slender Man." Imaginations were weapons that could be used for evil, as well as good. "We won't know until we ask her," Ellie said, "which is extremely problematic. Even though neither of us, in this capacity, are law enforcement personnel, questioning a juvenile . . . because if she *did* murder her brother, anything she tells us needs to be admissible. We'll have to tell the SACs."

"Yes. But we hardly want to call in the agents to grill the kid if she was tossing in birch leaves to summon a fairy godmother. We can clear it with Michael but it won't hurt if you simply ask her."

"Me." Of course her, but it wasn't an idea she relished. In fact her stomach screamed, *No no no!* Questioning people was not her forte. Questioning children, *definitely* not her forte. There was a reason she chose to work with fingerprints and bullet casings and other inanimate objects.

"You're her cousin. There's no legal complications, whatever she says to you. And for what it's worth, I don't believe she killed her brother. No child has that much acting ability."

Ellie felt better at this validation . . . a little. "We"—apparently they were *we* now—"need to ask this Gabriel and Tara if they actually *saw* Mason this morning, or not. And pin Becca down about this morning—what time did she get up, when did Mason wake, when he ate, when he napped, et cetera." And then ask again. And again. Try to catch inconsistencies in her cousin's story. Try to catch her cousin in a lie.

Rachael interrupted these thoughts. "But if Becca woke to

find the baby gone, made up the story to protect Taylor, why wouldn't she just open a window and call the cops right away? Why concoct this less believable story of Mason disappearing in the middle of the day when everyone was home? And why not erase or destroy this video?"

"Taylor might not have told her the details." But that *was* a good point. Maybe Taylor really had been summoning a dragon.

Images from the next day provided no surprises. The SUV left for Taylor's school, returning promptly this time. At 11:05 a.m., a woman with blond hair and fair skin pulled up to the front in a Jaguar, toting a diaper bag on one side, the other shoulder dipping toward a baby carrier. The carrier had been covered with a thin blanket even in the warm air. The woman also hovered at the door, at the lower edge of the camera's range before disappearing.

"I assume that's Tara," Rachael said.

"Neither of the best friends have a key to the house."

"Or don't bother to use it," Rachael said.

"True. Clearly, Tara had her hands full."

At 11:32 a.m., the Bentley pulled up to the kitchen door again and the handsome man emerged, knocked, disappeared inside. Another twenty minutes elapsed. Gabriel left in the Bentley, and just as it had the previous afternoon, Becca's SUV left the garage and drove away. The Jaguar remained in the drive. The SUV returned at 12:30 p.m.; shortly afterward, Tara labored under her burdens back to her car and left. Eight minutes and thirty seconds later, at 12:48, the Tesla drove up the drive and entered the garage. Hunter had a bit of a lead foot, Ellie noted.

Inside the house and away from the cameras, Becca would be caring for Taylor, Hunter unwinding after his trip. Ellie wondered if he would have gone in to look at his son. Ellie had grown up with school-age children, but there had never been a baby in the household. On television parents were obsessive about their kids, missing them terribly every minute apart . . . but maybe that wasn't reality. Maybe the four-month-old had been a bad sleeper, with everyone under strict orders not to risk waking him until he alerted them with a wail. She had so many questions, but right now, none of them seemed relevant. Only one remained: Who removed Mason from the house?

Assuming, of course, he was not still there. Blood relation or not, Ellie knew better than most that parents killed their children somewhere on the globe every day. They shook them too hard, or wanted to quiet their screams if only for a moment with a hand over their mouth. They needed to get them out of the way for a few hours and dropped too much allergy medicine in their milk. Or they turned away from the bathtub, the changing table, the top of the stairs, for just a moment and then panicked, fearing prosecution, the anger of a spouse, or that their other children might be collected by the state. The Carlisles wouldn't be the first to cover up even an innocent event with a story of a mysterious stranger somehow entering their home.

But that would not explain where the baby had physically *gone*. Hiding a corpse, even a small corpse, is not easy. And the cameras showed no movement outside until cop cars came screaming up to the circular turnaround in the front at 1:25 p.m. No one had left. And even if the baby had been discovered missing exactly when Hunter returned home, that gave them only thirty-seven minutes to remove the child and come up with a story. Or if Becca discovered the crib as soon as Tara left, maybe fifty. Not much time to experience a fatal accident, decide to conceal it, and plan a story that had evidently fooled both the local police and the FBI.

The scene outside the house continued with serene trees and the indifferent grass. Inside, chaos would have erupted.

She glanced at the former pathologist. Rachael's eyes seemed glued to the timestamp. Clearly, she wanted to know just how much time had elapsed—"When did the 911 call go out?" Ellie asked her.

"One-fifteen."

Consistent with Becca's statement.

"But," Rachael said, "did Becca *see* Mason—"

"Between the time she got home and Tara left?"

"Though Tara didn't seem to be carting out an extra baby."

They ran the tape back. The blanket had not been replaced and a white infant could be seen in the carrier, waving one pudgy fist. But whether it was Harper or Mason, Ellie couldn't begin to guess and she doubted the motion and the lighting would ever allow for the necessary clarity. Surely, Becca would have noticed her own baby being carted out by the wrong mother.

On the video more officers arrived and some remained outside, walking the grounds, apparently checking every window and bush. They crisscrossed the grass, certainly looking for tracks. Some hovered at the river's edge, pointing and milling about; more went into the woods. Eventually the unmarked SUV arrived, and two men in suits got out, one tall and imposing and the other lighter and leaner. Michael Tyler and Luis Alvarez.

"There they are," Rachael said.

"Have you worked with them before?" If Rachael could pick her brain, she could return the favor.

"Yeah—had them in my advanced shooting-scenes class. Have you known them long?"

"Never met them before today."

Rachael seemed surprised, though the Bureau had nearly

nine hundred special agents at the Washington field office. "Good guys. I've never actually worked a case with them, but from what I saw, I would feel confident in their abilities if I were your cousin."

"Good to know." *Even though they're turning our investigation over to a private lab.*

But she would cooperate. She had always been cooperative.

# Chapter 11

Ellie went to look for Taylor, leaving Rachael with the video system to make some notes and upload the relevant videos to the Locard server—including the video of Taylor. If the girl turned out to be guilty, it would be vital evidence that the owner of the system, her parents, controlled. It might disappear, like the eighteen minutes of the Watergate tapes, should Hunter and Becca feel that they couldn't risk losing their only other child.

*Dr. Davies doesn't trust us,* Ellie thought—*but why should she?* Lies came easily to people trying to protect a loved one. Hunter might have hired Rachael, but that didn't mean he owned her, any more than the Bureau owned Ellie. Hunter hadn't been there, but having seen the two of them together, she couldn't imagine Becca taking on the task of protecting her daughter without her partner. Michael and Luis would subpoena their cell phone records, but long conversations, or even short, hectic ones, would prove nothing. With this hearing consuming their lives, they'd have a lot to talk about under any circumstances.

She ran up the steps and found Taylor's bedroom—the

girl had left it out of the earlier tour. As large as the nursery, but with more accoutrements, like a four-poster double bed and a desk outfitted with a laptop, three speakers, and two large monitors. No sign of Taylor. Ellie took a quick peek at her bookshelves—as Rachael had theorized, there were several Young Adult books with vampires and witches and a whole series about fairies. But most of the fiction tended toward mysteries, from classic Nancy Drew to graphic novels featuring an anime crime scene photographer.

One title caught Ellie's attention—*Forty-Nine Ways to Kill Somebody*. The slender paperback offered exactly that, brief alphabetized descriptions of the pros and cons of stabbing (pro: quiet, con: messy) and car bombing (pro: not necessary to be present, con: requires serious mechanical knowledge). Oddly, each entry came with an illustration, all of an old-fashioned black-ink style more suited to nineteenth-century tomes. Ellie couldn't decide if she found it cute or disturbing. A child shouldn't have such a directory in her bedroom . . . *but*, at eleven, she'd have found it delightful in the same way that farts had been the most hilarious of topics.

Fanning the pages to check for any handwritten notations, she noticed that one page had been ripped out. Somewhere in the *D*'s, its entries would have fallen between *Defenestration* (throwing someone out a window) and *Entombment*.

*Drowning?*

*It's not Taylor.* The thought came strong and unbidden. Her little cousin had *not* murdered her baby brother.

She shut the book. It proved nothing, was circumstantial in the extreme. Even if Taylor *had* killed her brother, why rip out the page? She had no basis to collect the book; though if she left it there, Taylor—or Becca—might think to destroy it completely, especially if Mason's body turned up farther down the Potomac. He'd been so tiny, he might be washed out to sea before anyone spotted him—

Horrible thoughts. But none could advise her what to do right then.

She replaced the book carefully, leaving it flush with its neighbors and checking to be sure she hadn't left any telltale marks in the dust. She might tell Rachael and/or Michael about it, or she might not; she would wait to decide until after she'd spoken to Taylor.

A quick check of the other rooms did not reveal Taylor, so she moved down to the first floor, where voices lured her to the kitchen.

There, a crumpled beer can perched uncomfortably on the marble in front of Hunter. He and Becca and the tall, handsome Gabriel stood around the island crowded with manila folders, charging cell phones, and a large bowl of Doritos. Funny that no matter how lush the house might be, people still hung out in the kitchen. Ellie did not see Taylor, however, and started to duck out again to continue the search.

"Ellie!" Becca cried. "Come here, you need to meet Gabriel."

Gabriel Haller, as handsome in person as he appeared on security video, summoned up a courteously somber smile for Ellie and nodded politely. Black hair, fashionably neat with just enough length for a flirtatious style, topped a snow-white dress shirt and a loosened tie. Five-o'clock shadow covered slight dimples in lean cheeks. "I'm glad you could come and be here for Becca. This is such a terrible thing. I don't know how you two are still functioning," he said to the couple.

"Don't have a choice," Hunter said. "I've got the best working on it."

"I know, but—I hate that KidFun is . . . is why—"

Hunter growled a warning. "Don't. It's not your fault. It's not my fault. It's the fault of some sick wacko nutcases. The only thing we can do is get it done, get this bill out of committee one way or the other, and get Mason back." He spread both hands over his face and slid them into his hair. "Hell, maybe they're doing us a favor. You're hemorrhaging subscribers, as it is. If we postponed the vote, in six months you might as well license the game to Amazon and shutter your headquarters, anyway."

Ellie had no idea what they were talking about, but Hunter clearly didn't exaggerate. All three of them appeared miserable with worry and nights that had been sleepless, even before their child disappeared.

In the silence Becca went to the refrigerator and rummaged, emerging with a small bottle of Gatorade, a Diet Coke, and a bottle of some dark beer. She slapped the Gatorade in front of Gabriel, the beer beside Hunter, and snapped the pop-top on the Coke for herself, too preoccupied to even glance at her cousin.

Ellie opened her mouth to ask where Taylor might be and instead heard herself ask, "What's this hearing about?" Surely, the motivation for the crime should be able to point them in the direction of the culprits.

All three people looked at her as if they'd already forgotten her presence. She waited.

"Do you ever play video games?" Becca asked.

"Uh . . . I like *Mah Jong Tiles.*"

"I mean online, with other people?"

"No."

"Well, people do. Constantly, every day, adults and kids. You register, tell the platform your name and address and age, which the platform can sell to advertisers for directed marketing. Increases the spam in your in-box, but, hey, you can be a ninja storming a castle alongside a ninja controlled by a teenager in Japan. You can get on a headset and talk to that teenager in Japan."

"Right."

"Except you're twelve, and the teenager in Japan is actually a geriatric pedophile in Manhattan, who's going to talk you into sending him nudie pics. Or groom you into meeting him at the park. That's what legislation tries to prevent."

"Right. I've had a few cases involving online predators. So your bill will increase protection—"

"No," Gabriel burst out. "It . . . Look, maybe we should discuss this later. Maybe we shouldn't—"

*Talk about it in front of me, an outsider,* Ellie thought.

"She's fine." Hunter waved his hand at the woman he'd only really met an hour or so before. "She's family."

"Yeah. No problem," Becca said, her expression so neutral she might not have been listening.

Gabriel ran both hands through his hair, then cracked the Gatorade. "Okay. Most games have the chat bar so that teams can chat or individuals can privately message each other. For most kids this is the most fun part of it. They make friends—it's hard for us to imagine because we didn't grow up exactly like this, but they consider them really close friends—with kids in other parts of the country or even the world. It's fun for all of them, but especially for the ones who are restricted by location or poverty or even disability, it can be a lifeline. However, this is also where the pedophiles and bullies sneak in, and the next thing you know, your twelve-year-old is being blackmailed for nudie pics. It *is* a concern. But to ban it is essentially the government saying you can't talk to each other. It's a violation of free speech."

"Not exactly," Ellie said. "Only that they can't talk within that game."

"Yes. But the talking is a huge chunk of the game—turns out kids don't want to play if they can't talk."

Hunter said, "So games designed for children and teens are hemorrhaging money, while games designed for adults are going on their merry way—another reason why you can't tell me our rivals aren't feeding ammunition to the activists."

Gabriel said, not quite as bitterly, "Additionally, all this is doing is pushing children into adult games. They're lying about their ages, and pilfering their parents' IDs, to fool the requirements, rushing toward disaster. Three months ago a senator named Griffyn got a temporary ban passed that outlaws *any* DM, direct messaging, on *any* game designed for children or directed to children. We have adult players on our games too, but since the very name of the company is KidFun, it's going to be impossible to convince Congress our games aren't directed at children. If minors register to play adult games, the DM feature has to be disabled on their screens. The current bill before Congress makes the ban permanent."

Hunter said, "The wacko citizens groups like Child-Challenge *and* the adult gaming corporations backing them would love to see that happen. Destroy the competition and they can ooze right into that vacuum and suck up those profits. Since the temporary ban started, KidFun registrations have sunk by the day."

Ellie summarized, "So whoever took Mason wants you to throw the hearing, and instead of permanently repealing the ban, permanently install the ban."

Hunter made a face. "I guess so."

"Can you do that?"

"Sure. It's winning that's tough. Losing is easy." He didn't add any more detail than that. "Gabriel will be ruined. A two-point-five-billion-dollar company—of which I own thirty percent. Seven hundred and fifty million."

"Yep." Gabriel mimed cheer. "Might as well sell the office furniture and retire to Panama."

They lapsed into silence. Ellie couldn't help but wonder what loss they mourned more: Mason, or that 2.5 billion dollars.

"Maybe it's for the best," Gabriel said.

Hunter nearly spit out his beer. "How can you say that? You started KidFun."

"Yes, but when it's more about revenue and data mining than game design . . . that's not what I—"

"Oh, my God—just keep it together until after this hearing, okay? Then you can go climb a mountain in Tibet or do a sweat lodge with the Lakotas or whatever you need."

"Taylor's going to be disappointed," Becca said. "She's spent days rehearsing her statement."

Gabriel said, "Statement?"

"For the hearing. We thought she could talk about how much she likes the games, charm the pants off the committee. She'd—"

The plastic bottle clunked against the island counter. "Taylor? *Your* Taylor? Testify at a—the news will be there, you know. C-SPAN will broadcast it."

Hunter said, "Exactly! The best advertisement—if I'm willing to let my own kid play these games, it negates Child-Challenge's argument that they're so dangerous."

"But—it's a scary thing, sitting there in that hot seat. I've climbed Denali, and hearings make *me* sweat. She's *eleven*."

"Taylor? She'd eat it up. And eleven's the perfect age, old enough to stick to a script, but still got that wide-eyed innocent look."

"Doesn't matter now," Becca pointed out. "We're not going to dangle her in front of the kidnappers via a satellite dish. They've already got Mason."

"Where *is* Taylor?" Ellie asked. Enough of their regret that they could no longer use their child for a prop.

The three adults blinked in near unison.

"She's not in her room?" Becca asked. "Then she's probably outside . . . somewhere."

If Ellie had had something to drink, she would now be

the one choking on it. Was her cousin, having lost one child to unknown forces, *hoping* the other one might get scooped up too?

Becca added, "Tell her to be careful by the water. She can't swim. Signed her up for lessons three times, but the kid refused to get in the pool."

Ellie turned and walked out of the room.

# Chapter 12

Ellie left the house through the central rear door and scanned the area, promptly catching sight of Taylor's school uniform disappearing into the woods at the south edge of the lawn. She struck out across the grass to intercept.

Alone for a moment, she finally gave herself room to face one fact: None of this made any sense. *None* of it.

How does a child disappear from a house in the middle of the day when no one left the premises?

Why did Becca insist she stay part of the investigation when they had barely seen each other these past fifteen years? Yes, Ellie would have inside knowledge of the investigation, which Becca would want whether innocent or guilty.

How could radicals believe that a cryptic instruction to Hunter could change the course of a congressional committee vote in any permanent way? Surely, all the facts and figures KidFun would use to bolster their petition would have already been submitted. Wouldn't someone notice a 180-degree shift in their stance from *DMs are fine* to *DMs are irretrievably harmful*?

Becca and Hunter seemed exhausted and haggard over the

loss of their son, and yet instead of insisting the FBI camp out on their doorstep, seemed to disregard them in favor of a cousin and a private institute more known for training and research.

And why, after their home had been invaded and their child stolen, were they letting their other child wander around the large outdoors *by herself*?

Shock could only explain so much. Cluelessness could only explain so much. Ellie might be more accustomed to working with the dead than the living, but her gut had not stopped screaming at her that these reactions were not normal.

"Taylor!" Ellie shouted, nearing the trees. They were resplendent in hues of red and gold, oaks and maples and elms, but she didn't have time to appreciate the beauty. She focused only on the sliver of white shirt and dark blue skirt weaving among the trunks. A trail of weeds flattened into the dirt wound through the undergrowth, easy enough to follow. The soft odors of damp earth filled Ellie's head. Birds in the branches fell silent when she snapped a twig underfoot. "Taylor!"

Something with thorns caught at Ellie's thigh and bit, and she used two seconds to extricate herself without tearing her pants. This would have been much easier in winter or even late fall, after the leaves hit the ground, but right then, they provided ample coverage for the girl. Ellie could barely see twenty feet in every direction. The thick canopy overhead blotted out the sunshine.

Ellie walked on. The occasional broken branch indicated less used trails off to the sides, but nothing seemed fresh enough to follow. She didn't bother to feel annoyed at Taylor's refusal to respond. The family's life had been turned upside down in the past five hours, so no surprise that the kid would act out, and, possibly, she was always this way. It would be hard to get the attention of such busy parents. Ellie could look back now and doubly appreciate how hard her aunts and uncles had worked—her grandmother and their baking sessions, Joanna taking her to the theater for every musical comedy passing through Naples, Tommy and Valencia speaking Spanish over dinner every night to make her fluent. Taylor had every advantage in so many ways, but not in others.

The trees began to thin with more space between the trunks; more weeds and white bulbous mushrooms sprang up between them. Up ahead she could see a short open area and then another expansive lawn, manicured to within an inch of its life. Hundreds of yards beyond that, another massive home—or university, or state capitol, she couldn't quite tell. Apparently, she had reached the perimeter of the Carlisles' estate.

Ellie turned around. The birds were still silent, the brush and leaves completely still. Only the faint sound of tiny waves lapping at the edge of the river to her right made any sound at all. She could have been utterly alone.

But she felt pretty sure she wasn't.

A sudden instinct made her look up. There, nestled in the branches of a massive maple tree, sat Taylor, watching her with the limited curiosity of a cat watching a bird it won't bother to chase.

Ellie stalked over to the trunk of the tree, keeping her head down, schooling her expression. Taylor was acting like a normal kid, she told herself, and Ellie was invading her personal hideout.

Besides, if Taylor had thrown Mason into the river nearly seventeen hours before, then Mason was dead. Haste would not make a difference now.

So when Ellie reached the base of the maple, she grabbed a branch without hesitation and hauled herself up. She hadn't climbed a tree since leaving the mountains, but it wasn't highly specialized work. She progressed carefully, considering each branch for position and sturdiness before moving

up another rung, opting for dignity over speed. She aimed
for a thick branch opposite the bundle Taylor straddled. Another protruded from the trunk about a foot above it, pro-
viding a handy backrest.

Ellie settled in, said nothing for a minute or two. Then:
"Nice view." They were about fifteen feet off the ground.
The treetops were not as solid as they'd seemed from below,
and Ellie could see parts of the trail she'd just been on, part
of the lawn behind the Carlisle house and even, if she craned
her neck, the southeast corner of the house. But mostly the
river captured the attention, the blue shimmering in the sunlight, lined with trees only sometimes broken up by pieces of
lawn, somehow appearing more blue than it did in downtown DC . . . like everything in this neighborhood, perfect.

She stole the briefest of glances at Taylor. The girl had lost
the slightly mocking air she'd worn since they'd met . . . perhaps not entirely *lost*, but faded.

"Your mother and I used to climb trees like this," Ellie told her. "In West Virginia. We'd spend all day in the
woods . . . Well, the *house* was in the woods, so we could
hardly help it."

"Yeah, Mom said you lived with her when you were
a kid."

"Yes, for about three years. With her and your aunt
Melissa."

"Was it fun?"

"Sometimes." She'd meant to sound more enthusiastic
than that, but at least she'd stopped herself from saying no.
The woods had been fun, and the house tucked among them,
and the fresh air and the river and Aunt Katey.

Her cousins, not so much.

It should have been. Spending the gorgeous West Virginia
summers running up and down the hills with two girls close
in age, under the modern-day hippie parenting style of Aunt
Katey and her husband—it should have been a child's par-

adise. But growing up in a small town on an auto mechanic's wages, Becca and Missy felt the need to compete for everything—attention, clothing, accessories, gold stars from teachers, friendships. And the pretty little orphan cousin from "the big city" represented a prize to be won. Ellie's three years in the Kavanaugh household quickly became one long tightrope to walk, struggling to balance, often falling, and never reaching safety.

Go to the movies with Missy, and come home to find Becca in tears. Work on the never-finished tree house with Becca, and endure three days of cold silence from Missy. Let the popular boy in class flirt with you, and have your technique picked apart by both of them in a tag team effort. Becca had been the queen of tearful, screaming drama, but Missy had actually been worse. Her haughty disdain could strike terror into Ellie's preteen heart, an ice-cold stiletto of contempt. It had taken years for Ellie to realize it had never been about her, Ellie. It wasn't love for her that drove them; they had likely never loved her at all. But they'd needed *her* love, needed it to grow like they needed food and water.

The funny thing was, as they'd aged—as she knew from Aunt Katey and social media—Becca and Missy had grown close, sharing the clothes, friends, boys, thoughts, they used to fight over. That was how it should be—they were sisters, with more in common than they'd ever have with Ellie. Instead, *her* letters were never answered, her texts lost.

"It's so different from here," Taylor murmured.

"Yes. A lot different. You've been there to visit your grandma and grandpa, right?"

"Yes, two times! I had to stay there while Mom and Dad went out of the country. Gramps took me in a canoe on the river. Gram climbed a tree with me and we found a bird nest. There was a playground in the square too," added the girl who was too exceptional to play.

"Do they ever come here?"

The enthusiasm faded. "One time. Gramps kept walking around the house saying it's too big. Gram did the dishes, even though we have a dishwasher and the cook lady did them, anyway."

"That sounds like them."

"And Dad doesn't really like having houseguests." She swung both legs, hard scissors back and forth. "Mom says you lived with them because you were an orphan."

"Yes, that's true."

"She says you had to move in with them after your dad killed your mom."

"That's *not* true," Ellie said, though she'd heard the rumor before. "My mother wasn't killed by someone—she died in a car accident. My dad left me with my grandmother because he was afraid to raise a little kid all by himself."

"Oh," Taylor said. "Sorry."

To Ellie's surprise she *looked* sorry, enough to make Ellie in turn feel sorry for suspecting the girl of fratricide. The disappearance of her brother, her own preoccupation with mystery and mayhem—the kid probably had visions of bloody murder dancing in her head instead of sugarplums and party dresses and superheroes. They wouldn't be easily erased.

"I'm sorry about your brother. Do you miss him?"

"No. He was a dragon baby."

Too young for platitudes and white lies. Mason had only been around for a few months, a constant usurper of her position in the household. Why *would* she miss him? "Okay, but what does that mean?"

"It means he had to go away and live with the dragons." Taylor broke off a twig and threw it down in a hasty, impatient arc, as if that fact should be obvious. Clearly, she found Ellie's history more interesting than her brother's . . . or wanted to change the subject. "Mom said your mom went into the river."

"Yes. The car went off the road—but it was an accident."

"Are you afraid of the water now?"

A logical, but unexpected question. "No—I wasn't in the car, so—"

"Mom said you were."

"No, I wasn't. I think that was another family rumor." Ellie was sitting in a tree trying to get Taylor to tell her what she'd thrown in the river last night, not revisit Ellie's past. But, unbidden, she heard herself ask: "Does your mom mention me a lot?" *Did I mean* anything *to her?*

"No, I just heard her telling Dad that."

"Really," Ellie said. "When?"

The girl shrugged and picked at a piece of bark. "A while ago."

"Like, yesterday? This morning? Last week?" If Hunter could convince the FBI to defer to the Locard, could he also get them to send out a particular ERT member?

But Ellie really had been the only one available. She hadn't imagined her coworkers having been dispatched to the mall shooting, a bank robbery and a terrorism search warrant. Adam had done the dispatching, but he had never met Hunter . . . so far as she knew.

"I think last week," Taylor said after screwing up her face in abject concentration. "Can you swim?"

"Swim? Yes."

"Benjy couldn't swim. That's why he got drowned. But Mom said it was all right because he'd be all peaceful, and never hurt again."

Ellie could use this segue. "Yes, your mother mentioned you don't want to swim."

"I can't. I'll wind up like Benjy."

She wore an exaggeratedly sad face, but Ellie refused to be distracted. "That makes it even more important to be careful around water. Taylor, did you come out of the house last night?"

The girl's expression changed. Did Ellie imagine a cagey look in her eyes? "Sure. I had to say good night to George."

The stone lion. "But it was quite late."

"I couldn't sleep."

"But you went past George and out on the grass."

A blink, but no reaction. "Did you see that on the security video?"

"Yes, the security video. Why did you walk out to the river? You shouldn't play on the dock by yourself, especially in the dark."

Another pause. "I didn't."

"Taylor, I just said I watched the security video. I saw you."

"Look, there's a blue jay."

Ellie didn't alter her gaze. "Taylor, why did you walk to the river? What did you throw in it?"

The girl pumped her legs again, making distant leaves quiver. "I don't know what you're talking about."

"Taylor—"

"I don't know what you're talking about." The girl, Ellie thought, wasn't stonewalling because she felt panicked. The girl, Ellie thought, was enjoying the hell out of this.

"You threw something into the water. What was it?"

Taylor's hair swung over her shoulder as her head swiveled. "You mean like that?"

Ellie followed her gaze. Parts of the shore were visible, some open, some choked with plants and fallen branches. But almost directly across from the tree in which they sat, a dirtied white cloth floated among the reeds. A reedy weed had snagged it, kept it from moving into deeper water or landing on the mud of the shore. Thinner edges of the piece of cloth swirled around a swollen oval in the center.

Ellie leapt from her seat on the branch and climbed down the long trunk of the tree, descending in a fraction of the time it had taken her to go up. Muscle memories from childhood kept and saved her from a fall and a broken leg.

Thoughts sped through her mind all the while, with both the speed and clarity of lightning against a dark sky.

A corpse thrown in a body of water, despite common scenes on television, promptly sinks to the bottom. Air in the lungs is replaced with water, decreasing buoyancy and increasing weight—however, if Mason had been killed before immersion, his lungs might retain air, prompting the body to hover at the surface.

Her palms stung as they slapped from branch to branch. One set of toes missed a protrusion and her legs dangled in the air, bicycling for a toehold.

The body's natural bacteria then leaps into action, decomposing the flesh and creating gasses that will bring the victim to the surface. The water would be warm after the summer, which would make the process go faster.

She hung with both hands from one of the lower branches, then let go.

Not low enough—her legs crashed into the ground and she fell to both knees and one hand. The dirt and leaves smudged her jeans and a thorn bit into her palm.

But even with that, Mason would have only been dead for seventeen hours. Decomposition of even a small body wouldn't have proceeded that fast. He shouldn't be floating, not yet. Yes the relatively shallow, warm water could hasten what would normally take two to three days, but still. Besides, the Potomac was a river, not a lake. Any item should have been washed away, not still on the premises. Though it was caught. It was caught.

The weeds continued to grab at her as she ran, feet fighting for purchase on the covered ground, gaze probing the steps ahead of her for the least overgrown path to the water. Where did it—

*There.* About three feet down the sloping bank, tangled in the brown growth. A sodden baby blanket with—she could see as her shoe splashed into the water—orange cartoon bunnies with pink cartoon daisies.

The earth slanted sharply downward, so that the second step soaked her to the knee. The third brought the water to her hips as the depths of silt at the bottom claimed her boots, nearly cementing her in place. But she reached out and could just pull the wet cloth away from the bramble. Dirt had already soaked into the blanket, grainy under her palm.

She shouldn't move the body until it had been photographed.

Though that hardly mattered, since the water had clearly moved him from the point of entry.

She pulled the bundle, still mostly floating, toward her.

She should lift the whole thing into one of those undersized body bags, take it to the morgue so they could unwrap it layer by layer.

She grabbed the blanket and its contents, scooping it as one solid, sodden object. Her fingers felt the outline of what lay within the shroud with its bunnies and flowers.

And she breathed out, a slow breath.

"What's that?" came a voice behind her. Taylor had come down from the tree.

Ellie climbed out of the river. She took her time, determined not to slip on the muddy bottom and soak the rest of her clothing. No need for haste, now. She kept the bundle tucked in the crook of her right arm.

"Why'd you get your shoes all wet?" Taylor asked, watching this ascent with an expression designed to look innocent. It didn't, not that the girl cared. The falsely singsong inflections of her voice made that clear.

"Come on." She grasped Taylor's arm, not caring that her fingers smeared mud on the crisp white garment, not caring that her grip caused the girl to squirm. They marched the rest of the way back to the house in silence.

The three adults were still in the kitchen when Ellie knocked at that room's exterior door, using one foot, since both her hands were occupied. Becca saw them through the glass, set down her can, and opened the door. "What are you two doing? Why are you all wet?" she asked with a confused frown.

"I'd like your daughter to explain how this got in the water." Ellie held out the stiff form, the blanket falling away. A nearly life-size baby doll, its blond acrylic hair caked with algae and dead leaves. The rosebud lips had a hole in the center, a place to feed the toy baby its toy bottle. A frilly dress with puffed sleeves provided a contrast to the blanket.

Becca glanced at it and turned to Taylor. "Why did you throw your doll away?"

"I'm too old to play with dolls," Taylor said, and walked away through the dining room. Her footsteps echoed faintly in the air.

"Becca," Ellie said. "We need to talk about—"

Becca considered her cousin. "Could you take your shoes off before you walk anywhere else?"

# Chapter 13

Noah Thomas watched the green hills roll by, the trees with leaves just beginning to turn. They'd been driving for a good thirty minutes, but that didn't surprise him. Of course a camp would be away from the city, someplace with plenty of room. Millie had kept up a sporadic conversation, asking him questions the way adults do when they're trying to be nice. *How do you like your school? How long have you played baseball? What else do you like to do?* She seemed really interested in his favorite video game, *Blue Planet*. Maybe she played it, because she sure didn't play baseball. He'd asked a few questions himself about the structure of the camp and she couldn't answer a single one, didn't seem to know the difference between catcher and center field or how many of their kids got on travel teams.

"What do you like about the *Blue Planet*? My daughter, Tina, loved the unicorn meadow."

That figured, girls were always into unicorns. Noah described his avatar, who could breathe both air and water and had been reconstructing Atlantis. He had to collect the stones so he could make different buildings and occasionally fight off hordes of Krakens.

"That sounds really cool. Tina said it was so fun she couldn't stop playing."

"Yeah." They were way out somewhere now, the houses getting more and more sparse. The van turned down a road with no shoulders, barely two lanes wide. Trees closed in on both sides. Noah pictured wide fields, expanded diamonds where they could play all day without the neighbors complaining about the lights and the stupid soccer players running over the boundaries.

"You ever feel like that? Like you just want to keep playing all the time?"

"Sure. I guess."

"What is it your father does again?"

The question threw Noah off. He hadn't been paying a great deal of attention to Millie and her attempts at conversation, but he didn't think his father had come up before. So he hadn't said. Maybe she'd gotten mixed up—his father had arranged for him to come to this camp, so he'd probably chatted with Millie. His father talked to everyone. Noah took after his more guarded mother. "He's a software engineer."

"At KidFun, right?"

"Yeah." Noah had stopped telling other people where his dad worked. Too many kids had thought that meant he could give them the game for free, or at least a sizeable discount.

"He designed *Blue Planet*, didn't he?"

"Yeah."

"Maybe that's why you like it so much."

Noah considered this. He loved his dad, and Noah and his mom had heard about the progress of the design every night at the dinner table for months, so, of course, Noah had to try it. But family loyalty only went so far. "No, it's just a really cool game."

"It's designed to be. Those games are designed to keep you playing and playing. That's why there's never an end, only more levels. They want you to feel like you need to keep going, like you've never quite proven your skill. You always need to go one more step."

Noah considered this too, but not deeply. Wasn't that the whole point of a video game?

"It's like they're addicting. Do you feel like it's an addiction?"

Noah didn't have to consider this—he knew the answer. "No." Adults were always talking about how kids were "addicted" to their screens, and they needed to go outside and play and actually talk to their friends instead of texting, blah blah blah. Texting meant Noah talked to his friends twenty-four hours a day . . . How much more did they want him to talk?

"Have you heard of an addiction algorithm?"

Actually, he had—more dinner table conversation—but he didn't understand it, and had the vague feeling he didn't want to talk anymore. So he lied, a little bit. "No."

"It's the result of the data people like your dad have gathered from other games, and statistical analysis, and behavioral psychology. He's taken all that information and designed *Blue Planet* and *Lion's Reach* to use kids' minds against them, to make them want to do nothing else but play those games."

Noah didn't understand why she was talking about this. Did she want a discount too? He watched the trees pass.

But Millie went on. "Finn says it's all based on Skinner's box, behavior and reward. He taught a rat to press a lever to get food—turns out it's even easier to get someone to fork over real money for a virtual character in a world that doesn't exist."

*Who the heck is Finn and who cared what he thought?*

"First they set it up so that the game is cheaper if you 'earn' part of the money by playing longer."

Noah got to play for free, so he didn't really care about what would happen if he couldn't.

"Then present all sorts of loot to outfit your person, who doesn't really exist. You might not be cool, but in the game you can have the coolest clothes and the coolest car. *Then* they start varying the rewards, the bonus points and free loot when you get to a new level—which happens quickly at first, but then the game starts getting stingy, makes you *want* the reward even more. *World of Warcraft* has a bar showing your progress, to make you feel like there's progress even though you haven't gotten to the next reward. But there's the stick to go with the carrot—if you *don't* keep playing, you'll get punished . . . virtually, but even virtual punishment is no fun. Your crops die in *FarmVille*, and so on."

"Are we almost there?"

Instead of answering, she asked, "Did you know that games are *made* to do that?"

"No. I mean . . . yeah, but—aren't fun things *supposed* to make you want to keep doing them?"

"Not until it's affecting your schoolwork and you have kids with neck and eyesight problems because they never look up. Finn told me there's grown-ups who can't pay their mortgage because they get more interested in outfitting their avatar rather than themselves."

"I play baseball." Noah knew he sounded defensive. He wasn't a helpless troll, with no life outside a video game; after all, wasn't he going to camp? Baseball was outside, in real life, lots of fresh air and sunshine. Noah's mom commented on that fact at nearly every game.

Millie gave a little sigh, like his mom did when he was being funny, but she didn't think he was funny. "That's wonderful. Do you talk to your father about his video games?"

"Yeah. Is this it?" They had pulled onto an even smaller road, which seemed to have come to an end. A large house and an even larger barn sat way in the back, down the driveway, little more than two depressed tracks through weedy grass.

"Did he tell you that he designed this addiction algorithm?"

"I thought you said that stuff happened in *FarmVille* and *Warcraft*. Those aren't his."

That sigh again. "No. They're amateurs compared to him. He's perfected the technique in the KidFun games."

"Is this it?" he asked again, hoping mightily that she would say no, that they were just there to pick up some other kid. The place didn't make him feel warm and fuzzy, as his mother would say. Just that huge house and that even huger barn, with its faded flat red paint. No other kids, and as far as Noah could see, no other cars, no bleachers, and not even a diamond.

She slowed the van as they approached the barn.

"Could I have my backpack, please?" The first pangs of worry clutched at his stomach. Something wasn't right here, not right at all . . . that was it: no signs. A children's camp should have signs. A curving marquee at the front entrance, a sign for parents' parking and employee-only parking, restrooms, ball fields, where kids in the various age brackets should congregate.

"In a minute," Millie said. "You're such a nice boy. And it's nice that you play baseball. But you're their child—of course they'd be careful to keep you from harm, limit your exposure. It's other people's kids they don't care about. Other people's mortgages. Other teenagers' safety. Like Tina's."

A tall white man with an old-man beard, the gray kind that wasn't even on the bottom and with the cheeks still covered in fuzz, emerged from the house and moved toward them without pausing.

Irrational panic made Noah's throat close up. What could this be? Were they some weirdo cult that snatched young kids? Was it some kind of intervention, but why would they . . . When Ben's parents got divorced, they packed him off to some cousins in Ohio he barely knew, and by the time they let him come back, his house was gone and he had new bedrooms in two different places. Could that be like this?

"I really need my backpack."

His phone was in the side pocket.

Millie turned the van off and unbuckled her belt, watching him in the rearview. "In a minute. First I want to talk a little more about your father's algorithm."

The man was almost to the van.

# Chapter 14

"A doll," Rachael said.

"Yup. A doll." Ellie had changed out of her sodden pants and footwear. At least the crime scene van had her second "emergency" uniform and her old pair of work boots, all of which now smelled like the duffel they'd been stored in, a combination redolent of plastic and mildew. She hadn't had to use them since the time she'd jumped into the Potomac to save a drowning victim's dog, who had tried to rescue his master and then couldn't find a way out. Not part of her normal duties, but none of the cops at the scene had volunteered.

She'd happily jump in again, if only Mason could be rescued so easily.

"No explanation?"

"I asked," Ellie said. "I tried to emphasize, calmly—though the calm part was a bit of a struggle at that point—"

Rachael's lips curved up, but she said nothing.

"—that as much as everyone had been trying to shield her, something very bad had happened, and she needed to tell us the whole truth, even about things she thought might be embarrassing or unimportant."

"Anything?"

"Like talking to a wall. A brick wall. A brick wall with a layer of marble on one side and concrete on the other."

"At least her midnight ramble sounds like what we thought," Rachael said. "A kid playing some game that makes sense only to her. Can I get your contact DNA swabs? From the crib and window?"

Ellie only ground one tooth before she said, "Sure. Are you going to collect elimination samples from the family?"

Rachael labeled the swabs and stowed them in her kit, an oversized DeWalt tool bag. "I don't see a need at this time. We have access to CODIS."

*Yes, of course, you said that already.*

"So there's no need to further traumatize the family by sticking swabs in their mouths. We only care if a profile matches someone we *don't* know."

"Right. What do you use for your PCR? QIAamp?"

"MagNA."

"Okay."

"You don't like MagNA?"

"No, it's fine." Both products would amplify the tiny amounts of DNA into similar yields.

"It's what we have at the institute now. We could get QIAamp, but it would take a day—"

"Really, it's *fine.*" *Mental note, Ellie: Sensitive about choice of reagents.*

In the kitchen debate about the next day's committee hearing continued to rage, pausing only long enough to bid farewell to Dr. Davies. She promised to let them know if any DNA profiles matched any known offenders, and if the video analysts found something in the recordings that she had missed. She gave Ellie one last, knowing glance that Ellie felt entirely unable to interpret. *Good luck? Don't hide or destroy any evidence while I'm gone? MagNA really is better than QIAamp, anyway, and don't you forget it?*

The moment the door shut behind her, argument began again with Gabriel on one side and Hunter on the other. Becca escaped via the mundane chore of going out to get the mail. Apparently, despite the copious luxury of the neighborhood, residents still had to put on boots and trudge through the snow and rain to reach the box.

Or they could send their maid or gardener or nanny, unless the nanny was away visiting family in Asia. Ellie wished she could talk to Jenny Cho, who would certainly have a great deal of information about Mason. Maybe none of it would help, but maybe it would.

"It sounds as if they want you to say our controls gut COPPA," the dark-haired man said.

"I get that," Hunter told him. "But how can I? They don't. Remember, 312.7 says you can't make the child's participation in the game conditional on giving up personal information *unless* it's reasonably necessary. The personal information *is* reasonably necessary to keep them from online predators."

"But not online marketers."

"There's 312.8. You can release the information to third parties, as long as they keep the information safe. We can sell it to every toy company in the world—as long as they're not going to publish it on the dark web, it's all good."

Ellie quietly opened cabinets until she located a glass to fill with water. She might have learned a great deal about the committee process that morning, but it hadn't led her to Mason. Every type of legislative, oversight, investigative business of the U.S. government went through committee hearings, so that couldn't lead her to a set of suspects, like a vehicle description or an email address might.

"The corporate world leaks like a sieve."

"So it does," Hunter said. "But that's *their* problem."

"It's *my* game," Gabriel said. "So it *is* my problem."

Hunter's voice, always somewhere between flint and brick, hardened to granite. "You sound like you're on their side."

"No. I mean—I see what they're saying, but to go so far as to take Mason . . . it's terrifying. Say whatever you think will get him back. KidFun is—it's only money."

It wasn't only money to him, Ellie could see. He had probably founded the company in his garage with a few hundred bucks and nurtured it into a pride-bursting adulthood. It was, in a way, *his* child—one he would have to sacrifice to save someone else's.

Though it sounded as if he'd been considering some tough love for that child long before the kidnapping.

Becca returned, tossing letters and a pizza place flyer on the marble island. "Help yourself to the fridge, Ellie. There's diet stuff, juice, and Gabriel's stash of Gatorades."

"I'll share," the man said.

Becca began to open the envelopes with an evilly sharp, double-sided knife that could have doubled as a prop in *Game of Thrones.* She gestured at Gabriel with it. "Just keep Marty focused on the main point. If he says you've got five minutes, come in at four and a half. *Don't* tick off the guy with the gavel."

"It sounds like a trial," Ellie said.

"It's *exactly* like a trial," Hunter said. "There's a reason most lobbyists are either lawyers or employ a roster of lawyers. Everyone *thinks* my job is to sneak around passing out briefcases of money or season tickets to the Nats, but our job is to make sure that, first, what the client wants is not going to violate any existing laws. After that comes the creative part of the job—crafting an approach to the people involved. We have to create a sense of drama, get their attention, sometimes specific to the person, senator, representative, agency head. If we want a dam in New Mexico, maybe it will affect border security. If we want a dam in Iowa, they couldn't care less about border security, but care about nitrogen runoff from crop fertilizers. We have to find how our goals relate to their existing concerns. Sometimes they're in opposition, sometimes they don't relate at all. That's when we bust out the Nats tickets."

"Sounds . . . nerve-wracking."

He grinned. "Not to me. The worse the odds are, the more of a kick it is to win."

When the scream came, Ellie couldn't find its source, not immediately. The sound bounced off the marble and filled the room so completely that for a moment it seemed the house itself had let out a howl of pain. For one terrible moment Ellie thought her own throat had ripped loose, from frustration and despair and fear for a tiny, brown-eyed baby.

Becca had screamed. The piece of paper in her hands wafted to the counter and Ellie caught a glimpse of mismatched block letters.

She shot to her cousin's side and grabbed Becca's wrist just as the fingers reached to pick up the paper again. "Don't touch it!"

The single sheet of letter-size paper had been folded only twice, to fit into a five-by-seven envelope. Letters had been cut out from some printed item and glued to the page. A child would have recognized it as a ransom note.

# Chapter 15

The man from the house hadn't hurt Noah. Nor had Millie. All they did was talk. And talk, and talk, and none of it made any sense to Noah.

He had been right about this place not being a baseball camp, not even *pretending* to be a baseball camp, and clearly they no longer cared if he was fooled or not. That had to mean they were so far from anywhere else that he could yell his head off and it wouldn't make any difference.

But they couldn't be *that* far from other houses; he'd seen them on the trip. If he could get across the flat grassy areas to the forest, maybe he could hide there until they gave up. Then he could walk through the woods; he'd find someone eventually and they could call his parents.

He could probably beat Millie and this old guy in any race. Noah was fast. That's why his gym teacher had suggested he go out for the traveling team next year, not just baseball, but track too.

That plan would have to wait, since the sliding-door handle did not work from the inside. Noah tugged and tugged.

By the time he climbed around to the front seat, Millie had come around to the side and the man stood behind her.

She opened the passenger door. "Come on out, honey. No one's going to hurt you."

Noah dove to the driver's seat, reaching down to the floor, hands scrabbling along the dirty carpet—

"Looking for this?"

Noah turned. Millie held up his backpack.

"Don't worry about it, hon. I threw the phone out before we even left your school."

Noah thought back. She'd told him to get in, then walked around to the driver's side carrying the backpack. He could picture her reaching into the outer pocket, pulling out his phone, letting it fall out of her hand onto the school's drive—all below the edge of the windows so he wouldn't see it. It had probably been found by some other parent by now.

He shrank from her. Open the driver's door, head for those trees, neither of these people looked capable of long-distance—his fingers found the handle.

A man, a different man, younger, peered in at him, their faces separated by eight or ten inches of air and a pane of glass. Where had *he* come from?

The younger guy jerked the driver's door open. Noah, off center with his legs caught by the center console, nearly fell into his arms. The guy's meaty hand closed around his upper arm, almost but not quite tight enough to hurt. It both kept him upright and let him know he would not be going any-where soon.

The three of them guided him to the barn in silence. Noah heard eerie scratching noises and bizarre mutterings and his feet stopped, struggled until the two men nearly carried him the last ten feet. But when he could see the interior of the barn, it was empty.

A cavern made of creaky wood with a stripped interior.

The few openings, a second set of doors and two sort-of windows, but with double doors and no glass, all had long planks nailed over them in an X, like in movies he saw about zombie invasions. Bare bulbs hung from long wires, but they weren't on, since enough light poked through the cracks in the walls and roof, where the boards were no longer tightly joined.

At least there wasn't any torture equipment, he thought. No weird operating table where they meant to steal a kidney or a post where they were going to whip him until he gave them the access codes, like in a movie he'd seen.

But what *was* there made him equally nervous: a few straight chairs; four beat-up beds that seemed to be made out of old pipes, with bare, thin mattresses; a wooden table, empty except for a bottle of hand sanitizer; a Porta-Potty in one corner.

"Please sit down, Noah," the old man said. "We'd really like to talk to you."

Noah was not going to cry. He was not going to beg. He was not going to show weakness. But he also saw no way out, so he walked to one of the chairs and sat down. He did not say a word or ask a question. If he made any sound at all, it would come out as a sob.

The scratching and the skittering sounds remained outside and settled into an agitated clucking. Chickens, Noah realized, having heard them in a few TV shows. Barn, farm, chickens. What the f—

The man sat down as well, heavily, with that little sigh that old people eventually start making every time they get up or get down. He seemed to gather his thoughts for a moment and then began. "Noah, I know you're only a little boy, and none of this is your fault. I'm sorry you're suffering—well, at least being inconvenienced—because of what the adults in your life are doing. But you deserve to know the truth, so I'm going to talk to you like you're a grown-up."

Part of Noah fought to keep from screaming in terror, because this whole thing just got crazier by the second. The other part wanted to say something sassy and sarcastic. *You just kidnapped someone to hold them captive in this ratty old barn and you're going to talk to me like I'm an adult? I'm supposed to be, what, grateful?*

*Talk away, old man. Because the minute you open that door back up, I'm going to be out it and gone, and your goon won't be fast enough to stop me.*

"Megan probably already asked you about your father and his addiction algorithm."

*Who is Megan?*

The old man glanced at Millie as he said this.

*Is she Megan? Made sense that the fake name tag would have a fake name.*

"Your father uses his skills in behavioral psychology to make the game addicting, thereby maximizing the monetization. First your father establishes the daily quests and objectives and the rewards, like avatar accessories, dances, gestures, and so on."

As scared as he was, Noah took a moment to puzzle out "monetization."

"Then he figures out how to lock them into playing longer, with more expenses down the road, because there will be plenty of possessions for them to buy. They might be ordinary people in real life, but in this virtual world they can be outfitted like rock stars."

*Well,* Noah thought, *you gotta have a decent sword. Which would really come in handy right now.*

"Your father has formulas that help him decide all these things. He has manipulating children down to a science—literally. He has brilliantly hidden all these manipulations so that players feel like they have control over their participation in the game, over their choices in the game."

The Younger Guy, the goon, hovered halfway between

Noah and the open door. He looked bored, and Noah couldn't blame him. *What is the Old Guy's point? And most importantly, what does it have to do with me?*

Millie—or Megan, whatever—glanced at her watch. "I have to go. Finn says I have to pick up the next one by five."

What? They were going to take *another* kid? Or person? Would it be his *dad*?

Noah found his voice, and didn't even worry about crying. "Where are you going? Who are you going to get?"

"Don't worry, honey. It will be all right." Which did *not* answer the question.

"But . . ." She had kidnapped him, yet he didn't want her to leave—not if it meant he'd be alone with these two weird guys.

And then she was gone, and the stupid Old Guy was going on as if she had never been there. "This may all sound like, so what, big deal, this is just how games work—of course your dad structures the game so that kids want to keep playing it. That's his job, right? But his purpose is not to entertain kids—it's to make money off those kids without the kids even realizing that they're being used and coerced. It's a purposely created gambling addiction, purposely created by your father, and he has to be stopped." The guy shifted in his chair and leaned forward. "And that, Noah, is why you're here."

He'd wanted the guy to get to the point, but now—Noah wanted to crawl backward, go through the wall, do whatever it took to get away from this man and that calm, crazy voice.

"There's a good chance that you'll be returned to your parents . . ."

Chance? *Just a* chance? *What does that mean?*

". . . that your father will understand our demands and cooperate. I'm telling you all this so that you'll understand that we are not trying to harm you. We're not even trying to harm your father. We're just going to keep you here until he fixes the problems he's created."

A *chance* he'd go back home?

"I knew you'd understand if only we had a chance to explain things."

"When will I go? When can I leave?" He'd walk back to DC if he had to, didn't care how far it was.

"*Do* you understand?"

Of course not, but Noah had long learned that when adults asked that question, they weren't going to go away until you said yes. Otherwise, they'd just keep talking.

"Yes," he said.

"Good boy." The Old Guy beamed, sat back, then politely amended, "Man." With that settled, his face relaxed, so far as Noah could tell under all that facial hair. He and the Younger Guy both seemed to give little sighs, and the muscles in their necks and arms smoothed out. Noah waited. With luck they would leave now.

The Old Guy stood up.

"When can I leave? When am I leaving? Is my dad coming for me?"

"No." The guy tucked his chair under the table, as perfectly neat and square as if they were in a nice restaurant. "No one is coming here, because they don't know where you are. As for when you can leave—if you can leave—that depends on your father. If all goes as it should, tomorrow afternoon."

"*Tomorrow!* But," Noah added, struck with sudden inspiration, "if you let me talk to him, I can convince him to do what you say." He had no idea what, exactly, they wanted his father to do . . . *Probably pay them money, isn't that how kidnappings usually went? But whatever it is—*

"That's not possible, Noah. Your father will be informed of what he needs to do right now. We only wanted you to understand for the future." He was already halfway to the door. The Younger Guy walked out backward, always facing Noah as if Noah were some kind of ninja who could break a chair and throw the leg like a knife so it plunged right through the guy's chest. It would be funny if it wasn't so *not* funny, him scuttling like a crab away from something really scary instead of a ten-year-old who was about to cry.

Just before he slid open the heavy wooden door, the Old Guy called back, "I'm sure you're hungry. We'll bring you something to eat in a little bit. If you need anything, just give a yell. In the meantime relax. Your backpack is there, minus your phone. You might do your homework."

They slipped out and shut the door behind them. Even from thirty feet away Noah heard the simple clanks of a hasp or latch closing, with some sort of reinforcement to hold it in place. He was left with no one except some unseen chickens for company.

At least now no one could see him as the tears came.

# Chapter 16

The note said: *If you want the baby, put $500K in a black duffel bag and leave behind I Hate War at FDR Sep 9th ten am. Send someone else NOT you.*

Hunter and Gabriel now flanked the two women, saying, "What the hell?" and "What is that?" and "Seriously?" Ellie couldn't tell who said what. Hunter reached for the letter and Ellie stopped his hand as well, and again as he tried for the envelope. "Don't touch *anything*. These will have to be analyzed for fingerprints and trace evidence."

"A *ransom* note?" Gabriel asked.

Hunter let loose with a string of invectives that didn't seem to have any real focus.

"Where is my baby?" Becca cried, a sob strangling off the last word. Ellie put one arm around the thin shoulders in a fierce grip.

Ellie felt both relief and terror. Relief because a ransom demand, while horrible, made sense. Mason has been taken for a purpose, not by some baby-sacrificing cult or a woman desperate to pass him off as her own. Simply money. Give them money, they return Mason.

In theory, anyway.

But she also felt terror, because life rarely followed theory without some variation. Anyone ruthless and daring enough to take a child from his own bed in the middle of the day could be ruthless enough to destroy the evidence.

But the note . . . didn't seem ruthless and daring. It didn't specify denominations for the bills or demand there would be no tracking devices in the duffel or even tell them not to call the cops. It didn't leave them any instructions as to how Mason might be returned or even make a firm promise that Mason would be returned at all. But it also didn't include any threats to kill him if the very sparse demand wasn't met. Ellie had no real experience with ransom notes outside of television and documentaries, but the note didn't seem to track.

Becca appeared to voice her own thoughts when she said, in a dazed tone: "Who does ransom notes like this anymore?"

"It's like something out of a cartoon," Gabriel said.

"They've gotta be nuts," Hunter said.

"Maybe not." Ellie took the letter opener and used it to flip over the envelope. More cutout letters formed *The Carlisles* and their street information. No return address. A first-class stamp and the spotty ink of a postmark. "Handwriting is a lot harder to disguise than you'd think, and printers can have distinctive flaws in their mechanisms, or chemically distinct toners. If these letters are cut from something mass-produced and common in this area, it might not be a crazy way to do it."

"What's the matter with that post office?" Hunter snapped. "Don't they know a crime when they see it?"

Ellie said, "Letters are machine sorted these days—it's possible an actual human never saw it. Or they thought it was a joke."

"A *joke*?"

"I don't *get* this," Becca said, tears bubbling through her words. "If they planned to send a note, why not just leave it when they took him? Why mail it?"

Ellie agreed. It seemed a huge risk, betting that the envelope would be delivered on the right day. "Where's Agent Tyler?"

Gabriel said, "Ten tomorrow—what's 'I Hate War'?"

Ellie said, "The FDR Memorial?" The Roosevelt Memorial was a long walk of different displays and statues and fountains. Two large blocks of stone were engraved with those words in the section about a famous Depression-era speech.

Hunter had dialed his phone. After a lengthy conversation he put it in his pocket and said, "She'll be here in five minutes. She was just getting to 210."

"Who?"

"Dr. Davies. That's why I called the Locard. The cops, the FBI, they'd get that note analyzed in two weeks. We need it done in two hours."

Becca said, "But where is he? How do we get him back? Why don't they tell us *that*? Mason—"

Hunter Carlisle put his arms around his wife in a hug twice as fierce as Ellie's. Her cousin's stifled sob made her heart break.

"Is he dead?" came a voice from the doorway, and each adult turned. Taylor came closer, still in her school skirt and blouse, muddy smears from Ellie's hand having dried on the sleeve. "Did they find him?"

Ellie started to assure her, but had to break off to grab both of the little girl's wrists just as she'd already done to the girl's parents. Explaining about fingerprint analysis did not seem to help; Taylor couldn't resist the allure of a real live ransom note. "*Stop*. You cannot touch it, that's very important."

Rachael Davies appeared at the exterior door, and after a quick glance through the glass, she let herself in. On her heels came the two FBI agents, who had been conferring in the driveway upon Luis's return. A chorus of voices showered them with erratic facts, but Rachael seemed to grasp all of them in the first second or two.

She took a photograph of the letter and envelope—so did Ellie—then donned gloves and made both disappear into fresh manila envelopes, to Taylor's visible disappointment. "I'll have our techs get on this immediately. They won't mind a little overtime."

Ellie said, "They tell you to send someone else—I assume they mean not you or Hunter. Doesn't that seem strange?"

"What *doesn't* seem strange?" Gabriel said.

Maybe, Ellie thought, the kidnappers thought the parents would get too emotional, attract attention. Or they might be recognized by Becca or Hunter, someone known to them.

Michael Tyler said, "I can't advise you to pay or not pay—but is it even possible? Could you get that much money?"

"Of course," Hunter said. "Cash might be a little tough, but we could get Tara to—why five hundred thousand? Why not a round million? I'd pay it, I'd—we might need you to get the banks to open after hours—"

"Why a note?" Gabriel asked of no one in particular. "They texted Hunter. Why not send another text?"

"They might assume that after today's text, Hunter's phone would now be hooked up to machines at an FBI lab. Besides," Ellie added, "it's postmarked Monday."

"What?" Gabriel said.

"I noticed that," Rachael said. "They mailed the note before they took Mason."

"Pretty damn confident," Hunter snapped. "Not to mention their faith in the postal service. Who the hell *are* these people? It's gotta be someone who works for us. I told you I don't like that new guy who does the trees."

Becca spoke as if in a daze, as if this last blow might be one too many and she might be going down for the count. "But he's never been inside the house."

"From the trees he can see inside every room, there's so many damn windows in this place."

"He wasn't even here yesterday. Only the grass guy."

"Well, he wouldn't be, would he? He knew the layout and came through the woods. Got up to the house avoiding the cameras—"

"And somehow got through locked windows and doors without leaving a trace," Ellie said, mostly to stick up for the poor tree guy who wasn't even there that day. "It's possible—maybe he somehow got a key—but then, why mail the note? Why not just put it in the mailbox?"

"That would make more sense," Gabriel said. "It's too far from the house to get caught on the cameras."

"*Your* cameras," Ellie said to the couple. "But lots of houses have cameras, businesses, probably the gas station at the end of the street. They wouldn't have wanted to be caught on this road at all."

Gabriel still puzzled. "But why take the chance that the post office might confiscate the letter, or that the machines might lose it until next week?"

Michael cut through the theorizing. "Dr. Davies and Dr. Carr will see what we can learn from this note. We will help you with the banks and prep the equipment we'll need for the drop tomorrow. It's helpful that they didn't specify a type of bag—"

"We can't have cops leave this ransom!" Becca said. "These people will be watching—what if they panic and run away? We'll never get Mason back!"

"I'm sure they'll—"

"I'll do it," Gabriel said. "They can stay at a distance, give me a wire or whatever."

Hunter started to speak, but Becca said, "We can't ask you to. It might be dangerous—"

"No, it won't. They want the money, so they got no reason to attack me. All I'm going to do is drop the bag off and walk away."

Hunter said, "Thanks, buddy. I'd feel a lot better with you walking around with a bag of my money than some FBI agent I've never met." His voice felt heavy, weighed down by weariness, but then he thought of something, and turned to Michael and Luis. "No offense."

"None taken," Luis said.

His partner said nothing.

Rachael spoke again in the same brisk tone. "Okay. I'll let you know my results from the note as soon as I know myself. We can process the note with a number of dye stains, and an infrared spectrometer for the glue behind the letters."

*Of course you can,* Ellie thought. She didn't point out that knowing whether the kidnappers used Elmer's or Mod Podge would hardly help; Rachael wanted to make the parents feel they were in good hands, and Ellie wanted her cousin reassured as well.

"In the meantime you have a lot of cash to get together, which isn't going to be easy since the banks have already closed for the day."

Ellie knew what she was doing. Give stressed people a task, something concrete for them to do, to focus on. The same way her grief counselors would get family members working on funeral arrangements and contact information for loved ones and distant relatives.

"Dr. Carr," Rachael continued. "If you wouldn't mind

serving as family liaison, would you like to accompany me to the Locard? That way you could witness our analysis and be able to fill in your cousin on what we find."

Ellie knew what she was doing here as well. She wanted to get Ellie alone to grill her about Becca and Hunter. But asking a forensic specialist if she wanted to tour the Locard was like asking an economist if they wanted to go behind the scenes at the Federal Reserve. "I'd be happy to."

# Chapter 17

Sophie Tran made the last goal of the game, which made getting a goal doubly exciting. The high of triumph added inches to her leaps into the air as she bounced over to the drinks table, where one of the mothers had spread out paper cups of water and two bowls with cut-up oranges. No bananas, which meant it was Trish's mom this week, who had an allergy and wouldn't touch them. Supposedly, even the skin would make her break out in hives.

"Cool goal," her best friend told her. Lakeisha was always full of compliments—her dad was a psychologist and super big on positive reinforcement—but it still made Sophie do a cartwheel in the grass, the blades scratchy and dried out without rain. "Are you happy about the goal or *Leee— uhmm?*"

"The goal, of course."

"This was only a practice," Lakeisha teased.

"Still a goal!"

"Still a boy!"

They collapsed in giggles, winding through the narrow

trees that separated game fields from the parking lot. Then Sophie got serious. "Okay. So you're going to tell your mom that my mom is taking me to a quick dentist appointment, and then she's going to drop me at your place." Sophie's mom would believe that she'd been at Lakeisha's the whole time.

They ducked into the snack bar to use the bathroom so Sophie could wash the sweat off her face and change into her new jeans and her cutest T-shirt. She wished she'd brought a little makeup . . . She didn't usually wear it, but she thought about it, debated, changed her mind, then decided against it, and now regretted that decision. But she hadn't wanted to look like she was trying too hard. Didn't want to look as if she was trying at all. They were just friends, that's all . . . They were going out for ice cream with his *mom*, after all, so how serious could the date be?

Lakeisha held her bag for her while Sophie did all this, so she didn't have to set it on the gross tile floor, wavering between envy and concern.

"What are you going to do if it's *not* Liam?" She had asked this four times in the past twenty-four hours. "What if it turns out to be some middle-aged pervert who wants to traffic you?"

"Scream, kick him in the balls, and run. What else would I do?" Lip gloss. She at least had lip gloss.

"What if he tases you?"

"I won't get close enough in the first place. It's those benches over by the basketball courts. They're out in the open. I won't walk over there until I see him first. Why do you think I picked that spot?"

They left the bathroom, lowering their voices as they wound through tables of people eating fried potatoes, fried cheese sticks, and fried corn dogs. Lakeisha wrinkled her nose at more than just the smell. "What if he's just the bait?

You see him, think, 'Oh, that's Liam,' and go over to say hi and then *bam*! His old pervert handler jumps out of the bushes and they knock you out and stuff you in a van."

"No bushes there. You're just jealous."

"I know." Lakeisha was always super honest . . . all that psychology training. "He *is* super cute. But—"

"And I've got my parachute app." She would have it up on the screen and ready to go. One press of her thumb and it would send **I am in trouble, call the police** texts to five different people and provide location information, activate her phone tracking program, call 911, and turn on audio and video recording. It also locked the phone so none of that could be changed or turned off unless Sophie put in a special password, not her regular password. Short of a handgun, it was the best protection a girl could have . . . even though a lot could happen between that thumb press and the reaction time of even a highly staffed police department. Sophie knew that. She wasn't stupid.

But good luck talking her mom into getting Sophie a gun. The cell phone had been tough enough.

They reached the fork in the sidewalk. "I still think I should go with you," Lakeisha said.

"Don't have time—your mom will already be waiting, and if she sees me, the whole plan goes to hell." Sophie loved using mild swear words, but only mild ones. The really bad ones made you sound like a wannabe.

"All right. If anything goes wrong, or he doesn't show—"

"I'll text. We'll tell your mom the dentist got canceled."

"Got it." Lakeisha's honesty didn't always extend to parents. After all, it wasn't *her* lie, it was Sophie's, and you had to help your friends.

They hugged, and Sophie took the path to the basketball courts. Halfway there she looked back, but Lakeisha had disappeared.

From the curve by the mini-diamond, where the really little kids played T-ball, she paused to scan the area. The benches where she was to meet Liam sat empty. High school boys were playing ball, one kid whooping as the ball swished through the tubular net. Slightly behind her, a pudgy old guy who *could* be a pedophile bent over a tiny boy, gently guiding his arms to bat the ball off the tee. Two jock-like older boys, maybe college, came toward her on the sidewalk, holding an animated conversation in which every other word seemed to be the f-bomb. Wannabes, she thought, without bothering to specify what it was they wanted to be. Still, she backed way off the sidewalk, over to the chain-link fence surrounding the basketball court. The two guys walked on by, not appearing to notice her at all. She waited for them to pass. No would-be abductors there. Then she returned to the sidewalk. The benches were still vacant.

She rocked on the balls of her feet and kinda wished it *would* be a tubby old pervert coming to meet her. She'd dial the police before even walking over to tell him he was busted . . . Of course, if she wound up in a police report, she'd have to explain that to her mom. If he tried to grab her, she could hit him with the pepper spray—she'd better get that out of her backpack before even approaching—and *then* kick him between the legs. Maybe she'd pretend to fall for it, let him try to talk her into leaving the park with him. *I'm so sorry for lying about my age—and my looks and my school and where I live—but I was afraid you'd be angry and we've become such good friends, and it's still just me, and age is just a number,* and on and on and on, as if she would buy all that. Maybe she'd let him waste his time on her, in addition to the hours they'd already spent talking online and on her phone, like the way her mom strung along scam telemarketers. Then she'd say "Gotcha, sucker!" and tell him she'd recorded the whole exchange and streamed it live to Facebook. Watch his wrinkly old face fall.

Though she'd still have to explain stuff to her mom then.

Someone came and sat on the bench. Sophie stared, feeling at once exhilarated and a teensy bit disappointed. She'd actually been looking forward to taking on her very own internet predator. But no need.

The person on the bench was indisputably Liam. A skinny boy about her age, sandy-blond hair cut to stay a little messy, even when combed, dressed in jeans and a loose T-shirt with stylized writing that Sophie couldn't make out from that distance. And next to him stood a stout woman, with drab brown hair and a green polo shirt, who could only be his mom.

Well. Now that she *didn't* have to pepper-spray anybody, she wasn't quite sure what to do next . . . but then Liam noticed her and waved. Her heart sang as she continued up the sidewalk. But from the look on his face his heart *wasn't* singing, so she told herself to play it cool, switch out her wide grin for a small smile. "Hi. I'm Sophie."

"Liam." He stretched out a hand to shake hers, a little formal, but nice and polite. "This is my mom."

The woman had the warmth Liam lacked. Her brown hair brushed her shoulders in some sort of curls and her shirt read: CARSON'S CAR WASH. "Hi, Sophie. It's so nice to meet you. Did you just play a game?"

"Yes! Just for practice, though. The team rotations haven't started yet."

"Yes, I know. Liam plays soccer too—but, of course, you know that, you've been talking about it online, right? Why don't we walk a bit before we get some ice cream?"

And lacking any better ideas—why was it so much easier to talk to boys by message instead of in real life?—Sophie said, "Okay."

They strolled the circuit of the gaming fields, discussing Sophie's team, her coach's habits, Liam's team, and his school, somewhere south of DC, in a suburb she had never heard of. Liam's mother gently prodded when the conversation lagged, which Sophie thought was nice of her. She didn't think most mothers would put a lot of effort into encouraging a romance for their twelve-year-old, but maybe Liam didn't have a lot of friends. Given his conversational ability, that would not have surprised Sophie. But then boys often got tongue-tied when it came right down to it. They talked a big game around their friends, but away from that clique it became a different story.

They wound up by a slightly beat-up white van. "Ready for some ice cream?" Liam's mom asked, sliding the door open.

Sophie climbed right in.

# Chapter 18

The Locard rested on the shores of Chesapeake Bay, nearly an hour from downtown DC. But since the Carlisles were already twenty minutes southeast of the city, Ellie figured forty minutes each way and she didn't mind—she needed a break, needed a moment away from the Carlisle mansion and its dramas to assimilate what had occurred. A quiet hour or two humming along in Rachael's Audi would do nicely. Rachael would want to question her about Becca and her family under the guise of just making conversation, but that was okay. Ellie intended to ask all sorts of questions right back.

Rachael opened with a few softballs. "How long have you been with the FBI?"

"About eight years."

"Always in ERT?"

"I wish. No, ERT is a collateral duty. I applied as soon as I had my two years in. I'm in Organized Crime at the moment, but I've done public corruption, terrorism, and fraud." The last had been her favorite, the grifters and con men unique among criminals.

"Do any undercover?"

People always wanted to know that. "A few times. Not my forte—apparently, I don't have much of a poker face."

"Have you ever been to one of our courses?"

"No. One of my coworkers took your crime scene photography course last year. She spoke highly of it."

"Good." Rachael paused. Ellie could hear gears shift in her thinking. "You and your cousin seem close."

Ellie wanted to be truthful and deny it, but that would feel disloyal—and weaselly, as if she wanted to distance herself in case things went south. So she punted. "The whole family is tightly knit."

"She said you lived with them for a while, when you were young."

"Yes." Ellie took a breath. She always hated this part.

A ringing filled the interior, and the console display lit up with a photo of an older Black woman and **Mom**.

"Oh, sorry!" As a second ring sounded, Ellie watched her look around and pat her pockets as best she could while still watching the road, figure out that her phone was in her purse, and the purse was in the backseat, so she could either take the call via Bluetooth speakerphone, or decline it. She hesitated only one split second longer before telling Ellie, "I have to take this," and tapping she'd accept.

"Mamamamamama!"—it was shrieked at such a volume that Rachael quickly adjusted the knob.

"Hello, baby! What are you up to?"

The boy—Ellie guessed it was a boy—described building a house—Ellie assumed out of Legos—and that he had a Popsicle, which had been purple, and he wanted another one.

"Not until Nana says, maybe after dinner. Where is Nana?"

"She here."

"Where? Does she know you're using her phone?"

"Bye, Mama!" An abrupt *click*, and the car was quiet once more.

"He's got to stop doing that. He's going to call 911 or something one of these days and we're going to get in trouble."

Ellie found herself smiling along with Rachael. "How old is he?"

"Two and a half." Rachael goosed the car through a yellow light. "His name is Danton." She pronounced it as Dan-*tone*, not *Dan*-tun.

"Like the French revolutionary?" Ellie asked.

"Huh. I wouldn't be surprised."

She wasn't sure who her son was named af—

As if sensing Ellie's hesitation, Rachael explained: "Danton isn't actually my son."

"Oh, I'm—"

"He's my nephew. My sister died over a year ago."

"Oh." Stupidly. A decade of working with grieving families had not helped much—there were still no words.

Rachael didn't seem to need any, however. "I let Danton call me Mama because, well, I am now, and I can't see the point of correcting a toddler just for the sake of accuracy. I'm going to make it official, but . . . it's complicated."

Ellie didn't know if she should ask why. Would that be nosy or empathetic? It never came easily, being in someone else's house, having to learn the rhythm of someone else's family. Right back to where she'd been at four, at nine, at sixteen. "He's lucky to have you."

"He'd be luckier to have his mother raising him instead of an aunt. But thank you."

This part always required too many explanations . . . but the topic had come up and to run away now would be cowardly. "I have a lot of experience with aunts. My mother died when I was four, and my father took off. I lived with my grandmother for five years until she got too ill, then with various aunts and uncles. Aunt Rosalie from nine to eleven, until Uncle Wayne had a bout of PTSD. Then Aunt Katey and Uncle Terry—Becca's parents—until fourteen or so, when Uncle Paul and Aunt Joanna took me to Naples to attend a private high school."

"Naples, Italy?" Rachael asked with enthusiasm.

"As if. Naples, *Florida*."

"Too bad."

Ellie found herself laughing. "Plus some summers with my mother's cousins in Nevada when I was a kid and other cousins in California during college."

"Wow," Rachael said.

At this point Ellie normally expected to hear *How awful* or *Good thing you had such caring relatives.* But Rachael didn't seem to be able to manage anything beyond "Wow."

*No better than "oh,"* Ellie thought, and felt validated.

*But we are* not *bonding,* she told the universe. *This is not a bonding moment.*

Even though each and every aunt, uncle, and cousin had drawn her in with both arms, doing whatever they needed to do to make sure kin would not be abandoned to strangers—the same thing Rachael now did with her sister's child.

"Family is family," Ellie said. It wasn't a sensible comment, but—"I'm doing everything I can on this case because it's my job *and* because Becca is family. But you have to understand, that doesn't extend to covering up a crime. If I think for one minute she harmed her child, or Hunter did, or even Taylor did, I will say so." She turned her head, staring at Rachael as she spoke. "I would not hide any evidence to help them in that."

The car stopped for a red light, and Rachael turned as well. She considered Ellie for a long time.

Ellie did not break the gaze. Even though people looking you straight in the eye meant absolutely nothing about their honesty.

"I believe you," Rachael said.

*You do not. But maybe,* maybe, *you're trying to.*

The light changed, and they drove on.

"Unfortunately—" Rachael began.

"—we still have a seemingly impossible crime," Ellie finished. "If one of the three people living there didn't remove the baby, who did? And how did they get in and out without being caught on the cameras?"

"Which surround the house and cover the perimeter completely."

"You can get into the garage from the house without being seen. But you can't get in or out of the garage."

Rachael pounded the brakes as an SUV stopped short on a curving on-ramp. "Becca insists Gabriel was in her line of sight every minute during his visit, and she did check on Mason after returning from picking up Taylor. So Tara could not have taken him. Do you know Tara?"

"Never met her. Becca and I . . . have kept in touch, but we don't spend a lot of time together. I'd only seen Taylor once before today, which is a bit embarrassing. But we're so busy . . . demanding careers . . . time goes by before you know it." And Ellie didn't care to reminisce about the emotional tightrope she'd spent years walking between the two sisters and the damage inflicted with every fall. Adam had been right. She didn't even *like* Becca, in her heart of hearts.

And maybe Becca hadn't been too eager to have someone who spent her time amid blood and dust and death getting up close with the much more moneyed set of friends and clients. Perhaps she didn't want to see a reminder of her less privileged days sipping Carlisle champagne on the flagstone terrace.

So, even though they lived in the same city, a distance had been maintained. "I can't really say I know her well," Ellie went on, "as an adult. I don't know what her habits are or what their friends are like. I'm sure maintaining that social status requires a certain type of appearance. But I believe she's devastated about Mason—she's not faking that. She's not that good of an actress."

"I agree."

Ellie considered this with another sideways glance. "Thank you for not pointing out that she would *also* be devastated if she killed him."

"You're welcome. How well do you know Hunter Carlisle?"

"Not at all. Polite enough to me, but I've never encountered him outside of a few social occasions. At this point you've probably had a longer conversation with him than I've ever had."

"No problems you know of? Good enough dad, husband?"

"Taylor seems to be dying for her parents' attention, certainly not afraid of either, and Becca . . . This is going to sound like a family whitewash, but he and Becca seem to be on the same page, word by word. Lockstep—and not in a way like one controls the other, but as if they exist naturally on the same wavelength. It's effortless."

Rachael seemed to think this over. Ellie thought: Hunter and Becca were utterly united—even if it were only in their ambition to be DC's power couple—and it made their marriage enviably strong. Unlike hers. She had thought she and Adam were utterly united in a desire to spend the rest of their lives together. It turned out that Adam's desire had been for someone with more talent in the bedroom and less talent on the crime scene.

Rachael said, "So you're thinking if Becca and Hunter united to, for some reason, get rid of one of their children—they could probably do that too, as successfully as they get a bill passed for a client or researched for the committee."

The loyalty thing bubbled up again, but Ellie had too many concerns to mince words. "I think Becca is devastated over Mason. But I also think that if my kid had been kidnapped, I wouldn't be going to work."

"Everyone copes differently. That kind of icy calm probably makes her successful on the Hill."

Ellie adjusted the shoulder strap. "My problem is, 'icy calm' never described Becca. More like 'emotional outbursts of anger' describes Becca. 'Icy calm' was her sister Melissa's forte—*she* could do icy calm all day long. Becca, not so much."

"So you think her reaction is inconsistent."

"I don't *know*. I'm remembering a girl Taylor's age, so my assessment is badly out of date. Plus, I've never been up close and personal with a kidnapping for ransom. Have you?"

"I worked several kidnappings when I was at the Richmond crime lab." She didn't mention that she had *run* the Richmond crime lab. Ellie knew it because she had Googled for more details on Rachael in the bathroom at Becca's house. "But most were parental. We also had abductions."

Not really the same thing, where the perpetrator had no intention of bringing the child back.

"Only solved two of five there." As if on cue a cloud passed over the sun, flooding the car with a temporary dimness that matched Rachael's expression. "But only one actual kidnapping for ransom, and that was an adult, a CEO taken by a disgruntled former employee. I won't count the one that turned out to be a bunch of teenagers and their 'victim,' a willing participant trying to punk his parents out of money for pot."

"I know actual kidnapping for ransom is rare."

"In this country only about three percent of cases."

"What about at the Locard? Have they worked on any?"

Rachael picked up speed as the DC traffic thinned out and the landscape changed from solid structures to more open areas. The sun beat down, the days still long. "Only two that I know of, and they were both, um . . . cold."

Ellie immediately surmised: "The victims were dead."

"Both adults. An infant is different—they can't give a description, so they're not a danger to the criminals."

She didn't need to sugarcoat things, Ellie thought, but appreciated the effort. A baby couldn't give a description, but babies were also noisy, inconvenient, and easy to get rid of.

Rachael went on. "In one case the kidnapper got away with the ransom and we were hired to find him. In the other they didn't get the money and didn't escape either, but the two men wouldn't give up who their inside person had been, the corporate spy."

"And were you successful?"

"Yes, in both. In the first case we tracked him by trace evidence he'd left on the victim, and in the second it was a combination of office security video and cell phone records."

That would have made Ellie feel better, except they already knew video was useless and Mason was too young for a cell phone. And she hoped they'd never have a body.

# Chapter 19

Sophie ordered her favorite, mint chocolate chip. Liam got peanut butter, which Sophie considered a complete waste. She loved peanut butter, but only as peanut butter. She wasn't even crazy about Reese's Cups.

Liam's mom got coffee, which, as much as she loved coffee, Sophie also considered a waste of good ice cream. His mom even went back and got them all cherry slushies, since Sophie said she liked them too. Sophie's mother never let her get two things at the ice-cream place, said it was too much sugar. The sweet, cold drink seemed to perk Liam up as well, and he talked for ten minutes about *Lion's Reach* and the flaming axes in level six.

He was in the middle of the gorillas and how not to tangle up their vines, when his mother interrupted him midsentence to say, "You two met in the game, right? Liam messaged you in the live chat box."

"Yeah." Sophie sucked up about a tablespoon of the cherry-flavored ice and held it in her mouth to warm it up a bit before swallowing. You had to go slowly with slushies, or you'd get that pain in the head. They were sitting at one of the outside tables, with only a sidewalk separating them from the parking space and their van. Umbrellas sheltered them from the late summer sun. Other people roamed around them, in and out of the ice-cream place and the other stores in the plaza.

"You must have been relieved to see it was really him at the ball fields."

Sophie laughed, but Liam didn't. She told his mom how she had been thinking the same thing.

His mom said, "You can never really know who you're talking to online. A girl in Liam's class started chatting with a boy, or who she thought was a boy—"

"Oh, I've heard all the stories." Sophie wanted to get back to the gorillas. "I heard that in level eleven, the magic stone—"

"Sophie." His mom set her spoon down and gave the girl that "talking-to" look that adults get. "This is important."

She might be only twelve, but she knew better than to tick off the guy's mother. "I know. My mom tells me all these horror stories. And we have social media presentations at school every year."

"Online games are specifically targeted to children. Kid-Fun knows that children will be playing them. So do predators. My daughter, Tina, met someone online, because they started chatting through a game."

"*Fortnite,*" Liam said. Half of the peanut butter–flavored stuff sat in his cup, melting. He was probably ticked that his mom was butting in, and just as he'd been beginning to say more than one sentence at a time.

"Tina had no idea who this person was. He started out so nice, chatting about the game and strategies and their favorite snacks. Then he talked her into private messaging on a different platform—classic predator behavior."

Sophie nodded in a way she hoped implied sage knowledge. She really didn't feel like being lectured to about internet safety—Lord knew she heard enough of that from her own mother, and teachers, and even her soccer coach—but she wanted to be polite and impress this woman, no matter how much work it was.

The corners of Liam's mom's mouth got really tight, turning her lips into straight, thin lines. "He got her to feel romantic."

Sophie almost spit out the slushie she was warming up at this description. Of all the ways adults described what people did, she had never heard this one.

"She was only a little girl—"

"She wasn't little," Liam interrupted firmly.

"*Liam,*" his mom said, even more firmly. They glared at each other for a brief spell until Liam dropped his eyes.

Sophie squirmed. *Awkward.* She'd seen plenty of her friends fighting with their parents. Every parent seemed to have some weird hang-up. Jonathan's dad made him call every older woman "ma'am." Opal's mom made them pray out loud at every meal, even in restaurants. Michael's parents inspected his homework, every night, and signed off with their initials in the corners so that each parent would know the other one actually read it. Marjorie's mother freaked out if Marjorie even joked about eating meat, so they all had to be careful to never slip that Marjorie ate the meatballs every time the school served spaghetti.

So if Liam's mom was a little nutty on internet "stranger danger," no big deal. When an adult got like that, the only sensible thing was to shut up and let them yak. Then they'd be happy. So Sophie shut up and sipped more slushie. She loved cherry.

"She was very young," Liam's mom was saying. "This man talked her into meeting him at a park—just like we did with you."

Sophie felt her eyebrows knit. That—what was it called—

analogy wasn't correct. Sophie had been very careful *not* to meet a predator. Liam was exactly the same boy she'd been chatting with.

"You think you'll always be safe. You think you know all the right things to do. Your mother told you all the right things to do. Because your mother writes the protocols for how people get in the game, to keep all the bad people out."

Sophie wasn't sure how they got on a story about *her* mom from a story about Liam's sister, but here was a chance to shine. "Yes! My mom's company makes, like, when people register for a game, they have to answer those pop-up questions, like where you lived five years ago and what car you drive. That's *knowledge-based verification*." She pronounced the words carefully. The questions would make it hard for kids to pretend to be their parents and sign up for grown-up games with swearing and nudity. Sophie thought that might be a bit unfair, like adults were purposely trying to trick kids, but she'd never said so to her mom, and she certainly wasn't going to say so to Liam's mom.

"Sure," Liam's mom said. "She'll use facial recognition and make parents scan their IDs. She'll even make them give permission to search their identity through all online means, birth records, social media apps, school records, credit history."

"Yes," Sophie said proudly. Wasn't that *good*? Wouldn't that make Mrs. Liam—no, Liam's mom—happy, that Sophie's mom cared just as much about internet safety as she did?

But she didn't seem happy.

Sophie's dad also didn't seem happy when he and Sophie's mom argued about it.

Dad would say, *The automations of the platform will Google you, find you on other sites, like games and social media, and figure out who you are, how old you are, and that you follow Taylor Swift and not Marilyn Manson. Then it will use the information to sell, sell, sell, through targeted ads. It's bad enough that they do this to adults, but worse to do it to kids who don't know they're being brainwashed.*

And Mom would say, *So what if an ad for go-cart accessories pops up on your go-cart–racing son's tablet? You watch the Disney Channel, you see ads for toys and cereals. You watch a football game, it's beer and sports cars. Duh.*

And Dad would say, *That's just an excuse for profit-motivated data mining,* and then Mom would say, *You've been listening to your brother again,* and then they'd stop talking completely, until Sophie finished her dinner and left the room.

Liam's mom went on as though Sophie hadn't spoken, even though she had been looking directly at her the whole time. "She'll find out every single thing about the kids *and* their parents, but not to make sure that ten-year-olds are playing with other ten-year-olds. She'll gather all that lucrative data and it won't stop one pedophile from creating an avatar."

Sophie started to say yes and then wondered if the right answer was no. What was the woman's *point*? She looked at Liam, but he poked at his ice cream, now nearly soup.

"Finn sent me a white paper your mother published that said KidFun's verification procedures made kids as safe as they could possibly be. She actually wrote, 'As safe as they could possibly be.' But Tina," she said, "was never safe."

Sophie hoped she'd wind down soon. She was starting to feel slightly sleepy—odd, since Sophie's mom always said she *couldn't* have two treats because that much sugar would make her bounce off the walls.

"A white paper. It should be called a white*wash* paper."

What *did* happen to the sister? Despite herself Sophie had gotten a little interested in the story and wanted to know, but not know, what horrible thing the man did to her.

Sophie's straw made a loud slurping sound as she emptied

the bottom of her cup. How did she get to the bottom? She'd downed it too fast, because now her temple began to tingle. Ice-cream headache.

"Your mother is on KidFun's payroll, and yet she's telling Congress that her reports are entirely objective. On their *payroll*. KidFun pays for your fancy school and your big house and your soccer uniform."

"*Mom*," Liam said, really angry. But she ignored him.

"She tells *you* all the horror stories to keep you safe. But does she tell Congress the truth? Does she keep anyone *else's* kids safe?"

The words suddenly settled into a pattern, which became clear: Liam's mom was being really mean about Sophie's mom. Sophie didn't know what her problem was, but no boy was worth this. Not even one with cute, shaggy sandy-blond hair.

Screw Liam's mom.

She'd call Lakeisha and have her talk her mom into coming to pick Sophie up. They'd come up with some story about the dentist appointment. As long as she was at Lakeisha's house in time for a FaceTime call with her mom before bed, no one would ask questions.

The woman was still talking. "Your mother needs to tell everyone that what she's been doing is wrong. It's *evil*."

Sophie needed her phone. Where was her phone? In her backpack, right?

"She needs to go to that hearing tomorrow and tell the committee the truth. Tell them that suspending the direct-messaging ban will put every child in this country at risk. She knows it, and has known it all along."

"This isn't Sophie's fault," Liam said.

His voice seemed farther away than just the little iron-work table, as Sophie worked to find her backpack. There— by her feet. The phone was in the side flap. Lakeisha's number would be right on top of recent . . .

"Sophie's mother has to listen now. She certainly hasn't listened to anyone else. Finn sent her case data from all over the world—"

Sophie reached for the backpack. Stretching her hand down required all her concentration, moving those fingers down, down . . .

"That's all anecdotal," she heard Liam say.

"You don't even know what that means," his mother snapped. Her hands were on Sophie's arm, pulling her upright. For some reason Sophie couldn't raise her head all the way and it bobbled a little. The backpack remained on the ground, and Sophie tried to define "anecdotal" in her head.

Then the woman pulled her up to a standing position, one arm encircling her shoulders so tightly it hurt. Sophie's head continued to loll, but her knees at least partly supported her. What was going on?

"Liam," his mom ordered, "open the side door. Low blood sugar," she added, clearly speaking to someone else, since the tone of her voice changed abruptly.

All Sophie wanted to do was sleep. This made her calm and mellow and liberated her mind to put together some evidence: Mrs. Liam—no, Liam's mother, so she'd be Mrs. . . . Sophie didn't know what Mrs. she would be, but whoever she was, she had roofied Sophie's slushie. Only Sophie's, since both she and Liam were fine. They hustled Sophie away from the table and into the van parked right there, and some passerby must have seen them and looked at them funny, so Mrs. Liam—no—whatever—pretended Sophie was fainting, and tossed her on this bench seat inside the van's sliding door. Which was good, because Sophie could lay her torso along it and it felt as if she'd collapsed onto a fluffy feather bed while in the throes of complete exhaustion. Sophie sighed with pleasure.

*Parachute,* a voice in her head said. *Parachute!*

Her safety program. In her phone—all she had to do was hit the app. No, find the app, then hit the button.

The phone in her backpack—*Where is my backpack?* She tried to lift her head to look for it, maybe on the floor next to her, but her head didn't want to lift. Her hand didn't want to pat around for it either.

*OMG, did they leave my backpack at the ice-cream store? My phone, my homework, my lip gloss . . . did Liam's mom grab it?*

Didn't matter, because even if she had it, she wasn't likely to give Sophie her phone, just so she could call for help.

Bitch.

Sophie really should buckle the seat belt, because the buckle now dug into her ribs. And her mother was really strict about car safety. Just as fanatical as about internet safety.

Which, Sophie thought with a wide streak of guilt, hadn't worked so well. Because Sophie had just been kidnapped.

# Chapter 20

Rachael and Ellie discussed the relative merits of ninhydrin versus iodine versus diazafluorene through the Maryland countryside, eventually turning off the interstate onto a large road, then onto 423, winding past large swaths of forest and farmland, where houses tended to be large and widely spaced from each other. Just as the blue expanse of the bay came into sight, Rachael turned right and pulled down a bare-bones drive into a large parking lot.

They stepped from the car, arms full of bags and manila envelopes, and Rachael saw her passenger look around in slight confusion. The Locard, only two stories, could not be seen from the parking lot with all the trees in the way. But Ellie didn't ask. Rachael wondered if she didn't like to ask questions of anyone, or just of Rachael.

Letting a private lab take lead in the investigation had to be tough for her, Rachael knew. It certainly would have been for her when she headed up the Richmond Medical Examiner's Office. It wasn't ego that drove it, but the drilled-in training to keep third parties out of the crime lab, away from the evidence, minimize the chain of custody, reduce the number of cooks in the kitchen. Standard procedure.

She totally got it, but was still tired of having to tread so lightly through other jurisdictions. Just once she'd like to walk in and say, *Look, this is the way it is, we have twice the equipment and four times the expertise of your facilities, so please just get out of the way.*

Maybe someday, when retirement drew near, she would—but until then, she'd continue to play nice. Besides, Dr. Carr had proven much less problematic than she'd expected. News stories made her sound like a bulldog, but so far, she'd kept the fangs in check.

*So,* Rachael thought, *have I.* With both Ellie *and* with Danton's father, who had materialized without warning the evening before.

The day had been stressful, between an unhappy client complaining to the press that the Locard's findings had failed to implicate her ex-husband in the corporate theft and instead found some damning evidence against her, and the blood supplies not arriving for the bloodstain pattern interpretation class, Rachael had been looking forward to an evening of rocking Danton on the swing under the oak tree or admiring his collection of Hot Wheels. Yet she wasn't unaware of the strange car that had turned the corner in front of her and stopped, so that she had to drive around it to pull into her own driveway. Only one occupant.

She parked and got out of her car, expecting to be asked about the high-priced and unhappy client. But the man who walked slowly up her drive didn't dress like a reporter. She'd never seen a reporter dressed in fatigues, not in-country.

Tall, with a broad chest and high cheekbones under a hint of five-o'clock shadow. A resolutely blank, unresponsive expression. Long sleeves hid the tattoos and the muscles, since there wasn't a lot for an army demolitions expert in the Middle East to do when not blowing things up, except work out.

He stopped about eight feet away, then nodded. "Rachael."

"Jalen."

She heard the screen door slam behind her and prepared for the small train to hit the back of her legs and the cry of *"Mamamamamama!"* But instead of turning to swoop him up, she watched the man's eyes as he watched the boy. She expected—to be honest, wanted—a hint of distaste, perhaps of avarice at the sight of an opportunity he could exploit. But she detected only a widening of the eyes, the eyebrows rising like a deer in very welcome headlights. A look of *joy*.

Then the veil descended again, his expression expressionless.

She did bend to pick up Danton then, and he pointed at the man with a jumble of words that clearly formed a question.

"Danton," she told him, "this is your father."

It had been an interesting evening.

She put it out of her head. At least her child was home, safe. Mason Carlisle wasn't.

The smell of the water filled Rachael's head as they passed through the humid evening. She heard the waves lapping gently at the shore and could glimpse the water's surface through the trees.

She promised Ellie a short walk and led her to a nearly hidden opening in the forest, a wide asphalt path leading away from the parking lot. The path, hemmed in by growth, felt both cooler and more humid. She pointed out a small sign off the path to the left that read: SITE 1. "We have two 'body farm' type digs, to give our students practice with buried bodies."

"Of course you do," Ellie said, and chuckled to herself for some reason.

"Depending on the class and how long it runs, they might come out twice a day to observe the changes due to decomposition, or they might have to dig one up to get some experience in excavation and documenting an excavation."

"Very nice," Ellie said. "Okay, that sounds weird to say."

"But true."

Abruptly, the Locard loomed before them, impressively solid and rather nondescript at the same time. Two floors, constructed of stone, with large windows running its length. The trimmings had flair, sconces, and a curved edging under the gutters, but on the whole it looked like what it was: a school.

Concrete steps led up to an old steel door with a new electronic lock. Rachael flashed a key card at it and it swung open, a handy feature with their hands full. "The classes should all be done for the day and most staff will be gone. There will be a few diehards lingering, because they can't tear themselves away from their research, there always are. It's hard to find this building totally empty. I asked Gary Fernandez to stay, he's a real whiz with paper."

Rachael's low heels clacked against the gleaming tile, while Ellie's boots only squeaked now and then. Rachael pointed out the empty classrooms on the way to a stairwell, absurdly happy to be back on her home turf. "This main section at sort of the back of the campus—we came in the side—is all training rooms on the first floor and offices on the second. Both wings, on either side of the courtyard out front, are classrooms on the first floor, then labs on the second floor in this wing and research labs, which the students aren't usually in, in the other wing. If that makes any sense. I wish we had more time that I could show you around."

"That's all right. Obviously, this is more important."

But Rachael caught her gazing wistfully into a wet lab where a lone researcher fumed dollar bills and checking the label on a carton of fluorescent superglue left in the hallway. She even unbent enough to ask what the 3-D printer had been working on as they passed it, glowing and humming to itself in a darkened lab.

"For some reconstructions we need to create our own models. Mark is probably forming some needed piece for the nutshell, a chair, a weapon. Or he's making furniture for his daughter's doll house again . . . we might have to have another talk about that."

Ellie snickered.

They reached the document examination room. Gary Fernandez, the whiz with paper, appeared as short and rotund as a beach ball and about as cheerful. Rachael had known him for four years now and had never heard a discouraging word. Tucked in a corner of a brilliantly lit lab, he had prepared several bottles of chemicals and put fresh paper at the bottom of a fume hood. "Hello, hello! A baby, you say? Those are the worst cases. This it?"

He nearly danced with anticipation as Rachael produced the manila envelopes. He plucked a small plastic sac from a dispenser, broke it open, and removed two thin cotton gloves. Donning these, he spent a good five minutes simply staring at the note and envelope when viewed through a magnifying lamp. "Who writes a ransom note like this anymore? It's like something out of an old movie."

Rachael said, "They might have wanted to avoid printer toner. Or they like old movies."

Gary wore a disposable face shield, and it knocked against the magnifier again and again in an effort to get a better look. Then he placed the letter flat on a photo stand board, with the camera suspended above it. The camera connected to a computer wirelessly, and Gary could adjust the focus or the lighting. Ellie watched over his shoulder in silence, her gaze on the screen.

The page wouldn't lie flat, the way papers won't, once they've been folded. Gary wiped two magnetic bars with disinfectant wipes until assured of their sterility and used them to hold the corners of the note down. Then he turned a crank to raise and lower the camera and adjusted the distance, while program options allowed him to adjust the focus. He took many photos, including close-ups of the cut edges of each letter. The process seemed to take forever, but the pasted letters could be incredible evidence, a jigsaw match of the cut ends to the cut holes in the pages they came from. Of course, if the kidnappers had any brains at all, they would have completely destroyed the source document.

And they seemed to have brains, at least in some ways. Rachael thought they would probably keep the scissors, though. If the metal blades had a defect or two, that could be compelling ... not as good as the jigsaw match, but something.

After the painstaking photography, Gary used an alternate light source to hit the paper from various angles with light of various wavelengths. In Rachael's experience this didn't often help, but one never knew. He lingered over *NOT* in the phrase *Send someone else NOT you*, because it had been cut out as one word instead of letter by letter, as most of the others.

"There's something here," he muttered. "I see ridges, but ... "

The two women waited, squinting to figure out what he might be looking at. Finally Rachael broke: *"What?"*

"I see ridges ... it could almost be a patent print."

Most prints were called latent, meaning they could not be seen until developed with powders or dyes or even light. Patent prints, or plastic prints, were casts of the skin left in some malleable substance like putty or paint.

"It's the glue," Ellie said.

"Yes. I think the glue got tacky, and when your guy pressed the letters down with his finger, he left an impression, even through the paper. I don't know if it will be of any use—"

He meant that while there might be ridges, there might not be ridges with enough ends, splits, creases, pores, or scars to create a distinguishable pattern that could be compared to an identical pattern. Locating a fingerprint was only the beginning.

"Going to start with iodine?" Ellie asked the Locard expert.

"Can't beat an ancient classic. Like me."

Ellie thanked him for staying late.

"Not a problem. My wife has book club tonight. This way I can pick her up on my way home, since apparently the books they pick can only be read when accompanied with several bottles of wine. I read part of one once, and after that, the wine made sense. Besides, I couldn't pass up the chance to work on a real live ransom note. Usually, it's always wills. Wills, wills, wills. People just can't *believe* that Daddy left the estate to their rotten brother Ralph."

Iodine crystals were one of those odd substances that would sublimate, or change, from a solid to a gas without becoming liquid in between. The gaseous iodine would adhere to the amino acids in the skin's oil and sweat, turning the ridges left by a fingertip to a brown color. The advantage—or disadvantage, depending on what you needed— was that the color would soon fade and disappear. But it worked on any surface and would not damage or alter the paper.

Unfortunately, the crystals were also a carcinogen. Analysts used to sandwich them in between tufts of glass wool inside a glass tube, then blow through it with a rubber tube, forcing the fumes out the other end. Relatively safe, provided you didn't breathe in. Rachael usually went the simpler route and put the crystals and the paper to be processed in a large zip-top plastic bag and let it sit for an hour or two. But they didn't have that kind of time. Mrs. Fernandez would eventually run out of wine.

So Gary went the old-fashioned route with the glass tube and the rubber hose. With the note and envelope suspended from clips in the fume hood, the vacuum sucked away the dangerous fumes with a loud hum.

Three fingerprints leapt to life fully formed on the surface of the ransom note, with smaller fractions of the fingertips here and there.

"Probably Becca's," Ellie said.

Gary said, "Did she open the envelope? Then probably, since they look so fresh. There's two more faint ones."

"Super faint," Ellie agreed.

The rest of the paper remained blank. Surely, kidnappers would have worn gloves to create the note, but it had been labor intensive. First they had to decide what to say, then find the letters or words in their source document and cut them out, apply the glue without gluing gloves and letters together, then paste them down in a relatively straight line. What they might not have known is that latex gloves can, after extended wear, begin to adhere to the fingertip. A thin latex, the perfect layer of oil and sweat on the fingers, a lot of pressing down, and the finger's print could begin to show through the glove. Someone could possibly, just possibly, have left a print on the paper even while wearing gloves.

Smudges covered the envelope, though only one or two impressions had sufficient ridge detail. It would have passed through several mail carriers and containers before reaching the Carlisles' mailbox. Going through the mail system removed some of the kidnapper's personal control, but did put distance between himself—or herself—and the victims.

More careful photography followed. A small printer churned out printed photos at a one-to-one ratio.

The pasted letters complicated things in other ways. Ninhydrin was a liquid dye, which sometimes caused certain inks to run, and its reaction to glues and adhesives could be unpredictable. Gary needed to preserve any prints on the cut letters, but also lift off the cut paper and see what they could find underneath. Maybe more patent prints, maybe trace evidence if they got lucky and something had been caught in the glue. Gary had used a snake-neck tiny light to illuminate *NOT*, trying to get a better look at what might be a print in the glue, and photographed it as well as he could.

Rachael told Ellie, "Your cousin and Hunter let me take their prints. I was going to get Taylor's, but she'd already run off to the woods."

"Good." Ellie picked up the printed photos. "Let me have them."

"I got two sets of each. If you want to start with Gary's photos, I'll work on the print cards you collected through the house."

"Deal."

Gary Fernandez waved them toward a workstation stocked with jeweler's loupes and evil-looking "picks," five-inch-long thin metal skewers with wooden handles. They would help examiners keep their place on one print, while looking for the corresponding ridge in another.

Fingerprints were not Rachael's strong suit, so she happily took the better-quality impressions from the doors and windows. At least she assumed they would be better than the myriad, smudged blobs on the letter, but quickly learned that doors and windows, especially curved knobs and narrow latches, did not lend themselves to picture-perfect fingerprints. Bent over the loupes, her neck began to hurt, but she managed to identify several prints as either Becca's or Hunter's.

Too bad they didn't have the vacationing nanny's, or those of the cleaning staff, but at least it eliminated some that they wouldn't have to bother putting into AFIS.

She had begun with the prints from the jimmied window—if indeed it had been sabotaged and not simply broken. One was Becca's, one was Hunter's, and three were unknowns. She scanned those into the system, set it to search. It *might* go faster at this time of night, but probably not by much. Early on a Sunday a search might come back in an hour or two; during a busy weekday it could be twenty-four plus.

She didn't have Ellie's patience for the tiny ridges. "How's it going?"

"I'm reminding myself not to get my hopes up. Unless we find a miniature map to where they have Mason hidden under one of the letters, I doubt the note can help at all. Especially since every discernible fingerprint on the note, and one on the envelope, belong to Becca. Not Hunter's, not some unidentified person's. Only Becca's. Which tells us nothing."

"She opened it, unfolded it," Rachael said. "At least you kept anyone else from touching it—cut down on our work. Your work."

"And the print in the glue . . . I can trace a few ridges, but most taper out into vague wisps of gray scale. I don't think I'm going to be able to do anything with this." Meaning, *there was not enough information here to work with, and no amount of enhancement or filters or dyes or digital reconstruction could help.* Sometimes that was that.

*And here is a moment of truth,* Rachael thought. *Maybe the print in the glue* does *match Becca's or Hunter's. Maybe it matches Ellie. Maybe this is all some elaborate revenge or burst of jealousy of her richer, more successful, married-with-two-kids cousin.*

Maybe Rachael should take a look at that print herself.

But if she asked, it would be a declaration of war with Ellie as an enemy spy. Did she really want to—

Ellie passed the photo across the desk. "Would you take a look? Maybe your eyes are better than mine."

Rachael breathed out. "I doubt that, but I'll give it a shot."

Gary said, "Come and look at this."

The women crowded him again. He had put the note on a light board, so bright it felt like looking at an X-ray. Then he rolled a dark, thin plate over it to block most of the area, leaving only a space a few inches square.

The letters had been printed on a thin, off-white paper with jet-black machined letters. With the bright light behind it, Rachael could see specks of darker material in the paper mash, or dirt caught in the glue. In the middle of the *b* in *baby*, a short, rectangular capsule floated.

"What's that?" Ellie asked. "Is it in the paper or the glue?"

"Let's find out." He used xylene to dissolve the adhesive until he could pull off the *b* without tearing it. The solvent wet the paper, but evaporated so quickly that it only made the letter curl a little. The ink did not run.

"The xylene lets me separate the paper, but then it dissolves the glue. If there were any friction ridge impressions in it, they're gone, and I don't see a way to get around that. I never thought I'd be hoping criminals *don't* go back to certain crude techniques."

Ellie said, "If this were a TV show, you would analyze the glue, get a complete chemical profile including percentage composition, then run that through a handy database and find it's a boutique product only sold by a particular store, even though you still mysteriously have a sample of it in your database next to the Elmer's and the Scotch."

*So* true that Rachael had to smile. Gary Fernandez found this the most hilarious thing he'd heard that decade and hooted loudly. "Then, of course, you'd go to the store, they'd check receipts, and be able to tell you exactly when they sold the last bottle so you could look at their security cam and get a picture of your kidnapper."

"*That* would actually be more realistic. On television we'd have our tech whiz hack into the store's receipts from here, and find the sale and the person's driver's license photo."

Her gaze never moving from the bare spot of glue on the ransom note, Rachael said, "I don't know if our digital forensics person, Agnes, could really hack into anything. I'm not sure I want to know."

Gary transferred the spot of glue to a clear slide and said to Ellie, "I'm sorry. Your nephew is missing and we're making jokes."

"I made it first. And Mason is my second cousin. Or first once removed."

He focused the stereomicroscope, which functioned as an oversized magnifying glass, able to give them an extremely close look at a three-dimensional object.

"Is that a *hair*?" Ellie asked.

"Looks like . . . a piece of one." He used an incredibly fine set of tweezers to pull the microscopic fragment from the adhesive and rinse it clean in a drop of xylene. Then he did a "wet mount," wedging it between a glass slide and cover slip with a drop of water. Rachael held her breath until it had been secured in the water. Tiny hairs and fibers could be lost forever with one errant sneeze.

He moved the slide to a transmission microscope so they could see through the hair, the heavy brown pigmentation, and thick, clear cuticle. Caucasian, Rachael thought. And there would be nothing more she could say about it than that.

"No adhering cells," Gary muttered. "No root, so no DNA."

"Mitochondrial," the two women said in unison.

"And the likelihood that your kidnapper is going to be in a mitochondrial DNA database?"

"Extremely slim," Rachael admitted. Mitochondrial DNA existed in a cell organelle, not the nucleus, and so was present in samples where the regular nuclear double-helix type DNA would not be possible: fingernails, very old bones, and cut hair. This would be fabulous evidence—at the kidnapper's trial. Unless the kidnapper was also a missing person, their mitochondrial DNA would not have been uploaded into CODIS.

Gary left the slide where it was and worked to remove the *am*, as in *ten am*, where he had also seen a dark speck. It turned out to be dirt, which crumbled into fine granules when removed to a fresh slide. And behind the *F* in *FDR*, a shiny metallic square.

"It's reflective," Gary noted aloud.

"Glitter," Ellie guessed.

"Our kidnapper also used the glue on his craft projects?" Rachael said. "That might fit."

"He—or she—has other children. Or maybe works around children."

"That would make sense. Supposedly, the kidnappers' motivation is to protect children online."

Gary pointed out, "You ladies are assuming a lot from one tiny spot of what might be glitter."

"Spoilsport," Rachael said, and clapped him on the shoulder. "Do you think there's anything else under those letters?"

"A few more dark shapes, probably fibers."

Once more, it could prove wonderful evidence when they had a suspect. Until then, a red nylon fiber would be a red nylon fiber, and so on. Rachael said, "I'll get the DNA analysts working on the hair. The mitochondrial is worth a try."

"They'll come in now?" Ellie asked.

"There's two I know who will be more than happy to have Hunter pay for their overtime. Sorry—I'm not trying to gouge your cousin."

"They won't care. Because you're right, it's worth a try. Anything is."

Rachael guided Ellie out of the building. As Ellie walked, she texted Becca to let her know that the note had not provided any significant breakthroughs. Then she put the phone away and they moved in silence through the building and out the door before she said: "This isn't going so well, is it?"

Rachael didn't waste time on platitudes. "The ransom drop, that's our best chance. The FBI will be able to give us a tracker to put in with the money and another one in the duffel in case they dump it. They can make those things so tiny today—they'll never know it's there."

"Surprising that they—the kidnapper, or kidnappers— didn't warn us not to use one."

"They kept that note pretty simple. Maybe cutting out the letters or finding the right ones proved to be too much work. Whatever the reason, it makes coming up with a profile difficult."

"There's something I want to mention."

The odd wording made Rachael's scalp tingle. People only used such mild intros when what they were about to say would be pure dynamite. She took a deep breath . . . not so fortuitously, since they were passing the two body farm sites and the wind had changed. "Go ahead."

"I thought the lettering on that note looked familiar, but I had no idea why. I'm still not sure, but there's a book called *Forty-Nine Ways to Kill Somebody* in Taylor's room. It has old-fashioned type and slightly ivory paper in it. And it's missing a page."

"A page that might have 'not' in all caps on it?"

"I have no idea. It's in the *D*'s—the list is alphabetical—

and it *could* contain 'drowning.' " In the dark her voice seemed to drag behind her, wishing to be anywhere else.

"Okay. So it might be the same paper and typeface, it might contain 'not,' and Mason might have been drowned the night before his mother and two other adults saw him alive?"

Ellie smiled, barely visible in the dim light, but added: "Or say they did."

"So Taylor would have had to plan this, disguise her own handwriting sufficiently to address and mail an envelope, murder her brother and throw a doll into the water as well, and then Becca would have to talk their two close friends into helping her cover it up. *Possible*, I suppose."

"I could easily be wrong."

"I hope so." Rachael wasn't any more comfortable with the idea of an eleven-year-old psychopath than her companion.

"I do too," Ellie said.

Her voice couldn't quite hide the discouragement. It was a rough situation with an infant in the balance, even rougher when your own family members were counting on you to help, and even rougher when your coworkers might be looking at you askance, wondering where your loyalties rested.

This reminded Rachael of Ellie's personal history. She had been lucky to have loving relatives, just as Danton was lucky to have Rachael and her mother, but that had still been a lot of moving around for a little kid . . . if she could indulge in a little amateur psychoanalysis. Rachael had developed a keen interest in profiling in her postpathologist years, sat in on lectures on the topic at the Locard when she could and read all the texts. If left undisturbed, a body will freeze into the position it held at death, the muscles will tighten into an unbreakable stance that won't be pulled into a more cooperative shape without great force. This stage will eventually pass. Sometimes living people freeze into place as well, and the stage never passes.

Ellie's past had to affect her present, just as everyone's did. She must have always felt like a not-terribly-desired guest in other people's homes, a charity case to be tolerated and pitied. That was why she showed no envy of Becca's lifestyle; why even though she had tremendous expertise and prestige in her field, she didn't walk into a room as if she owned it; why she hadn't demanded Rachael's immediate eviction from her crime scene. Because she didn't think she deserved to.

*Well,* Rachael resolved, *she will never feel that way around me.*

As if to prove her point, Ellie now said: "I'm sorry you have to drive me all the way back to Becca's. I should have brought my own car."

"Nonsense. It was my idea, and it won't be so bad, now that rush hour is over. I want to go back, anyway. I talked to the agents while Gary was working and they're there now, coordinating the ransom drop. Besides, it gave us a chance to talk."

"You mean it gave you a chance to question me about my family," Ellie said as they climbed into the car. "I'm joking! I didn't mind—don't mind. Ask me anything. The problem is, when it comes to Becca and Hunter, I probably won't know."

"Well—good. Thank you." She did think of more questions on the return trip, which Ellie answered with apparent frankness, but they did not spark some new line of investigation. Mason remained missing, with the only lead a mysterious note that might or might not be genuine.

They discussed a plan to deal with Taylor's book, since the girl would certainly be in bed by the time they got there and they hardly wanted to alert the family of their very vague suspicions. If she was still up—possible given the chaos of the day—then Ellie would invent an excuse to get into the room. Offer to tuck Taylor in? Reading her a story would give her the perfect excuse to go to the bookshelf and . . . steal a child's book in the hope of convicting her of murder? She could say, *It looks cool, can I borrow it?* Or just look at the typeface again, and if Ellie still believed it to be the same, have the FBI get a search warrant?

They both agreed. Search warrant—the only way to make sure the evidence would not be thrown out by the legal system.

They reached the mansion. A black SUV had been parked in the curving drive before the center entrance, perfectly parallel with the curb, and Rachael made a mental bet that Michael Tyler had been at the wheel. Rachael parked.

"Okay," Ellie said, clearly steeling herself to go inside. "Now there's this."

She got out and headed for the door. Rachael followed, but not before noticing that Ellie had left a hair, too long and too red to belong to anyone else Rachael knew, on the headrest of the Audi.

That, she thought, might be useful.

# Chapter 21

*9:11 p.m.*

Ellie entered the kitchen to see Michael Tyler and Luis Alvarez, still as professional as ever, though Ellie thought the ties had been loosened by at least an eighth of an inch. "Tara said the Chase manager was super cooperative," Hunter had been saying as Ellie entered. "I got three hundred from our two money markets there."

"But we've got—" Becca said. Both of them seemed about to drop. The lines on Hunter's face had grown exponentially in the past few hours and Becca swayed on her feet.

"Way more than that in our accounts, yes, but you know the difference between money on paper and actual cash."

"Yes, yes."

Of course a bank wouldn't have that much cash on hand.

"She can get the rest in the morning. Barclays and AIG— managers will be meeting her. She'll bring it here then?"

"Yes," the shorter of the two agents, Luis Alvarez, spoke. "We have the black duffel bag with the trackers in the lining. That way the money will look clean, and that's always what they check first."

"Won't they . . ." Ellie began, then stopped—not to avoid ticking off the agents, but to avoid distressing Becca.

The other agent, Michael Tyler, did not hesitate. "Won't they dump the money into another container for just that reason? They might. They *should*, if they're thinking, but it's worth a try. And that's why we'll put additional trackers in the bands around the money. Completely imperceptible without an XF detector."

Becca rubbed her face, stretching the skin over the high cheekbones. "But if they do, they might hurt Mason."

"That's not likely," Luis said, but gave no support for the statement. Because, Ellie thought, there was no support for the statement. They had no reason to believe Mason was still alive, with no proof of life.

"They didn't even tell us how to get him back, once they do have the money," Becca muttered.

Hunter said, speaking almost absently, "That makes sense, though. If they named a location, the agents would have it staked out in advance to catch them. They could leave Mason someplace safe—"

"What's *safe*?" his wife cried.

"A fire department, a hospital, an urgent-care center. There's a million possibilities." He put his arm around her shoulders. "Then they're long gone by the time the place calls the cops and they connect him to us. But he'll be taken care of in the meantime."

It was a nice picture, baby Mason surrounded by nurses or buff firemen, cooing over the adorable infant. Ellie found herself praying with more force than she'd prayed for anything in her life, for that mirage to become reality.

Michael Tyler stayed brisk, part of the ongoing struggle to keep the parents motivated and calm. "We'll be back here by nine a.m. tomorrow with the duffel and the surveillance equipment. Gabriel Haller will be here as well. We can go over the plan with him once more. There's nothing anyone can do until then. I know it must seem impossible, but you all need to get as much sleep as you can. You won't be any help to Mason if—"

"Yeah, yeah," Becca said, and left the room without another word. She knew party line platitudes when she heard them, and had difficulty tolerating even well-intentioned ones. It was, Ellie knew, a family characteristic. The Beck clan took great pride in being realistic.

"I'm going to be here too," Ellie told Michael. At the other end of the kitchen island, Hunter spoke with Luis and Rachael. Ellie lowered her voice. "I've only worked three kidnapping cases, and they were all adults. Tell me the truth—is this normal? I mean—"

With kindness, and without condescension, he said: "I know what you mean. It does seem unusual. Most kidnappings are either someone desperate for a child, in which case they just grab them and disappear, or for money. They want $x$ amount of dollars, then you'll get the kid back. First there's a text demanding a political outcome to return the child, then a mailed note asking for a relatively small amount of money considering what the Carlisles have at their disposal. Neither bothered with instructions about calling or not calling authorities . . . I—we—don't know exactly what to make of it."

"Not to mention turning invisible to get in and out of here without leaving a trace."

"I still can't figure that one. I have a few theories, but nothing even reasonable enough to say out loud."

Ellie said, "Me too. Um . . . Taylor in bed?"

"Yeah. She crashed about an hour ago."

"Oh." If he ever figured out why she had asked, he might become less friendly in a hurry. "If you'll excuse me, I'm going to say goodbye to Becca before I leave."

"See you in the morning," the FBI agent told her.

*   *   *

Ellie padded up the hallway, her emergency pair of worn boots silent against the hardwood floor. Although it wasn't late, weariness had settled into her bones and she felt more than ready to go home to her boring post-divorce apartment on Twenty-Fifth Street. Right now, her boring post-divorce apartment on Twenty-Fifth Street seemed a treat: the first space she'd had that belonged entirely to her. She could stock, decorate, warm up pizza any way, or time, or how, she liked, and sometimes it felt delirious.

Though right now, she just wanted the pizza.

Yet she felt the same reluctance she always felt to leave a crime scene: Had she done everything she could? Had she considered every likelihood? Was there anything else she should collect before time wore it away? Might any other surface bear contact DNA? Fingerprints? Had they sufficiently grid-searched the lawn? Maybe the kidnapper had dropped something convenient . . . like his driver's license.

But she couldn't think of a thing. How do you find the fingerprints of a ghost?

Stop, she thought, and she literally stopped, her shoe giving a faint squeak. Once she'd moved forward through a scene, photographing as she went, she always liked to reverse and move back, photographing from the other side. All day she'd been looking for someone to come in from the outside. *Time to consider what you've been veering away from all day—that Becca and/or Hunter . . . and/or even Taylor . . . removed Mason themselves.* Someone *inside.*

She didn't bother with *why.* In a family there could be a million reasons. Given what she'd seen of infant deaths, the most likely reason was the one that had first occurred to her—an unplanned murder. One of them had shook the baby too hard, thrown him down. Taylor had drowned or throttled him and her parents covered it up to protect her. Becca had wanted him to sleep and overdosed him on Children's Benadryl.

Becca and Hunter were smart—very smart. That seemed evident from their occupations and their success. Even Taylor, according to her mother, was very intelligent. They would know that whatever story they came up with, a slip and fall, a SIDS death, would be disproven at autopsy. Their only chance was to be rid of the body completely.

But Mason was not in the house, and no one had left it. She knew from quick conversations that both the police and FBI and even the K-9 unit had searched the place from rafter to cellar, the garage, the cars, the fireplaces—there were four—under beds and inside closets. Mason was not on the property, and no one could have buried him in the woods or thrown him in the river without appearing on the video.

Not unless they had done so days earlier, and *both* Tara and Gabriel were in on the plot, since they'd both testified to seeing Mason *that morning*.

Two scenarios, both impossible: One, someone in the family killed Mason and magically got him out; or two, a kidnapper had magically gotten both in *and* out.

Usually, crimes came with more than one possible solution and the difficulty lay in choosing the correct one. Ellie wasn't accustomed to crimes that had *no* possible solution.

A quiet sound interrupted her thoughts, a breath so hushed she might have imagined it. At first she didn't know where it had come from; Taylor's door was closed and the light out, Becca's bedroom door at the far end of the hall remained open, the interior equally dark. Where was Hunter? Wasn't he still downstairs?

The sound came again. Mason's room.

Ellie crept forward, seized by the sudden hope that the kidnapper had returned to place Mason back in his crib, that when she looked again, the infant would smile and wave one chubby fist as the villain slipped silently out the window. Ellie would let him go, let him escape justice—as long as they got the baby back.

But it wasn't Mason or the kidnapper. Becca stood next to her son's crib, one hand on the railing, regardless of the fingerprint powder, the other pressed to her face as she cried.

Ellie stopped.

Becca wore what looked like a pair of thin sweatpants and a shapeless tank top, probably sleeping clothes, revealing the muscles in her arms and shoulders as they seized in a paroxysm of grief. Her head bent forward, hair parting to show the white skin at the nape of her neck, her mouth muffled by her palm to keep her sobs to herself.

Of course she wept, Ellie thought. She just lost her child and didn't know if she'd ever see him again.

She should hug her cousin. She should go in and put her arms around her and tell her that it would be all right and she would have Mason back in no time.

Problem was, Ellie didn't know if that was true. Did Becca weep because she thought she would never hold her baby boy again?

Or because she *knew* she wouldn't?

Cowardice washed through Ellie, and she backed away, one silent step at a time.

# Chapter 22

They washed dishes in silence—Rachael had missed dinner entirely, but her mother had always been a bit of a procrastinator about housework—until Rachael could stand it no longer. They hadn't had a chance to talk about the previous day's events until now. "You didn't have to ask him to stay for dinner."

Loretta dried a plate with exaggerated care. "You know we can't eat a whole loin. And it doesn't freeze well."

"That's hardly the point!"

"He's the boy's father. He's going to be in our lives, whether we want it or not."

"I *don't* want." Rachael knew she sounded petulant. But Jalen Williams represented a huge threat, a Scud missile aimed right at her cozy little house. As Danton's biological father, he could sue for custody at any moment . . . the thought filled her with a choking dread that crept up her insides and seized her heart and made it difficult to speak.

His relationship with her sister had been little more than a one-weekend fling while home on leave, the carelessness agreeable to both parties. Isis had never expressed much interest in true loves or soul mates . . . but it hardly gave him a moral right to the child that resulted. Did it?

She didn't care that he had been quiet and polite at dinner. He expressed appreciation of the food—for good reason—and had tried to make patient contact with Danton without overwhelming him. By the time the potatoes cooled the child had been talking gaily to him, the soldier listening with great attention, even though he clearly had no idea what the kid was trying to say.

He asked low-key questions, again without presumption or entitlement. He asked what Danton liked to eat, which were his favorite toys, had he been sick ever? Rachael enjoyed his discomfort; he didn't know what a parent would want to know, so he bounced over all possible topics. With every answer, deliberately short, Rachael tried to telegraph: *Don't even think about taking him away. Don't even think you can handle raising this boy. He's perfectly fine here,* perfectly *fine. If you even try it, I will fight you like a maelstrom and you don't want that.* Believe me, *you don't want that.*

But did he? Could he win that war?

Looking at him, she figured he could win *any* war. And biology had an automatic advantage. Possession of the right genes might be nine-tenths of the law . . .

"I don't know what I would do," she burst out, now ready to sob into the Dawn suds.

"He didn't say a word about custody. He's not a bad man. He wanted to see that his child is well cared for, which he is." Her mother spoke with a calm that didn't quite fool Rachael. "Now that he knows that, he can go back to his job, his life, and rest easy."

"Or he thinks that we won't fight him."

"He sure wouldn't walk away if he thought his boy was being raised by a couple of bitches, now would he?"

Rachael scrubbed au gratin residue from a pot and said nothing.

"But if he thinks the boy is fine, happy, healthy, then he can leave him in peace with a clear conscience. You catch more flies with honey—or, in this case, perfectly medium-rare beef loin. I'm right and you know it."

Rachael turned on the garbage disposal for a long moment just to listen to the violent grinding. Then she said, "You're right and I know it. But I don't want to catch him. I just want him to go away."

"I know, honey," Loretta said. "So do I."

Ellie slipped into the largely vacated kitchen, deeply unsure as to what she should do next. Offer to stay the night, borrow some of Becca's clothes? But her cousin surely needed some privacy, and Ellie longed for her own bed, even if she would spend half the night staring at the ceiling as usual. Sleeping well did not lie among her talents.

She should call her supervisor, fill him in, purely to justify her paycheck, and to keep up the illusion that she remained there as a professional and not a concerned family member—

"Did you say good night to Becca?" Hunter asked her. He stood alone at the kitchen counter finishing a beer.

Ellie lied without thinking. "I couldn't find her. And I didn't want to invade your bedroom."

"Oh. Did you get anything from that note? Dr. Davies said a guy at the Locard took it apart and found a hair and some fingerprints, but they weren't usable."

"Some fingerprint ridges, an impression in the glue. But not enough to be of any use."

"Huh." He drank from the bottle, swirling the liquid in his mouth a bit before swallowing. He did not seem impaired, only thoughtful. He was the man at the center of all this, at the center of Becca's life, and Ellie could have passed him on the street without realizing it.

"That's weird, isn't it?" He peered at her. "That note? Gluing pieces of paper like that?"

"It has its advantages." She relayed part of the conversation between herself and Rachael.

"But what do they *really* want?" he said. "A no vote at the hearing or a bundle of cash? Both? At least money is something I can understand, better that than some crazy old bat who just got on 70 and never looked back, who's already in Nowheresville, Kansas, telling everyone the baby's name is Jimmy."

"That's a good point," she said, though she thought it might not be, because professionals wouldn't be sentimental about a child.

"We leave the money, they give us Mason back. We go through with the hearing, they give us Mason back. That might sound naïve"—Ellie opened her mouth to defer, and he hastened to add—"but maybe not. They wouldn't want to keep him longer than necessary, to try to get us to cough up more cash. Babies are a lot of work . . . when they're not sleeping or eating, they're crying and needing their diapers changed. I speak from personal experience. Mason will be up every three hours, like clockwork. And then there's punishment, prosecution. That's cold."

This last came as a warning, as she had spied a few ounces left in the coffeepot and snagged a mug from the cabinet. Insomniacs should not drink coffee after lunch, she told herself . . . *but* it had been a rough day and she deserved something warm. The microwave could help her out. "Punishment?"

Hunter went on, reasoning out the possibilities from the kidnapper's—or kidnappers'—point of view. "They have to figure, if they . . . harm him, police will never stop looking for them. If I have the kind of money to pay a six-figure ransom, I have the kind of money to make sure of that. But if we get Mason back unharmed, our lives go on, cops go on to other crimes. In a month it's like it never happened."

"That's also very true." She tried the coffee, now heated to lavalike temperatures. "You've thought this through."

"That's my job, to think things through. What does my client need, why do current circumstances not allow for that, and what needs to change to make my client's needs advantageous to other people?"

She brought her nose to the cup again, gauging the heat. "Do you know what these people actually want you to *do* at this hearing? What to say?"

"I'm sure they want me to say that KidFun's present practices violate COPPA and 312, and that's bad, and you can't trust us not to do it again, so you'd better enact a permanent ban on direct messaging, addiction algorithms, and data retention."

"Can you do that? Say that?"

He blinked. "I can. It won't be true, but to get Mason back, I can."

A careful sip managed not to maim her lips. "Can you present the true information at a future hearing to reverse any permanent ban?"

"Someone can. Because the wheels of the legislative process grind like a sack of gravel in molasses, in fits and starts, and bills normally go from subcommittee to committee, and back and forth, and get changed and tweaked and discussed some more—nothing ever happens fast in the U.S. Congress. But this wasn't about their schedule, it was about mine. Ours. I need sales to get back on track before the auditors finish up the job we've already paid them to do. Without that, there isn't going to be a company left to *take* public. So the committee can schedule all the markup and rehearings it wants—KidFun might be around to participate, but I won't." He rubbed his face with both hands as if rubbing away makeup, removing the face he showed the world. She heard defeat in his voice when he muttered, "Maybe I shouldn't have invested so heavily in it . . . I got overly ambitious. But that's what I do. I get ambitious."

Ellie rinsed her cup and left it in the oversized farmhouse sink, alongside plates and silverware that might have been accumulating for days. Perhaps she should—

His phone rang. "Speak of the devil. It's Gabriel."

Ellie pulled open the dishwasher. Surely, it would not prove as complicated as the coffeemaker. Were these dishes clean or—

"*What?*" Hunter exploded, but not with anger. "What? Why . . . but . . . how old is he?"

Had Mason been found, or some hint of him? But why would that information come from Gabriel?

"I'm going to come over there . . . No . . . no, I guess not." He looked up suddenly, at Ellie, and apparently made a decision. "You're right, I'll stay here. But I'll have Ellie alert the FBI and Locard. Hang up, but keep me posted."

To Ellie, he said, "The son of one of our game engineers is missing. And it's the same people who took Mason."

# Chapter 23

*10:10 p.m.*

"From what we can tell, someone picked him up from school today." Michael Tyler filled her in with hushed tones in the meticulously decorated foyer of a large Georgetown row house. "The kid is ten. Dad works for KidFun, Mom was on a plane from Germany all day, was there on business. Both parents and the older sister—she's doing a semester in Paris, but we spoke on the phone—insist he would never have gone off with a stranger, and the school said there was a signed note in the office this morning with his father's known signature *and* the pickup person knew the number ID—a new number ID, they're unique to every nonparent pickup—texted to the father's phone. Except it didn't go to Mr. Thomas's phone. Video shows Noah leaving with a woman in a white van."

Through an open door at the end of the hall, she could see a couple seated on a modern leather couch. The deep worry in their expressions, their shallow breathing, and the way they held each other's hands, with a grip tight enough to crush, let her know these were Noah's parents. They were talking to Luis Alvarez.

"The parents—they're Darnell and Nakala—called every friend this boy has, a considerable list, but finally found one who said Noah got text messages from his dad to go to a baseball camp. Obviously, the dad never sent them, and doesn't know how someone could spoof his identity enough to fool the boy *and* the school. The dad went back there a few hours ago and found the kid's cell phone in the drive. It had been run over once or twice." He ran a hand through his short hair. We're all getting tired, Ellie thought, which did not bode well for the investigation. Tired people made mistakes. "We need you to take the cell phone, see if you can maybe get some fingerprints off it?"

After it had been run over by a car or two. Her thoughts must have appeared on her face.

"It's probably impossible, I know. And see if digital forensics can recover any of the text messages—if not, then maybe the Locard. If we can trace the number they came from . . ."

"And the parents also got a text?" Ellie asked. That's what Hunter had said. "We'll need to get their phone too."

"Yes. Come on."

He went up the hall. Ellie followed reluctantly—dealing with the bereaved or the irate or the unstable remained the job of cops and special agents; that was one of the things she liked when she got to work ERT. Her talents were better suited for work with inanimate objects. She got along fine with fingerprints and bloodstain patterns . . . people were too unpredictable.

Both parents looked up at them with a brief spate of hope, examined their faces, and the hopeful looks turned to disappointment.

Luis sat in a matching leather armchair, notebook open on his knees, speaking gently, yet leaning into their space as if trying to absorb their thoughts, as well as their words. "What does this text refer to—'confess and detail the addiction algorithm'? Do you know what it is they actually want you to do tomorrow?"

Darnell Thomas had loosened his tie, stress having dampened the collar. Nakala Thomas's fingers fluttered with the urgent need to *do* something; her mind would be racing from task to task in a never-ending spiral of plans to *get her child back* while fighting jet-lagged travel fatigue. She stared at the slim cell phone on the coffee table as if it were both a cursed thing and a lifeline.

"Yes," her husband said. "I do."

That was not what Ellie had expected to hear. Four people in the room stared at the man's downturned face, not one of them daring to breathe.

Darnell said, "It refers to the platform structures designed to keep kids playing. Structures like . . . for example, games having accoutrements. Daily quests and objectives and the rewards like avatar accessories, dances, gestures. There are plenty of possessions for them to buy, so they have to play longer to be outfitted like rock stars."

Luis asked, "Buy? With real money?"

"If they can get hold of a credit card, yes. They can pay outright or they can get a discount by playing the game a lot. It unlocks rewards more slowly."

Luis showed more comprehension than nongamer Ellie felt. Still—"But they're not buying real *stuff*."

"What's real anymore?" Darnell asked in a hollow tone. "There's a reason so many games use coins or gems as rewards, because what is valuable in real life seems equally valuable even when in a virtual world. Even a meaningless number, as long as it keeps going up, makes us feel like we're gaining value. It tricks players—children *and* adults—into equating them with real-world value."

"Where does an algorithm come in?"

"Timing, spacing, perception. The rewards come fast and furious when they start, moving up levels, earning extras. But then it takes longer and longer plays to get to the next level, and when you get a reward is no longer steady—unexpected rewards are very motivating, but only to a point, so some rewards are fixed and others variable, getting the best of both techniques."

Nakala said, "It's the reasoning behind the coding. Darnell is a behavioral psychologist."

He yanked on the tie again and the words came faster. "But we've hidden all these manipulations so players feel like they have control over their choices in the game, but it's illusory—the game progresses pretty much the same, no matter what choices you make. Actual control is not important. It's the *illusion* of control that's important. Think of *Tetris*. You don't really have any control over what drops from the top, but making the connections feels good."

"So, yes, we have manipulating people, children, down to a science," Darnell said. Now that he had begun on the topic, his analytical mind had to explain it thoroughly. "We offer loot boxes, a virtual box with a mystery virtual item, yet you have to pay real money for it—but once the attached credit card is entered, you can gamble on a mystery prize with just a click of the mouse. We might as well set kids in front of a slot machine. No one terms it a 'gambling addiction,' but that's exactly what it is. Like adults playing poker, kids can play themselves into crippling debt. A couple years ago a high school student with a part-time job and no car racked up nearly fourteen thousand dollars in tiny in-app purchases."

"They say it's 'manufactured addiction,'" Nakala said. "But so what? Everything online is designed to *keep* you online. Like Facebook introducing the News Feed or getting a magic coin when you move up a level in *Bejeweled* or Twitter posting What's Trending Now. Don't you want to see these tweets? Keep scrolling."

*Or TV channels having a million commercial breaks, but not between the end of one show and the beginning of another—because they don't want you to change the channel,* Ellie thought. *No matter what line of business you're in, it's easier to keep an existing customer than get a new one.*

"They take *my* kid over that?" Nakala said, her voice husky with fear and anger.

Her husband said, "It *is* manufactured addiction. It's also good business sense. Gabriel believes other gaming platforms are jealous and egging on critics from behind the scenes, which isn't hard when the whole fight is in the virtual world, anyway—a comment on a post here, forward a link through an anonymous email there. You can get anyone to do anything. All you have to do is find their buttons."

"And they found ours," Nakala said. Her fingers trembled as she pressed a fist to her mouth.

Luis summarized: "They want you to renounce this addiction algorithm at the hearing tomorrow so that the senators will vote to keep the DM ban and other measures in place. Can you do that? Until Noah's safety is assured?"

Darnell appeared surprised at the question. "Of course. I'll—I'll say whatever they want."

"Doesn't even make sense," Nakala murmured, clearly trying to make sense of the kidnappers' logic. "KidFun can propose a new bill at a new hearing. They going to kidnap children every single time?"

"I don't care," her husband said. "It won't be mine."

Ellie wasn't sure if he meant the children or the algorithm. From what Hunter and Gabriel said, it had sounded like

KidFun would go bankrupt after a no vote, which meant Darnell would be out of a lucrative job. He valued his child more. Good for him.

Luis went over the steps the FBI were taking to question school employees, enhance the video, list all registrations of similar vehicles, and examine toll booth records. He added, "We're going to take this phone to try to trace the text to its source."

*Burner phone,* Ellie thought. *It's already been destroyed.*

The FBI agent encouraged Darnell to make a list, check KidFun's memos and emails, try to find examples of the worst criticisms the company had received. Meanwhile, he dropped Darnell's phone into a paper envelope and handed it to Ellie.

Michael Tyler walked her out. "Please let me know what you get from it, as soon as possible. You have my card, right?"

"Yep." She started to turn away, then stopped. "How would the kidnappers know what Darnell's job is at Kid-Fun?"

He didn't seem to find this a smoking gun. "Company website. It has a page with the execs and their bios. But, sure, our kidnapper could be someone inside KidFun who thinks they need to be a whistleblower. Gabriel Haller is also making a list of critics, including ones inside the company. Any news at your cousin's house?"

"News? No." She should get going, get on the phone with dispatch to call in the digital forensic person on call, but hesitated. "Have you ever seen a radical group like this? Kidnapping kids to save kids from greedy corporate manipulators?"

"No. But I can't say I'm surprised." At her look he went on: "Every group thinks they're the white hats, riding in to

save people from themselves. They're not kidnappers or ter-
rorists, they're concerned citizens, and the only way to get
these greedy corporate types to think about harm coming to
children is to make it their *own* children."

"Whoever took the two boys means to force Darnell and
Hunter to go on national television, shred their personal in-
tegrity, and lose their livelihood. They won't actually be
standing off camera with a loaded pistol, like a military junta
in a presidential palace, but they might as well be."

"Exactly." A tight cord of muscle stretched angrily across
his jawline, suppressed rage seeking an outlet. "Maybe that's
why they're not concerned about the next round of bills and
the next legislative session. Money talks and lobbyists spin,
but C-Span videos live forever on YouTube."

She said, "But then where does the ransom fit in?"

"I don't know. My guess is that one member of the group
isn't motivated entirely by idealism. It's galling enough to
give in to one demand, much less two. But unless we can find
those kids, we don't have a choice."

She should get going. But for the first time they were
alone together, and Ellie grabbed the opportunity. "Why are
we working with the Locard? A private institute? It's an impressive facility, but what do they possibly have that the FBI
doesn't?"

"Time," he said. "The lab is overwhelmed with materials
from that mall shooting, and the Carolina serial killer."

"I know, but—"

"And the order came down from somewhere above to cooperate with Hunter Carlisle. Apparently, he has a friend or
former client somewhere on the upper floors. Not one that's
going to save him if he's guilty"—he watched her face as if to
gauge her reaction to this, but she didn't blink—"but
enough to indulge him where the Locard is concerned. And
I didn't protest."

He seemed like the type who would protest. She waited for his explanation.

"I've seen the Locard work miracles. And I trust Rachael."

*Then I guess I'll trust her too.*

"Besides," he added, "if the Carlisles are hiding something, why on earth would he hire them?"

They gazed at each other for a long moment. Then, holding the wrapped cell phones gently in one hand, Ellie left the house and headed for E Street.

An hour later a thirtyish man with a black beard trimmed to nanometer-level precision handed the crushed cell phone back to her. She had checked for prints with the alternative light source and tried a quick dusting with black powder, but got only a wonderful image of a tire track—which she had dutifully photographed, with scale, since the kidnapper might have purposely dropped it under their own tire to make sure. That would have been smart.

After that, she'd brought it to another part of the lab to meet the digital forensic tech who examined the cracked screen and scratched backing before locating the correct type of power cord to plug it in. He pushed the button on the side. Nothing happened. He pushed it again. Nothing happened.

"Well." He unplugged the cord. "I might be able to do something with it, but it will take a week or three."

Ellie knew the answer, but asked, anyway, "Are you sure? Isn't there anything you can tell me? It belongs to a kidnapped ten-year-old."

"I get that." He sipped coffee from a metal travel mug and envy rose up in her like a geyser. "That's why I'm not going to waste your time. Our equipment here is all about downloading and organizing and parsing computers and cell phones that work. Not about downloading ones that have been shredded. It doesn't have a media card, so I can't dig through the rubble and find it. I'm sorry, but my strengths don't help us here—what we need is one of those cluttered little storefronts where they fix your iPad after your kid drops it off the balcony. And they'd still take weeks."

"That's not going to work."

"Sorry. It's the best I can offer."

He sipped again, and this time she didn't think about coffee. "That's okay. I have an alternative."

*11:15 p.m.*

With the requested blessing of her supervisor, Ellie made her second trip out to the Locard Institute in what seemed as many hours. Rachael did not meet her there; as they spoke during Ellie's drive, she said her son was having a meltdown—someone did not have enough naptime today—and she didn't wish to leave unless absolutely necessary. Ellie heard a strain in her voice that seemed to go beyond dealing with the terrible twos. But Rachael arranged for the aforementioned tech whiz Agnes to take in the broken cell phone and see what she could do with it.

Ellie had also informed the FBI agents, who agreed to the plan. They could drive it out to the lab at Quantico, but since Agnes was geared up and ready to go, they decided to stay the course. Should Agnes fail, they would retrieve the phone immediately.

Things had changed, Ellie knew, in a low, subtle way that no one would ever say out loud. The possibility had never gone away that Mason had been killed inside his own household and the kidnapping story a badly constructed cover-up. But the disappearance of Noah Thomas, and the subsequent instruction to his father, verified the disappearance of Mason

Carlisle and the subsequent instruction to *his* father. Noah Thomas had definitely been kidnapped by a mysterious woman in a white van, and the phone that might have tracked his location ominously destroyed. So maybe Becca and Hunter *aren't* hiding anything. And maybe Ellie isn't a litmus test or a potential scapegoat.

The thought cheered her.

A GPS in the ERT van helped her find her way back to the impressive building and she wound through the forest path from the parking lot, trying to consider the dark woods as peaceful and not the stuff of many a horror movie. Actually, it *was* peaceful, and the path well lit to keep one from stumbling off the edge. Only the whiff of decay near the body farm ruined the idyll.

A figure hovered behind the same door she had entered with Rachael, its form visible through the glass. Ellie knocked, then stepped back as someone snapped the door open with an impatient force, overpowering the automatic mechanism.

A twentyish woman, all angular cheekbones of white skin and straight brown hair pulled into a severe ponytail, peered through old-fashioned cat's-eye glasses. "Are you Dr. Carr?"

"Yes. Are you—"

"Sign here." Agnes—for this could only be Agnes—thrust a form at her with two carbons under the top sheet, already completed with the Locard case number, the Metro PD case number, the FBI case number, the address of Noah Thomas's house, and *broken cell phone* written for the description. Ellie signed in the proper box, which Agnes had colored in with a yellow highlighter to avoid any errors. Agnes had already removed the evidence bag from her hand in a maneuver so deft she might have come from a family of grifters.

Ellie handed the form back. "Do you think you'll—"

"Yes, probably."

"Be able to get any call history or text—"

"Yes."

*Of course you will. Because this is the Locard.*

Agnes peeled off the top layer of the form and handed Ellie the middle copy. "I'll call you as soon as I have anything. Dr. Davies gave me your number."

"Thank you. We really appreciate you coming in on overt—"

But Agnes had already shut the door.

# Chapter 24

Sophie Tran woke up to see a boy staring at her.

She blinked, the picture not making any sense. What was a strange boy doing in her room? More importantly, she felt stiff, overwarm, a little hungry, very thirsty, and really needed to pee.

Then the rest of it crowded in. The boy was not Liam and this was not her room. It was a weird, dark cavern and she lay on a scratchy mattress without sheets or pillow, in all her clothes, including her shoes. Someone had thrown a soft blanket over her, which she didn't need, because it was stifling in the airless place, the late summer humidity crushing her chest and leaving a thin sheen of sweat along every inch of skin. She sat up—jerked upright really, and expected her head to hurt, but it didn't.

There was no one else in the—barn? The rough wood walls, the remnants of hay on the packed dirt floor, the *smell*—she might be a city kid, but this had to be a barn.

No one there but the Black kid, who sat on an identical

mattress about twelve feet away. He did not look at all familiar, though about her age and size. He said nothing and
didn't move toward her—more than that, he looked as miserable as she felt. Not a threat, she assessed. Another victim.

She had a million questions, but when she croaked out
the first words from her dry throat, they said only, "I have
to pee."

He gestured toward a big blue plastic box in one corner.
"There's that thing."

Sophie had used a Porta-Potty once in her life, that she
could remember, on a road trip to the Grand Canyon with
her mom and her aunt and a couple of cousins, and they'd
stopped at a gas station in the middle of nowhere and their
bathrooms were broken. She remembered it as hideous and
swore she'd never step in another one. But glancing around
at the dim, largely empty space, she very quickly guessed
that she had no more choice than she'd had at that gas station
and stumbled over to the corner. The barn was dim—a piece
of her brain figured it was early morning, the sun only beginning to come up—but inside the plastic toilet with the
door latched, and she made *sure* it was latched—no matter
how bad she had to go—it was nearly pitch dark. Somehow
she found the toilet paper and lined the top of the toilet seat,
because she'd pee her pants before she'd touch even her butt
to something that gross, and then finally she could let go.

The place stank, but the one in the Arizona desert had
been much worse.

Okay, now that she had a private moment to think: Liam
and his mom had drugged and kidnapped her, only to lock
her in a hot barn with a strange kid.

Why? Where? What should she do now?

As much as she didn't want to reenter that nightmare, she
didn't want to stay in the stuffy plastic toilet either, so she

used a liberal amount of hand sanitizer from a dispenser on the wall and turned the handle.

The boy hadn't moved, for which she felt grateful; she was too terrified right now to deal with much. He seemed to be waiting for her to get up to speed.

So was she.

She noticed the table without chairs had a ton of stuff on it that looked like—yes, food. And water! And another bottle of hand sanitizer, which she used again, since she'd had to touch the handle of the Porta-Potty to get out of it.

After that, a bottle of water—they even sat in a bucket of ice to keep them cold. She downed practically the whole thing, choking a little. The table had been spread with plenty of snacks—granola bars, Pop-Tarts, beef jerky, brownies, Chips Ahoy!, Doritos, a bowl with oranges, bananas, and apples, and a now-warm bag of mini carrots. At least no one intended to starve them, but they couldn't last long on that stuff. Snacks, her mother always reminded her, were a treat; they were *not* food.

She turned to the boy. "Where are we? And who are you?"

"I don't know, and I'm Noah Thomas."

Succinct and to the point. Sophie felt better. At least she was stuck with an ally, not an idiot or some sobbing baby.

He went on, speaking quietly, his voice controlled. "We're out in the country. We were on 270, but I lost track after that."

"You were awake? That woman—"

"Millie," Noah said. "I think."

Sophie realized that she didn't even know Liam's mom's name. She didn't even know *Liam's* last name. He had said he went to Westminster Middle School, but she had never verified it in any way. Despite the warnings of her mother and her teachers and every other adult in her life, Sophie had done the one thing they told you never, ever to do: She had gotten in a car with a stranger.

She wanted to cry.

Clutching the water bottle, she sank onto the mattress she'd apparently spent the night on.

"She picked me up from school. She said—" Noah stopped there.

"Soccer practice." It took all Sophie's self-control to keep her voice from breaking into a sob. Noah, she thought, looked younger than her. She couldn't cry in front of him, no matter how much pressure she felt in her chest with her heart beating so hard it was crushing her lungs. She had to be the big kid here. "She roofied my slushie."

"Yeah, the big guy had to carry you in here."

"*Guy?* What guy?" She knew he couldn't be referring to Liam, and though his mom was bad enough, the idea of some strange man she hadn't even seen *touching* her—

Something crunched outside, a heavy foot walking across weeds or maybe a few stones in the dirt. Her bed sat a good ten feet from the wall and yet it sounded like the steps were right behind her shoulder and she leapt up, whirling. "What's that?"

"That's the guy, one of them. The Younger Guy, I think. He walks around the whole place every so often. All night too."

That was why he'd kept his voice so low. Yet he related this with so little concern that she sat down again. If Noah, though clearly miserable and worried, did not seem terribly afraid, then perhaps she would be okay too.

"That's why we can't break out," the boy went on. "They put boards over the windows and that door, but they screwed them in. I bet they used bolts on the other side too, to make sure we couldn't just pull off the boards, because a lot of the wood is pretty rotten, so we probably could if they used nails. We could probably break through a few other places if we tried, but—"

"He's out there," Sophie finished for him. The kid had made a pretty thorough assessment of the situation. "How long have you been here?"

"Millie—whatever—picked me up at three-fifteen yesterday."

"Why?" Sophie asked, the tightness in her chest threatening to rise up and choke her. "What are they going to do to us?"

He gave her the sad look of someone who had been asking that same question for a very long time and no longer wanted the answer. "I don't know. She and the Old Guy talked all about my dad's coding for KidFun and how I need to tell him his algorithm is bad—"

"Yeah! She was saying all these things about my mom and the site protocols. Like, my mom's a bad *person* because of her job."

"I think they want me to brainwash my dad," Noah said. "But later they said, *if* I get to go home."

His voice cracked on "home," which Sophie totally got. "Then what do they want *now*?"

Noah had no answer.

They sat in silence for a few minutes.

Then they continued to compare notes.


7:30 a.m.

When Ellie returned to Becca's house, not bright but early enough, the forces were already marshaling. Tara Esposito had gained the cooperation of several bank managers, and she and Hunter stood at the kitchen counter stacking banded wads of cash. Ellie had only seen such a pile of bills a few times before, caches of drug lords tucked in cars and safes, and once, the walk-in closet of an eccentric heir to a moving-company empire.

"They're going to have a tracker on this or something, right?" Hunter demanded of her in lieu of a greeting of good morning. "They're not just going to rely on electronics?"

"The agents? They'll have several eyes on Gabriel and on the bag."

"As long as it gets Mason back," Tara said, then blushed, as if she'd made a social faux pas.

"How's Becca doing?" Ellie asked her cousin's husband.

"It was a rough night."

"Of course . . . is she up?"

"*I'm* up," a little voice said, and Taylor skipped into the kitchen. She still wore her nightgown, a worn flannel with a few ruffles and a pirate skull-and-bones print against a black background. Joining them at the counter, the stack of cash rested at nearly eye level to her. "Is this going to be enough to get him back?"

A pause, while no one spoke. Would it?

"That's what the note said," Tara said.

"We're going to try," Ellie said.

"Yes," Hunter said. "Go and get your uniform on, kid."

He put his hand on her head for a brief stroke, and she turned and skipped out again without another word. Hunter watched her go. "I suppose we're going to have to get her a therapist."

A knock at the door, and Gabriel Haller entered without waiting for a response, looking as if he'd had a rough night himself. The lanky man moved as if in pain, his face pasty and damp. Ellie wondered if he might be hungover. She couldn't blame him if the stressful day led to a nightcap or two—

"Dude," Hunter said, "you look like crap."

Gabriel climbed onto a stool at the island. "I know. Woke

up in the middle of the night with these aches and my stomach is killing me. Some sort of bug. Stay away from me—you *don't* want to catch this."

Tara went in to Mom Mode, stretching out a hand to touch his forehead, but he tilted away as if she might be radioactive. "Stop that! I don't have a fever. Kinda feels like food poisoning, but all I had last night was a peanut butter sandwich and it tasted fine."

He had dressed for comfort in a short-sleeved polo shirt, less formal than the previous day, and Ellie noticed a patch of dry skin along the underside of his forearm. "Could it be an allergic reaction to something?"

He followed her gaze to the scaly stretch of skin. "Nah, that's a skin condition, I've always had that. And I'm definitely not allergic to peanut butter."

"What about the jelly?" Tara asked.

"No J. Just PB."

Hunter remained focused on the need at hand. "You going to be able to do this today? It's okay if you can't. We'll find someone else. It really should be an undercover FBI guy, anyway. They get paid to get shot at."

"It's a lot of money to trust some government hack with."

Hunter nodded. "True."

Ellie, some government hack, took it as a mark of Gabriel's discomfort that he didn't even appear to notice the towering stacks of money on the counter. Instead, he ran his fingers over his face and tried to rally. "Yes. Got to be me—you or Becca can't do it, and you can't send her."

He nodded toward Tara, who joked awkwardly: "Why not? I'm tougher than I look."

Hunter ignored this. "Seriously—"

"I'll be fine," Gabriel insisted more firmly. "I'm just going to make some tea. I need something hot. And probably need some fluids too. I haven't felt like eating or drinking anything."

He helped himself to the electric kettle and the tea bags, and Tara retrieved a mug from a cabinet. Obviously, both spent a lot of time at the Carlisle house.

Becca appeared, dressed in a silk blouse and skinny pants, her hair up in a careless bun, looking fashionable, but even more worn out than Gabriel. Four people turned to her and she didn't acknowledge any of them, gazing instead through the glass in the kitchen door, where the two FBI agents approached the house.

"Here we go," she said, her tone grim.

# Chapter 25

Aisyah Kesuma sat on a concrete square under one of the umbrellas at Stead Park, watching her charge climb up the rock-climbing wall—the little one, not the semicircular structure where the handholds reached to nearly four feet in the center. Oliver loved to climb. He'd scrape a knuckle or two, but it wouldn't slow him down unless he got tired and wanted to call it a day; then it would be time for kisses and bandages. Until then, she knew better than to try to hold him back.

The nanny next to her, whose name was Nilsa, from Guatemala, told her how the landscaper's boy asked her to go see a movie that night. She wasn't sure what movie, and she didn't seem sure about the boy either; he might be too young. She thought he was younger than her, but how many years would be too many?

The considerable language barrier kept Aisyah from catching more than the general drift, but that didn't bother her overmuch. She enjoyed listening to Nilsa, whose animation always made Aisyah feel less alone in this vast country, even if she couldn't quite figure out if Nilsa spoke of the landscaper's son or a relative of the Laundromat supervisor. Some translation still escaped her.

Aisyah took an iced soda from her insulated bag, appreciating the shade under the blue umbrellas on such a hot day. Small children dominated the area in the morning, when school-age children were in class. At least eight toddlers shrieked with delight on the slides and the swings. She caught sight of Nilsa's client's boy, a big-for-his-age five-year-old, climbing up the spiral slide. Nilsa often told her that the kid should be in school already. However, if he went, then his parents might decide they didn't need a full-time nanny, so she kept her mouth shut.

Aisyah waved to another nanny entering from the far end of the park, aiming her stroller past a uniformed worker touching up the red paint on an umbrella pole. Aisyah made a mental note to keep Oliver at least twenty feet from that pole; the kid attracted staining liquids to his pants like a sandbur to a *kanga* skirt, and Mrs. Martinez chose his clothes so carefully.

She checked Oliver's location, found him pulling himself onto one of the saucer swings. Even from that distance and through a short iron fence, she could see the concentration on his face as he negotiated the hanging platform. He balanced by spreading himself across it—amazing that at such a young age he could master that. It must be instinct.

Nilsa went on, changing her topic from the boy and the movie to her favorite soap. She had described it before, but it took too much work to sort out who had married and who had cheated and who stole whose man. Besides, any minute now Oliver would rediscover the water park, the section of pavement with small sprays shooting up into the air. The pavement drained quickly, barely able to form puddles, but still she'd better whip off those little shoes before he soaked them through.

The other nanny, a blond from Austria, came closer.

The man painting the pole gave her a long leer, though Aisyah couldn't see why. A sweet girl, but one that liked sweets just a little too much.

Having mastered the saucer swing, Oliver instantly grew bored with it. She watched him slip off, budging only slightly as the thing rebounded to shove him in the hips. She waved at him, reorienting him to her position. *I'm here, I'm watching.* He either didn't see her or didn't care, because he went back to the rock-climbing wall.

The new nanny reached them, plopping herself on the shaded concrete bench. Her name was Katrin, or Karin, Aisyah was not yet sure. The little girl in the stroller could be her own daughter, blond and blue-eyed, but already with a fractious, demanding personality. As far as Aisyah could determine, the child didn't want to do anything that didn't involve screaming at a volume that brought tears to the eyes. But for once, the ride had put her to sleep, and they would have a few minutes of peace.

Oliver—he hung from a plastic rock handhold by one hand, which probably felt outrageously daring, though his toes were only a half an inch above the pavement. She bet herself that he'd last another sixty seconds before heading toward the water feature. He'd zigzag through the geysers, avoiding the spray, then get closer, then put his fingers in it, then his arms. In another quarter hour he'd be soaked to the skin, but she didn't care—it was worth it. She'd take him home for a quick shower and lunch, and then exhaustion would put him down for a good nap, while she cleaned up and got the morning's clothing dry. His parents would come home to a sunny little boy. And tomorrow she'd get up and do it all over again, because that was the price she paid to live here.

An easy price. When she'd come to this country, she'd been at least 60 percent sure the employment agency would be a scam and she'd be locked up in a whorehouse and beaten until she escaped. Instead, she'd been given a green card and a job. Her employers did not beat or rape her. She had enough to eat and her own room to sleep in. And most of the time she enjoyed every minute with the energetic little boy, now that he'd outgrown the biting and throwing-toys stage.

"And he has a motorbike," Nilsa was saying.

"On the TV?" Aisyah asked.

"No! At the Laundromat."

The man repainting poles had moved to the next one, nearer the climbing wall. Aisyah tensed her legs, preparing to spring up. Oliver loved men in uniform. And wet paint.

"It's going to be hot today," Karin or Katrin said. She had one foot on one wheel of the stroller, rotating it back and forth as if that might simulate movement, but it became a series of jerks instead of a rocking and only woke the child up. The little rosebud mouth opened before the eyes did and emitted a sound that could only mean all the forces of hell had descended to commence tearing her limb from limb.

"Oh, my," Karin or Katrin said, her standard response to anything the child did.

"*Dios mío,*" Nilsa said. "*Qué le pasa a esta chica?*"

The little girl decided to flee, and threw herself forward from the stroller. She nearly fell out, her nanny having once again neglected to buckle her straps, so that her tiny hands now dangled around Aisyah's ankles.

"I get," Nilsa offered, and in one smooth motion whisked the girl up and out of the stroller, holding her against one shoulder and patting her back more gently than Aisyah would have expected from Nilsa's frequent complaints—not that it helped much, the screaming did not abate by so much as a decibel.

Aisyah looked around for Oliver. The tough little boy had

a soft core when it came to his peers, often trying in his sweet but awkward way to comfort those afflicted with scraped knees and bruised feelings. And she needed to get those shoes off if he headed for the puddles.

He wasn't on the rock-climbing wall. She bobbed to look around Nilsa; between her and the stroller and Karin/Katrin, she had been boxed in. But she couldn't see Oliver in the fountains either.

Her heart increased its pace, the preliminary to panic; she had felt it before, when he'd darted away through the aisles at Whole Foods, when he sailed his scooter into the street in front of the house. But nothing bad would happen. She would find him in the spiral slides or pretending to ride one of the metal seals by the water feature. She stepped up on the bench.

There were more children in the park than she had thought. He wore an orange shirt today, she reminded herself—look for the orange.

None.

He must be in the water feature. She couldn't see all of it from her vantage point. She walked along the bench to get around the other two nannies, now asking her what was the matter. She moved quickly—not running, not overreacting—to the low iron fence and jumped it in one smooth motion. First she went to the spiral slides, where Nilsa's boy still climbed up one backward, irritating the other children waiting to descend. Oliver might be imitating him, hiding in one of the bends of the slide where he couldn't be seen. She poked her head in and was nearly decapitated by a pink-clad toddler.

He must be in the fountains. She sprinted through another fence, calling his name, no longer concerned about overreacting. Seven different children ran around the water feature in varying stages of wetness. None wore an orange T-shirt.

Though he was clearly not present, she crossed the area, anyway, scanning, calling his name. Her sharp tone alerted and startled the other parents and nannies, but that was all right, they would help her look. Every one of them had pictured themselves in the same panic, had mentally trained themselves for such a day. She reached the far end, the expanse of ball field, utterly vacant at that hour. She circled around the building—perhaps he had wandered to the basketball courts, watching larger kids play there, but they were as empty as the field. Nilsa and the new blond nanny met her there, their voices a cacophony of concerned questions she couldn't answer.

Then she saw the paint.

The small can of red paint, which the maintenance worker had carried, now lay on its side on the concrete, a few spatters leading to the abandoned brush.

Aisyah began to scream.

### 8:45 a.m.

Sophie and Noah had scouted out every inch of the barn, cataloging every decent gap in the slats that could give them a view of the outside (several), the loosest boards (quietly pressed and pulled, only after the horizon had been scanned and they'd listened with great attention for the Younger Guy to make his crunching rounds of the area, though the stupid chickens—now awake—probably made enough noise to disguise theirs), and how many Little Debbie Cosmic Brownies remained (five).

"He went back to the house for a while before. He's got to have to go to the bathroom or get a drink of water once in a while," Sophie said, turning her head away from the crack she'd been peeking through. She already had a splinter in her cheek, she could feel it, and tried to pull it out with her fingers.

"Uh-huh," Noah agreed, still peering, his voice low, though he had the man in his line of vision. "He stopped talking to the Old Guy on the porch and he's coming back. That van is coming back too."

"The same van?"

"Yeah."

Sophie groaned. No help there, no rescue, only Millie who had kidnapped them in the first place. She gave up on the splinter and made a decision. She was the oldest here and needed to take charge. "Okay. The next time he goes back to the house, we'll wait until he goes inside, pull out that board over there, and run to the woods. They won't see us from the house."

"Unless someone's on the second floor," Noah pointed out.

Sophie checked the height of the barn roof. "This is as tall as the house. So it should block us."

"Maybe." They crossed the dirt floor and considered their target, a rickety board that seemed thinner than those in the rest of the wall, as if it had been tacked on as a temporary fix to keep animals from escaping. It had been screwed in at the top, to a beam about level with Sophie's chin, but attached at the bottom with a thin nail with no head. If they pulled from the bottom edge, the board slid right off its nail. Even if they couldn't pull it right off the wall, they should be able to pull it away far enough to wriggle through the gap.

"He won't know we've gone until he comes back and walks around the whole thing again. That could be a long time." Younger Guy didn't seem too energetic. But he also didn't stick to a schedule and made his checks at random, which made it harder to plan.

The chicken coop had been attached to the front corner

of the barn. Noah had been too scared to notice it when he'd been hustled inside, though he didn't phrase it like that. The birds made a great burglar alarm, getting restless and squawking whenever Younger Guy approached, but they'd react the same way if Noah and Sophie emerged from the barn wall.

Noah moved his hands, still trying to estimate the field of view from an upstairs window to past the barn along the meadow to the tree line. "If anyone's looking, they're going to see us at some point."

*Is he afraid?* "Doesn't matter. We don't have much of a choice."

"True." He spoke so calmly that she knew he wasn't afraid to try; he simply chose to be thorough. "We'll have to run as fast as we can, give us as much time to get into the woods—"

"I can run fast. My coach says I'm the second fastest on the team."

"What team?"

"Edgewood Soccer."

"I play baseball," he said. "I go to Virginia Prep."

His tone implied that baseball was more of a real sport than soccer. Sophie had run into the attitude before . . . and it could be what her mom called a "hot button." She opened her mouth to ask how fast Noah could run, because she bet she could beat it—even though she knew that was a little unfair, because she was twelve and he was only a little kid, so, of course, she could probably beat him, though the attitude annoyed her enough that she felt like being a little unfair— when the large barn door opened. Younger Guy stuck his head in, cautiously, as if he thought Sophie and Noah might bean him with a shovel, which Sophie would totally have done, if they had left anything in the barn that could be used as a weapon. But he looked around, saw Sophie and Noah, and withdrew. Then Millie walked in, carrying a little boy. Real little, like Sophie's cousin's age, like three or four. He had jet-black hair and an orange shirt, and was crying that fake little on-again, off-again cry that little kids did when they wanted something and you weren't giving it to them.

"I've brought you another playmate," Millie said.

# Chapter 26

"What do you think?" Michael Tyler asked his partner. They were both dressed as tourists, an easy disguise in the sixth most visited city in the country. Pull on a pair of athletic shoes, lose the tie, and dangle a camera around the neck and they were as convincing as they could get. Which did not mean Michael didn't feel like a complete dweeb. He had tried to persuade his boss to let him throw on his old army camo so they could look like soldiers on leave, but, of course, any garb that might actually be comfortable would not meet bureau standards. And, soldiers might spook a skittish, low-life kidnapper.

The cameras, however, might come in handy—even though there were no less than three teams of agents equipped with long-range directional microphones, video cameras, Stop Sticks to disable a vehicle, and both a bike and a motorcycle (plus a helicopter on standby) in case alternate forms of pursuit were needed. The teams were spread along the memorial area, one at each end and another in the ball fields between the memorial and Ohio Drive. Though since the memorial itself sat on a stretch of land between the National Mall Tidal

Basin and the Potomac River, perhaps they should have lined up a boat as well.

"I don't get it," Luis Alvarez admitted. "Are we dealing with a nutcase, an amateur, a professional, or a group of political rivals more extreme than Stalin and Tito?"

"At this point I am not taking any bets. Except one: I'll bet our guy didn't think there would be this many people here at ten a.m. on a weekday. Look, there's *another* field trip."

Thirty small children in uniforms shredded the air with high-pitched voices as their teacher patiently tried to tell them about the thirty-second president and something known as "the Depression."

The unusually designed Franklin Delano Roosevelt Memorial stretched along the edge of the basin between the Dr. Martin Luther King Jr. and Thomas Jefferson Memorials. Instead of a single structure it consisted of stone walls, water features, twenty-two carved quotations, and bronze statues ranging from figures standing in a bread line to the president's dog, Fala. There were plenty of stone benches and shade trees to make the tour relaxing and pleasant.

"Odd choice for a drop," Luis said. They sat on a bench in the shade, the basin somewhere behind them, facing the walls with the WWII quotes about hating war. The "I Hate War" phrase had also been carved into two huge, roughly rectangular stones with one propped on the other in the open area in front of the wall and water. This created a small cubby under the larger of the stones. "That duffel under there is perfectly visible to anyone walking up to the quotation, especially that bunch of four-foot-tall munchkins. I thought they did field trips at the end of the school year, not the beginning."

"It's open here, though—the location. Not like they're in a building or something with only one entrance, like Lincoln or Jefferson."

"Yeah, whoever grabs it can run either east or west, go around the back of that thing to the field, but eventually they still have one road out there and the water here. It boxes them in."

A breeze floated through the trees, showering them with leaves already beginning to accept the inevitable death. Michael pulled one out of the back of his collar. Two young women and a young man moved across the plaza, all dewy skin and boundless enthusiasm, discussing an office in which they interned. An elderly woman strolled with a cane, smiling indulgently at the group of second graders, most of whom were climbing on any large stone or bench at hand, instead of listening to their teacher's summary. A lone man approached from Michael's right.

"Why are we sitting here again? I hope it's not because we're FBI agents waiting for a kidnapper to come collect his ransom."

"Of course not. We're just innocent history-buff dorks. But we're old and tired."

"Speak for yourself," Michael said.

"We're doing the circuit. Started at the Washington Monument, through the World War Two and Vietnam Memorials, up the steps to see Mr. Lincoln and use up a bunch of pixels on the view over the reflecting pool toward the Capitol. Then the Korean, the MLK, and by the time we got here, we're plumb tuckered out."

" 'Plumb tuckered'?"

"*Plumb,*" Luis insisted. "Because we've got to get to the Jefferson yet."

"Then why are we wearing sunglasses in the shade?"

"Sensitive eyes." For increased verisimilitude Luis took his off and made a show of wiping them with the bottom of his shirt. "Ellie Carr couldn't get anything off the phone?"

"Not prints. I didn't expect her to. Someone at the Locard is working on the data."

"Probably Agnes. You trust her?"

"Agnes? She scares the crap out of me."

"No, Dr. Carr. She's the victim's cousin. I can't believe the AD didn't think that was a conflict of interest." He meant the assistant director of the Criminal Investigation Division.

"He asked what I thought, and I told him—she's the best, and I stood there when she first walked in and realized the victim is a blood relation. She's either an A-plus-list actress, or she had no idea her cousin had married one of the richest men in town and lived in a palace. They haven't been hanging together a whole lot, in other words. I'm no psychic, but they did not seem close," Michael replied.

"A list. There's no 'A-plus list.'"

"If she was acting, then there is now."

The man wandered closer. He walked without urgency, a backpack weighing him down. As he entered their section of the plaza, Michael could see the tattered shoes and a hole in the T-shirt under the long-sleeved flannel. A homeless guy, or a guy pretending to be homeless, just as Michael pretended to be a tourist?

"It's a crapshoot, either way," he went on, thinking out loud. "Her emotional connection might make her work wobble. Other than *that*, assuming Mason and Noah were disappeared by the same people, for the same reasons, then her connection to the victims makes no difference."

When Luis made his wife angry or exasperated, or giggly or even amorous, she would call him "*diablo*." He liked it. Someone always needed to play devil's advocate—it kept the investigation honest. "If you take Noah Thomas out of the equation for a minute, though, what happens to our assumptions?"

Michael played along without pause. "Then the more likely explanation is that the Carlisles, either purposely or accidentally, killed their son, and Hunter sent that text to himself."

"Yes."

"In that case, even if they're not close, even if there isn't much of a connection, if Ellie realizes her cousin killed her baby and hid the body and came up with this not-terribly-believable story about him disappearing from his crib in the middle of the afternoon, she might help her cover it up. Blood is blood. *Or* she might consider her cousin a distant acquaintance who's on her own. Ellie's built up a hell of a career and a hell of a reputation. She'd think hard before throwing that away over a few nanometers of DNA."

"And maybe her cousin doesn't know that, and spills the truth to her, which could be *very* good for us." Luis waved his hand at the bronze statues off to their left as if discussing the president's choice of canines. "'Nanometers.' Look at you, talking all sciencey-like. Plus she's cute."

"Who?" Michael said, while knowing quite well who, because they had a similarly themed discussion at least six times monthly.

"Ellie Carr."

"Don't care."

"Then you need to get your pulse checked, bro."

Michael fiddled with the camera they'd given him without actually changing a setting or taking a picture. "Don't care. Last time I met someone cute, I married her. She took my car, all the furniture, and my kids."

"This one strikes me as having better taste—too good to touch that two-door econobox thing you drive with a stick and a disinfectant wipe." Luis checked his watch without moving his arm. "It's ten-to."

"I know. We'd better move on." Michael kept his gaze on the shuffling man while facing directly ahead at the quotation wall. It made his eyeballs ache. At least standing up gave him a reason to turn his head.

"I hope that's our guy. But if he really is homeless, he's not going to pass up that duffel. We might have a problem."

"We also might have a problem if he *is* our guy and one of those kids finds it first."

Luis stood up as well, making a show of checking for his camera bag. "Aw, man. What do you think they are, second grade? Luke just started second. I can't believe the math they have those kids doing now. Fractions! They're learning freaking fractions. In the second grade!"

"Word of advice." Michael had two girls in middle school; of Luis's two, Lucas was the oldest, with Thiago only in kindergarten, putting Luis firmly in the position of advice recipient, not issuer, whether he liked it or not. "Don't try to help them. You'll only make things worse."

Two little boys climbed on the *I Hate* stone, unaware that they stood atop a duffel containing half a million dollars in cash. The teacher paused in her recitation of facts and Michael could imagine her internal debate: *It's a chunk of granite, unlikely to be harmed by fifty pounds of sneaker-clad child, and since the benches are also made of stone, the structures could be reasonably equated in a seven-year-old mind. However, those particular stones are, technically, part of the memorial and should be treated with respect—*

The lady with the cane settled herself next to the statue of Fala, perhaps assuming it would be the kids' next stop and she would have a good view of the tykes. Or the bad knee made for frequent rest periods.

*—unless they are meant to be interactive, in which case the designers had* planned *for children to climb on them.*

The homeless guy drew even with the stones, appearing to ignore the granite blocks, the children, the teacher, and Michael and Luis completely. He shuffled along, leaving Michael to form other possible scenarios: The guy was no one, zoned out into his own world; the guy was the advance team and would report to someone else as soon as he rounded the wall with the "We Have Faith" quotation; the guy was here for the duffel, but had made them as something other than tourists. Michael raised the camera, clicked, getting a photo of the man, just for the hell of it.

"Don't take pictures of the kids," Luis warned. "Everyone will think you're a pedophile."

The teacher solved the problem of her climbers by wrapping up and telling her students to move on. Some of them quickly spied the statue of the Scottish terrier and zoomed off. The two boys on the *I Hate* stone likewise leapt to the ground in foolishly bold arcs and followed suit, leaving the duffel unnoticed. The homeless guy cleared the plaza as Michael relayed the information to the situation coordinator, so the western team could check to see if his actions remained consistent.

A teenager on a skateboard rattled his way around the wall to the west, a skinny boy in a sweat-soaked T-shirt. He glanced at the school group, ignored the agents, and continued on his way east without hesitation.

Michael and Luis moved slowly in a northwest direction, careful to note where they could not be seen from any telephoto lens. The kidnapper would have to enter that particular square of area to notice them. But they couldn't linger. Michael knew darn well that, in any clothing, they looked exactly like what they were. They'd have to trust one of the eastern teams to mosey over and pick up where they left off.

The teacher tried to explain FDR's press club speech quote about the necessity of the Second World War, which proved too difficult to summarize within the students' less-than-a-minute attention span, and, besides, most were too occupied with sneaking past the teacher to pat the dog statue's head. The group moved on, the beaming lady with the cane bringing up the rear.

The skateboarder kept going. The homeless guy did not reappear.

Four Asian tourists moved through, following a private tour guide. None so much as glanced at the *I Hate War* stones, with the not-well-hidden duffel bag full of half a million dollars in cash. Michael and Luis moved to the bench against the west wall.

Adrenaline faded, and self-doubts flooded in. Had they been made? By the homeless guy, the skateboarder, the woman with the jogging baby carriage who had gone by at a breakneck pace shortly after they had arrived? One of the second graders?

Did the kidnapper get held up, by insidious traffic or some last-minute emergency . . . like having accidentally killed Mason? Michael didn't want to think it.

"It's ten-thirty," Luis said.

"I know."

Had they ever intended to show up at all? Had this always been nothing but a distraction, to keep the agents focused on the city, while the perpetrators whisked the baby out of the country entirely? But if they weren't interested in the money, then why *this* baby? Both parents swore there were no exes or lovers involved.

Maybe it was the same woman who had taken Noah Thomas. She'd been slick enough to spirit him from his well-secured school without notice; perhaps she'd figured out a way in and out of the Carlisle mansion. Then it all must relate to the hearing.

As crazy as DC could get, as corrupt and backstabbing as opposing forces in a political battle could prove to be, Michael had never heard of one group kidnapping the other group's children to force a committee vote to go their way.

"Partner," Luis said, "I don't think anyone's coming."

# Chapter 27

"We should have gone," Becca said, pulling a gray suit jacket from a rack in her closet, a closet as big as the entire bedroom Ellie had shared with Becca and her sister, Melissa, in Haven, West Virginia.

Ellie perched uncomfortably on a lumpy ottoman next to a wall of floor-to-ceiling shoe racks. "I know this must be frustrating for you, but it wouldn't be worth the risk."

Becca didn't bother arguing. They had discussed it with the FBI agents, of course. Since the note had specifically forbade Becca and Hunter, there would be nothing they could do there except blow the agents' cover.

But that didn't make it easy.

"What about this one?" Becca held the suit jacket to her chest, examining her reflection in a large trifold mirror.

"It's very nice."

"You said that about the last two."

Ellie turned her palms up. "You know me—I don't know Burberry from Armani."

"I thought you might have picked something up in the past twenty years. And this *is* Armani."

"It's very nice," Ellie teased, and felt an iota better to see a small grin on her cousin's face. "Is it important what you wear to committee hearings?"

"No . . . normally it's usual DC attire, professional but decently comfortable. But this one—what do I have that screams *competent, knowledgeable* and most of all *I'm not only here because my husband and I have to give up the millions we were to reap from the outcome in order to get our son back with no guarantee that we actually will*?"

"That's a lot to ask from a suit."

Becca hesitated, then threw the gray jacket back on the rack and dug between the hangers to retrieve another in a slightly darker gray. "You're right. The Kiton, then."

"Won't the committee wonder why you're at work when—after what happened?" Ellie asked as gently as she could. Of course, now that they intended to lose the hearing, it might not be so bad if the senators wondered how the parents of a family-friendly gaming organization could focus on work when their children were missing.

Becca tried on the jacket, checking her reflection in the mirror. "They don't know."

"They don't—"

"We can't tell them! It would be instant, crazy news coverage—who knows what the kidnappers would do if they saw the story splashed all over? And they would definitely cancel the hearing."

And without the hearing Mason and Noah wouldn't be returned.

The hardwood beams underneath Ellie's feet trembled in an apprehensive hum as someone tore through the bedroom to the dressing area, and Hunter burst through the doorway. His obvious fury made both women jump—Becca sank into the other ottoman like a wrecked ship slipping beneath the waves.

Ellie's heart pounded a refrain: *Mason isn't dead. Mason isn't dead. It can't be.*

"Two more kids are gone," he told them.

*9:48 a.m.*

The arrival of the little boy—Millie said his name was Oliver, and that they should look after him—put a definite crimp in Noah and Sophie's escape plan. He was too short to run fast, and yet too big for either of them to carry while sprinting at the same time. And he was noisy as hell—he hadn't stopped either screaming, crying, or talking since his arrival. He could talk in sentences, but couldn't comprehend that they had no idea what was going on either. They were bigger, so they *had* to know. So when he asked them where his mommy was and why they couldn't take him home, and they said they didn't know and were stuck there just like he was, he simply asked the same questions again. And again. And again. Sometimes in English, sometimes in Spanish.

Sophie stepped up to play mommy, because interspersed with the questions had been mentions of pee-pee. Noah watched her guide him to the Porta-Potty, something the kid seemed to hate as much as they did, but after many calm promises of help, she got him up on the toilet seat. At least Oliver was potty-trained. Noah had seen the inside of his little cousin's diaper once, and he wanted *nothing* to do with that sort of thing.

How long did Millie think he and Sophie could take care of a toddler like that, with nothing but granola bars and bottled water and Little Debbies? Eventually all three of them would need a bath and clean clothes and actual protein. His mom's insistence on a shower every night drove him nuts, but after a whole night in the tolerable but ceaseless humidity, he promised he'd never argue with her again. What was *wrong* with these people?

The plastic door swung shut, muffling the constant conversation, so that Noah could press his face to the planks at the other end of the barn because Millie and Younger Guy were having a conversation. Or more like an argument.

"How much longer?" Younger Guy asked.

"Four o'clock. It's the last on the agenda for today. Then we'll know if they've listened or not."

She tried to walk away from him but he stepped in front of her. "*Then* what?"

"Then we know whether we have a world fit for our children to live in."

"I meant what about them?" He waved a hand at the barn and seemed to look right at Noah, startling him into jumping back so that he missed what Millie said next. Inside the plastic box, Oliver protested to something with another shout.

*They can't see me*, Noah told himself, and pressed one ear to the sliver of gap between the wooden planks. Then he covered up his other ear with his hand, and tried to blot out every other sensation. If he covered one eye as well, he could peek through a different gap without straining his eyeballs . . . much.

". . . and right now, they're comparing notes," Millie said.

"Do you really think they'll do it?"

"Of course they will. We have *them*." She hitched a thumb toward the barn, and the gesture gave Noah a chill even in the heat. She was going to make them do something. Like the bad guys made the prisoners of war talk about how bad the U.S. was in that movie about Vietnam that his dad had been watching one time. Or maybe make him and Sophie tell their parents they were going to be killed if they didn't send a bunch of money. Or maybe there was something only he and Sophie knew, and Younger Guy would cut them with a knife and pour salt on it—he had seen that in some ancient movie before his mom made him turn it off—and torture them like that. Noah's heart pounded.

Millie said, "They'll see the light when it's their own kids' safety they have to think about. Finn says—"

"Finn again! You don't even know who Finn *is*!"

She gave him that patient look, the kind Noah had seen on his own mother many a time. "I know I would never have noticed the data clause if he hadn't contacted me. And I know we couldn't have done this without him."

With one hand on the guy's shoulder, she added, "I never said this would be easy. But for the sake of your children, it has to be done. And *they* are the key."

She walked off. Younger Guy stood there for a second. He turned back to the barn, but didn't approach, only stared at the barn door behind which Noah cowered. Then he stomped off to a slight hill opposite the door and sat down under a tree. From there he watched the barn with an unhappy frown.

A brief reprieve. Noah turned from his stance to see Sophie washing Oliver's hands with hand sanitizer. The kid kept up a constant chatter, but didn't seem to *say* much, communicating mostly in grunts, shouts, unintelligible syllables, and finger pointing. Sophie unwrapped a protein bar for him, earning a moment of relative quiet as the kid chewed, wet tracks still visible down both cheeks.

"We've got to get out of here," Noah told Sophie. "Something bad is going to happen to us."

*9:48 a.m.*

Rachael Davies yawned as she opened the door to her office. She'd returned there the night before after driving Ellie back, helping the DNA analyst prepare the tiny fragment of hair caught in the ransom note glue for analysis . . . even though the analyst already muttered to herself that even handsomely paid overtime was still overtime and overtime sucked. Then she had to bail on that, even, when Danton had not settled down to sleep after Rachael's mother had read him three stories and answered his interminable questions about where his mother was. Rachael hated that her absence had brought on the meltdown, and hated the worry that she might be overtaxing her mother. Loretta had raised her kids, done her time. She shouldn't have to raise her grandchildren as well.

But things don't always go as planned, do they?

She dumped her purse and briefcase stuffed with training-session proposals on the desk and switched on her coffeepot, wondering if she'd have time to check on her research project during the day. She'd been working with the DC Medical Examiner's Office to collect small samples of brain tissue from the recently deceased to see if there were any chemical abnormalities, especially in the brains of suicide victims. But she probably wouldn't have time to visit the pathology lab, with Mason Carlisle still missing and another boy gone as well.

The hallways grew noisy as students milled about, preparing for that day's seminars, comparing notes and networking. The current slate of training classes would end on Friday, with a two-week break until the next session began. As much as Rachael enjoyed the energy of meeting and sharing ideas with trainees from all over the world, she also liked the catching up she could get done when they all went away again.

The DNA lab, spotless and gleaming, made her eyes ache with its relentless fluorescent glow. The analyst on overtime had already returned, only slightly less grumpy as the night before. As soon as Rachael entered, she said, "Nothing."

"No mitochondrial?" That sucked, but mDNA could be temperamental like that, and it had been a very small piece of hair.

Nearly all DNA analysis used the double-helix strands found in one's chromosomes, located in the cell's nucleus. However, some of the body's cells, though they start out with a nucleus, later destroy it as part of the maturation process to make room for more pressing structures. Red blood cells and platelets lose their nuclei, and hair, outer skin cells, and finger and toenails destroy the nuclei to make room for the sturdy keratin structures that will make them tough.

"Oh, I got a profile. But it doesn't match anyone in our database."

That was to be expected. The mitochondrial database had a fraction of the profiles that the nuclear DNA database had. A very, very *long* shot, but worth a try.

Mitochondria, the kidney bean–shaped organelles found in cells, function as the cell's generators and produce chemical energy to power everything the cell has to do. But mitochondria have their own DNA, a rudimentary circular structure called a plasmid. As the cell divides by mitosis, the mitochondria and its DNA divides by simple fission. It replicates without recombining; in a fertilized egg the only mitochondria present will be from the egg, not the sperm, so that a child inherits only their mother's mDNA, passed down unchanged through the maternal line.

"So unless you have someone for me to compare it to, there's nothing more I can do for you. I was going to run a demo this morning, anyway, give the students some real-time observation. Usually, I have one of them volunteer a hair or fingernail, but if you—"

"Yes." Rachael pulled out an envelope containing Ellie's red hair, the one she had plucked off her passenger headrest.

She handed it to the analyst, who filled out a quick receipt and had Rachael sign off. "What is this?"

"Just a hunch," Rachael said.

# Chapter 28

10:45 a.m.

"Kieu Tran just called me." Hunter spoke so quickly that Ellie had trouble making sense of the words. Yet he didn't shout; his voice stayed low, controlled, thoughts and strategies churning behind them as steadily and rapidly as a server bank in a temperature-controlled vault. "Her daughter, Sophie, pulled the old trick, told her mom she was staying at a girlfriend's, but she really met a boy, or was supposed to meet a boy. The girlfriend got more and more worried and had just confessed to her mother when Kieu called for a bedtime video chat. Of course she had been having nightmares of a pedophile ring and didn't connect it to KidFun, until she got a text this morning."

"Oh, my G—what the hell do they want Kieu to do?"

"Something about the security verification procedure. They want her to say it's just a data grab. This can't be happening," Hunter exploded, grabbing his hair with both hands and walking around in a circle. "This can't be *happening*."

Ellie wanted to echo the sentiment. She'd examined and

tested everything she could, and yet the situation kept get-ting worse. "You said two kids."

Hunter stopped pacing, sucked in a breath. "Jason Mar-tinez's son, Oliver. He's three. Snatched from a playground. Jason was there when Darnell got the text about Noah, so he contacted everyone immediately, but Jason hasn't gotten a text yet."

Becca's expensive suit jacket slipped from her hand. "Has Gabriel told everyone at KidFun that they need to put their kids under armed guard—"

"Yes," Hunter cut her off. "He did. But I'll bet that's it. There won't be more."

"How do you *know*?"

"Because Kieu, Darnell, and Jason are the three scheduled to speak at the hearing today. Just them and Gabriel."

An abrupt silence as this sank in. Why hadn't Ellie thought of that yesterday? Since the whole drama centered around the hearing, surely, kidnappers would focus on the people speaking there. From what she'd spent all night reading, agendas and list of witnesses had to be submitted in advance for committee meetings, and not changed without difficulty.

She also had read a great deal on gaming practices and on-line safety. "What will they want Jason Martinez to say?"

Hunter roused himself from his own thoughts to say without patience, "Who knows with these wackos?"

Becca murmured, "Jason is an advertising lawyer."

For a second or two Ellie thought that meant he took out billboards about his law practice.

"He deals with the use of data collected by the program."

Ah. "And its sale to advertisers."

A flicker in Becca's eyes: surprise. But Ellie had read quite a lot during the night; chronic insomnia provided ample op-portunities for education.

Her cousin said, "There's a number of issues to data collec-tion. Half the critics say we need to collect more to keep out the pedophiles pretending to be tweens, the other half say anything we collect is a violation of privacy and discrimination, as if it's discrimination to pitch Barbies to little girls. Say you're running real estate ads for an expensive development and you target the ad only to go to whites, or only people who live in certain zip codes. Now *that's* discrimination. But pitching toys to children?"

Business talk seemed to lower Hunter's blood pressure, if only by a millimeter or two. "They're talking about the registration requirements that Kieu wrote into the game platform to make it *safer*. It's insane."

Becca said, "Exactly. Gathering the data from kids playing the game to verify identity and keep out the trolls and pedophiles is vital. Yes, we'll sell it to advertisers, but so what? What did Mom do when we asked for Super Sugar Crisp instead of shredded wheat?"

"She said no," Ellie dutifully replied.

"Exactly," Becca repeated. "No online protocol can take the place of parents paying attention. These people are insane, and they're grabbing all our kids. I should never have let Taylor go to school today."

Hunter said, "The school's aware. They're not going to let anyone other than you or me get near her."

Becca ignored him, saying to Ellie: "I wanted her to have a normal day . . . and if something went wrong, I—wanted to protect her."

Which meant, *If her brother turns up dead, I don't want her to be here when we find out.*

"Hello?" The voice came from the first floor, faint and wavering. The three people in Becca's dressing room stared at each other for a split second, then nearly got caught in the doorway as they dashed toward the stairs.

Gabriel Haller sat at the dining table, the informal one attached to the kitchen. Under a sheen of sweat his skin had turned pasty white, and his fingers trembled without pause.

He leaned over the table, propping an elbow on its surface to keep himself upright.

*Mason's dead,* Ellie thought. *They* did *find his body.*

"I don't know what happened," he said, answering their main question before anyone found the courage to ask it. "I don't know where Mason is. I left the ransom and came here. Have you heard?"

Ellie fished Michael Tyler's card from her pocket, then dialed. He and Luis had been replaced by another agent, and it had been an hour and no one had arrived to collect the ransom. Had the Carlisles been contacted?

They were also, Michael added, monitoring all hospitals, fire departments and other safe havens for reports of infants left, but so far, none had been.

She disconnected, and had to relay the disappointing news to Mason's parents.

"I did exactly what they said." Gabriel rocked slightly as he spoke, his skin taking on a slightly greenish hue. "I left it under the stones and got out of there. I didn't even look back. My vision's been all wonky, anyway. One of the agents wanted to drive me back, but I wouldn't let anyone take the Bentley—"

Hunter said, "It's not your fault, man. Thanks for trying—I don't know what the hell these people want."

"Especially as sick as you are." Becca put a hand on Gabriel's forehead and asked about symptoms and treatments. He said he'd had to pull over on the way home to vomit, and now he was dying of thirst. Becca hastened to get him a glass of water.

*He isn't rocking,* Ellie thought. *He's shivering.* His body twitched in involuntary spasms. There were illnesses that could cause such a rapid decline, but not many. There were also many nonnatural events with the same effect. "Call an ambulance."

"No," Hunter said. "He's got to make that hearing. We *all*

have to make the hearing. They don't want the ransom, they want the hearing."

"That's not going to be an option."

Hunter ignored her. "We'll get you some aspirin and a hot toddy, pal. You'll be fine."

"No," Gabriel said to Ellie. "It's just the flu. I'm going to be there when we tell the truth about the company."

"It's not the truth!" Hunter snapped.

Gabriel did not respond. When he reached for the glass Becca held, he slid from his chair and onto the floor in a slow-motion avalanche of arms and legs.

"Call an ambulance!" Ellie ordered her cousin as she grabbed Gabriel's wrists to pull him away from the chairs and table. This gave her room to get him completely on his back, stretched out on the gleaming wood floor—a hard surface, not the plush carpet so thickly padded it might as well be a bed's mattress.

Gabriel did not breathe. She checked his airway—clear—and put her ear to his chest, blocking her other ear to be able to detect even the slightest heartbeat. His dress shirt felt damp, and she could smell the accumulation of sweat in its fibers.

Nothing.

Though grateful for the quiet moment, Ellie realized she hadn't heard anyone dialing 911 and barked again: "Ambulance!" as she felt along Gabriel's breastbone, positioning her hands. "Do you have an AED?"

Hunter said, "No. What's the matter with him?"

Ellie began to pump the man's chest. *One—two—three—*

She heard Becca direct the 911 operator to their location. Then Becca knelt across from Ellie, her skin turned nearly as pale as the sick man's. She said his name in a stricken tone, once again stroking his forehead.

*—twenty-nine—thirty.* Ellie stopped and listened again. Nothing.

She tilted his head again, pinching his nose with one hand and holding the jaw with another.

"What's the *matter* with him?" Hunter shouted.

Ellie put her mouth—acutely aware that the man may have collapsed due to some communicable disease, though she didn't think so—over Gabriel's slack, dry lips and puffed two deep breaths into his lungs. She turned to see his chest fall . . . *Good, at least his airways are not obstructed.*

She restarted compressions, trying to ask for the ambulance's ETA without losing count. But Becca didn't know; in her distress she had tossed the phone aside, and when relocated, the 911 center had disconnected. Just then, however, they all heard a firm knock, followed by yet another questioning: "Hello?"

*Good,* Ellie thought, *get some pros in here because he's not going to—*

But paramedics didn't arrive through the open doorway. Dr. Rachael Davies did, and took in the tableau before her with a raised eyebrow. As she crossed to the fallen man, she said, "Sorry to barge in—but I talked to the FBI agents and they were headed here—"

"What's happened?" Hunter demanded.

"Nothing. No pickup, no sign of Mason." She knelt across from Ellie, gently nudging Becca out of the way. "What happened to him?"

"Flulike symptoms since last night, shivering, vomited, thirst, sweating." Ellie reached thirty, listened, breathed into his mouth, and started over again.

"Medical history?" Rachael asked of Becca and Hunter, her tone so firm it shaded into harsh. "Any possibility of drugs?"

They both said no to drugs, and no to any medical issues, so far as they knew.

"This doesn't make sense." Ellie continued to push on the unresisting flesh, knowing that the window to save his life grew narrower every second. Soon it would close completely—if it hadn't already.

"No, it doesn't. Need me to take over?" Rachael asked her.

"No." She had a rhythm going, a system . . . not that it seemed to be working. They needed a defibrillator, they needed a medevac, they needed the operating theater of the best hospital in the country or—

Rachael suddenly abandoned her, but then Ellie saw why. A strong young woman in a pair of BDU pants knelt in her place and told Ellie, "Taking over when you finish that set."

"Twenty-eight, twenty-nine," she counted aloud, then took her hands away and let the paramedics work. They intubated Gabriel, then took a scissors to the expensive dress shirt and applied the AED pads—one defibrillator to his right side under the collarbone, and the other to the lower left. The EMT hesitated over a wide patch of scaly, hardened skin, no doubt wondering if it might affect delivery of the charge, decided it wouldn't, and pasted the flat white oval to his side.

"Clear!" she said loudly, and hit the button.

Gabriel's body gave a start, but the glowing pinpoint on their portable EKG settled back to a single, unchanging line.

They tried again, then finally bundled him onto a gurney and sped away with sirens blaring, and Ellie felt the utter certainty that it would all be for nothing.

Gabriel Haller was dead.

# Chapter 29

Rachael Davies donned a Tyvek apron, following it up with long sleeves with elastic at both ends to slip over her silk blouse. A mask and a face shield completed the ensemble. Good thing the DC Medical Examiner's Office kept the building nice and cool . . . Tyvek could be miserable in hot weather.

"Thank you for letting me attend," she said to the pathologist assigned to Gabriel Haller, a gray-haired woman with olive skin and an unpronounceable name.

"No problem. It's a light day, for a change, so we've got room around the tables. We *finally* finished work on the mall shooting victims. And when the FBI asks for you to be here, my boss isn't likely to argue."

They went out into the hallway, where Gabriel Haller's mortal coil lay under a sheet on a stainless-steel gurney. Rachael helped her maneuver the rolling table into the autopsy suite and up to one of the bays where the lip of the gurney could connect to the sink.

The doctor began to make notes on a clipboard while her assistant, a young man with dark skin and dimples peeking

out from behind his mask, collected the dead man's fingerprints. "I couldn't even catch everything they said. Something about missing children and a congressional hearing?"

Rachael tried to summarize the events so far—not an easy
task, when they didn't even make sense to her, finishing
with: "So this man had been feeling sick since last night, but
this morning dropped off a ransom payment and then drove
himself back to the parents' house, where he collapsed of an
apparent medical issue."

"That's bad timing," the assistant said as he squirted dish-
washing liquid over Gabriel's body. He followed this with
water from a rubber hose attached to a sink faucet, and then
washed every inch of skin with a sponge.

"That's suspicious timing," Rachael said.

"Anybody else sick?"

"No."

"No history?"

"Not that I know of."

"Contamination? Botulism? Salmonella? Bad drugs?"

"No clue at this point. They're checking his house now,
but he lives alone and was out and about yesterday, so who
knows what he consumed?"

"Huh." The doctor scribbled more notes. Then the hesitation in Rachael's voice, some atypical timbre, made her re-
consider. She gave her fellow pathologist a sharp peer.
"You're thinking poison. Like a Russian spy or something?"

"Well," Rachael said, "yes, given the extremely rapid decline of an apparently healthy man. The symptoms don't follow a familiar route—"

"And the timing."

"And," Rachael said, "the timing."

"What's this on his skin?" the assistant asked, scrubbing at
the wide patch of thickened, rough skin. The largest patch
covered a six-inch diameter, with some smaller blotches elsewhere on his torso. When they flipped the body over to

scrub and examine the back surface, Rachael saw that the most pronounced areas were over his elbows.

"A couple of things could cause that," the doctor said, unimpressed. "It's probably a form of ichthyosis."

"Easy for you to say," the assistant joked.

"See the mosaic lines on the calves? It's a mild form, really, not that bad. A little bit of exfoliation now and then probably kept him comfortable." The two of them turned the body faceup again. "It can be a lot worse, where the scales cover the sweat glands and the person gets itchy because the skin's trying to sweat, and can't. They get large red patches all over, which can dry out, crack, bleed, and ooze. Which would be a pity," she added with a glance at the dead man's face. "He's a good-looking guy."

"Is it contagious?" the assistant asked, examining his gloves with a nervous eye.

"Nah. It's genetic. And I'm sure it didn't kill him."

"I'd like to know what did," Rachael said.

Other than the various patches of dry skin, Gabriel Haller didn't have a mark on him. The doctor and Rachael saw no bruises or pinpricks that would indicate an injection site or any other kind of trauma. He could have a blow to the head that produced an undiagnosed concussion, but that would be obvious when the doctor pulled back the skin over the cranium. His hands made it clear that he worked at a desk, with manicured nails and no sign that he had been in a struggle.

Rachael hovered at a respectable distance as the doctor cut her way through the chest cavity to examine the organs. She cut apart the lungs on a polyethylene cutting board, using a large bread knife. She expected to see edema, or blood clots, associated with poisoning, but the edema present were small and not pervasive. Poisons or drug overdoses often produced foaming in the lungs, but those were cases of sudden, acute poisoning . . . Given that Gabriel had felt sick for at least twelve hours, foaming would have been absorbed by the system.

Ellie had been thinking the same thing, Rachael knew. But neither of them wanted to guess aloud about poison in front of Becca and Hunter. Ellie had told Rachael she would talk to her cousin about checking any foodstuffs, after the body had been removed.

Rachael hadn't asked because she didn't trust them. First their child disappears from their house, and then their close friend drops dead in their dining room. It had been made clear that a great deal of money depended on KidFun and the result of the hearing. Add in an emotional factor, like children, and motives could get murky.

As the heart was dissected, she, likewise, observed the valves and walls, smooth and regular. The coronary arteries did not give the characteristic crunch of arteriosclerosis when cut.

Things got more interesting when they came to the largest internal organ, the liver. It looked fatty with obvious signs of necrosis, which seemed odd in someone relatively young and in good shape.

"Alcoholic?" the assistant suggested.

"Too acute," Rachael blurted before remembering that she was no longer the pathologist.

The doctor either did not notice or did not take offense. "No, this isn't a cirrhosis that developed over time. This is a direct hepatotoxin." She used a scalpel to slice off smaller portions of the meat to send to histology. There the tissues would be fixed and sliced in order to make slides so that the doctor could examine the organ on a cellular level. "So whatever it was attacked the liver and not the heart."

Rachael said, "Probably coagulopathy actually killed him."

"That narrows it down. Any idea how the poison got into his system? Is anyone else sick? If so, they're going to have to get to the hospital, like, last night . . . if they want to live."

"Not so far. It's going to be hard to track down—as far as I know, he lives alone and I have no idea where all he went yesterday."

"Or the day before," the doctor said.

True, Rachael thought. Some poisons took a long time to kill. But by the time the victim sought help for their symptoms, the internal damage had already caused irreversible organ failure. Gabriel Haller had been strong and healthy. If he had gone to the hospital at the first sign, he might have been saved—depending, of course, on how much poison he had ingested. But with the kidnapping and the upcoming hearing, he had doubtless tried to push himself through it and fulfill his obligations regardless. And it had killed him.

She told the pathologist how FBI agents were searching his townhome and interviewing his staff to create a timeline of his every movement for the past forty-eight hours. With luck they might find something that could lead them to a suspect, or, on the chance that this had been some sort of accidental exposure, a source. But that would mean his death during this chaotic time had been pure coincidence.

And Rachael didn't believe in coincidence.

# Chapter 30

Gabriel's death had left Hunter reeling. He paced through the house on a rampage, usually on his phone, directing staff members to various tasks in an attempt to fill the void left by KidFun's CEO and most visible spokesman. He worked with a desperation Ellie more than understood: The ransom money had not worked. The ransom of coerced testimony was all they had left.

Becca remained calm, but it resembled hopeless despondency more than resignation. The twin shocks of *not* getting her son back without any indication of remedy and her friend dying on her dining-room floor had knocked her so far off kilter that Ellie had no idea what to say or do. She could guess at many explanations for the kidnapper's failure to collect the ransom, all of them bad, and clearly Gabriel had been more than a family friend. The Carlisles' financial future had been tied up with KidFun; and without Gabriel, that future, already threatened by the kidnappers, tottered on its axis. So should Ellie ask about Gabriel to take Becca's mind off Mason, or make up something hopeful to say about Mason to distract her from Gabriel?

Neither option seemed particularly helpful. Instead, she simply gathered up the peel-off backings and other packaging left by the EMTs on the glossy wood floor and stuffed them into the kitchen garbage can, next to the cardboard coffee cup she had dropped in there upon arrival and Gabriel's Gatorade bottle from the night before. Had anyone in the family eaten anything since yesterday? She should ask. Both Becca and Hunter seemed shaky, probably hypoglycemic. But before that—

"Did Gabriel eat or drink anything here yesterday, other than this Gatorade?"

"What?"

Ellie pulled on a glove and plucked the bottle out of the garbage, moving to her bag to get a fresh paper sack and repeated the question. "Did you have any of this?"

"What? No. I only buy that stuff for him, no one else can stand it."

"I'm going to take it all. We'll have to check it for contamination."

Becca shrugged, not even summoning up a reply of "whatever."

"Any other drink? Food? Did he bring you anything?"

"No." Becca pressed a tissue to the corner of one eye, its edges shredded into confetti. She had been bursting into small sobs, interspersed with logical discussions of what to do next.

Ellie passed her the box. She could probably sneak upstairs and check that book from Taylor's room, but it seemed beside the point, now. Suspicions might have lingered around Becca and Hunter, but they certainly hadn't abducted Noah Thomas or Sophie Tran or Oliver Martinez.

Michael Tyler stood at the marble island, removing the last of the tracers from the bundles of cash. The money once again stood in neat piles; he hadn't said so, but the special duffel bag belonged to the FBI and no doubt needed to be returned to inventory.

"I'm sorry, sir," he said to Hunter, "but you or Mrs. Carlisle will need to count it and sign a receipt."

"I don't have time for that!" Hunter snapped. "Becca, get Tara over here. She can put this back where it belongs."

Becca dutifully tapped her phone's screen once again, and a rap sounded at the door. Rachael Davies entered, took in the scene with one glance, and did not waste time on pleasantries.

"Gabriel Haller died of organ failure, specifically the liver and kidneys—the result of poisoning."

Ellie didn't even bother to think *I knew it.* This case already had kidnapping and extortion—why not murder as well?

Was it possible there were two different anti-KidFun groups? One kidnapping kids and the other happy to simply murder the CEO?

"Poisoned?" Becca said. "How does *that* make sense?"

"Most likely, at some point yesterday," Rachael went on. "It had to be a massive dose, so he would have felt the effects sooner rather than later. His stomach contents were largely empty, so we couldn't tell when he'd eaten last—probably felt too nauseous. The ME will send out the samples, of course, but that will take a while. We have every chemist on our staff trying to isolate the compounds."

Michael said, "Luis has established something of a timeline, but there's still some gaps. He lives in Georgetown, neighbors saw him yesterday morning, and he spent a few hours at the KidFun office in Leesburg. He came here yesterday about eleven, stayed less than an hour." He looked at Becca for confirmation.

Ellie's cousin sniffed into a fresh tissue and nodded.

"According to his office, he had lunch in their conference

room with four other people regarding the hearing tomorrow. They had food brought in, and he didn't consume anything that wasn't also ordered by at least one other person. The cans of soda were sealed, bottles of water, as were the snacks. Of course he also had water and coffee at the office, but no one else is ill, so someone would have had to doctor his cup or glass specifically. Cleaning staff emptied all the trash last night—less than helpful. He came back here in the afternoon, as we all know, then returned to the office until late." He said to Hunter, "He called you about Noah Thomas. Did he sound ill?"

"No . . . I thought he sounded a little *pained*, but I figured he was worried about Noah."

Michael continued: "His coworkers had all gone home at regular quitting time, except for two assistants. Those two said he seemed uncomfortable and refused their offer to order in dinner for him, but they chalked that up to the pressure of today's hearing. They left by six. According to their security system, he swiped out of the parking garage at ten-thirty. He swiped back into his secure Georgetown row house at eleven, which didn't leave him a lot of time to make any stops. He didn't leave the townhouse until this morning. Given the time he left, he most likely came straight here."

Ellie said, "And was sick by that point. We all commented on it." She told Rachael and Michael that she had collected the Gatorade bottle.

Michael said, "Product tampering would be a hell of a coincidence. But stranger things have happened."

Ellie's cousin leapt to her feet as if her chair had given her an electric shock. "You think those bottles—we've got to get rid of those, right now! Taylor might have—"

"Taylor hates Gatorade," Hunter said, still texting.

Becca ignored him and yanked the fridge door so hard the condiments rattled. She grabbed the closest bottle and peered at the neck of it. "Looks okay."

"I'll take them," Rachael said diplomatically, and she and Ellie bagged up the four small bottles.

With that project taken over, Becca heaved a shuddering breath. "I have to get myself together. We have to pick up Taylor soon and she can't see me like . . . this."

"There's more," Rachael said, folding the top of the bag with a crisp pleat, and her tone made everyone refocus. Her gaze swung from Becca to Hunter and back. "You are my clients, so I must keep you informed of every detail. But this is something law enforcement needs to know as well."

The other four people in the room held a collective breath. Ellie had no idea what the woman would say, but clearly it would be something worrisome.

"My DNA analysts have finished working with the fragment of hair caught in the glue in the ransom note. Because it's only a piece from the hair shaft and has no skin cells attached, nuclear DNA was not possible. Therefore we could only do mitochondrial DNA, which is a plasmid—" She looked around, apparently realized that everyone either already knew what mDNA was or didn't need to know at that point, and condensed: "It didn't match anyone in our limited database. However, we compared it to a sample from Mason's sheets, and it matched."

"How can that be?" Hunter asked. "The note was mailed before he was taken."

"Yes." She stopped, as if to let them start filling in the blanks.

Michael said, "It had to be someone with access to Mason, to know how to get in and out of this house undetected. It's not inconceivable that his hair had gotten on them or their clothes at some point."

*And we're back to the original hypothesis,* Ellie thought. The parents were the most likely suspects. The hair strongly implicated someone in the household. The odds of a doctor or a family friend or someone who briefly held the baby winding up with a hair that just happened to fall into the glue of the ransom note were too outrageous . . . It was much more reasonable to think the note had been constructed by someone like the still-absent Jenny Cho. Or—

"Was it a vellus hair?" she asked Rachael. "On the note?"

The woman nodded approvingly, as if she'd expected the question. "We can't be quite sure. It's very fine."

Becca asked what that meant.

Ellie said, "Vellus hairs are those very soft, fine hairs babies are born with. A child's permanent hair slowly takes over, usually by age two or so. Your expert couldn't tell from the cuticle?"

"He didn't want to commit," Rachael said.

*And neither do you, because*—"Mitochondrial DNA is passed intact through the maternal line. So if the hair is not Mason's, it could be Becca's. Or Taylor's. Or," Ellie added, "mine."

"That's ridiculous!" Hunter said. "That makes no sense. Besides, if someone had been close enough to our family to get Mason's hair on them, they could have gotten Becca or Taylor's too. I hate to say it, Becca, but maybe we're wrong about Jenny. Being out of the country gives her a perfect alibi."

"It's not Jenny," Becca said wearily. "We have other people in this house regularly besides Jenny. The cleaning staff, the cable guy—we had one small dinner party last month, thirty guests and a team of caterers, then extra cleaners the following day. It could be anyone."

Hunter had a new theory. "Maybe it's someone from the schools! Their staff would know where the kids live, what time they get out, how to circumvent pickup security, who their parents are."

Michael shot this down with a courteously worded arrow. "Taylor, Noah, and Sophie go to different schools. Oliver

Martinez wasn't even in preschool, and Sophie was lured away from a soccer practice."

"So someone higher up on the school system organizational chart."

"*School!*" Becca burst out. "We have to pick up Taylor in a few minutes. I've got to go." She jumped up as Michael said, "We can have agents—"

Hunter said, "Are you kidding? That school has security so tight, they'd call the cops on *you* if a new person wanted to pick up my kid."

Becca said, "No! No matter what the school does, I drilled this into her head. She will *not* leave that school with anyone except me or Hunter. She'd be terrified."

"Of course. We will accompany you, however. In a separate car."

"Good idea," Hunter said.

# Chapter 31

*2:10 p.m.*

Glen Echo Academy could have been used in movies as a stand-in for Oxford, except that most of its clientele had not yet topped five feet. Boys and girls alike wore dark blue pants or skirts with a pinstripe, white collared shirts, and blue ties with red diagonals. Despite the impressive building and the manicured lawns and the row of luxury vehicles waiting for them, they were still kids at the end of a school day, and many shirts were badly tucked, ties loosened or awry.

Glen Echo Academy's end of day process rolled on in its controlled chaos. The line of sleek, expensive cars idled, waiting for their cargo. Ellie had offered to drive, but Becca insisted, so Ellie rode shotgun and wondered how to explain this use of FBI time to any future auditors . . . not that it really mattered. She would continue her role as a human litmus test regardless, wouldn't leave now—even if her job depended on it. How much did she really want to work for Adam, anyway?

They were amicable and had kept the worst of their history out of the office, but still, would it be different when he became her supervisor? Not for the first time she wondered if that might be why they hadn't yanked her from this case, if Adam were waiting for it to all go south so he could justify firing her. She had been biased, unprofessional, so emotionally involved that she either helped Becca to get away with it or did such bad work that the kidnappers got away with it. If he didn't really want to work beside her every day either, he might be waiting for her to fail.

"Do you see her?" Becca asked. The tears for Gabriel had dried, but her voice still quavered with the shocks of the past twenty-four hours. "There's the car pickup dismissal officer."

"There's the *what*?"

"The teacher assigned to release the kids. They have to know every authorized pickup person by sight—they keep it classy here, no numbers or codes. For Taylor that's me, Hunter, or Jenny, and it nearly requires an act of Congress to make additions or subtractions."

"Wow."

Becca stepped out of the SUV and waved wildly to a ponytailed young woman who scanned the perimeter with a tired but razor-sharp gaze. The woman waved back, then spoke to someone behind her, inside the building.

Ellie's cousin dropped back into the driver's seat and the air-conditioning. "Remember when we were kids and we just walked out of school and no one paid any attention to where we went?"

"Yep."

"Between pedophiles and acrimonious divorces—and we have plenty in DC—those days are over."

With all the children in the same clothing and of approximately the same height . . . Ellie trained her eyes to find a skirt, a drag-behind backpack, and a long braid. There—no.

"I don't know what to make of Mason's hair on the note. Though we've said all along it had to be someone who knows the house," Becca said.

"Mmm-hm." *But it might not be Mason's hair.* Three kids by the fountain . . . but none with Taylor's book bag. A longish braid by the side steps . . .

"They had to be really confident to have mailed that note before they even took him."

"True." The kid towing her wheeled backpack down the short flight of steps could be Taylor. A little stocky, the braid twitching while the ponytailed woman broke up a scuffle between two boys. Taylor Carlisle's tie remained perfectly centered, and she chased no one. "Is that her? On the steps?"

Becca peered. "Yeah, that's her. I can see that neon scrunchie from here. Would you go get her—I'll signal the dismissal officer. I'm going to have to move up in another second. And the other parents are probably wondering why there's a car with a guy who's not picking up a kid behind me. They'll be calling the cops on him in another minute."

Ellie had to laugh at the idea of a concerned parent reporting Agent Tyler as a suspicious person. She slipped out of the SUV into the afternoon heat and headed for Taylor. The well-made car had muffled the noise that now exploded around her, shrieks and honks and the pounding of little feet along the sidewalk. She stepped onto the grass, feeling guilty for walking on such perfectly green blades, wondering what Rachael wasn't telling them. Ellie had examined hairs in her day, and felt certain any expert should be able to tell the difference between newborn and mature hairs.

Dr. Davies suspected someone in the Carlisle household constructed that note. Someone like Becca, or Taylor—or her. Ellie had not been aware of Mason's existence until after the note had been mailed, but Rachael had no reason to believe that. Or the FBI agents. For all they knew, Ellie could have been following her cousin's life from afar, keeping up with the society pages and the congressional news, using the law enforcement agencies she worked for to keep tabs on them, sinking into envy of her rich cousin with the famous husband and the beautiful children, all the things that Ellie didn't have—

Up ahead, a teacher manning the sidewalk patted Taylor's shoulder, and they took a few steps down the sidewalk—*not* walking on the grass. Had Ellie missed a sign to that effect?

Or, perhaps, Rachael and the FBI agents thought Ellie and Becca might still be sworn besties, the way they were at twelve, when there was nothing they didn't know about each other. If that were so, Ellie would be exactly the person to whom Becca would turn for help covering up her crime. Or her daughter's crime.

Taylor and her teacher turned away from her at the sidewalk, away from the line of pickup cars. And Ellie's chest seized up with a terrible foreboding.

"Taylor!" The name ripped from her throat unbidden, cutting through the cacophony of voices around her, and her body erupted into a dead run. Her feet slammed at the trimmed grass, and in her state of heightened awareness, she could hear tiny divots as they were dug up by her toes. The groundskeeper would be mad.

Up ahead, both Taylor and the teacher—woman, probably not a teacher—turned. The girl's step slowed, but the woman reached out with more than a friendly pat this time. She clamped one hand on Taylor's forearm and nearly wrenched her off her feet.

The woman began to run, giving Taylor no choice but to run as well, still dragging her wheeled book bag behind her.

Ellie screamed the girl's name again, not so much for Taylor's sake, but for Becca's, and Michael's. They must have seen, they must be pursuing as well, but she couldn't take even a split second to glance behind to see.

Only thirty or so yards separated them. Surely, she could—

The woman tried to pick Taylor up, forcing her to drop the book bag, but now Taylor struggled. Ellie saw her pushing at the woman's shoulders with both hands, heard her yelling. The woman's pace slowed—Taylor was four and a half feet and eighty or so healthy pounds.

But Ellie saw where they were headed. A white van idled at the curb, the side door slid open. A man stood next to it, watching this drama with both fists pressed to his mouth—not a man, a boy.

The woman couldn't make it, not with Taylor. She made a decision and let go of the girl, unceremoniously dropping her in the grass and speeding off without a hitch in her stride. Taylor barely stayed on her feet, only to be nearly pummeled by Ellie in midflight.

Ellie grasped Taylor's shoulders. The girl sucked in a breath, too terrified even to cry. "Stay with your mom," Ellie ordered, seeing Becca approaching only steps behind the FBI agent. Then she turned and ran after the would-be abductor.

This woman knew where the children were. She knew where Mason was. Ellie's lungs already ached and her muscles protested from the brief but intense activity, but she would not let her get away.

A last burst of speed and she grabbed the woman, wrapping an arm around her waist and taking her down like a defensive end at the Super Bowl. *I'm glad we're on grass,* she thought as they fell, hoping the earth would keep her from a broken elbow.

But it still hurt plenty when the woman landed on it. Ellie's face slammed into her back, getting a noseful of her dark blue dress—sweat and dust. Then Ellie was up, utilizing her advantage, and her Academy training came back to her in a burst of muscle memory. She locked her feet over each of the woman's thighs as she sat on the small of the woman's back.

But the woman pulled her hands in and used them to push off the ground. She had the muscles to lift both herself and Ellie, like a bucking horse, at least until Michael Tyler snatched them back out from under her again, cuffing her wrists at the small of her back so deftly that Ellie heard the twin clicks before the woman's face hit the grass once more.

Ellie leapt off her as if she were radioactive, her heart pounding so hard she thought it might never catch up. Then she remembered the man at the van—the boy.

She got her feet under her and spread her arms, instinctively bodychecking Taylor and Becca from further attack, but the boy hadn't moved from his spot by the van.

"Don't hurt my mom!" he cried.

# Chapter 32

"Where are the children?" Michael Tyler asked. The interview room had been well insulated and stripped as bare as any on television—four walls, a door, three chairs, and a camera in each corner beaming the proceedings to a monitor in the next room *and* to the forensic lab where Rachael and Ellie could listen. The lack of décor gave the interviewee no way to distract themselves from the hard questions asked . . . and also nothing they could pick up, throw, or use as a weapon.

Though the woman before him didn't look dangerous. Around forty-five, fifty, she seemed all maternal middle age, with a thickened waistline and slightly dowdy hair . . . though her expression didn't match. With cold disdain she said, "What children?"

Luis said, "Your son will be charged as an accessory."

The only information she had spared so far was that the boy was her son. His name was Matthew. Hers was Megan. She sat with her arms wrapped around herself, supporting her breasts under the shapeless prison dress. They had collected her clothing along with her purse, van, and child. Ellie and Rachael had been interested in the trace evidence her dark blue dress might show, while Michael Tyler wanted the psychological benefit of confiscation. The suspect needed to know who had control over the interrogation and who didn't; Michael wanted her to feel vulnerable, separated from everything in her life, up to and including her own choice of underwear.

Ellie and Rachael pored over the clothing and the van as he spoke, three floors down in the secure forensic garage. The van had been old and basic, without anything as wildly helpful as a GPS or a map with notations in the glove compartment, but they seemed to think the dirt in the tire treads or the bugs on the windshield could be clues to the children's location. He wished them luck.

Somewhere in the back of his mind, he wondered if Ellie was more comfortable with yesterday's roles reversed and Rachael now on Ellie's home base. He had been concerned about their professional friction—couldn't blame either one, the whole case was unusual—but today they seemed to be getting on like a house ablaze.

"We'll charge him as an adult," Luis went on.

"But he's not—"

"He's fourteen. We've charged kids younger than that, and federal aggravated kidnapping? At a bare minimum, twenty years. By the time he gets out, all his friends will have already done college and marriage and kids. They'll be working on their first divorce and he'll have no resources and no education to speak of."

"Matt didn't do anything."

"He was serving as your getaway driver in the kidnapping of an eleven-year-old. Maximum sentence, he never gets out. He dies in prison, an old man, without ever having had a high school class or a prom date, a fiancée, a grandchild—"

She clearly cared about her son, but she also clearly thought they were bluffing. "You can't do anything to Matt. He's just a little boy."

The good cop role in their partnership had been abandoned, and Luis' anger seeped through his words. "Who has helped you kidnap four children, almost five."

"Four—"

"He's the pictures Sophie saw online, right? The Liam she thought she was meeting?" Sophie's BFF, Lakeisha, had told them all about "Liam."

A hairline crack shot through the façade. "That wasn't his fault. I did that."

Michael shifted his weight and the chair frame under him groaned its protest. "Thank you for being honest about taking Sophie. We knew that, anyway . . . you and Matt and your van were seen at the ice-cream shop where you left her phone. We also have you on camera abducting Noah Thomas. But Oliver Martinez—was that Matthew?"

The slender boy didn't match witness descriptions, but eyewitness testimony could be notoriously unreliable. The mind went back, colored in details, might make an ordinary workman bigger and badder when seen through the hindsight of frightened parents.

"No."

"So, who was it?"

She stared, but this time the disdain faltered a little. Her gaze fell to the tabletop.

Luis leaned forward with an impatient sigh. "Somebody else from ChildChallenge? Because we've spoken to them. They said you haven't been an active participant in over a year."

Disdain flooded back. "They had no stomach for doing what was necessary."

"They said they kicked you out, asked you not to return."

The crossed arms left her fingers wrapped around the opposite bicep. Now those fingers tightened until the skin underneath them went pale. "I wasn't going to waste time with do-nothings."

"Fine. But what about the baby? Who's taking care of Mason?"

Her head came up, and she did a great imitation of not knowing what he was talking about. "Who's Mason?"

"Four innocent children," Michael said. "If anything happens to even one of them, you will be looking at the death penalty. I'm not saying that to scare you. It's the truth."

She met his gaze. "They are innocent. Their parents are not. All we want them to do is tell the truth."

"Who is we?"

"I'm not going to tell you who my colleagues are."

"Then tell us where the children are. We can't begin to negotiate with you until we get the kids back safely."

"I've already done all the negotiating I plan to. Their parents tell the truth, prove that they're worthy of *being* parents to these children, and they'll be returned." She checked her watch. "They should be getting the texts with those instructions right . . . about . . . now."

"What does that mean, 'the truth'?" Luis had regained control, his voice again calm and steady. Michael wanted, with a desperate passion, to leap over the table and throttle the woman.

She smiled without mirth. "Let me tell you a story."

"No," Michael said. "No stories. Where are the children?"

She went on as if he hadn't spoken. "My daughter, Tina, was a typical teen. Loved 'liking' her friends' posts. Glued to her Instagram account. Enjoyed playing video games. She was a sweet girl, a very girly girl—not interested in shoot-'em-ups, liked the ones with unicorns and kittens and fairies. She started playing a KidFun game, *Blue Planet*. The original version, just as Darnell Thomas began to pump up all the bells and whistles to make it ten times as addictive."

"Noah Thomas's father."

"That's his job. His *job* is to ensnare as many children as possible in the name of the almighty dollar. His own son is an addict and he doesn't even care."

"So you kidnapped Noah to—what? Force Darnell Thomas to redesign a video game?" Michael had encountered many, many motives for crimes in his time, but this one was brand-new.

"Back to my daughter," she continued, maddeningly calm. "Where is Noah?"

"She loved *Blue Planet*. Played it every second she could. Her homework got as sloppy as her bedroom. I couldn't get her out of bed in the morning, not because she was sleeping, but because she was playing that game on her phone under the covers. Thomas *perfected* that addiction algorithm."

"Where—"

"But that wasn't the worst part."

*Never let the suspect control the interview.* There were many times when Michael liked to let the suspect talk—for hours, days if necessary. Give them enough rope, and it would eventually tangle around their feet and take them down. But right now, they didn't have time—those kids could be starving, dehydrated, suffocating in an underground chamber.

But despite himself, Michael waited.

"She found friends through the game, people she talked with online. Instant messaging. Instant connection."

"Megan—"

"She started talking to a boy. Who she *thought* was a boy. Someone who loved the game as much as she did. Then he loved her jokes, the same school subjects she did, the same music, the same art, her cat, her opinions—and, of course, her photos."

Michael could guess where this story would go. Sexual predator, convinced the girl to meet and that it shouldn't matter that he might be thirty years older than he said he was, because they were friends, soul mates, right? Or he convinced her to send nude pictures, then blackmailed her to send more. When she refused, he posted them online, maybe even sent them to her mother. The girl's life became a nightmare, her future a trial. Maybe she couldn't face it and spiraled into self-destructive behavior. Maybe suicide.

Stories like that had become so common, he could write it himself. "I understand. You think if you can defeat the bill allowing direct messaging, it would save children like your daughter. But—"

"No."

"I—what?"

"The direct messaging is just a distraction. A flourish of the magician's cape to get you to look in the wrong direction." When the two FBI agents said nothing, she raised one eyebrow. "Have you *read* the bill?"

"No," Michael said. "No, because, I'll be honest, I don't give a shit about the bill. I'm here to bring those missing children back home to their families, the ones you—"

"The data collection is what it's really about. It's in the fine print," she added, as if throwing a bone to his ego. "Presently, there are rules against gathering the demographics of the players—the platforms can ask only what they need to know to make sure the game is appropriate to the user, and they're supposed to destroy any information they don't need, once that's done. Such as the kid's age, location, grade, gender, hobbies—all the things that are gold to advertisers. And advertisers are the real gold of the platform. The in-game purchases might bankrupt a few players, but the *real* money comes from the corporations that would love to market directly to an eleven-year-old Hispanic hockey-playing boy who likes dogs and Cheetos rather than a generic eleven-year-old in Anywheresville. Comparably, targeted marketing has an astronomical ROI. You see?"

"Yes. So what?"

"The thrust of the bill is to make direct messaging safe, to make the whole game safe, by confirming the player's identities, asking for the parents' IDs, for them to show their face on webcam so they can be compared to their social media via face recognition, to obtain every factoid of the kid's life in order to make sure the eleven-year-old really *is* an eleven-year-old. Sounds like they're trying so hard to be responsible and keep everyone totally safe, right?"

"Where are the children, Megan?"

"What do you think is going to happen to all that data? By current law they need to erase it once the registration process is done, but do you *really* think they're going to take that gold and throw it to the bottom of the ocean?"

"Where are the children, Megan?"

If she felt any pressure from his single-minded questions, she concealed it with more cool than Bond, James Bond. "In this bill, in its fine print, there's a clause to retain the data indefinitely. To, of course, check against future registrations, flag the user if they lie about their age to get into a different game, if they use a friend to pose as their parent. Makes sense, right? Tracking a person through their growth and the changes in their life—he's getting too old for G.I. Joe, let's start him on alt band T-shirts and P90X workouts."

Luis tried: "I understand your concern, but—"

"We're handing them permission to gather every detail of your child's life and sell it to the highest bidder. *That's* what this bill is really about. And the lobbyist's wife will make sure no one will bother to read the fine print. She'll hustle this right through, keep it very simple for her bosses like she's oh so efficient. You don't have to read it, I've prepared a summary! Darnell Thomas created the algorithm. Jason Martinez disguised the data retention policy to look innocuous. Kieu Tran exploded the amount of information the players have to fork over in order to keep playing, layering it into the levels to make it seem fun instead of a massive invasion of privacy."

"You think KidFun is using child-safety procedures to il-legally sell users' private information to advertisers? Is that what you want them to confess to the committee in order to get their children back?"

"Yes." She sat back, perhaps pleased that he finally got it.

"And then you'll release their children?"

"Yes."

Luis said, "What if their statements don't match what you want to hear? What will you do to the children then?"

A flicker of one eyelid, but nothing more. "They will. If they're such *loving* parents. They'd hardly want the buying public to know what hard souls writhe behind KidFun's family façade."

Michael feigned incredulity. "So you think we're going to take you to the Hart Building to listen to their testimony and see if it meets your standards?"

"Of course not. But my colleagues will be monitoring. Committee hearings are streamed live, you know. There's no way for you to find everyone who's watching."

The unfortunate truth: Her team could be anywhere, the kids could be anywhere—in the state, the country, the world. Speaking of data, they needed Megan's—her home, her job, her friends, her bank accounts, her emails, and her texts. They had nothing but a van with a registration that came back to a defunct bakery on J Street and a son too ter-rified to speak. Her purse contained nothing personal and her fingerprints did not match anyone in the system, not even job applicants. If Michael couldn't get her to crack . . .

"I'm sorry about your daughter and whatever the man did to her, Megan, but—"

"He *stole* her. She was a happy, bright child. He took her away from me like he had a *right* to!"

"—but that doesn't justify harming other children."

"I'm not harming them! I'm *saving* them!"

"From their own parents? No matter what you hold them

responsible for, that doesn't justify taking it out on innocent children." She saw herself as a savior to these kids. He had to shatter that image. "They did nothing to you. Oliver is only three and he has epilepsy. If he has an attack—and I can't imagine what would bring one on more than being ripped apart from his family—he could die."

This surprised her, but not in the way he intended. "That's not true."

It wasn't, but he had been out of ideas. "Yes, it is. You spent so much time stalking the parents, maybe you should have done a better job on the kids. Sophie Tran—"

"None of them have any medical issues—and I thought negotiators weren't supposed to lie to suspects." She stated this as incontrovertible fact. Michael felt a stirring of more than embarrassment—here was a clue here, if only he could tunnel over to it.

"How could you possibly know that?"

"Finn assured me of it. They're strong, perfectly healthy children. A day or two in a—a day or two won't hurt them."

"Who is Finn?"

If this had been a slip, it didn't concern her. "He's my source, the one who alerted me to the data collection catch in the first place. He's been invaluable."

"Fabulous. Who is he?"

"I don't know."

"How is that—"

"He only contacts me online from a free email account. I know absolutely nothing else about him, and I don't want to."

Her words were so steady, her gaze so calm, it made Michael think all those words were as true as they were unhelpful. Finn probably did not have the children or she would have encountered him physically at some point. Finn might be an inside man, someone at KidFun who worried about their agenda, or he might be a true believer in the fight against online child exploitation. He might even be from another gaming platform, using a member of a lunatic fringe to ruin rival KidFun's fortunes without having to get his own hands dirty.

Luis said, "It's going to go very badly for you if you don't help us in saving these children."

"They *are* save—"

"Where are they?" Michael demanded, losing what little patience he had left. "I don't care about greedy gaming corporations or the committee hearing or whatever wacko has loaded you up and pulled the trigger. I just want to know where the kids are."

"I'm not going to tell you," she said, uncrossing her arms with the satisfied air of one who holds the highest hand at the table. "And you can't make me."

# Chapter 33

The white van now rested in the middle of the FBI's foren-sic garage like a starlet just emerged from a limousine on Oscar night, the star of the show, extra bright under the spotlights. Ellie approached, wearing a Tyvek jumpsuit. Nice to be back in her own lair, but she absolutely hated having to swaddle herself in the baggy, awkward, unflatter-ing, and sometimes stifling-hot plastic-coated protective clothing. Worse, the lives of four children might be depend-ing on her to tease some useful information out of this hunk of old metal.

Once she started, however, the decade-old habits took over. No matter the urgency, the evidence had to be pho-tographed and documented before she could search. She snapped still photos of the exterior, the handles, the license plate, VIN number bar, dents, scratches, and significant dirt. Then she opened the doors and continued.

Rachael, meanwhile, had begun the paperwork, listing their names, location, date, time started. Then she picked up an alternate light source. Working wherever Ellie wasn't, she moved the wand over the interior. Fingerprints could sometimes fluoresce enough to get one's attention, and other bodily fluids, but unfortunately, so would cleansers, some synthetic fibers, and many other items. She told Ellie that most of the fluorescence she found belonged to large, ill-defined areas of vague reaction, most likely cleaning products used on the upholstery and carpeting or a characteristic of the fabric's construction.

They worked quietly in order to hear the interrogation of Megan, streaming to a nearby monitor via a secure hookup. They hoped she would blurt out a helpful fact—like an address—and make their work redundant. Or, perhaps she'd say something that would make sense in the context, something that would turn their findings into clues. But listening to the woman rant about KidFun didn't raise Ellie's hopes.

Once done with the photos, she took a closer look at the tires. Three were worn Michelins, the tread sanded down to near-dangerous levels, but the fourth had been recently replaced. The deep grooves in the new Firestone on the rear driver's side yielded a tablespoon of dirt and debris. She used a plastic pick to pry the stuff out and drop it onto a sheet of clean paper, while Rachael used clear packaging tape to lift the most recently deposited hairs and fibers off the upholstery.

After that, they each took a side and dusted the vehicle with fingerprint powder from grille to rear bumper, obtaining several prints, but not nearly as many as they would have, had the exterior been new and clean. Years and lack of care had roughened up the finish and the fine coating of dust and water spots made for poor retention of prints. Of course the oppressive humidity of a DC summer hadn't helped either.

While the exterior of a (clean) car is a great surface for prints, the interior is usually a different story. Other than the windows, which adults tend not to touch too often, the rearview mirror, and perhaps the radio screen, every other surface tends to be fabric or textured vinyl—too rough to hold prints of any quality. But they tried.

Ellie stopped inwardly complaining about the Tyvek suit, knowing that without it she would be coated in black powder of such tiny particles that it would be invisible until smeared. She reminded herself *not* to touch her face for any reason until she could get to a ladies' room and wash the entire thing. Otherwise, she'd be walking around with dark smears across her skin, of which no one would inform her until the maximum amount of embarrassment had been reached.

Just another hazard of the job.

Through it all they listened to Megan talk, praying that she would say something useful.

Anything.

Michael and his partner took a quick break, then regrouped in the hallway. Luis told him, "I checked with research, they traced the former bakery owner, who's now running a restaurant in Brooklyn. He says he sold his old delivery van a year ago for cash to 'some guy,' didn't know said guy, never changed the registration. He gave a description which could be the one who snatched Oliver or could be about any other guy in the world."

"Let's hope the two docs come up with something. Ready to tackle the kid?"

"Yeah . . . we'll go softball. I've had Duffy babysitting and he says the boy is answering anything and everything, totally cooperative—unfortunately, doesn't know much. He gave their address and there's a team there now, but so far, they're coming up empty. There's no sign of the kids having been there and no records relating to another property. No communications with her 'colleagues.' She doesn't even own a computer or tablet, doesn't have a car. She's got bank accounts with small amounts, apparently getting by on some sort of pension or trust fund payments, but nothing out-sized."

"The boy's got to know something. His mother doesn't seem like the type to keep her thoughts to herself."

"Let's find out." They strode into another interview room, this one meant to put someone at ease rather than intimidate. It had a window, a couch, end table, lamp, even magazines. Comfy, but also on camera, also streamed. Matthew sat on the sofa and the two men each took a straight chair. He seemed a picture of anxiety, legs pressed together, arms pulled into his body, leaning forward with his elbows propped on his knees as if he no longer had the strength to hold himself upright.

"We need you to tell us where those kids are, Matt," Michael said.

"I don't know." His voice described all the misery he felt. "I'd tell you if I did."

"Where does she meet her—friends?"

"I don't know. She talks on the phone to them a lot." Techs upstairs had the phone now, but said it would take time to get around the passcode. The son didn't know it and insisted he would tell them that if he did as well. "She met a guy in a park once, when I had a soccer match."

"When was that?"

"Last year. I mean, school year—May, I guess."

"They ever come to your apartment?"

"No. Unless it's when I'm at school." He rubbed one red-rimmed eye, the picture of exhaustion.

"You don't have a computer at your apartment? Tablet? Smartphone?"

Matthew shook his head to each, touched a growing pimple on his chin. "You guys took my phone—it's one of those super-basic things that old people use. No data."

Luis said, "Your mom doesn't own a car. Does she ever borrow one from somebody?"

"No. We take the Metro everywhere."

"Who's Finn?"

A blink. "This guy she talks to online. He told her all about the KidFun people. He lives in Japan, though."

"*Japan?*"

"He said that's why he mostly contacted her at night."

Michael did some quick calculations and found that consistent with international time zones. "What has she told you about these children?"

The boy gave a classic teen shrug. "That their parents are not keeping them safe. That their parents are exploiting them and all kids, and if this bill passes, it will be like a billion times worse than it already is. She's . . ." Words failed him.

A nutcase, Michael thought.

Luis said, "We realize she's a little fanatical on the subject. She told us about your sister."

Matthew covered his face with both hands and groaned, loudly enough that the two men exchanged a glance.

Luis said, "I know it must be a painful memory—"

"*No.* No, it's not, she—she just goes on and *on* about that."

"Do you think she's doing all this because of your sister?"

"No. Yes, probably, but—look." The boy spoke with sudden force. There might be a great deal he didn't know, but he knew this. "There's nothing wrong with my sister. Tina met a guy online, they started dating, she married him. She's perfectly happy, but Mom, well, he took her baby girl away from her, so he's a terrible guy."

What?

Michael always worked to keep expression from his face, but this time he couldn't help it. He turned to Luis, jaw slack. The daughter was *alive*? "Where *is* your sister?"

"She lives in Richmond. She's a nurse."

Luis leaned forward. "How old was she when she met her husband?"

Another shrug. "She's twenty-four now, so—twenty-two?"

"How old is her husband?" Michael had been picturing a middle-aged pedophile.

"He's pretty old," Matthew conceded, screwing up one eye in concentration. "Like, twenty-seven?"

The two agents exchanged a glance, reassessing. Luis said, "And—your mother knows this, right? That Tina's safe? Happy?"

"Of course she knows! Tina comes by to visit, takes us to breakfast sometimes on Sundays. Mom won't even talk to her husband, but I do. He's an okay guy."

"The way your mother spoke of her—"

"That's what I mean! I'm so sick of hearing about it. Mom's convinced that she was brainwashed by the internet somehow and that's why she left home. My mom"—he paused, caught between loyalty and honesty—"is a little crazy."

*3:35 p.m.*

Rachael had paused to take a call. Ellie heard her say, "Really? Are you sure . . . Sorry, sorry. But how? Wasn't it sealed?"

She disconnected. Ellie waited for an update, but Rachael stared into space, lost in thought. "Well?" she finally demanded as Megan's interrogation concluded.

"My lab completed the tests on Gabriel's samples. He was killed with an amatoxin, amanita phalloides."

"Death caps?"

"Yeah. Mushrooms."

"Are they sure?"

"That's what I asked, and got an earful. Which translated to: Of *course* they're sure."

"It would have to be a massive dose, to work so fast. Usually, people linger for days, can even be saved if the situation is caught early enough. Any idea how it was ingested? What was in his stomach?"

"It had been largely empty, so it was hard to tell. But they tested everything at his townhouse that seemed recently used." Rachael seemed to be watching her with great attention. "It turned out to be in the Gatorade."

Ellie felt her jaw fall open. "What? How . . . Wait, that bottle was sealed. I heard it crack when he opened it."

"My toxicologists pulled the bottle and looked at the cap under the stereomicroscope. Apparently, it had been resealed. Caps like that are connected to the ring around the neck of the bottle with tiny plastic bridges that break when you twist it. Someone melted just enough new connections to make it seem sealed. If he had looked at it under magnification, it would have been obvious, but who would do that?"

"Huh. So it looks like product tampering."

"Maybe."

Ellie shook her head. "But right before the hearing? Way too coincidental."

"I couldn't agree more."

"Plus with a product sitting in someone else's house?" Ellie was thinking out loud. "Someone from Megan's group got into the house to take Mason. Did they take the time to leave a doctored bottle as well? And were they trying to kill Becca or Hunter? For all they knew, Taylor might drink it! But how would they know that size and flavor would be there? Unless they saw Becca buying it at the grocery, or worked somewhere that delivered it."

"Jenny, the nanny, would know," Rachael said. She sounded as though she had no enthusiasm for the idea. "And she would know only Gabriel liked them. She's also out of the country with the perfect alibi and could have coached Megan on how to get into the house without getting caught. But what possible motive would she have?"

"I don't know." Ellie tried to fight the wave of despair trying to wash over her. "None of this makes any sense. It feels like we're still missing a huge piece of this puzzle."

"I agree. What made you collect the bottle? We would have never known where the poison came from if you hadn't collected it."

"Force of habit, I guess." *Because I think my cousin isn't telling me all she knows, and neither do you.* Ellie had no rational explanation for the quaking at the rock bottom of her stomach, and her words sounded lame even to her. "I figured it had to be poison and knew we'd be looking for a pathway. That was the only thing I'd seen him consume, and those drinks clearly were there for only him."

She couldn't identify the look on Rachael's face. The Locard dean had either decided that Ellie was completely innocent of all involvement—or was the mastermind behind the whole inexplicable scheme. But in the meantime, they had no choice but to go back to work.

Rachael swabbed the steering wheel and each interior handle for contact DNA. The swabs all turned black from the fingerprint powder, but that would not preclude getting a profile. The powder wouldn't interfere with the results.

Meanwhile, Ellie constructed the vacuum with its sterile filter screen and gave the van carpet the cleaning it had needed for at least a year. The dust, fibers, hairs, and dirt filled up the clear plastic section between the hose and the motor.

All the while she wallowed in the acute awareness that *this was taking too long.* Usually, such work was done after a suspect had been apprehended or a victim found, and the evidence gathered to build a case. The circumstances here were different. The fates of four young children depended on her correct interpretation of this evidence *right now.*

At the back of the vehicle bay sat a series of tables, outfitted with microscopes, stereomicroscopes, and everything else they could need to pick apart trace evidence and package it for further analysis. Rachael had already started on the dirt from the rear driver's-side tire.

Trace evidence was a bit like buried treasure. If the dirt, for instance, had only bits of asphalt or a stone or two, perhaps the kind of clean mud that could be picked up anywhere in the country, it would not help them. But if it contained something more specific, perhaps it could narrow the search to an area: a mineral only found in a certain quarry, a paint only used at a certain factory. The actual soil could give them a clue as well, but they'd probably need to find a forensic geologist for that level of detail. Again, they did not have time for that.

"There's fine shards of glass here, in two layers. There's something on each layer, running at right angles—how much you want to bet it's transparent semiconductors and these are pieces of Noah Thomas's cell phone screen?"

"I will not take that bet," Ellie said, settling down at another stereomicroscope with the vacuumings. "Could ICP identify the shards as matching his phone?" She referred to glass analysis via inductively coupled plasma spectrometry.

"The model, probably. I don't know how much variation there is from phone to phone. It could prove this van abducted Noah . . . except we *already know that*." She ground out the last three words. Frustration gripped them both.

"Yep. Great evidence for a trial—which is really not our concern at the moment."

"What do you have?"

Ellie said, "Lots of stuff. Animal hairs, human hairs, pollen . . . and feathers."

"Maybe Megan has a dog and a bird?"

"I don't think so. The hairs have a long root, but not quite like a dog's, and it's so thick. I think it's a horse's, or maybe a cow's."

Rachael sat back. "Really?"

Ellie scooped some of the debris—there was plenty—into a new petri dish and handed it over to her. "Take a look at this."

For ten minutes they used plastic picks and tweezers to examine items, transferring some to slides and making wet mounts to use the transmission microscope, using their phones to look up reference images for comparison.

"Definitely a cow's," Rachael said. "And I think some bits in the tread could be manure."

"Plenty of farms in the area. She's abducting the kids in this van, so she's got to be taking them to where they're being held. Or a transfer point, at the very least. I think I have pea pollen over her."

"What?"

"Peas. Like green peas. They sort of look like little hoagy rolls—at least according to my great good friend Google."

They worked in silence for a while, picking minuscule bits of plant and animal life out of the piles and separating them into the plastic dishes. One or two pieces of a certain leaf could have been picked up anywhere, but a goodly number of one particular species would be more significant.

*Had* to be, because they really needed a break.

All the while a monitor broadcasted young Matthew's interrogation as he explained about his mother's obsessions and how a mysterious benefactor named Finn gave her all the support she needed to put them into action.

Ellie had accumulated a pile of small seeds. "I've got a bunch of this. It looks familiar, but I can't quite place it, and searching football-shaped seed brings up a tidal wave of possibilities."

Rachael glanced at it. "Dill. I ought to know, my mom uses enough of the stuff."

"That makes sense—why I wouldn't know, I mean. Not a fan."

"Lots of twigs, pieces of branch . . . too small for me to tell . . . You found any white flowers?"

"Yeah," Ellie said. "Pieces of something white, like a cluster of thin stalks."

"Me too. Crushed, but . . . I think I recognize it. I think it's black cohosh."

"That grows wild, doesn't it?"

"Yes, but it's also cultivated as a dietary supplement. I had a suspected food-tampering case last year, a woman thought her husband was trying to poison her because after meals she'd have nausea, dizziness, wonky vision—turned out she was drugging herself. She'd been taking black cohosh because she thought it would ease symptoms of menopause."

"Ah." A fascinating tour through the microscopy of botanical samples, but Ellie wondered if any of it could help.

"Some people have no ill effects, but some do."

"It's everywhere through these samples. That's an awful lot for just a patch in someone's yard."

"You're thinking a commercial crop," Rachael said.

"Maybe. A farm that produces peas, dill, cohosh, and cows. And chickens—there's too many feathers to belong to a household pet, unless they live in the van."

Rachael's words came faster and stronger as the first ray of hope edged through their gloom. "A farm, even a commercial one, could be isolated, away from the road, no neighbors in sight."

"And still within easy driving distance." The hope moderated. "There are an awful lot of them, once you get outside the city."

"We need the agents. They have the manpower." Rachael picked up her phone.

All this work would prove unneeded if Megan would tell them where to find the children. But from the woman's behavior, from her boldness in trying to take Taylor when she had to know law enforcement would be monitoring the family, from her willingness to use her own son . . . Ellie didn't think she'd give up.

"They should start with ones that have closed, even temporarily. Harvest season is beginning, but I doubt they'd be having customers come to the door while they're hiding a bunch of stolen kids," Ellie suggested.

Her own phone lit up with a text from Becca: **Anything happening? Hearing starts in a half hour.**

As if Ellie might have forgotten.

# Chapter 34

*3:30 p.m.*

Sophie Tran hated it when adults assumed that because she was a girl, she existed for them to dump their kids on. She had a number of aunts and uncles who did just that: The second they stepped into the house, it was: *Go and play with Sophie*, em—as if she really wanted to hang out with their first grader.

And now here she was, a freakin' *prisoner*, and still assigned that role. Clearly, it had been left to her to figure out how to feed, clean, and amuse a traumatized three-year-old who had a *lot* of questions and didn't hesitate to ask each and every one. Noah was nice to the kid, telling him not to worry in a soothing tone he hadn't used with Sophie, but feeding the boy the rest of the brownies and wiping off the little hands with the sanitizer was up to her. She used the brownies whenever the tears came and Oliver had decimated their supply. More than that, he had seriously disrupted their escape plans.

The preschooler could sure walk okay—he hadn't stopped moving around the barn since he'd arrived—but she doubted he could run very fast on such tiny legs. They'd either have to go slow, or . . .

"If we waited until dark, then we could get across the field without anyone seeing us."

Noah shook his head. "Younger Guy sat out there all night."

Despite the heat in the barn, Sophie stifled a chill. The idea of that horrible man first carrying her and then watching the place she slept all night long filled her with a panic she couldn't name. "He has to sleep sometime."

"Yeah, he laid on a cot out there. But he could wake up at any time."

"What's a cot?"

"It's a . . . fold-up bed. Like a hammock, only it doesn't swing."

"Oh."

"Besides, once we got to the woods, we don't know where to go, and we wouldn't be able to see anything."

"We don't know where to go now."

"We can at least follow the sun, so we know we're going in the same direction. Not walking in circles."

Oliver interrupted, coming by to pat Sophie's knee to get her attention. "Where my mom? I want to go home."

"I know, kid. We all do. We're going to run away from here and try to find her, okay?"

He considered this, the tiny nose wrinkling in concentration. "I not supposed to run away."

"This is different. We want to run *to* your mom."

Still confusing, but if it involved his mother, he was in.

"Let me pick you up," she said, and, being a very small child, he did not find this request strange. She had held plenty of babies—at any large family gathering her nana would find one to thrust into Sophie's arms, then stand back and beam. *It's a baby! Isn't that great? Wouldn't you like to have one or two or five?* Sophie would hold the tiny human long enough not to hurt Nana's feelings and then give it back. They were cute, but not *that* cute.

Oliver, however, seemed a lot heavier than he looked. Maybe he was denser than she had expected, or maybe when she picked up her little cousins, she wasn't planning to make a frantic escape across open farmland carrying them? That might color her observations.

She let the kid slip to the ground again and considered asking Noah, now peering out the crack by the door, if he could take him. Noah was skinnier than she was . . . yet he played sports like her, so he probably had a lot more muscle than she could see.

But Noah turned and gestured for her to join him. She scurried up to another crack to see both Younger Guy and Old Guy in conversation, not four feet from the barn door.

"I don't know why she's not back," Old Guy complained.

Younger Guy said, "Probably ran into traffic and stayed there. It's about to start."

"That wasn't the plan," Old Guy said in the furious kind of tone her one uncle used sometimes, the tone that made her aunt look really worried. "And she's got the damn van!"

She felt a shove and a soft head as Oliver pushed in between her and Noah, not to be left out of whatever the big kids were doing.

"So, what do you want to do?"

The gray-haired man thought a minute, then said, "We don't have much of a choice at this point. We'll have to take my car."

"Are you sure? If she's been compromised—"

"One way or the other . . . it's time to get rid of *them*."

"Finally!"

Each head swung until they stared at the barn door, and

Sophie swore they could see through each crack and crevice into her very brain.

A terrible certainty seized her.

"They're going to kill us," she said to Noah.

*3:51 p.m.*

Rachael stood over two FBI agents' shoulders as they each searched for where the children might be. The one on the left searched commercial farms in Virginia and Maryland. The way the white van had been popping up to steal children in the city made Rachael believe Megan's headquarters could not be too far away. There weren't too many large ones within reasonable driving distance to DC, but many of the small, artisanal farms that catered to the city dwellers' desire for healthy, "clean" foods.

The agent on her right searched the states' business license sites, cross-referencing the names of farm owners and operators with the names of ChildChallenge activists and those of other civic groups with concerns about online kids' games. Not that they had a roster or some such thing—they had only the names of members quoted in the media or those who had pushed their protest activities until they came to the attention of law enforcement. Megan had not, and there were no matches so far.

Michael Tyler paced behind the three of them, tapping options on his phone, checking texts and emails, hoping for a clue.

"Here's one that mentions black cohosh," the one on the left said. "But . . . no cattle. No chickens."

Her partner said, "Put it in the middle section of the list. Maybe there are chickens for the owner's personal stock. They might not mention it on the website."

Rachael stood there, feeling useless, acutely aware of

every passing second. They were trying to narrow locations in two states down to one likely spot. And there was Delaware, right over the Chesapeake Bay Bridge, and Pennsylvania—

Her phone buzzed at her hip and she checked the screen. Agnes, the digital expert. "What do you have?"

Agnes, of course, would not take offense at the abrupt greeting. She *would* have taken offense at *Hi, how are you?* as a waste of her time. "I've gotten what I can out of Noah Thomas's phone. No calls the day of his disappearance, but there were texts from his father regarding this baseball camp."

"But they weren't from his father."

"Right. Someone spoofed his number."

"That's ille—" She realized too late how stupid that sounded. "What did the texts say?"

Agnes read them all before ringing off, very quickly, in case any of it meant anything to Rachael.

Which it didn't . . . except for one detail. "Michael."

The agent stopped his pacing, while Ellie simultaneously rejoined the group, having returned from a bathroom break.

"Whoever texted Noah Thomas pretending to be his father knew Noah had an iPad Pro."

"So? Every kid must have a tablet these days, and obviously they knew who his father was. That was the whole point. They even knew how to foil that particular school's pickup procedures," he answered.

"They also knew his father's personal phone number. Surely, he keeps that off the internet."

"You think Megan's group has a spy at KidFun?" Ellie asked. "Someone close enough to the execs to know what kind of tech their kids have?"

"It would make sense. They found Sophie via the game,

that's simple enough, but they knew which playground Oliver's nanny took him to every day and went prepared with red paint. Sure, maybe they just followed her for a day or two—"

Ellie said, "Or they had a lot of inside information. They were confident Noah wouldn't question the idea of a baseball camp, wouldn't call his parents directly at some point."

Michael said, "The school has a strict no-phone-conversations rule during the school day. Parents have to call the office and actually pull their kid out of class or recess if they want to speak to them."

"But how would they know Sophie wouldn't tell her mother about Liam?"

Rachael said, "That's a little less risky, given how much preteen girls love keeping secrets. If her BFF hadn't spoken up, we *still* wouldn't know what happened to Sophie Tran."

"I think that's it," the agent on the left-side terminal said, more to her partner than the people waiting behind the two of them. "That's everything within seventy miles that has peas, cohosh, dill, free-range chickens, and fresh corn-fed beef."

The one on the right checked his list. "I've got nothing. None of the owners comes up on the list of activist arrests."

"How many places we looking at?" Michael said. "Twenty? Thirty?"

"Three," the female agent said.

The furrow between the tall man's brows smoothed some. "Really? Only three?"

As she wrote the addresses and owners' names on a piece of copy paper, she added, "One has apparently shut down, though."

The other agent had been reading over her shoulder and checking his own lists. "License is still active. Should have renewed last month, but they have a grace period."

"Their website hasn't been updated in over a year and the home page has a note about appreciating all their past customers. It might be a dead end."

Michael snatched the piece of paper, a lifejacket to a drowning man. "Or it might be perfect."

Ellie said, "I'm coming with you."

"No." He looked at her face and softened his voice by a half tone or so. "These people are serious enough to kidnap four kids—who knows what they'll do if confronted?" She bristled until he added, "Besides, if this isn't the place, we'll have to go on to the next place. And they could all be wrong and the kids are just in a messy house with people who go to a lot of farmers' markets."

"I know, but . . ." She stopped, obviously unable to think of a good enough *but*.

"I'll make sure the scene is disturbed as little as possible until you can process. And"—he gazed at her directly, his eyes dark and piercing—"I'll call you immediately if we find Mason."

*Alive or dead,* he meant. "Do that."

As the FBI agent turned to go, Rachael said, "I'm going to the committee hearing. I can't do anything more here, and if Megan's group is planning a confrontation, it will be there."

Ellie said, "Let's go—it might be faster to walk."

"In this heat?" Rachael said, and punched the button for the elevator. "Not on your life. I'll drive."

# Chapter 35

*4:10 p.m.*

Rachael had no problem finding a parking space near the Hart Senate Office Building. At four o'clock a good deal of DC workers had already finished their meetings and packed up their work to take home; schools' field trips were over and the tourist buses on their way back to hotels. The whole building smelled like paper and floor cleaner.

A text to Becca brought her out to meet them. A few minutes later they were cutting across the center atrium, Ellie's boots squeaking on the polished marble floor. A sculpture rested in the center of it, black sheet metal cut into shapes and bolted together, almost as if a little boy had built his own rocket ship out of a cardboard box.

Ellie began: "What is—"

"*Mountains and Clouds,*" Becca said. "The name of it is *Mountains and Clouds.*"

Most of the flat pieces of metal ended in a sharp peak at the top. "I see the mountain part. The rest of it, not so much."

Becca led them through a series of gleaming hallways, occasionally greeting coworkers or acquaintances. She did not bother to introduce them, there wasn't time.

Everyone they passed seemed busy, relatively young, and nicely dressed, Ellie thought. Some seemed too young to work there or anywhere, and she wondered if they were interns or if she was just getting old. Even the middle-aged men and women moved with more energy than expected, and all wore clothes that were businesslike, not luxurious, but with a uniform tidiness. Men wore ties. Women's blouses were tucked, often into skirts. As a world it differed from Ellie's daily experience of cargo pants, plainclothes detectives, undercover narcotics officers, paramedics, bad smells, and blood. A world she suddenly missed. It might not be as hygienic, but it was home.

Becca hustled them through a door into a cavernous room of dark paneled walls and somber wall sconce lighting. Heavy draperies covered floor-to-ceiling windows. A curved bar of the same deep wood spread across one end of the room with at least twenty-five comfy-looking desk chairs behind it, more than half occupied by men and women in suits. More chairs lined all three walls behind this structure. On the floor in front of it sat three less impressive-looking folding tables covered with black cloth, and rows of padded stackable metal chairs.

Clearly, nothing had yet begun. Occupants milled in some type of hanging out posture in these last minutes before the hearing began. Some texted or checked email; some typed on laptops; one read the paper; at least three were on the phone; the rest either chatted with each other or conferred with assistants who hovered over their shoulders. From the numbers Ellie estimated that each senator had at least one assistant in attendance, all to be seated behind the curving desk in chairs lined up along the walls to wait like chambermaids at the queen's bedside.

Hunter stood at the front right table. There he conferred with a willowy woman with jet-black hair and Asian features, a tall Black man, and a heavyset man with dark hair and reddened eyes. Their haggard looks and miserable expressions told Ellie they must be Kieu Tran, Darnell Thomas, and Jason Martinez, trying to figure out exactly what to say in order to get their children back.

Taylor sat at the table, bent over a notebook, creating a sketch in colored pencil. Becca pointed them toward this table and then returned to the dais, behind the huge, curved desk. Taylor had been taken home, calmed down, and pumped up. In fresh clothes and her hair tied back in a bow, she did not seem to bear any ill effects of nearly being kidnapped. As Ellie watched, she looked up and beamed across the room at her mother, happy to be in the thick of things with the grown-ups.

Hunter saw Ellie as they approached, and stepped away from his colleagues. He strode to them quickly, perhaps keeping them out of earshot of the two parents. "Where are the kids?"

Their lack of response answered his question.

"You don't have them yet? Megan didn't confess?"

"We have some good leads," Rachael told him in her calm, commanding tone. She described the winnowing process and that FBI agents would be arriving at the farm at any moment. "Of course we can't be sure that's the right place, but it's well worth a try."

"When will they get there? Will they call us—you—anybody—right away? Hell." He started to glance at the KidFun parents, seemed to prevent himself. "They're so afraid of what's going to happen if they don't say whatever magic words those crazies want to hear. Jason is about to collapse and Kieu is having chest pains."

"We don't get that impression from Megan," Rachael said. "I don't believe she ever intended to harm the kids."

Hunter checked his watch. "Sit with Taylor. *Don't* tell the others who you are."

"But they already—" Darnell Thomas had seen Ellie at his house the previous evening, though they hadn't been introduced. But Hunter had already gone to join Becca for a brief, intense consult.

Ellie watched them, unable to read the expression on her cousin's face. Concern, annoyance, and a touch of . . . relief? Ellie had been correct when speaking to Rachael the day before—she still thought of Becca as she had been at twelve. Becca, now an adult, had outgrown the volatility of childhood, the wearing of her heart emblazoned on one sleeve, and now Ellie had no idea at all what might be in her cousin's mind.

She saw Becca point, subtly, at two different senators, a woman from New Mexico three seats to the chairman's left and a man from Minnesota two seats to his right.

She and Rachael sat at the table with Taylor and the three execs, Ellie wondering how this would look when the news clip was played at any future trial. No matter who would be on trial, the image of her seated with the victim's family would be a testament to her *non*-lack of bias. But she had already been biased by blood, and they wouldn't need photos to prove that. Not that she and Becca looked alike in anything other than the general shape of the nose and jawline. Their eyes weren't even the same color, blues and browns scattered equally among their mothers' clan of Becks. But then eye color didn't work the same way as, say, mitochondrial DNA.

Kieu, Darnell, and Jason had seated themselves and continued talking without noticing the two women.

Ellie did not say anything to Taylor; the girl was quiet and occupied, best to leave her that way. But this lasted only a second or two before the girl looked up; her face glowed to have another family member present. "Hi! Are you going to testify too?"

"No, I'm just here to ... to listen to everyone." Saying *I'm here because one way or another, something bad is going to happen, and I need to be here when it does* hardly seemed like a good idea. The girl chattered on about her mother picking out what clothes to wear. If the afternoon's trauma had frightened her at the time, the bustle of the hearing had erased it.

"They don't usually let kids in here, but I'm more mature than everyone else my age," Taylor informed her.

*And your parents are understandably terrified to let you out of their sight,* Ellie thought as Hunter sat and laid one arm loosely around his daughter.

"That's right, sweetie, but you have to be super quiet. Once we start, no talking or even whispering. Got that? It's very important."

"Right."

"All those people sitting in all those chairs, we want them to listen to us, right? Not sleeping or reading the paper or scrolling Facebook memes."

"Right."

To Ellie, Hunter discreetly nodded at the man in the middle of the dais, the committee chairman. "That's the guy *not* to tick off, Becca's boss, the senator from Missouri. You might have the votes, but he has the gavel. He sets the agenda. If he doesn't like you, you might not even get into this room."

"But you did. I'm sure being married to the policy advisor didn't hurt?"

He took no offense to this. "Of course not. Anyone in government winds up across from their own spouse at some point—DC is a small town with big buildings. Minor conflicts of interest are inevitable. And not relevant here, since she only advises. She doesn't get a vote."

But advisement could be more important than a vote. Who had the ear of the king? Government had always been about access.

The hundred or so chairs had been set up in mostly perfect rows, though only thirty or forty were occupied. Most seemed like DC types, clerks, perhaps interns or students, dressed in ties or skirts and conservative shoes. Two had the skinny notebooks often used by cops and reporters.

The knot clustered around a different table appeared in more casual clothing, but much less casual in attitude, armed with notebooks and folders of clippings. Ellie pegged them for a group of concerned parents, yet they did not pay particular attention to the KidFun execs, so she doubted they were part of Megan's group. They looked around at everyone, equally, as if unsure where or from whom the action might begin.

The man with the gavel gave it a pound or two. Hunter patted Taylor's shoulder absently, warned her that they'd have to be quiet now, and whispered something to Kieu Tran.

"I can't risk my daughter—" she began, but he continued to whisper, to both her and the other two executives. Then they sat back, no less concerned but apparently reassured enough to continue.

The chairman began by thanking his colleagues (and their staff, which she thought was a nice touch) for their presence, and thanking each of the presenters by name. This included the KidFun execs, a man from ChildChallenge, and two women from Campaign for a Commercial-Free Childhood and the Center for Digital Democracy. The chairman expressed his condolences for the death of Gabriel Haller, "who passed away this morning." This elicited a gasp from those at the other table, who clearly had not been informed.

Had that only been this morning? It seemed a century ago.

He went on to give an overview of the agenda. The three other presenters would speak first and then they would move on to Darnell Thomas. He also warned everyone present, sternly, to silence their cell phones. Violations would result in immediate eviction.

"Why is he talking so much?" Taylor complained to her father.

"Because this is how things are done. You have to be quiet now."

"Yeah, I know," she muttered, and went back to her drawing of a winged dragon. Ellie thought it quite good and wished she had one-tenth of that artistic ability, especially at Taylor's age. Even drafts of her crime scene sketches could have been made by a five-year-old, but—good for her—CSI positions were not awarded on artistic merits.

The dragon carried something in its talons, and Ellie squinted at the humanlike form. It had a face and arms and fingers, but the torso and limbs seemed oddly foreshortened, out of proportion to the head.

It looked, she realized, like a baby.

# Chapter 36

*4:27 p.m.*

Sophie and Noah decided that if they each took one of Oliver's hands they could get him to move much faster, even if they had to sort of drag him the way parents sometimes swung their kids between them. They couldn't afford to be particular about how they made their escape, not anymore.

Old Guy had disappeared somewhere, and as Noah and Sophie watched, Younger Guy finally walked off toward the house. They didn't wait for him to get all the way to the porch. They would need every second they could get.

The loose board could be swung to one side and tacked in place using its own nail. Sophie squeezed through first, the rough wood planks scraping her ears. She had read that if your head could fit through a space, then the rest of the body would too, which didn't really make sense because your shoulders were much wider than your head. But her head made it out, eyes blinking in the bright daylight.

Then she dragged her back and her chest—for once, she *wasn't* happy about her growing breasts—through the narrow opening, wood fibers raking along her body and ripping small tears in the nylon fabric of her shirt. But if she, the biggest, could make it, the others could too. Besides, she feared that if Noah went first and she couldn't fit through, he'd leave without her. She wouldn't blame him if he did.

"Hurry, Sophie," Noah urged.

"I'm *trying!*"

The stupid chickens started up before she even got her boobs out, squawking and cackling. She saw that there were only five or six of them, with a narrow coop attached to the wall of the barn and a six-foot-square pen made of chicken wire. Maybe they thought they were going to be fed or maybe a new person to look at was the most exciting thing that had happened to them in months, because they would not shut up about the human being oozing through the barn walls.

"Move, Sophie! Someone's coming!"

Younger Guy must have come back. Maybe he heard them move the plank, or the chickens alerted him. She put her palms on either side of the opening and shoved off, trying to free her hips. Her feet scrambled against the dirt floor, trying to gain leverage, and she accidentally kicked one of the boys. Oliver, to judge from the aggravated howl.

"He's coming in!"

They didn't have a chance now. With a heart plunging to her knees, she realized she had to wiggle *back* into the horrid barn and move the plank back before Younger Guy got inside, so they could stand there and pretend they hadn't been trying to escape, hadn't even thought about it, despite the rips in her clothing and the scrapes that were already starting to bleed.

Her shoulders were still outside with the raucous chickens when the door opened. Through the gap she watched a new guy run in, and OMG, he was way scarier than both Younger Guy and Old Guy put together, a huge man with thin black hair and a scar on his temple.

Sophie pushed with all her might and tumbled out of the barn.

# Chapter 37

"I wish Michael or Luis would let us know if they found the kids," Rachael whispered to her.

"Me too." Ellie checked her screen, though a vibration would have alerted her to a text or call.

"I feel so helpless."

Ellie didn't bother repeating that she did too. She leaned closer to Taylor and asked, "Is that a baby?"

"Yes, that's Mason."

Ellie chose her words, but there were only so many ways to ask it. "Where is the dragon taking Mason?"

"Back to where he lives."

"Your house?"

"No," Taylor said with a touch of impatience. "Where the *dragon* lives."

"Okay. Why?"

As if it should be obvious: "Because that's where Mason's supposed to be."

Hunter gave Ellie a split-second scowl, but she didn't know if he didn't want her interrogating his child or if he didn't want her encouraging the child to talk during the hearing.

The woman from the Center for Digital Democracy stood up, and spoke for several minutes about the pervasive presence of online gaming in children's internet use, statistics showing that a full quarter of all U.S. children engaged in online games, and the addiction algorithm that Darnell Thomas had explained the night before. Her dense speech only lasted three or four minutes. Becca had told her that the most valuable commodity senators have is time—it absolutely could not be wasted. So nearly every witness, unless otherwise arranged, would stick to five minutes or less. It made sense—give experts free rein and they could go on forever. Ellie could happily expound on the basics of bloodstain pattern interpretation for an hour or two or three.

Three senators asked questions about the incentives and virtual "prizes" used to keep the kids hooked and extend playing time. The senator from New Mexico asked if making a game too fun to put down wasn't the point of the game.

Though after listening to Darnell Thomas explain his work, Ellie wondered where fun left off and blatant manipulation began.

It *was* just like a trial, with the proposed bill or resolution or amendment on the hot seat. She had never really thought about it, and assumed that bills were written up and read by the members of Congress, then voted on. But no one could possibly read every word of the ten thousand–plus bills sent to Congress each year, even if they were so inclined. Ellie doubted that even the most conscientious would be so inclined.

Instead, first they assigned the proposed legislation to committees; the committees took the role of both a detective unit, investigating, researching, consulting experts in the field, *and* the jury that would eventually decide the bill's fate. The trial/hearing gave them an opportunity to question/cross-examine the witnesses, both saving the senators the need to read every word of the documents and giving them the opportunity to ask for facts that perhaps the submitted documents had glossed over. The pro vs. con witnesses sat at separate tables.

The committees were necessary because, like a trial, the company representatives and other interested parties were not unbiased. They *did* have a dog in this fight. And while the experts hired might be impartial, those hiring them—like prosecutors and defense attorneys—might choose only those sympathetic to their cause. But also the committee could request any witness themselves, should they have concerns about one side loading the deck.

And after that, the committee would vote, but only as a grand jury, deciding whether the item has enough merit to get to the trial jury vote of the entire Congress plus the president. They served as gatekeepers, just as detectives have to decide if they have enough to ask for an arrest and the prosecutors have to believe they can present a sufficiently compelling case to a court process. As Becca had said, time was the most precious commodity of the senators, the experts, the committee, the Congress, the president, and the taxpayers footing the bill for it all. If the item in question would waste it, then the group would cut their losses and let it "die in committee."

The senator from Minnesota asked if an addiction algorithm wasn't just sensible business practice—the same question Darnell Thomas had posed.

Ellie thought: Becca's job as policy advisor would be to research the issue's details, the pros and cons. A vital and necessary position, just as attorneys had investigators to go out and do the legwork, run down witnesses and get their statements, check records, and so on. The senators couldn't possibly have time to do that themselves, not for every issue they had to debate—there were ten or twenty different committee hearings every day, three days a week. A senator would serve on two or three. It added up to a lot of information and a lot of time.

So policy advisors would give them a summary—and maybe a hint of what needed clarification. The question might sound familiar because Becca had fed it to the committee. It was her job.

Hunter's job, as he had explained, was to treat the hearing like a drama, to create interest and tension with a well-written script.

The woman from Campaign for a Commercial-Free Childhood spoke about data mining by online gaming concerns. The games asked for much more information than they needed merely to be sure the player was age-appropriate, gathering all sorts of demographic facts—not for safety, but in order for advertisers to bombard the kids with targeted pitches. Yes, advertising might be a fact of life, always filling children with the idea that they *have to have* these shoes or this toy or this waist diameter to be happy, but that didn't mean consumers had to make it easy for them.

"But," the senator from New Mexico asked, "aren't platforms required or at least advised to verify that the player is who they say they are? Some now asked for FaceTime with the kid's parents or at least copies of their ID cards, with the goal of keeping the kid in only age-appropriate games and to make sure the kid really *is* a kid."

"Yes," the woman said, "but all that data is supposed to be destroyed after verification is complete, not sold to advertisers." Her passion on this topic seemed more than genuine; her voice became tight and shrill, nearly tearful.

*And she is right,* Ellie thought. Hunter and Becca had said so, and had also made it clear they had no intention of discarding such lucrative information.

"There have been cases," the woman went on, "where the

data wound up on the dark web as a flea market of victims for every pedophile out there."

"*What* cases?" the senator from Minnesota asked.

As she paged through sheaves of paper looking for the answer, another senator asked about the verification process and how many platforms were conducting such thorough examinations.

Kieu Tran leaned toward Hunter, and Ellie heard her whisper: "What am I supposed to do, just agree with her? The cameras are running. W—whoever has the kids is going to know instantly what happens here."

"Just tell the truth," Hunter said.

"I'm not risking my child!"

"Of course not. The FBI's following a lead, we should be hearing from them any minute."

"Noah?" Darnell Thomas asked.

"It's going to be fine," Hunter said, an apparently unwarranted sentiment that reassured no one. "Just hang in there. I'm going to see if I can get an update."

He left the table and headed for the back of the room before Ellie could ask where he planned to go.

The man from ChildChallenge stood up and related several tales of school-age children, both girls and boys, having been lured into a "relationship" via direct messaging with someone posing as a friend. Online gaming provided children entertainment and communication across cultures and borders, but it needed to be locked up as tightly as a school building in this age of mass shootings. He went a little over his five minutes and the chairman gave him the fish eye, but didn't cut him off.

The senator from New Mexico checked her notes, then asked with an uncertain air: "Did your organization have a member named Megan Anderson?"

"No—wait. Yes, we did." His expression grew wary. "We

received another inquiry about her today . . . She was asked to leave the group about a year ago."

"She is no longer with your organization?"

"No."

"Why not?"

Another senator interrupted to ask who this Megan was, and why had she come up? A different senator who had been surreptitiously scrolling through his phone set it down.

The woman from New Mexico persisted. "Why not, sir?"

"She got—radical. We wanted to picket the headquarters of companies like KidFun. She wanted to slash all their tires. We wanted to monitor proposed bills and amendments, like this one here. She said we should hire hackers to install ransomware on their website, and use the ransom payments to give all parents of minors a free mirroring program to transmit them a copy of every interaction their child had online. We found her ideas a little . . . concerning."

"Are you aware that four children of KidFun execs were abducted yesterday?"

The man's face froze, his mind taking those words and trying to rearrange them into a pattern that made sense. At this task, his mind failed. "*What?*"

The two women next to him appeared equally confused.

The scattered spectators murmured, the reporters scribbling furiously. Every senator sat up straighter. The chairman gave a single, sharp rap with his gavel.

"Megan and other ChildChallenge members kidnapped the children in order to force their parents to change their testimony today. Those are some of the parents right there." She pointed at three executives. All three paled and looked around in near panic, wondering what this revelation would do to their children's safety.

Where had Hunter gone?

"Ma'am," the man said, "I have no idea what you're talking about."

"That's not going to be sufficient, Mr.—"

A door banged at the back of the room. Excited footsteps made Ellie turn—to see Sophie Tran and Noah Thomas making a beeline for their parents, who leapt to their feet, stumbling over their chairs to get free. Behind them, Hunter strode along with a satisfied smile on his face, carrying Oliver Martinez, though once the little boy caught sight of his father he nearly leapt from Hunter's arms to get to the floor and run.

Michael Tyler followed with a much less happy expression. He probably hated the lack of proper procedure in this case—the children, as any victims would, should have been separated and their statements obtained, a process that could take hours. They should have been checked by doctors and counselors, given a private moment to be reunited with their families. But not even he could have resisted the plea of such children for the only thing they wanted—to feel their parents' embrace once again. Luis, however, couldn't help but beam.

The screams and excited chatter as Noah and Sophie were also swept up told everyone in the room what had just occurred. The chairman didn't even bother to ask for order right away. Ellie noticed Becca filling him and the other senators in on who was who, pointing from the dais.

Create drama. Get their attention.

Rachael clapped Michael on the arm in congratulations. "Thank heavens for black cohosh and green peas."

"*Mason,*" Ellie demanded, though she already knew the answer from the heavy way he turned to her.

"No. There's no sign he was ever there. The two men we caught on the property denied any knowledge of him."

"But—"

"I don't know why they'd lie, when they admitted taking the other three."

*They would if Mason had been killed,* she thought. But

the children seemed fine. Sophie's shirt had some small tears across the back with thin scratches on the skin underneath, and all three appeared dirty and wearied beyond exhaustion, but otherwise physically unharmed.

"Not that they could deny it under the circumstances," Michael went on. "According to what they started blurting out as soon as we showed up, they were about to drive the kids to Sophie's ball park and let them go. The hearing had begun, the KidFun execs had been taught a lesson, project ended. I think they knew things had gone sideways when Megan didn't return with Taylor. They were afraid to call her phone and have us trace it, and assumed she'd confess and give it all up—their only chance was dumping the kids and running far and fast. One or both of them had been panicking enough to call in an anonymous tip about where the kids were. We were practically there by the time the office relayed it to us, but clearly someone had lost their nerve."

"Yes, but 'dumping the kids' could have meant—" She stopped, realizing Taylor stood at her elbow, though she seemed to be asking too many questions of her father to overhear. "Why did you bring them here?"

"I know," he said. "Hardly protocol. I guess your cousins and KidFun have deep pockets and many friends, and this is a city that's accustomed to making allowances for people who think they're too unusual for usual procedure."

"We've got two doctors and the child trauma team on their way here," Luis added.

Last-minute rescues aside, the business of the country went on. The chairman eventually rapped his gavel and said, "Let me get this straight. Someone kidnapped these three children and demanded their parents do—what?"

"Make statements to agree with our esteemed colleagues"— here Hunter waved a hand at the table of child-safety advocates—"and say that our games manipulate children into addiction and our security procedures are designed to gather data for advertising."

*Except that's actually true,* Ellie thought. *Isn't it?*

"That's the craziest thing I've ever heard," the chairman said, and suggested that the KidFun execs take their children home. When Hunter asked, he gave the lobbyist permission to present the execs' statements with the assurance that he could handle any follow-up questions. Apparently lobbyists were not normally permitted to present testimony at hearings, though Hunter partly qualified as an owner of the business.

Luis guided the execs and the three children toward the door, to the waiting arms of the FBI doctors and debriefers. It wouldn't be a simple matter of going home for a shower and some dinner and a bedtime tuck-in to undo all the damage, but the reunion itself did most of the work.

With the children returned, the threat over, the KidFun agenda was back on. Get the ban thrown out, reinstate direct messaging, and require users to overshare the personal info that would provide so much lovely advertising revenue. Hunter could now play to win, and win big.

But *Mason* hadn't been returned. Ellie tried to catch Becca's attention, somehow express her sympathy, but Becca's head stayed bent over the paperwork in her lap. Taylor continued to draw, apparently not connecting the appearance of the three kids with the disappearance of her brother.

"I think this is an excellent illustration of the kind of over-reaction that we see from people who supposedly care about protecting children," he began. When the man from Child-Challenge began to object, he was warned to wait his turn in accordance with committee rules.

"It's also an excellent illustration that dangers to children can come from anywhere. Noah Thomas had been lured through a simple text message, not an online gaming platform created by hard souls interested only in commerce."

Though, Ellie thought, Sophie *had* been tricked via a game, using the direct message feature. She wondered when Liam first contacted the girl. It must have taken some time to gain her trust. Megan had been planning this for a while.

But how would she know what game Sophie played? Kids all used screen names, right? Maybe profile pics, so Megan would know when she found the right girl. That the child of a KidFun exec would be playing KidFun games seemed a very likely bet. But KidFun produced close to a hundred different games—what did she do, cruise through each one until she stumbled onto Sophie's participation?

"We know that there's three types of lies," Hunter was continuing. "Lies, damn lies, and statistics. We can make numbers say anything we want, but here's the ones compiled by the Center for Child Advocacy. When these extra verification measures, such as requiring copies of the parents' IDs and FaceTime interviews with the players, were introduced, complaints of inappropriate contact plummeted from nineteen percent to two."

And, as Rachael had asked, how did she know Noah Thomas had an iPad Pro? She could have guessed, but that would risk mentioning the wrong one and tipping the boy off.

Hunter held up his fingers in a 1960s peace sign. "Two," he said again.

*Keep it simple. Give them a short statement that will stick in their minds, even if they don't really understand it.*

*Even if you make it up on the spot,* Ellie thought, *would anybody check?*

He violated the "simple" rule a second later by relating the number of children in the country who play online games and a few biographies of kids who were isolated by geography or disability or bullying, for whom the online interactions were their only outlet. A few bad apples shouldn't ruin it for children like his daughter. He gestured toward her with the clear message: If this were harmful, would I let my own kid do it?

Two senators had follow-up questions for Hunter regarding the advanced verification procedures and how they differed from current practices.

The two women from the advocacy groups tried to ask a few questions, but didn't get very far. The man from Child-Challenge sat with his head in his hands, no doubt overwhelmed with thoughts of damage control, wondering if repair was even possible.

Finally, finally, the chairman tapped his gavel and declared the hearing concluded. The senators voted by ayes and nays, the bill winning approval to move to the full Senate floor by a tally of seventeen to five, with one abstention and five absent. The man from ChildChallenge left before the echoes of the gavel faded, rubbing his forehead with one hand and texting with the other. The women from the other two organizations walked out with matching and dazed expressions. Taylor toured the other side of the huge, curved desk, scavenging pens and mint candies left behind and declaring each find in her piping voice. Hunter had gotten what he wanted. It didn't matter if the bill passed Congress in the next year— it only needed to pass the committee now. The stock price would go back up, and the IPO would make him a large fortune. He flashed his wife a smile, triumphant. She returned one that seemed only weary instead of jubilant. It had been a very long two days, and she still didn't have her child back.

# Chapter 38

*6:41 p.m.*

*And why* didn't *she have Mason back?* Ellie thought as she watched her cousin use the fancy coffeemaker to make a celebratory cappuccino. It wasn't champagne, but still the party mood lingered. They'd pulled off a great success against a boatload of odds—Gabriel's death, executives distraught over their kidnapped children, Taylor's near abduction. With all that working against them, they'd accomplished their goal.

But their kid was still missing.

Why didn't they seem, well, devastated? Why had Becca not rushed from the dais as soon as the other children appeared, convinced that Mason couldn't be far behind? Yes, she had gained a lot of self-control since their teens, but *still*.

And Hunter—he had had a few minutes to deal with the fact after meeting Michael and the kids outside, and he did seem to have utter focus when it came to his work and its effect on his 750 million–dollar investment. But, again, *still*.

Now Hunter had been on the phone with Tara for ten minutes with all sorts of instructions about this overseas account and some T-bond fund. He had shown a surprising love for comfy clothes, and had ripped off the tie instantly upon their return and now padded around the kitchen in sweatpants and bare feet. Taylor danced around in her hanging-with-grown-ups outfit, until she noticed his attire and ran off to change as well. Rachael had headed back to the Locard, and Michael and Luis to the FBI building to finish the paperwork for the arrests of the two men and Megan. Charging them with kidnapping, extortion, and several other crimes would be a much longer process, one that could wait until Monday to begin. They'd be back, though, since they'd forgotten the special duffel bag made for ransoms, with the hidden trackers inside. It still sat on the kitchen counter, next to Taylor's notebook.

Ellie should go to her apartment—there was nothing more she could do at the house, and the family might want some privacy after two hellish days. So did she.

Yet she leaned against the marble island, pretending that she wanted some caffeine, and let her mind worry over these inconsistencies like a loose string on a sweater. Too many other ones might unravel, but she couldn't stop pulling.

Hunter had been incensed the day before at his son's disappearance, and Becca bereft. Both of them flummoxed when the ransom was ignored. It wasn't as if they didn't care about Mason.

So, why weren't they more upset at this setback?

And then the answer came to her with a clear and startling certainty: They already knew.

They knew exactly where the three children were and that Mason was not among them. They knew because they had arranged it.

But why? How? Where was Mason?

And why was Gabriel dead?

Ellie turned and left the kitchen, heading for the back

staircase. Becca watched her go, her lips parting to ask where she headed, but Ellie hustled past her and she did not follow. Hunter was still on the phone.

She took the steps two at a time.

Light showed under the rim of Taylor's bathroom—few people desired privacy more than preteen girls—and Ellie crossed to the bookshelf. *Forty-Nine Ways to Kill Somebody* sat right where she had left it, the page between *Defenestration* and *Entombment* still missing. She carried it over to Taylor's nightstand and clicked on the light as the sunlight outside began to fade. She'd taken a photo of the ransom note with her phone and used it to compare the font and the page color, knowing that the color might not be perfect. It seemed to match perfectly. It didn't prove anything, of course, but between that and the fragment of hair caught in the glue, it certainly indicated that the ransom note had come from inside the house. She had no doubt that Gary, the whiz with paper, could prove it—analysis of the paper fibers, the ink, maybe touch DNA from Taylor's fingers.

But to what end?

She paged through the rest of the book. She expected to find an entry on poisoning and did (pro: need not be present; con: obtaining a poison), though it did not contain any surprises. *Obtaining a poison would not be difficult when they grew in your backyard, with a textbook on mycology in Becca's study to help you along.*

It did not describe how to reseal a plastic screw top, but that wasn't pediatric neurosurgery either. Take a soldering iron or a fork or a paper clip, heat it enough to melt plastic even just a little, and go around the top to create new connections between the cap and its lower ring under the threads. A decent magnifying glass would give it up, but who inspects every plastic bottle they crack open?

Especially when a friend hands it to you, in a place where you feel safe.

Book in hand, Ellie shut the girl's door and padded down the steps, the thick carpet absorbing the sound of her boots. She should get out of there. School her face back into its sympathetic cast, say her goodbyes, maybe apologize for her failure to bring Mason home, but say she'd keep working on it, would never give up.

She pulled her phone out of her large pants pocket. The book might fit there. The cargo pants could hold quite a bit. She took the steps, trying to fit the pages into the cloth cavity with one hand while texting Rachael with the other: *I have book. Sure it matches note. Mason is—*

"What's that?" Becca asked, waiting at the bottom of the stairs.

Ellie drew in a breath. "Taylor's loaning me her favorite book. She thought it could help me in my job."

At the sight of the cover, Becca's face became still, and that, in itself, told Ellie everything she needed to know.

Becca said, "She loves to show off her worldliness. You ran off in such a hurry."

"I wanted to tell her what a brave girl she'd been today, getting away from Megan." She brushed past her cousin, so close she could feel her body heat. She needed to get with Rachael, regroup, decide on a course of action. She wished Michael Tyler had stayed at the house, someone with a gun, someone armed with a more potent weapon than the small knife she carried to cut through plastic crime scene tape and open boxes. He or Luis would be back, but when? "I'll leave you guys alone. You must be exhausted. So am I."

Becca wasn't buying it, she could tell. Her cousin followed too closely, too quickly, and alerted her husband the moment Ellie crossed the threshold into the kitchen. "*Hunter, I think Ellie has some questions.*"

He'd been texting, but dropped the phone on the island and took a single step to his left—setting his body directly in her path to the door. Yet his words sounded entirely natural. "Really? About what?"

Ellie was now neatly trapped in the aisle between the island and the counter, Hunter at one end, Becca at the other, Ellie's attention divided between the two and nothing to use for self-defense except a vastly overpriced coffeemaker and some tiny kebab skewers.

Screw it. She wouldn't back down this time.

"For starters," she said to Hunter, "how did you know her name was Megan?"

# Chapter 39

"What?" Hunter asked, and for once, his perfect self-confidence slipped. Unsure of what to say, the lips parted, the brows grew closer to each other. "What are you talking about?"

"When I got to the hearing, you asked if Megan had confessed. No one knew her name until halfway through her interrogation."

"The FBI agent told me."

"No, he didn't." She wasn't 100 percent sure of this—it wouldn't have been unreasonable for Michael to call Hunter and ask if he knew of a Megan, but he hadn't mentioned it and the agent had not had time to spare for phone calls. In any case Hunter's discomforted expression gave him away. "Becca fed that senator from New Mexico Megan's *last* name, which I didn't even know. Becca, you didn't ask a single question when Rachael and I arrived. You didn't ask who the woman who had almost kidnapped your daughter was, you didn't ask if the children had been found. Neither of you asked about your own son, when you should have been assuming that Mason had also been kidnapped by Megan's group. *Neither* of you."

She stopped to let them explain. *Please explain,* she thought. *Tell me my childhood BFF wasn't behind the abduction of four children.*

Neither of them said a word.

"It all makes sense now." Inside her pocket her phone gave a tiny buzz, still on vibrate mode from the Senate hearing—probably Rachael texting her back. Ellie went on, pressing while they were off-balance. "How Megan knew exactly where to contact Sophie, what might tempt her— surely, you both heard all about Kieu's daughter from her, countless meetings to prepare for the hearing and the IPO auditors, maybe a company picnic. Parents talk about their kids, especially when those kids are, in a way, beta-testing your product. Darnell would have chatted about his son's favorite electronics and his obsession with baseball. Both of you would know about Megan's threats. She wasn't going to go away, so you decided to use her, *Finn.*" She accused Hunter with that final word. He didn't deny it, and no longer appeared discomforted. His mind had already leapt ahead to damage control. They had a problem, and would require a solution.

Ellie was the problem.

"According to Megan's son, the mysterious Finn knew *everything* about KidFun. Where the execs lived, where their kids could be found, the parents' phone numbers, photos of the houses, kids, cars, nannies, schools, when who would be out of town on business. Finn just handed it to her on a charcuterie board."

Becca finally spoke. "That could have been anyone at KidFun—someone in HR, a secretary, the guy who services the copy machine. It's a gaming company, not the CIA."

"True. That's true. But *you* two had to get the ban

dropped before the final audit before the IPO—after that, you didn't care about games and direct messaging because you would have already cashed out. The secretary or the copy machine guy might have lost their jobs, but they didn't have seven hundred and fifty million dollars riding on that hearing."

"That isn't proof," Becca said.

Also true, so she pressed on: "At the hearing you sarcastically referred to KidFun as 'hard souls.' Megan also spoke of making the 'hard souls writhe.' Most people would either reference 'cold souls' or 'hard hearts.'"

"That's not proof either," Hunter said.

"No. But Megan's phone with her communications from Finn—you—*is* evidence. And Rachael has it."

"Who works for me." It seemed to pop out, his arrogance impossible to control.

"Who works for the Locard, founded on the principle that every contact leaves a trace. That applies to digital contacts as well."

"Sure. Good luck with that."

"She doesn't need luck. She has Agnes."

"But *why*? Why would we do that?" Becca demanded.

"Exactly," Hunter said. "*Why* would I coerce my own execs into slamming the company?"

"You both told me why—a hearing is theater. You have to create drama, establish a hero and a villain. Human beings are simple and, more important, pressed for time. Give them a narrative that presses the right buttons, and they'll open the door for you. You needed that joyous family reunion to happen right in front of the senators, so they could see the overwhelming love KidFun execs have for their kids—no one would doubt their intentions after that, direct messaging and data mining be damned. These are hardened career politicians, but there wasn't a dry eye in the house. Child-

Challenge had been thoroughly discredited, and the other organizations guilty by association. You won the battle *and* the war."

Hunter shook his head. "It would be the wrong kind of drama if the execs told the committee that we're purposely addicting kids and selling their data to advertisers."

"The truth, in other words? Yes, you'd hardly want to do that."

They both seemed to relax, shoulders dropping a few millimeters, yet waiting for the kicker.

"But you never expected it to get that far. You never thought Megan would actually *do* it. You thought she was a middle-aged, delusional nutcase who couldn't pull off the theft of a pen from a bank counter. You thought she'd send some nasty emails and leave a digital trail, vandalize the offices and smile for the security cameras, call in a bomb threat using her own phone. Whatever she did, how mild or how outrageous, whether the police caught her at it or she got away scot-free—*anything* could then be used to discredit ChildChallenge at the hearing, which was your only goal. Take a potential threat and turn it into an asset. The same way attorneys might needle an expert witness until they lose their temper on the stand. At that point it ceases to matter what they did or what they said. All that matters is perceived credibility. As Darnell said, you can get anyone to do anything online, where nothing is real—so everything is. You only need to push the right buttons."

Neither of them said anything. She could swear Hunter looked a little proud.

"But she didn't get caught. She actually grabbed a child—*your* child, you thought—and left the authorities without a single clue. You knew right then your creation had slipped out of the lab and out of your control, but what could you do? Call the cops? How did she convince you that she didn't have Mason? Or did you even care?"

"She didn't have Mason," he said stiffly.

"I know," Ellie said. "We'll get to that later. But you did know she had three other children and you did nothing. You—both of you—let her terrorize small children and their families because it served your purposes."

"How did it do that?" Hunter said. "We were losing that hearing! We came *so* close to losing, and you think I arranged a nick-of-time rescue by the FBI to pull it out in the last inning? If they'd been late, if they even got stuck in DC traffic, then the hearing would be over, my own execs having worked against me and lost their own livelihoods in the process—"

"You didn't expect Megan to hold out. You figured a nutcase like her would crack as soon as we caught her. And you knew we'd catch her, because *you* sent her, me, *and* the FBI to Taylor's school at the same time. How else could Megan spoof the pickup procedures for the school? Because the child's father arranged it for her."

He shook his head. He and Becca both faced her with identically crossed arms, a unit to the last. "Not even I could have pulled off that timing."

"The timing was overly ambitious, but that's what you are—*overly* ambitious. And not impossible at all, not with an anonymous tip to the FBI. Why would the kidnappers call when they were still at the farm, before they'd gotten away? The kids didn't know who they were. They could have dropped the children off somewhere so that the farm would never be connected to their ordeal and then melted back into the landscape. No, *you* called, creating the perfect storm of melodrama and misdirection."

Becca finally spoke: "Ellie, this is insane. You're my *family*."

"I know!" She had to ignore the pain in her heart, had to ignore it or she wouldn't get through this, and having begun, she had to get through it. "That's what makes this so miserable. But Taylor is *yours*, and you would have let her go through the trauma, even briefly, of being—"

"Never!" Becca burst out, the famous temper surfacing at last. "I had eyes on her the whole time! I pointed you at her! I insisted the agent come along."

"So you knew," Ellie said.

A brief but total silence pressed down as if a thick blanket had been thrown over the tableau, the thumping of Ellie's heart against its cage the only movement in the room.

Becca's voice cut like a sword carefully whetted. "Ellie. Are you still mad that I have a mom and you don't? Or that you're not my best friend anymore? Where is this *coming* from?"

Ellie ignored this too.

"In case you haven't noticed," Hunter said, "I don't have my son back! He wasn't found on Megan's farm or whatever. So if I'm the criminal mastermind behind it all, where is my kid?"

His self-satisfied aura cracked on this last word, real emotion and real fear behind it.

Ellie said, "That's what's been confounding me all this time. Nothing seemed consistent, nothing made sense. Now I see—the facts didn't fit together because they *weren't* related. We had three separate crimes—the abduction of the three children, Gabriel's murder, and Mason's disappearance."

"Abduction," Becca corrected.

"Disappearance."

"*Murder*?" Hunter burst out. "Gabriel wasn't *murdered*. He had—it was some weird virus or aneurysm . . . wasn't it?"

"Destroying angel," Ellie said.

"What's that?"

"Ask your wife. The one who handed Gabriel the Gatorade, knowing that no one else in the house would drink it.

The one who minored in mycology, the study of mushrooms. Who had to notice the amanita growing in your woods."

He looked to Becca for a denial. Ellie didn't think her expression had changed one iota, but clearly her husband knew her much, much better than Ellie ever had. What he saw stunned him.

"What? Wh—why? Why Gabriel?"

"He was backing out!" All the emotion she'd kept stuffed down inside her for two days erupted, and Ellie caught a glimpse of the young, always emotional Becca. "He wanted to cancel the IPO! He *wanted* the hearing to kill us—the last thing he said was he'd tell the *truth* about the company! And all because he had cold feet over the algorithm and the data mining. The whole company would go down the tubes because he had an attack of conscience! Everything we'd done, the risks we took, would all have been for nothing."

"That was just talk. I could have controlled Gabriel!"

"I couldn't take that chance."

"*You* couldn't? You didn't even think about talking to me? What do you think is going to happen to the company now?"

"That's your complaint?" Ellie said. "That she made an executive decision?"

"Shut up." And that quickly, he put his wife's upgrade from kidnapper and extortionist to killer out of his mind and moved forward. Damage control. One glance at Becca and they were a team again. The Gabriel problem had been in the past. The Ellie problem still stood in front of them.

Ellie took a breath, turned her face toward her first cousin. "Are you really thinking of a way to kill me, Becca?"

A pause. "Of course not."

But the pause robbed the statement of any conviction. Had they both moved closer without appearing to, or had she only imagined that?

Ellie pulled the book out of her pocket. The best defense, after all . . .

"Maybe you'll want to consult this for suggestions," she goaded.

"What's that?" Hunter asked.

"The source of the letters on Mason's ransom note."

Once more, he stumbled. "Wh . . . How is that possible?"

"Because the plan had been put in place before you left town, the letter mailed before you left. It must have been tough for you," she added to Becca, "mailing that letter, committing yourself to go through with it. Of course if you changed your mind, all you had to do was be sure to get the mail—not tough with Jenny out of town, and I'm sure Hunter here doesn't concern himself with mundane tasks like that."

"What are you talking about?" Becca's fingers gripped the island counter, knuckles white.

"The timing worked perfectly, but it wouldn't have mattered if it hadn't, if it arrived a week or a month later. The letter was only a distraction, meant to confuse. That's why the strange amount—enough to sound convincing, but not enough to really cause an inconvenience."

Hunter was still trying to puzzle this out. "Why would Becca—that doesn't make any sense at all."

"Her hair got caught in the glue before it dried. I believe Rachael knows it's not a vellus hair—Mason's—though it could be Taylor's. Are we meant to think it's Taylor's? Is that why you used her book? Tell me you weren't trying to frame your own daughter."

"Becca?" Hunter asked, his voice abruptly uncertain.

"Of course not!" she snapped at her husband. "I would never!"

Ellie kept it up. "You didn't think of simply using a newspaper or a magazine?"

Becca's shoulders slumped, not under her cousin's accusing gaze, but her husband's. "Who gets magazines anymore?"

"You said Taylor reads the *Post*—"

"Online."

"Stop!" Hunter shouted. "Where is Mason? Where is my son?"

Ellie looked at her cousin. "Do you want to tell him? Or should I?"

# Chapter 40

Becca remained as silent as if she were a teenager again, uncertain, caught but hoping she could brazen it out, anyway.

Ellie prompted, "He's going to find out sooner or later."

"Becca? What's she talking about?"

Becca said, "Don't listen to her. She's just running off at the mouth, trying to get herself out of this kitchen after making all these accusations. Just let her leave. She can't prove a word of what she's been saying."

"But she knows—"

"It doesn't matter what they suspect. It only matters what they can *prove*."

Was she trying to save Ellie? Or herself?

It didn't matter, because neither plan worked. Hunter would not be distracted. "But where is *Mason*?"

"I don't know!"

Hands clenching and unclenching, he took two more steps toward his wife. Unfortunately, it took him two steps closer to Ellie. Maybe he'd pass her entirely and she could run out as they argued, get in her car, and escape the house.

And then what? Leave her cousin at the mercy of her very

irate husband, who was about to get a lot more irate once he learned the truth? Maybe have another murder take place— for Taylor to stumble across?

Though Hunter, so far, had only terrorized a few families. It was Becca who had committed the cold-blooded murder. Perhaps Ellie should worry about Hunter's safety.

Or her own.

Hunter stopped a foot away and, snake-quick, reached out to wrap one hand around Ellie's throat. He squeezed, and she instinctively punched him (which did nothing) and kicked his shin as hard as she could (which caused a grunt and a wince).

If she'd really wanted to do damage, she would have kicked his knee out, dislocating the joint. She meant this struggle only as a warning: She would not be manhandled, not even by a technical member of her family. She did not want to get in a fistfight with Hunter; first, she would lose, and second, she wanted both of them to keep talking.

He let go, but didn't move. "You'd better tell me where my kid is, if you want to walk out of here."

She looked to her cousin, to give her one last chance to confess voluntarily.

"Well?" Hunter demanded.

Time was up. "Look at the drawing. Taylor's notebook."

He glanced down at the opened book, next to him on the island, at Taylor's illustration of a dragon carrying off an infant. "So what? She's always drawing stuff."

"Don't you wonder why she called Mason a 'dragon baby'?"

"Because she's jealous of the new kid. So what?"

"It's not jealousy. Mason has ichthyosis. A condition that causes scaly patches on the skin, trapping sweat glands under its scabs. Nothing serious, easily controlled by a skin care routine of lotions and exfoliations. But genetic."

Hunter said, "What, that patchy stuff . . ."

"Yes. That Gabriel had."

The tumblers fell. He had to see the connection, but clearly didn't want to. "So?"

Ellie said, "Mason has it too."

"You've never even *seen* Mason!"

"No, but Taylor has. The *dragon* baby." Ellie pointed again to the drawing. "See the red patches along the baby's arms?"

"There's nothing like that on Mason. He's my kid. I know what he looks like." But he glanced at his wife, quickly, waiting for confirmation. He didn't get it. Becca focused on Ellie, and Ellie alone.

Who said gently: "Yes, but I'm willing to bet you leave bath time and changing diapers to the nanny or to Becca. It's only been four months, and you're out of town a lot. A *lot*."

His resistance began to show a few cracks. "Becca. Tell her this isn't true. There was nothing wrong with Mason."

"No." She spoke without an ounce of conviction. "No, there isn't."

Ellie continued: "Jenny Cho had to know, and Mason's doctors and nurses would have seen the condition during his checkups. That was another reason this had to be done while Jenny remained safely out of the way. *Maybe* to help her out, give her an ironclad alibi, but maybe so that she would not be here to be questioned about Mason's medical conditions. She might have even known about Gabriel. But this way Megan and her group will be blamed for his disappearance, case closed, no reason to talk to Jenny at all."

Hunter couldn't hide from this truth any longer. He turned to his wife. "Gabriel? Really? *Really?*"

She stared at the table, at her daughter's drawing of her son and the dragon.

Ellie said, "Did you even think of what this would do to Taylor? Wondering for the rest of her life what happened to her brother? If he was alive? If whoever took him would come back for her?"

"Don't be ridiculous," Becca said. "Taylor is *happy* he's gone. Now she's got us all to herself again."

"Maybe you really believe that," Ellie said. "It's still inexcusable."

This sparked fire. "What the hell would you know about having children? About having a family?"

Hunter also spared no sympathy for his daughter, too focused on his own humiliation. "Gabriel? Really? You—you did—"

Becca could have argued with Ellie all day and never cracked her iron shell, but she didn't last thirty seconds under Hunter's eye. "It was only a few times! You were gone so much—it didn't mean anything! I could get him out of our lives, but if you ever knew, ever suspected, you'd reject Mason and you'd leave me. Our lives would fall apart, the house, the accounts, the projects. It wasn't worth it. I had to let the baby go. *And it killed me.*"

Her voice broke on the last four words, so heartfelt and so piteously that Ellie almost wanted to turn away and write this off as a family conflict to be worked out among the parties themselves.

Almost.

But a man had been killed.

"She loves you," Ellie told Hunter. "She murdered Gabriel to keep you."

"My *friend*?" The words burst out in ragged shards, and this time he did brush past Ellie. "You two were *pretending* around me, knowing all the time, making a fool—"

Ellie was free. She could run now, and they probably wouldn't even notice. But then Hunter's hands went around her cousin's throat, and as strong as the running and the spinning and the aerobics might have made her, Becca didn't stand a chance against his mindless rage. Her cousin was bent backward over the table, legs trapped, arms pulling uselessly at his biceps.

Ellie grabbed one of Hunter's arms and tried to pull it away, the effort a sneeze in the hurricane of his fury. He did stop killing his wife long enough to shove Ellie away; her hip slammed against the marble countertop and her spine popped loudly enough to be heard over Becca's gasps.

Ellie needed a weapon. A gun might make him rethink his strategy, but, of course, she didn't have one. Knives abounded, and she could stab him, but that would only make him turn on her, unless she actually killed him.

The knife block included a pair of scissors, and she pulled it out. Yanking the plug of the expensive coffeemaker, she cut the cord at its base. Then she approached the struggling couple and found the outlet at the end of the island.

Ellie had no idea if this would work. It might kill him. It might just make him mad. Madd*er*.

It might kill him and Becca both.

She inserted the plug into the outlet. It didn't have a GFI, she had to hope it dated to some far earlier remodel, before the stainless-steel Sub-Zero and the Simonelli. With luck it would at least startle Hunter into rational thought before the circuit breaker tripped and cut the power. And before he turned around and strangled Ellie instead.

Becca's feet were kicking, but losing strength.

Ellie touched the wire to Hunter's right ear, careful to hold it well back from the hot ends. There had not been time to strip them—

A tremor ran through Hunter's body, down to his bare, grounded feet.

*"Daddy!"*

Taylor stood in the doorway to the dining room, her eyes huge, both hands held out in front of her as if she could push her father away from her mother.

Then the lights went out.

The circuit breaker had tripped, but in the dying light from the windows, Ellie saw Taylor's mouth open for another scream, which didn't come. Instead, the girl turned and ran, springing away as fast as any rabbit.

The hands around Becca's neck loosened, then fell. Hunter stepped heavily to one side and slid awkwardly into a chair as Becca rolled over, sucking in breath as quickly as she could, coughing, then sucking again.

Ellie heard the rear veranda door clatter against its stops as if thrown by great force, and was in motion before she even realized what her body might be doing. Always smarter than her, it had reacted to the danger before she could form the thought.

*Taylor!* Distraught, horrified, unable to swim.

Ellie burst out of the back door, across the flagstones, past George the stone lion and his no-name partner. Taylor's pajamaed form was already three-quarters of the way down the lawn with no signs of slowing.

*Turn right,* Ellie prayed. *Turn right and go to your tree. Climb your tree to your special alone place. Don't go to the dock.*

The girl kept on straight, the short legs moving with unbelievable speed.

Behind her she heard the veranda door slam once more, and a more solid sound, like the *thunk* of a car door.

*Don't go to the dock. Don't go off the end of the dock. Don't be like Benjy, it's not really that peaceful.*

Taylor didn't turn toward the woods. Her bare feet hit the planks of the dock with a slap so loud it made Ellie wince.

*"Stop!"* Ellie shouted. Or thought she shouted. Her heart beat too loudly for her to hear.

It was a long dock. It would take her a while. A splinter might slow her down, the hard wood too painful after the soft grass.

Without the slightest hesitation Taylor disappeared off the end.

Ellie reached the boards only a second—it had to be only a second, it couldn't have been longer—after her, could just catch a glimpse of the white print pajama set in the water, already downstream from the jumping-off point by several feet. She had to do what Taylor had done. *Don't hesitate, don't slow down. No time to take off shoes. I don't know what real difference shoes would make, anyway—*

She hit the water in a most inelegant dive, more or less smacking her face and stomach onto the surface. The sting distracted her from the shock of the water, which, while not exactly cold yet, wasn't exactly warm either. She tried to breathe and managed only to get a mouthful of the Potomac. It didn't taste great.

*Where is she?*

Ellie's body was longer, stronger, she should be within reach with one more kick—but her fingers felt only water, that nothingness heavier than air.

She kicked harder, tried to lift her head out of the small waves. There—a flash of white against the greenish-brown flow. Ellie gave a frantic sprint, legs and arms in a panicked rush.

Something grabbed her foot.

She wouldn't have believed her body could get any more mindlessly hysterical, but it did. She flailed wildly, kicking against the tendrils, until the submerged tree branches around her ankle flowed and gapped.

Another push, and her hand touched cloth. Ever so briefly, before the current took it once more out of her range, but enough to know she hadn't imagined it. Her water-blurred eyes saw the whitish shade below the surface, and then she had hold of it.

With both hands she grabbed the girl's torso and hefted her upper body out of the water. This pushed Ellie below the surface, but only for a moment. Her legs scissored—maybe taking off the shoes *would* have helped—and she managed to get both their heads into the air.

Taylor had gone completely limp; Ellie had no idea if the girl was breathing. She tried to grasp the girl's back to her chest, looping one arm across her from armpit to armpit in the classic lifeguard carry. But, to be honest, Ellie had no idea how lifeguards dragged the rescued to safety. Though Aunt Rosalie had worked hard to teach her, Ellie wasn't much of a swimmer.

With the set sun below the horizon, the shadow of the trees turned the riverbank to a deep darkness. There were no inlets or cleared land in sight and the current felt much stronger than she had expected. She struggled toward the shore, her kicking legs tangling with Taylor's lifeless ones. Ellie didn't bother shouting for help; there would be no one to hear.

A very small but grassy sliver of bank appeared ahead and Ellie aimed for it. Easier said than done, but the water grew slightly shallower and calmer near the edge. She talked herself toward it with Aunt Katey's mantra: *I can do this. I can do this*—though she was not at all sure that she could.

*Where is the river bottom?* She should be able to reach the bottom, stand up, and pull Taylor out, but still her feet flailed in nothingness, without a toehold.

She heard a voice.

"Here! I'll get her."

A dark figure appeared on the slope, only two feet away. Once more, she pushed the girl's body upward. *Taylor should breathe, she should be able to breathe.* This once again shoved Ellie under the water's surface. *Where the hell is the bottom?*

Taylor was torn from her hands and yet she couldn't pull herself up, her feet finding only silt that didn't give enough purchase and even sucked her down farther. Her hands were in the air, breaking the surface, but the rest of her needed to breathe and couldn't, and her legs had done all they could.

The soaking water, her flailing limbs, the smell of algae and lichen and restraints, and suddenly she was four years old again, in the backseat of a car, slowly sinking into—

Just as her lungs gave out, someone grasped her wrist and yanked.

Somehow she knew it was Michael Tyler before she opened her eyes. He crouched halfway in and halfway out of the water, fighting for balance in the uncertain, shifting wet earth of the riverbank. Behind him she caught a glimpse of Rachael holding Taylor as she coughed up water. Behind them Becca stood with her hands to her face, screaming with a raspy, damaged throat, one long wail of animal despair. For her daughter or for herself, Ellie couldn't tell.

Ellie could do nothing to help, coughing and coughing to expel water from her lungs, her largest ambition at the moment to keep from throwing up on Michael. It might have been less likely if he hadn't kneed her in the rib cage trying to haul her weakened body up onto the grass, but she wasn't about to quibble.

Her face in a pile of branches, she rolled into a ball, hacking wet breaths onto the earth. When this finally slowed, she could hear the noises of someone else doing the same.

"She's okay," Michael told her. "Taylor's all right."

# Chapter 41

Rachael Davies stood in her front yard, supervising her helper as he cared for the chrysanthemums. Danton held the garden hose with both hands and great concentration, always fascinated by the cascade of clear liquid it produced and how it could take different forms depending on how one held one's fingers over the end. But his experimentations always seemed to end with one or both of them in dripping clothes, and this morning Rachael had to make sure it wasn't her.

Danton waved the hose.

"On the plants, honey. The plants need the water, not the wall."

"Much."

"Yes, that's *mulch*."

"Fower."

"*Flower*, yes."

And suddenly Jalen Williams materialized alongside them on the sidewalk. It unnerved her that someone six-five, with bulging biceps and bike-racing-champion calves, could

move so unobtrusively . . . Did the army give ninja training now?

"Hello—" he began, but then Danton, with his hose,
turned toward him and he had to take a quick two steps to
his left to keep his pants dry. Danton dropped the hose and
squealed in delight, arms raised in a demand to be picked up.
Rachael twisted the nozzle and shut off the water, mostly to
keep herself from snapping: *What the hell are you doing
here?*

By that time Danton had already wriggled back to the
ground and dashed as fast as toddler legs could take him
through the front door, no doubt to find some toy that the
visitor simply *had* to see. Rachael fixed the man with her
neutral face, waiting for an explanation.

"Sorry for not calling first, but I'm on my way to the air-
port and I wanted to see Danton one more time.

"Oh." Not *I'm glad you did*, because, of course, she wasn't
glad at all. *No offense, Jalen Williams, but I hope I never see
you again.*

A pause. Then a rush of words she already knew to be un-
characteristic: "You're doing a great job with him. I mean, I
know you know that, but I wanted to say it. He's lucky to
have you and Loretta."

And Rachael felt one tiny string of the straitjacket around
her heart stretch and loosen. Her mother had been right. He
simply wanted to make sure his boy was well cared for before stepping out of his life—

"But I don't intend just to walk away," he continued.

She blinked. The straitjacket laced up again, even tighter.

"I'm not going to be one of those guys who just drops
some sperm and figures the rest isn't his problem. I want to
be Danton's dad. I want to be everything for him that a dad
should be."

*And what makes you think—*

"But I have another year to go on my deployment, and I

don't want to mess up what you've got going here. I do *not* want to mess that up."

"Then don't." *Simple as that.*

Replying as steady as granite, he said, "I don't intend to. He's happy, he's stable—I want that for him. I want him to know exactly where his home is, but I also want to be his dad. My plan is to leave everything exactly as it is."

"Good."

"Until I get back Stateside. Then we'll see—"

"Oh, the hell—"

"—about some sort of shared custody, visitations, something."

She could feel her face flushing, a sort of white-hot wave of blood welling up from deep inside her. Rage, or fear, it didn't matter which.

"We'll work it out. I just want him to be happy. I don't want to take him away from you."

She managed to take some air into her lungs, just a crack.

"But I don't want him taken away from me either," he finished.

She didn't trust herself to respond, could only watch as Danton returned with a toy car in each hand, both of which had to be explained carefully, in largely incomprehensible language, to the tall stranger. Jalen listened, asked a few questions, then shook his son's tiny hand with solemn reverence. He gave Rachael a nod, picked up his olive drab duffel, and went out to the rental car parked at the curb.

Only then did Rachael suck in a deep breath and snatch her little boy up, holding him to her, feeling his skinny but strong arms wrap around her neck, smelling his special baby shampoo mixed with a hint of Play-Doh.

A year. She had a year before the army demolitions expert came back and blew up her life.

The car pulled away and a 1960s era Mustang in slightly faded burgundy pulled into her drive. A convertible, she noticed, and hoped Ellie wouldn't want to put the top down in this heat.

Danton squealed at the thrill of having two visitors in the same morning and waved his cars at the emerging woman.

"This is your car?" Rachael asked.

Ellie beamed. "A college graduation present to myself. It's a '65."

"Um . . . are you sure it can make it?"

"Of course it can," Ellie said. "Trust me."

The drive from Washington, DC, to Haven, West Virginia, took Ellie five hours, but through incredibly scenic areas, including a national park (Shenandoah) and a national forest (George Washington and Jefferson). This prompted Ellie to spend four miles wondering why such men had to share a location. Hadn't each deserved a forest of his own? And maybe Washington got to keep his first name in order to distinguish the man from the city?

And, in the sunny daylight, the roads only occasionally wracked the nerves with a shoulder crumbling off into a sheer gorge or a bridge suspended hundreds of feet above a valley of water and treetops.

"Sorry about the space," Ellie said to Rachael, who sat with a copy paper supply–size box on her lap.

"It wouldn't be so bad if it weren't—Taylor, what's in here?"

The girl yanked out one of her earbuds. The backseat barely had enough room for the eleven-year-old next to the suitcases and boxes. "What? That? It's books."

"Well," Rachael said to Ellie, "I can't argue with a girl who reads books."

"As long as they don't produce deep vein thrombosis. Thanks again for coming with me."

"No problem. I felt like I wanted to see this to the end. And I wanted to talk to you."

Ellie had been too discombobulated to question Rachael's accompaniment on this trip, and now wished she had. There were few more ominous requests in the known universe than *I want to talk to you.* "About what?"

"A job," Rachael said without preamble. "The Locard needs a crime scene instructor. Our current one is leaving to continue her research at a body farm in Utah, so . . . you would have an office, two classes per session, and we can talk about your areas of research and getting you whatever resources you might need. You would also be expected to participate in our private contract work."

Meaning, work like finding a rich lobbyist's missing child.

Ellie drove two more miles in wordless surprise. *The Locard wants* me? *The* Locard?

A place with all the equipment and materials she could possibly need? A place that worked on the most baffling, most unique—and, as an added benefit, where her ex-husband would *not* be working. She wouldn't have the threat of transfer to another office should staffing demand it. Most of all, she'd be able to do forensic work *full time*—

Rachael misinterpreted her silence and assured her, "You don't have to answer today. Let's just deliver our charge first."

"I'm not a 'charge,' " Taylor said.

"Sacred trust?" Rachael tried.

The girl considered this, then nodded. Then she noticed a freeway sign and read the announcement of a tunnel ahead with so much excitement she nearly danced in her seat. Or at least in the space allotted her by three suitcases and four boxes.

Ellie guided the car into the tile-coated tunnel cut into a mountain with less enthusiasm, trying not to think about the weight of the rock and stone suspended above her. *Keep your eyes on the road and ignore everything else,* her aunt Joanna always said. Joanna had taught her to drive, having had much more patience than her husband, Paul. Everyone in her mother's family had taken the time to teach her a skill or leave her with a memory to carry with her every day of her life. Even, sometimes, ones she didn't want.

And now, that family would have to teach Taylor. The eleven-year-old had shown surprising resilience as she lost both her parents and her lavish home in less than a week. Her parents' crimes weren't an appropriate subject for such a young person, but Taylor demanded honesty. She had nothing left.

Ellie wished her relatives had been as honest with her; if they had, she might not be just past thirty and still wondering how her mother had truly died and where her father had gone.

Taylor went on, "Hey! Here's that bridge!"

The roadway over the New River soared close to nine hundred feet above the rushing water. *Keep your eyes on the road . . .*

"Gram took me on a picnic in that park once! There's a trail with stone steps and a patio with these magnifying telescopes that you can use if you put a quarter in. Gram said when I got bigger I could get a raft and go down the river in the waves."

Ellie felt a little better to hear the enthusiasm in the girl's voice. A little.

When she pulled into the gravel drive of the little house in which she had spent few but formative years, Taylor burst from the backseat before Ellie could kill the engine. Aunt Katey appeared on the porch. She'd heard the gravel, always did. She wore a brightly colored blouse and her good yoga pants, her long graying hair brushed and pulled back with jeweled clips.

The house seemed smaller than Ellie remembered; of course, she'd been smaller herself. The oak trees had crowded in over the years. One of the three steps to the ground sagged in the middle, but the porch had been freshly painted, the wooden railings a newly bright white, as if in preparation for Taylor's homecoming.

The girl flung herself at her grandmother, and Katey enveloped her in a hug twice as fierce. They had a quick, hushed conversation before Taylor skipped around her and into the house. The wooden screen door swung shut with one quick *bang*.

Ellie pushed herself forward, made her feet move, while Katey waited. Rachael stayed at the car, doubtless giving her the privacy needed for this incredibly awkward family reunion. Would Aunt Katey strike her? Scream at her? At a very minimum tell her never to set foot on the property again? That she had no right to consider herself part of—

And then she was there and Aunt Katey enveloped her in a bear hug as tight as the one with which she'd just welcomed Taylor. Ellie had no choice. She collapsed into uglycry, nose-running sobs.

"There, there," Katey murmured, patting Ellie's back just as she had so often done fifteen-plus years before. The faint scent of ginger grass pulled Ellie back through time.

"I'm so sorry!"

"You did what had to be done. It wasn't your fault," her aunt comforted.

"But—" With shuddering gasps, ineffectively wiping her face with both hands, Ellie made an effort to speak like the grown-up she now had to be. "But—"

*But I put your daughter in jail,* she wanted to say, and couldn't make herself.

Because it wasn't true. She hadn't put Becca in jail. Becca had done that herself.

Aunt Katey put both hands on either side of Ellie's face. "You did the right thing. Just as we always taught you."

That only made Ellie cry again.

But Katey produced a few tissues and Ellie found herself

saying, "Maybe in time . . . maybe after . . . I could talk to you about my mom. I remembered something. I remembered about the crash and the water—"

The screen door gave another *bang*, and they both looked up to see Melissa. Becca's opposite in many ways, heavy where Becca had the wiry limbs, fair where Becca had raven locks, but identical in their thorough disdain for people who crossed them. She gave Ellie that look now, that cold, haughty stare that said: *You lent Becca your book before you gave it to me. You sat with Becca on the bus instead of me. You sent my sister to jail.*

*You're not really my best friend.*

But Ellie wasn't twelve years old anymore.

She climbed the steps to the porch and looked at the baby in Missy's arms. A dark-haired little boy with a round, cherubic face.

"Hello, Mason," Ellie said.

# Chapter 42

The ride back stayed largely silent, and Ellie hoped Rachael at least enjoyed the view because the company wasn't much to speak of. Rachael, however, seemed comfortable, diplomatically giving Ellie the mental space she needed to acclimate to what had happened. Begin to acclimate. It would take a while.

Finally, though, Rachael stirred and said, "In all the excitement you never did explain how they got Mason out of the house."

Ellie merged into a center lane. "Tara, of course. Becca told me most of it last night. She, Tara, and Melissa made the plan well in advance, so Tara and Melissa knew exactly what was going on the entire time. Gabriel left that day, having witnessed that Mason had been alive and well, then Tara left the house and promptly passed Mason off to Melissa in an out-of-the-way parking lot. Becca told me Melissa was out of the country, but no one ever checked—why would they? Melissa didn't seem to have any connection to the household other than as a distant relative. . . ."

"I can see a sister doing anything for a sister, but a friend, even a close friend—risking a kidnapping charge?" Rachael mused.

"But it wasn't. It's not kidnapping when the mother hands you the kid. At most it would be custodial interference, but they both knew that even if caught, Hunter would never want the public embarrassment of pressing charges. Now that he's going to jail for his own plot, it's very unlikely Tara or Melissa will be charged at all."

Rachael thought this through. "Melissa could just deny all knowledge, say her sister asked her to watch her baby for a while. But Tara also lied to the FBI."

"True, and she could be prosecuted for that. Personally, I think she's a sweet woman who honestly believed she was acting in Mason's best interest. And Becca can be very controlling . . . She has a way of treating any objection with such disdain that you feel stupid for arguing. Even at twelve, she had that down to an art."

"But you do know that. You've known her that long, so why did she want you right in the middle of her own house? Wasn't she afraid you'd see through her?"

"Apparently not." Ellie goosed the Mustang, her gaze locked on the road "And for good reason, because I didn't. Not for a long time. Even if I had, I'm *family* . . . I think she really believed I'd protect her, no matter what."

"Family is everything." Rachael said that quietly, as if speaking to herself. Then she went on: "But what was Becca's endgame? Let Melissa raise Mason? Wouldn't Hunter—and Taylor—see him eventually, figure it out? Was she going to keep them separated forever?"

"Not really as hard as it sounds. Hunter had no interest in Becca's West Virginia relatives. I don't know how she planned to handle Taylor . . . I think she might have told Taylor eventually, maybe thinking Taylor would keep the secret in order to have her parents to herself again, but that's just my theory. Missy always wanted children but doesn't have a partner, so she leapt on board with the plan. Aunt Katey, of course, would do whatever her girls needed."

"Family."

"Family," Ellie said. "Hardly a great plan, but the best Becca could do. More to the point she had to do it *fast*—any day Hunter might see the patchy skin. He knew all about Gabriel's condition, they'd played sports together, swam, changed in locker rooms. And maybe, *maybe*, Hunter might not have been able to father a child. The medical forms on his desk mentioned tamsulosin."

"Prescribed following prostate cancer," Rachael said. "I didn't see that."

"I didn't point it out. Didn't want to be prying into their medical history."

"Cancer wouldn't necessarily have rendered him sterile—that's not a common reaction."

"Yes, but if he ever thought about it, he might have wondered about that eleven-year gap between children . . . though for all I know, that could have been by design, and Becca could explain the pregnancy as a birth control mix-up. Doesn't matter—that's pure speculation. But Mason's skin condition was quite definite. Becca had to do something, and when Hunter came up with the plan to push Megan into actions to discredit ChildChallenge—"

"Risky in itself."

"I think Hunter thrives on risk. It didn't have to work perfectly, it didn't *have* to work at all, but when she actually went through with it, he figured he had a slam dunk. With the hearing so close, the temptation to use her as the big reveal proved irresistible."

"Until his own kid disappeared."

"Exactly! Hunter had to think Megan had taken him, despite that *not* having been the plan—but maybe he couldn't immediately text her to demand an answer in case she wondered how he could have known about it. He wasn't supposed to be 'Finn.' So Hunter hired you, both to make himself look innocent and so he could aim you at Megan if she didn't give Mason back. He also had to consider the possibility that it was a real ransom-induced kidnapping unrelated to his plot, in which case he genuinely needed your help.

"If he did find a way to ask, Megan would have told him she knew nothing about Mason—but he also knew how unbalanced she was. He couldn't know for sure, right up to the end. He had to keep all the balls in play whether he liked it or not, the hearing, Megan's group, and the Locard, until something shook out."

Rachael snorted. "That's a lot of juggling. So Megan sends the other parents the texts, designed by 'Finn.' But she hadn't taken Mason, so who texted Hunter about the hearing?"

"Becca. She was in on the kidnapping plot from the start, so only had to add a few lines to the script. Two can play that burner phone game."

"He was in my office when he got the text," Rachael said. "It stunned him. He had to think Megan had gone off the res, but he couldn't be sure and could hardly complain to the FBI that 'she wasn't supposed to take *my* kid.' He just had to play it out."

"He figured he couldn't be connected to her, in any way."

"He may be right. Agnes is working on Megan's phone, but no breakthroughs yet."

"He should have destroyed the burner as soon as she got caught. He probably dropped it down a storm drain on the way to the hearing, when we were all at the FBI poring over Megan's van. Could Agnes do anything with mine?" After Becca caught her texting Rachael, Ellie had clicked on her camera app to record video before sliding it into her pants.

The screen only recorded the inside of her back pocket, but with the microphone peeking out, the audio could pick up at least some of the action. Unfortunately, that phone had gone into the river with her.

"She's got it in a box of rice right now. We'll see. At least Gary is sure he can match the paper and lettering in the ransom note with the book, once it dries out. But—why the ransom note at all? Why a text *and* the note, if Becca did them both?"

"Because Mason wasn't going to be found with the others."

"Ah," Rachael said. "Mason's case had to be different. The note would send us in another direction—maybe a simple kidnapping for ransom, maybe one of Megan's group making a cash grab. Maybe it was an unrelated ransom-motivated kidnapping, but one of Megan's group somehow knew about it and decided to piggyback on it and force Hunter to throw the hearing. The note would always leave a trail of possible, never-answered questions to why Mason's fate turned out different than the other three kids."

"Yup. Listening to Hunter's Megan-versus-KidFun plot, Becca saw an opportunity. First, get the nanny out of the way, both to give her an ironclad alibi and to make sure no one could question her about Mason's medical conditions."

Rachael sipped from a travel mug of coffee, purchased at their last pit stop. Ellie had already drained hers in record time, like the three before it. The insomnia had been out in full force the night before, her brain turning over and over every nightmarish nuance of what she had to do. "Yes . . . every time Jenny came up, Becca would insist she had nothing to do with it."

"As with Tara. Becca did her best to make sure her friends would be safe. When the mother herself said Tara had left with Harper, and only Harper, who would question it?"

"I knew her gait seemed off when she left the house. My theory had been that Harper hadn't been there at all—but then Gabriel said he saw the little girl."

"Oh, yes, it was Harper in the baby carrier. They simply took out Tara's all-organic diapers, piling them in Mason's nursery, and put the sleeping Mason in the bag. Then Tara drove away to meet Melissa. I should have wondered more why Becca hadn't called her mother or sister, why they weren't blowing up her phone or showing up on the doorstep."

"Organic diapers."

"They were stacked on the changing table, when Becca told me herself she thought organics were a scam." Ellie shifted the Mustang more abruptly than it liked and it whined a brief protest. "All this time I've been wondering how Becca could possibly focus on a—albeit incredibly lucrative—political maneuver, but now it makes complete sense. The plan had already been executed, her part completed, Mason safe. She missed him, but had no reason to be worried. Before I ever got to their house, she had already moved into the next phase. Pulling off the hearing was all she needed to worry about.

"Hunter was in the opposite corner. He had put his plan in play, but was stunned by Mason's disappearance. That's why he seemed more frantic, but less grieving, than Becca. And more erratic—his brain must have ping-ponged between questions. Did Megan have Mason? Why? Why wouldn't she say? Did some unknown kidnapper have him? Why didn't they collect the ransom? Had Becca and/or Taylor done something to him? But he had to be so careful not to appear to us and to Megan to have more information than he should have. Both he and Becca had to act baffled in front of you and the FBI."

"And you," Rachael said.

"Yes. And me."

"But if Mason was out of the way, why did she have to kill Gabriel? No offense, but there she moves past desperate mother and into cold-blooded killer."

Ellie had always prided herself on not shrinking from reality. Yes, her flesh and blood had been very cold, indeed. "Gabriel's existence would always be a threat to her secret, but more than that, he was going to give up the lucrative parts of the online gaming empire. She and Hunter *had* to keep the price up until they could sell out. Otherwise, the entire thing was for nothing."

"But to murder her lover, the father of her child—"

"To us, ice cold. To her, a logical choice. I hate to sound cynical, but the truth is, people murder inconvenient lovers, even parents of their children, all the time. If she were a man, you wouldn't even think to question it."

"Huh." Rachael said in surprise. "You're right. But how could Becca give up her child? She wasn't poor or addicted. Would a divorce really be so impossible? I couldn't . . ."

"That's because you're a typical mom, who can't conceive of being separated from your son under any circumstances." Rachael wasn't typical, since Danton had been her sister's child, but clearly that made no difference to her. "Not everyone's emotions are that clear-cut. Becca saw her choice as this. She could lose Mason and keep her beautiful life, or keep Mason and lose her marriage, partial custody of Taylor, and home. She might have a great job, but the real money is Hunter's. He's got the family money and the company, the stocks, the bonds. She'd be perfectly comfortable with her own estate, but comparatively . . ."

"Comparatively, a pittance in light of his wealth."

"And status. So she had to choose. *We* see a pathologically ambitious woman who would sacrifice her own child for wealth, but I believe Becca saw herself as standing on the roof of the embassy in Saigon lifting Mason into a helicopter, just to get him to a better place."

"Really." Rachael's voice echoed her disbelief.

"That's what I think. But I *am* biased." She pulled into Rachael's drive, switched off the engine. On the swing under the oak tree, Rachael's mother read a story to Danton, whose eyes had closed in the afternoon warmth.

Rachael watched them. "I still can't see it."

"I know," Ellie said. "And I like that about you. About that job. . . ."

"You don't have to decide n—"

"I'll take it."

# NOTES AND ACKNOWLEDGMENTS

I'd like to thank my fantastic agent Vicky Bijur and Kensington editor Michaela Hamilton and their teams, who helped guide me through a rough two years.

I'd also like to thank my nephew Brian, who explained IPOs and SPACs.

I very rarely make things up out of whole cloth, but I was desperate and therefore must confess: I made up the XF detector.

I discovered that the world of children's online gaming and legislation regarding same are vast and rapidly evolving topics. I barely skimmed their surfaces in this book, though assisted by a great deal of online articles and podcasts. I especially appreciated Jerri Williams's *FBI Retired Case File Review* podcast, and feel sure that working for the FBI's Evidence Response Team is much more exciting than I make it sound in this book.